THE ASSISTANT

WINTER K. WILLIS

CONNECT WITH WINTER

Winter K. Willis is a pseudonym for our two-person writing team. We like to think of it as our band name. We love telling our characters' stories and hope that you enjoy reading them.

For info on our latest releases, sign up for our newsletter at www.winterkwillis.com

ALSO BY WINTER K. WILLIS

THE WIFE INSIDE

HOW THE AFFAIR ENDS

BEHIND THE NEIGHBOR'S DOOR

THE PERFECT GIFT

THE PERFECT EX-WIFE

THE LAST CHANCE

PROLOGUE

The sun is slipping below the horizon, casting a golden haze over the dense evergreen forest. Beth trudges behind Jason, her feet crunching on the forest floor.

"Why are we taking this ridiculous route to the lake?" She asks, her voice laced with irritation. Her eyes dart around the thick ferns, half-expecting a bear to lunge out at any moment.

Jason halts abruptly, turning to face her with that trademark smirk she simultaneously loves and hates. "You've been to the lake a million times. Don't you want to see it from a new angle? It's about the adventure, Beth."

She rolls her eyes and swats him on the shoulder, harder than necessary. "Adventure? You mean, get mauled by a bear before dinner? Yeah, hard pass." Her gaze flicks toward the looming shadows. "Are you even sure this is safe?"

Jason shrugs, unbothered. "No idea. That's what makes it an adventure."

Beth huffs but quickens her steps to stay close, refusing

to let him out of her sight. "Just so you know, if I die out here, I'm haunting you. Forever."

Jason laughs but doesn't reply. Ten minutes later, they push past a final curtain of ferns, and the lake stretches out before them. The stillness is unnerving. The water looks like molten glass, perfectly reflecting the fiery hues of the sunset.

"See?" Jason says, gesturing grandly. "You've never seen it like this before."

Beth's breath catches. "It's beautiful," she admits, her voice barely above a whisper. She steps closer to the water, mesmerized by its eerie calm. But then her eyes snag on something a few yards out — a splash of red near an over-turned canoe.

"Jason..." Her voice wavers as she points. "What is that?"

Jason follows her gaze, squinting. "Probably nothing. A buoy or a life jacket or something. Come on, let's swim."

Beth ignores him. Her heart thuds painfully in her chest as she pulls out her phone, hands trembling. She opens the camera app and zooms in on the floating object. The image comes into focus, and her breath stops.

Her scream tears through the stillness, echoing across the lake. Her phone slips from her hands and plunges into the water with a quiet splash. Beth doesn't notice — her wide eyes remain fixed on the body across the lake.

DETECTIVE JOHN HAWKINS pulls up to the lake. The beach is swarming with police, and divers in wet suits are carefully retrieving the body from the water.

He steps out of his car as Officer Mills, one of the first officers to arrive on the scene, approaches him.

"What do we have?" Hawkins asks.

"A deceased female. She appears to be in her thirties. We don't have an I.D. yet."

"Does it look like foul play?"

Mills shakes his head. "Hard to say so far, but I don't think so. This area? It's most likely she was out on the water at night, fell out of her canoe and drowned."

Hawkins frowns. Something feels off. This time of the year, he already felt it was too cold for night canoeing. "Are those the two who found her?" Hawkins nods toward the two teenagers sitting on a log, huddled under a blanket.

"Yeah, that's them," Mills confirms.

Hawkins walks toward them, pausing as the divers reach the shore with the body. He studies her for a moment — early thirties, close to his age. He sighs. Aldercreek is a small town where crime is rare, let alone a suspicious death. Hawkins knows that it's going to be a long night.

1

EDEN

I turn toward the register and take a few seconds to myself — only three more hours. I can do this. I take a deep breath and turn back toward the bar. I set the cash in front of one of my regulars.

"Can I get you anything else, Bill?" I ask.

"No, sweetheart. I'm good for now," he says. "Today's your last night, huh?"

"Yeah," I nod. "It is time to move on."

"Well, we're sure gonna miss you around here," he says as he takes a sip of his drink.

I smile at Bill. He comes every day like clockwork, around 10 p.m., and each time, he's wearing practically the same thing, almost as if it's a uniform: dark slacks and a plaid button-up shirt. His thinning gray hair is tucked under a ball cap, but wisps of it escape, peeking out on the sides. He's probably in his sixties, although I've never asked him. I'm a pretty good judge of people, though. It probably comes from the years I've spent in this place, mostly being an observer in other people's lives.

I've witnessed it all. First dates, breakups, honeymoons,

twenty-first birthday parties — and one thing is true about all of them: I feed them alcohol, and it always heightens whatever emotion they're feeling at the time. It's like a key to unlocking their deepest and darkest thoughts. People will share things with me that they would normally not even share with their best friend. I don't know if it's because they're intoxicated or if they see me as safe because they don't really know me, but whatever the case is, let's just say I've learned the most about people by listening to them spill their guts.

I grab a rag and wipe next to Bill. He watches me silently as I work. I can tell he's thinking about something. I clear my throat. "Couldn't sleep again tonight?" I ask him.

He shakes his head. "I always try to go to bed around nine, but I've learned not to try too long, or I'll just end up lying in bed the whole night."

"Well, we're always happy to see you here," I tell him as a loud noise erupts in the corner of the bar.

I glance at the booth, and the three girls sitting there are cackling loudly.

Bill looks over at them and back at me. "Good luck with that one," he says. "Looks like they've already had one too many."

"I know," I sigh. "I almost didn't let them come in, but they begged me."

I lay the rag down and walk towards the high-backed booth. I pause in the middle of the nearly empty space and look around me. The Hillside Lounge is not the fanciest bar in the Capitol Hill neighborhood of Seattle, but it's also not the worst. Our customers say that it's cozy and relaxing. The walls inside are made of brick, but almost every square inch is covered with local artwork. Artists hang their artwork for free in hopes of selling a piece to one of our customers. I like the vibe the artwork gives to the space. It's eclectic and always changing. Vintage neon signs that add a touch of nostalgia to the atmosphere are interspersed between the artwork.

I'm sure gonna miss this place. It's been home to me for so long. I force myself out of my reverie and continue walking toward the booth.

"How are you doing, ladies?" I ask mainly as a formality because it's clear that they are heavily intoxicated. There are two brunettes and a blonde. They look like they've had the best night of their lives.

The brunette closest to me turns towards me and smiles, but before she can even speak, she busts out laughing again. "I think Janice has had a little too much to drink," she giggles.

I look at the other two faces and quickly ascertain which one is Janice. She's the other brunette leaning back against the booth, staring up at the ceiling.

"Everything is spinning," she moans.

"Let me grab you all some water," I insist, not even waiting for them to agree.

I come back a couple of minutes later with a tray of three glasses of water and set one down in front of each of them. Janice looks even greener than she did when I left, if that's even possible.

"Which one of you is driving?" I ask, really hoping that they are not planning on driving themselves. The last thing I need is for one of them to get a DUI and then for me to get in trouble for over-serving them.

The brunette near me speaks up. "Oh, we're not driving. Our rideshare is on its way."

Relief floods my body. At least I don't have to worry about taking their keys or something like that.

The blonde girl looks at me. "Janice drove us here, but she's obviously in no position to drive us home. I offered to take her keys and drive us myself, but she wouldn't let me."

"That's probably smart," I say.

Janice begins to push her way out of the booth, trying desperately to get by the other brunette, a look of panic on her face. The brunette stands quickly and gets out of her way.

"Where's the bathroom?" She asks, clearly on the verge of losing her entire stomach. Her hand covers her mouth as she desperately tries to hold it in.

I point towards the back of the bar, but it's too late. She grabs my shoulders and proceeds to empty the contents of her stomach all over my apron. This is what I get for being nice. I knew I shouldn't have let them in.

Instead of pushing the sick girl off of me, I take it and try to make sure she's done before escorting her and her friends to the bathroom. Most people would think this is crazy, but this is not my first rodeo. This is a sick dance, and the best thing you can do for yourself is confine it to one place rather than clean the whole bar because she expelled everywhere in her path.

While they are in the bathroom, I toss my apron; then I clean and disinfect everything at the scene: the booth, the chairs, the floors. I make sure every crack and crevice is spotless.

I am scrubbing the legs of a table when I hear one of the girls' squeaky voices. "Could I have a double vodka soda?" She asks.

Resisting the urge to backhand her, I stand up and simply stare at her, dumbfounded.

She takes the hint. "Oh, okay," she says disappointedly.

I shake my head as I walk to the staff room behind the

bar. Drunk people are sometimes clueless about how far gone they are, and then this happens. It's a good thing I brought a change of clothes.

I remove my white button-up shirt and black slacks and replace them with jeans and a well-worn T-shirt. I'm definitely not meeting the dress code right now, but I don't really care. It's not like I can get fired.

Holding my breath, I look in a mirror, expecting to see whatever came out of that girl on my face and in my hair. Thankfully, I am spared. However, my chocolate-brown skin is drained of its warmth. My usually voluminous, curly fro looks deflated. It's been a long day. I look at my watch. Just two more hours, and I'm done with this place for good.

I grab the mop bucket from the supply closet and head back out into the bar. The three girls are gone. In their place is a wad of cash on the table. I quickly count it and put it in my pocket. At least they tipped well. That's not normally the case when the customers are wasted. Sometimes, they even forget to pay entirely.

I dip the mop into the soapy water and begin disinfecting the rest of the floor.

Bill walks up to me and puts his hand on my shoulder. "We're sure gonna miss you, Eden," he says.

"I'll miss you too, Bill," I say genuinely. The customers are probably what I'm going to miss the most, the nice ones, at least. Definitely not going to miss having to be somebody's toilet. "Are you heading out?" I ask, genuinely sad to see him go.

He nods. "I'm finally getting tired, and I'm going to take advantage of it."

I set down the mop and give him a huge hug. He stands stiffly, his arms pressed to his sides, but I keep hugging him. Eventually, he softens a little and wraps one arm around my back. Tears well in my eyes. I didn't expect to get emotional about this. I step back and punch him lightly on the shoulder. "You take care of yourself, Bill."

"Oh, I will," he says. "Don't you worry about me."

I watch him as he exits the bar and the door closes behind him. His exit makes the reality of the situation sink in. Tomorrow, I won't be coming back.

The next few hours pass uneventfully. A few random customers wander in, get a drink, and wander out. As soon as the clock strikes two a.m., I turn off the lights to the bar and walk out the front door, locking it behind me for the last time.

2

EDEN

I step onto the sidewalk and inwardly groan. The streets are wet, and the sky drizzles a light mist of rain. Typical Seattle weather. I wrap my coat around me and put my hood over my head. The wind blows almost violently, making it feel colder than it actually is. I hate walking alone in the dark, especially in this kind of weather, but I have no choice. I could have driven my car to work tonight and spent an hour looking for parking, but nobody has time for that. Besides, it's good to get the steps in.

As the rain stings my face, I find myself tempted to call a rideshare, but that would defeat the entire purpose of walking here in the first place. My home is only a few blocks away. I can do anything for a few blocks.

I take my pepper spray out of my purse and hold it in my right hand as I walk down the street. Thankfully, I don't live too far. It shouldn't take me more than twenty minutes to get home.

When I'm only a block from home, I hear footsteps behind me. Is someone following me? My heart rate increases. "Stop being so paranoid," I berate myself under my breath. "Not every person on the street is out to get you."

I glance behind me and see a dark figure walking in the same direction as me. It's probably nothing. Probably just someone who's trying to get home, like me. I pick up my pace, trying to shorten the distance to my front door. After several steps, I glance behind me again. The person has also picked up their pace. I feel an immediate rush of dampness under my arms and at the small of my back. My heart beats faster. What if they are trying to get me? Why would they walk faster if they weren't attempting to catch up with me? I unlock the pepper spray and prepare myself to aim it directly at their face.

The footsteps sound closer now, echoing loudly in the darkness. I take a deep breath. I can't keep running away. I'm not going to just live in this kind of fear.

I turn around to face my stalker head-on and aim the pepper spray at the face of the person approaching me.

"Leave me alone," I yell. My voice is steady and strong, masking the untamed fear I feel rising inside my chest. I put my finger on the trigger, and just as I'm about to spray it, the person raises both of their hands and yells, "Eden, don't. It's me."

"Derek?" I ask, slowly lowering my hand.

"Yes," he says. "I didn't mean to startle you, but you've not been answering my calls. I couldn't figure out any other way to reach you."

"Dang it, Derek. I almost pepper-sprayed you. You idiot." I take a deep breath and force my heart rate to slow.

"I can see that," he says.

I take a long look at him. He really is beautiful. His skin is almost mahogany in color. His locs hang past his sharp jawline and are sprinkled with mists of water that annoyingly shine in the streetlight. I take a step toward him, magnetically drawn to him. I miss him, but I can't do this. "What do you want, Derek?" I ask.

"I just want to talk. Please," he says earnestly.

"We're not together anymore."

"Trust me, I know," he says. "I can't get you out of my mind. All I'm asking for is a few minutes of your time. Please," he begs.

I cross my arms and stare at him. I wasn't quite fair to him when I ended things. Maybe I do owe him a little more of an explanation. At the same time, there's a part of me that knows I should just walk away. Giving this situation any more of my time will only make it harder for me to leave.

He stares at me with those puppy dog eyes that I've never been able to say no to. "Please, Eden, just a few minutes."

I silence the little bells going off in my mind that are warning me that this is a bad idea and shrug. "Fine. We can go to your place," I say. What can a few minutes hurt?

3

EDEN

I should have known better. The moment we step foot into his apartment, I am transported back to all the good times Derek and I had.

"Can I get you a glass of wine?" He asks.

I nod, knowing deep down that it's a bad idea.

He grabs two glasses from the cupboard and sets them on the counter. He opens the fridge, grabs a bottle of pinot grigio, and pours a hefty amount into each glass.

"What, you trying to get me drunk?" I tease.

"Maybe," he says, giving me a wry smile.

He sets the glass in front of me, and I take a long drink, practically downing half of it in one go.

"Dang, Eden," he exclaims. "Take it easy."

But I can't take it easy. Just being here is making me wish I had been able to make a different choice. I never wanted to break up with him.

Derek walks over to me and puts an arm around my waist. I should push him away, but I don't... I can't. I love him too much.

He puts his other hand on the side of my face and forces me to look at him. "You know I love you, right?"

I nod, unable to speak.

He leans forward and kisses me. The kiss is gentle and soft. I'm going to miss this. Derek's kisses quickly become more passionate. It's as if he wants something from me that I'm not sure I should give.

I push him away weakly. "I thought you just wanted to talk."

"I do, but is that enough for you? It's not enough for me."

I stare into his chocolate-brown eyes. I know what he means, and I know that I feel the same way. Finally, I nod my head, certain I'm going to regret it.

DEREK and I lie next to each other in his bed, staring at the ceiling. My body is exhausted. Tears prick my eyes. He rolls onto his side and stares at me. After several seconds, he wipes a stray curl off of my forehead.

"Eden," he says. "Look at me."

I blink hard to rid my eyes of the tears and turn my head toward him.

"I need you to be honest with me," he says. "I thought what we had was special. A once-in-a-lifetime kind of love, you know? You didn't have to end things. I'm willing to wait for you."

I nod and look away. Just the sight of him makes me second-guess my choice. "I know," I whisper. "But it's not that simple. I gotta do this by myself." I take a deep breath and look back at him. "I'm leaving tomorrow," I say softly.

Sadness fills his face. He grabs my hand. "Please don't do this. You can figure out a way to move on without leaving," he pleads.

I shake my head, tears threatening to spill from my eyes. "You know I can't do that. I will never forgive myself if I don't follow this through. And if I know you're here waiting for me, it will stop me from doing what I have to do. I love you, Derek, but I will never be good for you if I don't do this first."

"You know I had to try," he says resignedly. "You're the only woman I'll ever want, Eden."

"I don't know if I'll ever be back, Derek. You should really try and move on," I say gently.

He nods, but I can tell he doesn't want to. As much as I love him and as much as I want to stay here, I know I can't. This path was laid before me years ago, and I have to walk it no matter what I leave behind.

I swing my legs over the side of the bed and stand. I hunt the floor for my clothes and find them wadded up in the corner of the room.

Derek gets up and walks to the kitchen, pouring us glasses of water. As soon as I'm done dressing, I walk into the kitchen. He hands me the glass of water, and I down it in one gulp.

"Thanks," I say, placing the glass on the counter.

"I hope this isn't forever," he tells me.

"Me too, but you can't stay behind and wait for me. I can't have that pressure."

"Just know I love you, Eden. I always will."

"I love you too, Derek," I reply. He steps towards me and gently kisses me on the lips. It's soft and tender and feels like a final goodbye.

I pull away and quickly step toward the door. I don't look at him for fear he will see me crying.

"Wait," he says. "I have something for you."

I turn and look at him as he heads back into the bedroom.

He emerges a few seconds later with a brown box and hands it to me. "Don't open it right now. Do it later when you're alone," he says.

I take the package and tuck it under my arm. "Thanks, Derek, you really are the best." I don't even try to hide the tears anymore as they freely flow down my face.

"You can call and text me anytime you need someone to talk to," he says as I open the door.

I nod, unable to speak. Walking away from him is one of the hardest things I've ever done, but I know I must do it.

I step into the hall and towards the elevator without even looking back. If I look back, I know I will stay the night, and all my plans will be ruined.

As soon as I get to the elevator and the door closes, I take a deep breath and wipe away my tears. As hard as it is to leave, I know if I don't, I won't be a whole person capable of being in a healthy relationship. I have to do this so I can someday live.

4

EDEN

I open the door to my empty apartment. I just finished packing all of my stuff into my car. The only thing that remains is my bed. I either gave away or donated everything else. I can't fit my bed in the car, so I'm not bringing it with me. Aldercreek has a thrift store. I'll just find something when I get there.

It's still dark outside. The sun hasn't yet begun to peek over the horizon. I had planned on staying here one more night and leaving in the morning, but after spending time with Derek, I don't think staying another minute is wise. I am on the edge of talking myself out of this. If I do that, I will never be able to move on. Besides, it's just after four a.m. I'm barely going to get any sleep as it is. I pull the sheets off my bed and stuff them into a garbage bag along with the comforter I've had ever since I was a child. I double-check each room to make sure I leave nothing behind. Every room and closet is already empty.

I take one last look around. I'm going to miss this place.

I lock the door and quickly walk down the stairs. The sound of rain pelting on the metal roof above me fills my ears. The moment I step out from under the covered walkway into the parking lot, I'm drenched.

"Dang it," I say as I cover my head with the garbage bag and rush to my red convertible. The car was made way before I was born and has almost three hundred thousand miles on it. Thankfully, it still runs well. My sister and I always dreamed of having matching convertibles once we could drive. It was all part of a grander plan to live together in a cottage in some small town far away from where we grew up.

I got mine just after I graduated from high school and got my first real job. It has been well loved. There have been moments when it has broken, and I've thought about getting a new car, but I've made so many memories in this thing. It has been my constant companion for so long that I can't imagine letting it go.

I open the back door and throw the bag onto the back seat. The door creaks as I throw it shut and rush to the front. I get in the driver's side seat and exhale, wiping the drops of rain from my face. I pat the dashboard. "We're going on a trip, Ruby," I tell her. Initially, she was a bright red color, and the name suited her. Now, the red has faded, and there are dings and scratches all over her. She doesn't look very ruby anymore, but I don't care. She's always going to be Ruby to me.

I start the engine and turn on the windshield wipers. They barely move fast enough to keep up with the rain pelting down. I grip the steering wheel as I pull out of the parking lot onto the dark streets.

When I get to the freeway, there is no traffic. It is lined with dense forests that keep out the moon's light. My headlights are my only guide. I worry on several occasions that a deer will stray out in front of me, and I won't see it in time to stop. I'm on high alert the entire time I'm driving. I really should have waited until morning, but if I had, I might have never left.

THE DRIVE IS SURPRISINGLY UNEVENTFUL. By the time the sun peaks over the horizon, I'm pulling into the parking lot of a four-story apartment building nestled on top of a hill overlooking a valley.

I park my car and walk into the building, quickly finding the manager's door. I knock several times and wait. An old blond-haired woman opens the door. It's clear I've woken her from her sleep.

"I'm so sorry to bother you," I tell her. "My name is Eden. I'm leasing the apartment on the fourth floor, the one that overlooks the valley. I got here earlier than expected, and I was hoping I could get my key?" I ask.

"I.D.?" She asks.

I grab my wallet and hand the I.D. to her. She doesn't know that it's a fake.

"You already sent all the other paperwork. Let me just copy this, and I'll grab your key."

Before I can respond, she shuts the door in my face, leaving me in the hallway. I stand there for several minutes before she returns with the keys and my I.D. She hands them to me and shuts the door again, immediately locking it behind her.

That was too quick. How does she even know for sure I'm the tenant? I've never met her in person. We've done all the necessary paperwork via email. I look around me. What I see answers the question for me. The carpets in the hallways are worn thin, and the walls have scuff marks all over them. I don't think anybody really cares about this place, which suits my purposes perfectly.

I climb the steps to the fourth floor, my legs burning by the time I reach it. I unlock the door and peek my head into the apartment.

"Hello?" I ask, my voice echoing around inside. It's empty and dark. I turn on the lights and quickly check all the closets in each room to ensure they're empty. As soon as I am satisfied that there's no one hiding in the corners of the unit, I breathe a sigh of relief.

I step to the window that overlooks the valley and look outside. Large houses cover the side of the hill; some would even call them mansions. Each house has several acres of minimally developed property. It's as if each family has its own oasis in the woods.

I run back down to my car and grab several of my bags, hauling them up the stairs. I place the load in the middle of the living room and run back down the stairs for a second load. It doesn't take me long to finish the job. I don't own much anymore.

As soon as I bring the last bag into my apartment, I close the door and lock it behind me. I hunt for my black bag, finding it at the bottom of the pile. I unzip it and pull out a pair of binoculars. I open the sliding glass door, stepping out onto the patio that overlooks the valley. I put the binoculars to my eyes and move them around, adjusting them until I spot it — a large Victorian-style home sitting in a small development about half a mile away. A man and a woman are sitting on their porch, sipping coffee. I get out my notepad and start taking notes.

7:04 a.m. The couple is awake and drinking coffee on their back porch. It looks like the wife is wearing some kind of house dress underneath a long down jacket, but the man is already dressed in his suit and tie.

I watch for several minutes until the wife stands and walks back inside before writing again.

7:30 a.m. The wife leaves the back porch and walks back into the house. The husband is still sitting outside with his coffee.

I grab a folding chair and set it up on the porch. I sit in the chair and wrap myself in a blanket. Thankfully, it's no longer raining, but it's still cold.

I continue to watch them, taking notes anytime I observe something new happening. My eyes feel heavy. I'm not sure I can keep them open much longer. I set the binoculars on my lap, and before I realize what is happening, I drift off to sleep.

5

LIV

I take a long, deep sip of my coffee. I love mornings like this. Mitch and I are sitting on our back porch in silence. It's cooler now than it will be when the sun rises, and there's a slight breeze. In just a few hours, the sun will be fully in the sky, and it will be almost too bright to enjoy this space, but now it's perfect.

Our house sits on a large lot that borders the forest. Occasionally, we see deer and other wildlife wander onto our back lawn. This is exactly the life I had dreamed of having. I love being able to watch nature from a distance and, at the same time, experience all the luxuries life has to offer. It's really the best of both worlds.

I spend the next twenty minutes focusing on my goals for the day. I have an open house today at eleven and three appointments for showings scattered throughout. Every detail about my day is planned down to the minute. I always say that without a plan, you are bound to fail. I will never fail.

Mitch sits on the chair next to me, reading the newspaper. He's already dressed for the day and looks as handsome as usual. He is precisely the kind of man I always thought I would marry. When I was in middle school, I wrote a list of the qualities I wanted in a husband. As I got older and started dating, I didn't vary from that list one bit. I waited until I found a man who had checked every box.

We were in an A.P. Economics study group together during our senior year in high school. I knew the first time we met that he was the one. It took some planning and scheming, but several years later, we were married. We haven't had any issues since, at least not any that we can't handle. He's just as I thought he would be: ambitious, strong, and wildly successful.

The alarm on my phone goes off, and I know it's time to move. I take one last sip of my coffee and rise from the chair.

"I'm gonna head inside and get ready," I say to Mitch.

He looks at me and nods, his eyes running up and down my body approvingly. "I'll be right in," he says, taking another sip of his coffee.

"Seriously, Mitch?" I ask, rolling my eyes. I know that look. We've been trying to have a baby for a year and a half, and that's the *let's do it right now* look, but I don't have time for that. I'm gonna have to let him down gently again.

I walk upstairs to my room. Mitch and I sleep in the same bed, but I have my own room for my clothes, along with my own bathroom. It's easier that way. Besides, this is a five-bedroom house; what else are we going to use the other bedrooms for?

My clothes are already neatly hung on a hanger in my bathroom. I prep everything the night before. I must make my mornings as streamlined as possible. I can't afford to deal with a wrinkled shirt or missing stockings as I get ready. I usually have appointments all day starting at nine am, and it's essential that I be on time.

I carefully apply my makeup and put on my clothes. I'm looking in the mirror, putting on the finishing touches, when Mitch walks in and wraps his arms around me.

Is he really this clueless? Does he think I'm going to do that right after I've gotten ready for the day? I push him away. "Not now, Mitch," I say, annoyed.

"But I think you're ovulating," he says. "Your lips always get bright pink when you're ovulating, and this morning it almost looked like you were wearing lipstick."

"Well, that's probably true," I say. "It is that time of the month, but if we do it now, both of us will be late for work."

"No one's going to die if you're late one day, Liv," he says.

I glare at him. "How could you even say something like that? You know how important this is to me. I'm trying to build an empire here. My brokerage is one of the best in Aldercreek, but we aren't without competition. I can't let my guard down for even one day if I want to achieve my goals."

Mitch looks at me, disappointed. I can see the weariness on his face. Trying for a baby for so long is taking its toll, and I feel myself softening just a little.

I put my hand on his shoulder. "Tonight," I say quietly. "I am free from eight to ten p.m. We can do it sometime then."

"Can't we ever just be spontaneous?" He asks, frustrated.

"People who don't plan don't achieve the things they want in life," I tell him. "So, no. Even this has to be a part of the plan."

He sighs and runs his hands through his hair. "Fine," he says. "Tonight it is."

I can tell he's not happy. He'll get over it. He always does.

He silently leaves my bathroom. I hear the garage door opening a few minutes later. I glance out the bedroom window and watch as he drives away.

I slip on my heels and look at myself in the mirror for the last time. "Perfect," I say to my reflection.

I walk down the stairs to grab the salad that Nadia, our helper, made for me for lunch. Walking into the kitchen, I see her cutting vegetables on the island. I like her. She's a hard worker. She keeps to herself. Her English is not that great, so sometimes, it's hard to communicate with her, but we figure it out.

"Good morning, Nadia," I say.

She looks at me and nods, a shy smile forming.

I grab my salad out of the fridge and turn to her. "Don't forget I left the new lunch plan for Mitch on the fridge. Please don't deviate from it. His numbers were slightly elevated at his last appointment, so we must ensure he is eating the proper combination of foods."

I place the salad in my bag and look back at Nadia when she doesn't respond. She startles and quickly begins to pull down her long sleeves. Before she does, I notice a bruise on her arm, almost like a handprint.

"Yes, Mrs. Mitre," she says quietly.

I look at her long and hard. Why is she so nervous? Where did that bruise come from? I consider asking, but I don't have time for her answer.

I glance at my watch. I have to be at work in twenty minutes, and the brokerage is nearly ten minutes away. As my daddy always said, being on time is late.

I stare at her for a few more seconds and decide to let it go. I'm sure it was just some accident.

"Please don't forget about the lunch plan," I tell her. "It is very important."

She looks at me and nods. I can see tears forming in her eyes.

I shake my head as I walk out of the house. She really

needs to get a grip on her emotions. It is not appropriate to cry on the job. I'll have to speak to her about this later, but right now, I have more pressing issues.

My first client this morning is a wealthy businessman looking to move to the area. The types of homes he is interested in viewing today could earn me quite a paycheck. Everything else can wait.

LIV

I open the car door and place my bag on the passenger seat of my mid-size car. It's not the exact type of car I would have wanted, but it's nice. The seats are leather, and they give the car an air of luxury, but it's just not my dream car. Someday, I will have the best, classiest car in Aldercreek.

I pull out of the garage and start driving toward the office. I check the time. I've got eighteen minutes before my first appointment — just enough time to get coffee on the way.

I pull up to my regular coffee stand a few blocks from my house. It's a small, independently owned shop that makes some of the best coffee in the area. I roll down my window.

"Good morning, Liv," the lone barista says to me.

"Good morning, Tawni," I reply cheerfully. She can't be more than twenty-one, but she's been working here for as long as I can remember. She must have started when she was in high school. Her face is young and beautiful, and she's always dressed a little provocatively. I'm sure Mitch and every other man in this city comes here just to look at her, but I don't care. No matter how hard she tries, she will never be as successful as me, especially working at a coffee stand. In fact, I pity her a little bit. She has her looks going for her but not much else. Even those will fade someday.

"Would you like your usual?" She asks.

I nod and watch as she pours the oat milk into a metal container and steams it. I don't do dairy anymore. Haven't for a long time. Oat milk is my alternative milk of choice. While the milk is steaming, she pulls two shots of espresso and expertly combines the two in a paper cup.

"Here you go, Miss Liv," she says. "A double tall oat milk latte, just how you like it."

I take the cup from her and carefully place it in my cup holder. "Thank you, Tawni," I say. I pay and give her the regular twenty percent. I make sure to do this because if I keep the public servants happy, I can potentially get referrals from them later.

As I drive away, I can't help but wish I was young again like her. There are so many things about this life that I would have done differently. Mostly, I would have started working towards my goals earlier, but when I was in college, I was so wrapped up in getting married that I didn't really start my career until my mid-twenties. Don't get me wrong, I love Mitch, and I'm glad we're married, but if I had started when I was her age, I would have been unstoppable.

I take a sip of my latte. Perfect, as usual.

Ten minutes later, I pull into the parking lot of a mid-sized shopping center. The brick facade of the buildings gives it a classy vibe, even though it's really just a glorified strip mall. All of the shops look basically the same from the outside, but some of the most exclusive boutiques in town are located here.

My little brokerage is nestled between a children's boutique selling exquisite French-imported clothing and a high-end pilates studio. In addition to the boutiques, some of the best restaurants in town can also be found here.

Even at this early hour, the sidewalks are full of people. I watch as stay-at-home moms push their kids in strollers, chatting with each other. This is the spot where the upper-middle-class members of our community congregate.

I was ecstatic the day the *for rent* sign went up outside what is now my brokerage. I knew that moving my company here would put me on a different path, so I jumped at the opportunity even though the rent was significantly higher than the rent at our previous location. I was convinced that operating in a wealthier neighborhood would bring wealthier clientele and that the increase in rent would quickly not even be an issue. For the most part, I was right. The space is small, but it's all mine. At the rate we're growing, I will have to find a new place in just a few years to house all the agents that work for me.

I stare at the sign I had custom-made and put up just last week. I love it. It says L. M. Brokerage in simple gold lettering. It's evidence to everyone who reads it that I have made it.

I grab my bag and my coffee and step out of the car. As soon as I do, I notice a car pulling into one of the parking spots I pay to reserve for my clients. I pick up my pace. I have to get inside before him. I refuse to ever have one of my clients waiting for me. I must always be on time.

EDEN

I have been watching Liv from my little balcony window for three days now. Every morning, she follows the exact same routine.

First, she sits on the porch with her husband, drinks her coffee, and goes back inside. Next, she leaves in her car at precisely the same time every day to head to her office.

I've followed her in my car each time, staying back as far as possible without losing her. I'm pretty sure she has no idea I'm there. She's so wrapped up in her own little world that she doesn't even consider those around her. That makes following her easy. I don't really have to be that careful.

She always stops at a small coffee stand. I presume she gets the same thing each time, considering the rest of her life is so orderly. After the coffee stand, it's straight to work.

She arrives at the office within the same five-minute time span every day, like clockwork.

Today, I skip that whole following her part and drive straight to the complex where her office is located. I park at the end of the lot, close enough to the brokerage that I can still see the front door, but not directly in front of the building. I want to be able to watch without being seen.

A tall, brunette woman approaches the front door. I haven't seen her before. She's dressed impeccably in a pencil skirt and light blue blouse. Her high heels and manicured nails complete the look. Her hair is pulled back in a bun, and as far as I can tell from this position, there's not a single stray piece of hair. She's the brunette version of Liv.

I watch as she unlocks the door and lets herself into the office, eventually turning on the brokerage's lights and flipping the door sign to *open*.

I look at the clock. Liv should be here soon.

My phone vibrates in my lap, and I pick it up, hyperaware that if I get too distracted by my phone, I could miss Liv's arrival.

It's a message from Derek. *I've been thinking about you. I hope everything's going okay. I miss you.*

A sharp pain forms in my chest. He has no idea how much I miss him, too. I close the app and put the phone upside down so I can't see if he texts again. I can't allow myself to be emotionally invested in things with him right now. I have to remain focused and vigilant.

I look around the complex, taking in everything. The past few times I've been here, I've been so focused on Liv that I didn't have the chance to take note of my surroundings. It's a nice place but a little too bougie for me.

I notice a clothing store a few doors down from the brokerage. The mannequins in the window are dressed in gowns made of taffeta and silk. One of those dresses probably cost the same as my entire haul yesterday at the local thrift store, where I bought an air mattress along with a few necessities for the apartment. It seems almost immoral to spend that kind of money on a single piece of clothing.

I watch as two women enter the store, one of them pushing a stroller. I shake my head. They live a life I can't even fathom. Somehow, I have to figure out how to fit in here. My shoulders sag at the weight of it all. It seems almost impossible.

I look around the parking lot. By the south entrance, I notice a huge gray rock. I don't know how I've missed it the last few times I've been here. A memory immediately comes rushing back. I've seen that rock before. This place used to be mostly just woods. In my memory, the rock was covered in a spray-painted message that read *Happy Birthday, Janiee!* Below the wording was a giant number seven.

A few feet away from the rock stood a gas station on a lonely highway. It was the only gas station in Aldercreek and the only place for miles for visitors driving through town to fill up. I wonder what happened to it.

I'm pulled from my memory by a flash of blonde getting out of a car. Liv is dressed no-nonsense as usual. Her crisp blouse is buttoned up nearly to the top, with only the top button left undone. She isn't one of those real estate agents who tries to sell homes with her looks. She takes the business and her knowledge of local real estate seriously. Her perfectly bleached hair is flat-ironed and hangs straight around her face. She confidently walks into her office, but not before taking a few seconds to stop and stare at the sign with her name on it. Geez, this woman is full of herself.

I wonder what goes on in there all day. Who does she talk to? Who is she friends with? Who is she dismissive and rude to? There's so much more about Liv that I need to know. I need to find a way to get closer to her.

8

LIV

I walk into my brokerage to the smell of freshly brewed coffee. It is impeccably clean, just as I like it. I hire a crew to clean a couple of nights per week, so nothing ever looks out of place. At the reception desk, there is always a large vase full of white roses. They are a symbol of order. I keep the same ones on my kitchen island at home. I change them often before they wilt or even get the slightest browning. I know that when people walk into my office or my home, they will feel confident that we have everything under control, including the clutter and the dirt.

"Good morning!" I yell from the front door.

"Back here making coffee," Sandy yells.

I walk to the sizeable glass-walled office in the front corner of the room, unlock the door, and set down my purse on the desk chair. The office is perched on a small platform raised just a few feet off the ground so I can overlook the rest of the agents and ensure everyone is on task. Plus, it helps to psychologically remind my employees that I'm in charge. I had the builder install shades that I can close when I want some privacy, but I usually leave them open.

The rest of the office is filled with neatly arranged desks in cubicles. I currently have four other agents besides Sandy. Most of them come into the office for a couple of hours during the day but spend the majority of their time either showing houses to clients or knocking on doors to get new listings. We have weekly staff meetings to discuss sales, listings, and marketing strategies. I always insist that each of them makes attending that meeting a priority. Otherwise, I really don't care how they spend their time as long as they hit their monthly quotas.

When new agents join the firm, they are placed on probation for the first six months. During that time, I set them a goal and meticulously track every move they make. If they do not meet or exceed that goal by the end of the six months, they are dismissed. It's one way I ensure that we never have dead weight in the office. My agents are some of the best in the business.

Sandy comes out of the back room with a cup of coffee in her hand. "Good morning, boss," she says in her sweet Southern drawl.

We met five years ago at a local auction and quickly became inseparable. Within six months of knowing each other, I convinced her to get her real estate license and join me at my brokerage. She doesn't sell many houses, but she helps me in other ways by taking on some of the office management tasks that I literally can't stand, like making coffee for our clients. She and her husband didn't really need the money, but she was bored, and I needed the help. She is the only one I don't hold to my high standards for agents. She's my best friend. She could sell one house or ten houses a month, I don't care.

She takes a sip of her coffee. "You'd never believe my morning," she says, almost giddy.

"What are you talking about? It's just after eight o'clock. What could have already happened?"

"I know, but one of Blaine's friends flew into town last night. We met him for dinner and found out that he's thinking about moving here."

"That's convenient," I say, slightly jealous. I never get clients that easily.

"Well, of course, I offered to help him look for a home. He had meetings with clients scheduled all day today, but I convinced him to get up early and view a couple of homes before his first appointment. You would not believe his budget; it's unreal."

I eyeball her skeptically.

"I took him to the empty mansion on Hillhurst Street."

My eyebrows rise. "You took him there before eight in the morning?" I ask, surprised.

"It's empty," she says, waving her hand at me. "Nobody's gonna care."

"You run the risk of one of the neighbors calling the cops on you," I tell her.

She shrugs. "Nobody pays attention to anything in this town. It's so safe that they could be robbed right under their noses and wouldn't notice."

She's probably right. Aside from two drownings in the local lake that were deemed accidents, we've barely had any crimes committed here for as long as I can remember. The only thing I have heard about in the past few years is the occasional spray-painted business wall, most likely perpetrated by the local teenagers. Most of the people who live here are law-abiding citizens.

"Well, tell me about the showing," I say.

"He loved it. You should have seen the look on his face. I

wish I could get my husband to look at me the way these men look at million-dollar homes," she says, laughing.

"Oh, I'm sure he does, but you just don't realize it," I say dismissively. Sandy and Blaine are the perfect couple. I've always looked up to them.

She stares at me skeptically. "He barely acts like I even exist sometimes."

I ignore her. She's prone to dramatics. "Well, anyway, finish telling me about the client."

"Right," she says. "I think he's going to make an offer."

"That would be an amazing win for the brokerage," I say. "And for you, too. Stay on top of it."

"Of course I will, Liv. I'm good at this. I know I don't sell a lot, but you know when I do, I go big. You don't have to worry," Sandy reassures me, taking another sip of her coffee. She looks down at my empty hands. "No coffee this morning?" She asks.

"I didn't have time. Mitch and I got into an argument, and I left five minutes late."

"I made plenty in the back. Help yourself."

"I think I will," I reply, feeling a headache forming in my temples. I'm sure it's caffeine withdrawal. I've been drinking caffeine at the exact same time every day for years now, and any time I skip it, I get a monster headache.

As I pour my coffee, I hear Sandy turn on the television in the corner of the office. I used to argue with her about turning the television on during the workday, but I gave up a long time ago. Sandy is obsessed with knowing local gossip, so I acquiesced and now allow her to watch the news for thirty minutes daily.

"The Aldercreek mayoral race is about to heat up as local area candidates are putting in their bid for this year's election," the newswoman announces.

I walk back into the office with a cup of coffee in my hand.

"You know, you really should run for mayor," Sandy says. "You would be great at it. Not to mention, you've lived here your entire life, so you know everything about the town."

Of course, I want to be mayor; why wouldn't I? This community needs a woman's touch to move it in the right direction, and I know I'd be perfect for the job. However, I can't just come out and say that. Nobody likes a braggart. I need to play it cool. "You really think so?" I ask.

"Of course, you would be the best mayor," she responds encouragingly.

What Sandy doesn't know is that I'm planning on filing the paperwork for my candidacy in the next couple of weeks. I've already made up my mind. However, I need her to be one hundred percent behind my decision. I'm no fool. I know I'm going to need strong allies if I'm going to win. She obviously thinks it's a good idea, but her comment was made off the cuff. I need her to believe she was the one who convinced me to run because then she will be fully invested in the outcome. When the sheep are invested, it makes it easier to lead them both to pasture and to slaughter. They will follow me anywhere I decide to take them.

I wave my hand at Sandy in mock dismissal. "Nobody wants to see me as mayor, at least not right now. Maybe in ten years. I'll reconsider once I've further established my business. By that time, maybe people will see me as a serious candidate."

"You have no idea how people see you now," Sandy says. "You're envied by so many. I think you'd be a shoo-in."

I pretend as though I'm seriously contemplating her words. "You think so?" I ask, hoping to sound uncertain.

"Liv, have you looked at yourself lately? You're perfect, and you would be perfect for Aldercreek."

Perfect. I can see in her eyes that she means it. I've got her.

"I'll think about it," I say. I force my face to look serious, but inside, I'm beaming.

9

EDEN

Over the last several days, I've been continuing to follow Liv. It's been more of the same predictable routine. She leaves the office only between the hours of ten and twelve or again between one and three to meet with clients. At precisely twelve fifteen, she walks to a nearby cafe called Dotty's, where she picks up her lunch. From my car, I can see it's a salad, but I'm not sure what kind. All I know is that it looks exactly the same every day. After work, she heads directly to a local bar to meet a client. Today is no exception.

She exits her office precisely at five o'clock and locks the door behind her. She gets in her car and pulls out of the parking lot. I stay a reasonable distance behind her, but at this point, I know exactly where she's going. I don't have to follow her, but I do, just in case she veers from her routine. She doesn't. Ten minutes later, she pulls into the parking lot of Dave's, the nicest bar in town. It's one of those classy places that is dark inside. The only light comes from candles and lamps placed on every table. The floors are rich mahogany, and the bar itself looks like it was hand-carved. It kind of seems out of place for a small town like this, but the average income of the population here is obscene, so it makes sense.

Liv doesn't immediately head inside. Instead, she waits in her car until she sees her client approach the front door. She gets out of the car and flags them down, shaking their hand outside and escorting them in.

It's clear she is a creature of habit. I have almost completely memorized her movements — at least the ones I can witness from afar. Somehow, I need to get inside her life.

I pull my laptop out of my backpack and connect to the restaurant's Wi-Fi. I pull up Liv's brokerage website. Liv's headshot is front and center of the page, her bright white teeth shining in her camera-ready smile. Her email address is posted prominently underneath her photo. I quickly jot it down in my notebook.

I log into the email account I made just for this purpose and start a new message. *Dear Ms. Mitre, I'm a businessman from Seattle looking for a weekend home...*

10

LIV

As I walk into Dave's, I smile and nod as my new client describes his perfect home. He looks like the typical guy I work with. Probably was in a frat at the university. He probably pays a little too much for his haircuts but is too embarrassed to admit it.

"I'm really just hoping to find an oasis from the city — a place where I can relax on the weekends. Maybe I'll even invite a few friends sometimes," he says. "I imagine Aldercreek kind of being like the Hamptons, but for Seattle."

"I like that analogy," I respond. "I think I'll use it in my marketing. It's very true, though. The amenities Aldercreek has to offer are world-class. Fine dining, a highly-rated golf course and country club, not to mention the high-scale handcrafted homes you have to choose from."

My client continues describing his list of wants. He has a condo in the city that he will use during the week, and this will be his weekend home.

These men from Seattle are all the same. They're either high-powered attorneys, work in tech, or they work in the financial sector. Many of them are worth millions, and they have more money than they know what to do with, so they start buying up real estate.

I can already predict it. He'll buy a home here that he will barely occupy. Don't get me wrong, he will come here every weekend for the first few months, and he will love it, but the commute will start to wear on him, and eventually, he'll be here maybe once a month, if not less.

That is, until he has a family. Once he has a wife and kids, he will feel much safer having them out here in our small town than having them live in the city. He'll move his family to Aldercreek, where the kids will be raised primarily by their mother, while he commutes to and from Seattle every single day. A few nights a week, he'll stay in that condo downtown when he has a work dinner or is getting drinks with a client. At least, that's what he'll tell his wife. He'll raise his family here, and he will feel like he's done right by them because of our highly-rated schools and low crime rates. The kids will grow up knowing small-town life, and he will feel safe having them isolated from the rest of the world. I've seen it dozens of times.

This client is just starting out on his journey. Phase one is to convince him to buy much more house than he needs so that he is already prepared for the day he has a family.

"I hope that's not too much to ask for," he says.

I haven't even really been paying attention to what he's been saying. Oh, I've been pretending to take meticulous notes of everything he's been describing, but the truth is, I don't really even need to listen. I can read him like a book. I give him a broad smile and shake my head. "No, of course not. I can find you exactly what you're looking for."

From the moment I shook his hand in the parking lot, I

began making a mental note of the properties I would show him based on the car he drove and how he was dressed. I know I shouldn't profile like that, but it works.

By the time we sit for drinks, I have several properties in mind. I allow him to talk, though. It makes him feel heard, and when I show him homes tomorrow, he'll think I paid attention to every single detail. Being good at selling houses is less about marketing than it is about psychology. What a client says they want and what they need are two different things. I focus on what they need and then make them believe it's also what they want.

I glance at my watch. It's five-fifty — time to leave. "I'm so sorry, but I have to get home. I already have several homes in mind that I can't wait to show you tomorrow."

"Oh great," he says enthusiastically. "One o'clock, correct?"

"Yes, sir," I say as I put down some cash for the drinks and grab my purse. "It was lovely to finally meet you after spending so much time going back and forth over email." I extend my hand, and he shakes it firmly.

"Likewise. Have a great evening," he says, returning to his drink.

I exit Dave's and get in my car. Before backing out of the parking lot, I create a quick itinerary for tomorrow's home showing tour. I write down the houses in the order that makes the most sense so we can get through them as quickly as possible, starting with the house I am most excited to show him.

If I were a betting woman, I would bet money that my client would pick the first house I show him and not want to look at any others. In just those few short minutes I spent with him, I've been able to ascertain exactly the type of man he is, and I know the perfect house for him.

My commute home is quick. There's no rush-hour traffic like there is in Seattle. I open the garage door. Mitch is already home. What is he doing here already? He almost never gets home before seven. He runs the largest construction company in town and is usually swamped managing the job sites until well past six.

A realization hits me like a ton of bricks — he wants to be intimate. I know I promised him I would this morning, especially since I'm supposed to be ovulating soon, but I don't know that I have it in me now. It's not that I dislike making love to my husband. Once we get going, I generally have a good time. I do love him, and I find myself attracted to him, but it just seems to take away so much time from the other things I need to do. The longer we're married and the older I get, I find it more of a chore than something I do for pleasure. I look at my watch. I can put this off for a couple more hours. I'll just tell him I've got work to do first.

I open the door to the house, and Mitch is nowhere to be found on the first floor. He must be in his office upstairs. I breathe a sigh of relief. Maybe I can avoid him for a little while.

I walk into the kitchen and find Nadia cleaning up the dishes from the dinner she prepared for us. The food is neatly put away in small glass dishes in the fridge. We'll eat this meal for the next couple of nights until she cooks again.

"Good evening, Nadia," I say to her kindly.

"Hello, Mrs. Mitre," she responds. She doesn't look me in the eye when she says it, which I find quite strange. She's always been shy and quiet, but she's never been impolite.

I stand and stare at her for several seconds, trying to read her body language to figure out what's going on. Is she hiding something from me? She's impossible to read. I must pay closer attention to her in the next few days. Maybe she's stealing from me. I make a mental note to check all of my things to ensure they are still present.

If she's not stealing, what else could she be hiding? I push the thought to the back of my mind; I have more pressing things to worry about.

I grab the premade dinner from the refrigerator and pop it in the microwave. "This looks delicious, Nadia. Thank you," I say.

"You're welcome," she says quietly as she rinses dishes and puts them in the dishwasher.

I grab a wine glass out of the cabinet and fill it halfway with my favorite pinot grigio. I allow myself to have one glass of wine every night with dinner, but no more. It's important to me that I keep my figure and my faculties. Too much wine, and I say and do things that I regret. Just as I pull my food out of the microwave, Mitch enters the kitchen.

"Dinner smells amazing," he says, grabbing his own container from the fridge.

He walks up behind me, his food in one hand and wraps his other arm around me. "You ready for tonight?" He asks seductively.

"You're gonna spill your food, Mitch," I say, trying to wriggle away from him.

He sets his food down and wraps both arms around me.

"Mitch, Nadia is still here," I hiss. "Not now."

"Nadia, you're dismissed. We can finish the dishes," he says, not even looking at her.

She quickly grabs her things and exits the kitchen, not bothering to dry her hands.

"You made her uncomfortable," I tell him, frustrated.

"She'll get over it," he says, caressing different parts of my body.

I sigh, setting down my plate of food and my glass of wine. I turn around towards him, allowing him to kiss me long and deep. I might as well get this over with. Dinner can wait.

11

EDEN

I check my email at seven a.m. At the top of my inbox is a response from Liv. After several back-and-forth exchanges, we set a time for her to meet with the wealthy businessman the following day. Of course, she picked Dave's for the meeting, as I expected she would. Little does she know that things aren't going to go exactly as she has planned.

LATER THAT NIGHT, I sit on my back porch and observe Liv's evening routine. I've done this every night since I arrived. From my vantage point on the balcony, I can see through their back windows into the kitchen and the living room, but not much beyond that. For most of the night, I don't see anything at all. I usually observe until the lights dim. Liv often leaves the house at least once each night to run errands, but in the past few days, she's been a recluse, never venturing out after dusk.

I spend several minutes watching her navigate through the same routine. There's nothing new; it's the same old boring night. I check the map on my phone and find a local Chinese place. I can't justify paying for most of the restaurants in this town. So much of the fancy food in the suburbs is overpriced without the taste to back it up. At least in the city, if you buy something expensive, it tastes amazing. I'll give this place a try, though. I have been craving Chinese food for a while now.

I leave the notepad on the porch and hop in my car. I roll down my windows and allow the fresh air to blow my hair. In the distance, I can hear the marching band playing at the local high school football field. It's not quite football season, so I imagine they're practicing for a competition or a parade.

I pull up to the Chinese restaurant. It's exactly what I had expected. It's small and simply adorned. An older Chinese woman greets me at the counter and tells me that she owns the restaurant and that the man in the back cooking the food is her husband. She looks excited to see me. I look around the restaurant and realize it is entirely empty. I hope I'm not her first customer of the day.

I smile at the woman kindly. "It's nice to meet you. I can't wait to try your husband's cooking."

She flashes me the broadest smile I've ever seen and promptly takes my order. I order egg foo young and chow mein.

The woman excitedly hands the ticket to her husband as I pull cash out to pay her. She hands me back my change. I leave all of it in the small tip jar on the counter next to the register.

She smiles at me gratefully. "I'll be right back," she says as she walks to the kitchen to help her husband pack the food.

In less than ten minutes, my order is ready. I grab the bag from the owner and thank her. The entire time I was in the restaurant, not a single other person came to order food. How much longer can they go on like this? I feel bad for them.

I open the food cartons as soon as I get home and eat directly out of them. The food is decent but nothing compared to the restaurants in Chinatown in downtown Seattle. The egg foo young is fresh, but the sauce is overly sweet. The chow mein is greasier than I prefer, but it's edible. I eat half of each order and put the rest in the fridge for tomorrow.

My apartment is not furnished at all. Besides an air mattress I bought to sleep on, I have no table, chairs, or couch. I eat my food on the floor. I sleep on the floor. I journal on the floor. I don't plan to be here long enough to make this place fully mine, but maybe getting a few more things from the thrift store would be a good idea. I could just go to the regular store instead of a thrift store, but what's the point? Besides, old habits, I guess. I make a mental note to go back sometime in the next few days.

I take out my journal and write down notes from the day. I try to remember everything I failed to write down earlier, which isn't much. I'm pretty meticulous, but a few times, I used the binoculars and forgot to take note of what was happening. I have made it my nightly routine to spend five to ten minutes filling in those gaps so my record is always complete.

I should sleep, but I'm just not tired. Thoughts of my observations of Liv swirl around in my mind. I need a distraction. I look around the bare room when my eyes land on the box Derek gave me just before he left. He told me to wait until I was alone to open it. Well, I couldn't be more alone than I am right now.

I grab the box and use my keys to slice into the tape he

used to seal it shut. I sit on my mattress and open the box. My eyes immediately fall on the stack of cash tied neatly with a string. I shake my head. Of course, he would do something like this. He's always trying to take care of me. Maybe I won't have to pull more cash out of my account after all.

I rifle through the rest of the contents. Several tiny flash drives cover the bottom of the box. I push them to the side to reveal another fake I.D. with my picture but a different name than the one I'm currently using. I'm amazed at the quality. As usual, it looks like a real one. I'm convinced no one would be able to tell it was fake.

A pang of sadness fills me as I think about the man I left behind. He is so good to me, and I will miss him deeply. I lay down on my air mattress and try to sleep, but I can't. I toss and turn for what feels like hours. Eventually, I sit up, impulsively grab my faded black sweatshirt and my keys off my bed, and head to my car. I'm not going to sleep; I'm just lying here. In my experience, I've found it's best to distract myself for a couple of hours and then try again.

I pull the sweatshirt over my head as I walk toward the car. The sweatshirt has the year nineteen eighty-nine imprinted on the front in bold white numbers that are now cracked and fading. It's not the prettiest sweatshirt, but it's comfortable and reminds me of home.

As soon as I sit in my car, I think about Derek again. Generally, on nights like this in Seattle, I would drive to his house. He'd massage my shoulders, and we'd spend time together. This would be enough to distract my mind from whatever was keeping me awake, and I almost inevitably fell asleep in his bed.

I wish I could call him. Seattle's barely more than an hour away; I could be there before midnight. That would not be fair to him, though. I told him I needed to do this by myself, and going to him just to help me sleep would confuse us both.

I put the keys into the ignition and turn on the car. I don't know exactly where I'm driving. I have no real destination. I guess I'm just going to drive.

Fifteen minutes later, I find myself at a fancy business park on the opposite side of town from the strip mall where Liv works. The sign out front reads *Mason's Medical Insurance*. The buildings have the same aesthetic as the stores in the strip mall. It looks like they were possibly built by the same builder. The facades of the buildings are covered in red brick with fancy white moldings, giving them a timeless appearance, but I know the truth.

This was not always a business park. In fact, just a few years ago, there used to be a trailer park here. A hundred trailers were lined up in makeshift streets. The roads were made of gravel that would kick up dirt every time a car drove down them. The kids who lived in the trailer park ran wild and free, often playing tackle football in the gravel or climbing the nearby trees.

I shake my head. I wonder what happened to those kids and to those people. I stare at the empty parking lot and feel a pang of sadness. This is what towns do to people who they feel aren't worthy. They pave over any memory of them and erect stores that sell wares that those people could never even have afforded if they wanted to. They erase their existence as if they didn't matter.

I shouldn't have come here. I don't feel better now than when I was back at my apartment. In fact, now I feel worse.

12

PIPPA

Pippa Halloway is the type of person you don't trifle with. Although she is a five-foot-flat Filipino woman, people view her as a giant. Her jet-black hair is swept into a no-nonsense French twist, and she's wearing a power suit that adds to her formidable appearance. She stomps up the school's front steps, irritation evident on her face. Her head is held high, and her heels click loudly with every step.

She looks at her watch; it's eleven a.m., not even lunchtime yet. The last thing she needs today is to deal with some nonsense at Bobbi's school, but here she is. As she reaches the front door, she slides her sunglasses to the top of her head. She enters the building and pauses in the entryway for a few seconds, surveying the hallway. All the students are in class, and it's eerily silent. She spots a sign hanging from the ceiling with an arrow pointing to the other end of the hallway that reads *Office*. She continues to stomp down the linoleum floors of Aldercreek's only high school. Her heels echo in the hallway, warning every person in the office that she's coming.

As she steps into the carpeted office, her heels are silent, but it's too late. Everyone has been adequately warned that she's here. The secretary looks up at her, concerned. "Mrs. Halloway, thank you for coming on such short notice. I believe Principal Evans is waiting to see you."

Pippa barely even looks at the secretary. She has far better things to do than deal with low-level employees; at least, that's what she makes people believe. She acts as though she's out of everyone's league in this building, but it's all just a facade. Deep down, she is wildly insecure and doubts her own worth. However, she never allows anyone to see her insecurities. To the outside world, she looks like she has everything figured out.

She walks straight to the principal's office and, without even knocking, opens the door. The principal, a round woman with bleached blonde hair and too much makeup, sits behind the desk. Next to the principal is an older woman with a short, curly brown haircut that ages her probably ten years. Pippa assumes she is Bobbi's teacher. In front of the desk sits Bobbi, her sixteen-year-old daughter. Her arms are crossed over her chest, and she's uncharacteristically slumped in the chair.

"Mrs. Halloway," Principal Evans says, "please come in. We were just finishing here."

Pippa steps into the room and closes the door behind her.

"Please take a seat," the principal says.

Pippa refuses. Instead, she crosses her arms in defiance of the request. "What exactly is going on here?" She asks the principal.

"Well, Mrs. Thompson," she gestures to the woman sitting in the chair, "believes that Bobbi may have forged her father's signature on a permission slip."

"And why would she think that?" Pippa asks, annoyed.

"As you can see, Mrs. Halloway," the principal says, handing a white piece of paper to Pippa, "the signature at the bottom is eerily similar to Bobbi's own signature at the very top. Bobbi likes to use a lot of flowy and loopy letters, which are also found in the signature below."

Pippa grabs the letter, stares at it, and tears it up. She glares at the principal. "How dare you accuse my child of forging anybody's signature. You have absolutely no proof. All you have is a mere assumption, and you dragged me all the way here in the middle of the day for this? I had to leave a client in the middle of a meeting. You really think this was worth it?" She asks, her voice rising. Her hands are firmly on the desk as she leans towards the principal.

Bobbi watches, half-amused and half-afraid. She wonders how her mother can make someone feel like they're about to melt with just a glance.

"I'm sorry, Mrs. Halloway. It's our policy to investigate all matters such as this. We weren't trying to inconvenience you," the principal says, clearly shaken by Pippa's intensity.

Pippa shakes her head. "This is ridiculous. You are targeting my daughter for no logical reason."

The principal looks almost hurt by the accusation. "Mrs. Halloway, we would never..." but her words trail away as she looks at Pippa.

"You know I'm an attorney in this town, right?" Pippa asks.

The principal nods.

Pippa looks at the teacher, who cowers in her chair. "I'm also running for mayor of Aldercreek," she says. "The last thing either one of you wants to do is get on my bad side, and making false accusations about my daughter is a sure way to do that."

Principal Evans sits straighter in her seat. "Mrs. Halloway, it is our job to make sure that our students are safe while they are both on school grounds and off. This is why we require parent or guardian approval for all activities that occur off school grounds. You do understand why that's important, right?"

Pippa glares at her. "Of course I do, but you are wildly mistaken about this accusation. That's her father's signature. For you to say otherwise is a joke. Come on, Bobbi, we're leaving," Pippa says.

Bobbi gets up hesitantly, unsure if she wants to be in her mom's presence while she's in this kind of mood.

"Now," Pippa says forcefully.

Bobbi moves quickly to stand next to her mother.

Pippa continues. "I will be taking her home for the rest of the day. I hope that tomorrow when we come back, you will think more deeply about the things you choose to accuse my daughter of. Let's go, Bobbi," she says, grabbing Bobbi's hand. Her grip is solid and tight.

She pulls her out of the office into the school hallway without a backward glance.

"Ow, Mom, you're hurting me," Bobbi whispers as they walk down the hall.

"Don't say a word to me, young lady. We will discuss this later at a more appropriate time," Pippa says firmly.

Bobbi immediately stops talking.

As they finish their walk down the hall, all that can be heard is the echo of Pippa's heels and the muffled sounds of Bobbi's shoes on the linoleum floor.

13

LIV

I try to schedule a meeting with a prospective client after work every day. I always plan my meetings at Dave's. The drinks are good, the atmosphere is refined, and it gives my clients a view of the life they will get if they move here.

I usually get to the bar at least ten minutes early but wait in my car. I don't sit in the bar because I don't want my clients to think I've been waiting for them for long. It always makes them feel bad. I also don't want them to get there before me and wonder if I'm standing them up, so I sit in my car and watch the door. As soon as I see someone walking to the door who looks like their picture, I quickly get out of my car and stop them before they go in.

I make it a point to know exactly what all my clients look like before I meet them. I fully vet them using their social media accounts or anything else I can find. I must know precisely who I am dealing with. I always print a large color headshot from one of the pictures they have posted and hold it in my lap while I wait. It's rare that I don't recognize them the moment I see them. I also vet them because I'm not willing to waste my time on somebody who doesn't have enough money to sustain the lifestyle here.

Justin, the man I'm meeting today, seems to have all the right criteria. His social media page is filled with pictures of him on various boats on Lake Washington, on a ski trip to Whistler, and multiple evenings out at some of the most exclusive restaurants in Seattle. These are all the things I would expect to see of a wealthy client.

I look at my watch. I've been waiting here for him for fifteen minutes. He's late, or maybe he got here before me, and he's already inside. The thought causes me to panic. If he's been waiting for me this long, I've probably already lost him.

I quickly grab my bag and exit my car, locking the door behind me. As soon as I step foot into the bar, it takes a moment for my eyes to adjust. When they do, I look around, but don't see anyone that matches the photo I left in the car. I walk up to the bar and sit on a stool. I guess I'll wait inside just this once.

"Can I get you anything?" the bartender asks. "Your usual?"

"No, thank you, not yet. I'll have water first, please."

A girl sitting two stools away from me leans over. "I've never been to this bar before. Do you have any recommendations?" She has very big hair, but her curls are mesmerizing and defined. She looks like an underdressed high-fashion model. She definitely can't be from around here.

"Everything here is great, really," I respond, distracted. I quickly glance at the door before turning back to the girl. "They only use top-shelf liquor, and I find it really makes a difference. My absolute favorite is the Moscow Mule. I only allow myself one when I'm meeting clients, but they are delicious."

"Have you ever tried it with pineapple?" the girl asks.

I stare at her in surprise. "No, I haven't," I say. "It does sound interesting, though."

"You should. It kind of kicks everything up a notch, you know?"

I look around the bar one last time to see if I somehow missed my client when I scanned it earlier, but it's clear he's not here. I glance at my watch; it's nearly six o'clock. I sigh. Why not? It looks like my client is not going to show, but I could still have my drink. "Johnny," I say, getting the bartender's attention.

He turns towards me. "You want your Moscow Mule now?" He asks.

"Yes, but can you add pineapple to it this time, please?" I ask.

"Sure," he responds as he attempts to try and hide the look of shock that spreads across his face.

I'm a creature of habit. I've gotten that Mule every day for years now.

To his credit, he quickly hides his surprise and gets to work on my drink. He sets it down in front of me, along with a napkin. It looks exactly like the drink I'm used to, but I am pleasantly surprised as soon as I take my first sip. It is sweeter than a regular Moscow Mule, but the pineapple gives it a nice tropical hint. "Wow, that's good," I say, looking towards the girl. "Thank you. Are you a bartender?"

She shakes her head. "No. I used to be, though."

How could somebody that young have something that she used to be? It seems far-fetched. I would have guessed that she's just starting her career, not on to her second one. "Well, wherever you learned this, it is definitely amazing."

"I know, right? It just adds that little extra something."

She takes a sip from a tall glass of water. "Are you waiting for someone?" She asks.

"Yes, a friend, but I'm not sure they're coming. They're already several minutes late."

"Why don't you move down a stool, and we can have a drink together? If your friend comes, they can sit on the other side, and I'll pretend like the two of you don't exist."

I hesitate. I don't know this girl, but she did suggest one of the best drinks I've ever had. I sigh. "Okay, fine." I get up and slide my drink down the bar to sit beside her.

She gets the bartender's attention and orders a Moscow Mule with pineapple. The bartender brings it a few minutes later, and she takes a long sip. "It's been a long time since I've had one of these. It's definitely hitting the spot."

"Are you new to town?" I ask.

"I got here just a few days ago. Still trying to figure out what I'm going to do with myself," she says, laughing.

"Well, you will love it here. This is the best-kept secret in the Pacific Northwest. How do you like it so far?" I ask.

"I love it. Especially this place. It's really nice."

"Oh, I agree. It is the best bar in Aldercreek. There's another bar called the Brick House on the other side of town. It's nice, too, but it just doesn't have the classy vibe of Dave's. I'm a real estate agent, and I always take my clients here the first time I meet them so they can get a sense of what we have to offer."

"That's cool," the girl says.

I can tell she wants to ask more, but suddenly, an alarm goes off on my phone. I look down and quickly turn it off. It's my reminder to end my meeting and head home. "I'm so sorry. I have to go." I take another long sip of my Moscow Mule and drain the rest of it. "I hope to see you around," I say.

"Yeah, me too. It's a small town. I can't imagine we won't see each other somewhere." She flashes me a genuine smile.

I grab my purse and force myself to leave, walking quickly to the car. She seemed nice and kind of cool. I wouldn't mind hanging out with her again. It's so hard to have female friends at this age, but she seemed drama-free, which I need — especially as I consider running for mayor. I can't be the center of any gossip. Maybe when I see her again, I will suggest we go to dinner sometime. I open my driver-side door and put my purse on the passenger seat. At least this meeting wasn't a total waste. However, I need to do a better job of vetting my prospective clients. I can't afford to be stood up like that again.

14

PIPPA

Pippa grabs her handbag and double-checks her reflection in the bathroom mirror. "Come on, Bobbi," she says. "It's time to get breakfast."

Living in a hotel has not been ideal, but it does have its perks. The major one is that she doesn't have to make breakfast every morning before school for Bobbi. The hotel they've been staying at has a free buffet. Considering their current financial situation, Pippa is grateful for anything she doesn't have to pay for.

Bobbi steps in front of the mirror and double-checks her appearance as well. "Are you really going to let me go back to school today?" She asks.

"We have to seem as though nothing has changed. You know that. So yes, you're going to school," Pippa says, irritated. "You're lucky they didn't suspend you and only gave you a warning, or you would be forced to stay home."

"Mom, that whole thing wasn't fair. Can we please talk about it?" She begs.

"Later," Pippa says. "Finish getting ready."

Bobbi rolls her eyes at her and exits the bathroom.

A few minutes later, they leave the hotel room and walk down to the hotel lobby, where the buffet is served. Pippa takes a small scoop of scrambled eggs and fat-free yogurt. Bobbi fills her plate with pancakes and sausage, all the foods that Pippa hasn't touched in years. She can't remember the last time she could eat like that and not gain a ton of weight in the process. Getting old kind of sucks.

Bobbi follows Pippa to the area with tables, and they sit across from each other in one of the booths.

"Okay, now's your chance. Let's talk about what happened yesterday," Pippa says. "Why in the world would you do that?"

Bobbi looks at her mother angrily. "Are you serious?" She asks, challenging Pippa. "You're always working, so I never even have two seconds to ask you about these kinds of things. And Dad is obviously not around. What else was I supposed to do? You're the one who keeps telling me to make things seem normal. So I signed his signature," she says, shrugging. "I didn't want to be the only one not going on the field trip because I couldn't get my permission slip signed."

"We have breakfast every morning together, Bobbi. I know I work a lot, but you could have asked me then," Pippa says.

"I kept forgetting in the morning until after you dropped me off at school. I tried to have you sign it two days ago when I got home from school, but you didn't come home until after I went to sleep. I really had no choice, Mom."

"Well then, you need to get better at forging our signatures. Nobody can know that we live in this hotel or that we are broke if I'm going to be elected mayor of Aldercreek. You can't have any more attention be drawn to you."

Bobbi sighs. "I know, Mom. That's why I did it," she says.

A hardened expression crosses Pippa's face. "I still get so angry about what your father did to me. He left us with nothing, forcing me to spend hours away from you just to make ends meet. I wish it wasn't like this, Bobbi. I do. I miss spending time with you."

"I miss it too, Mom," Bobbi says, grabbing her hand. I know most girls want nothing to do with their moms at my age, but I don't feel that way."

Pippa squeezes back. "As soon as I'm elected mayor, hopefully, our lives can go back to the way they were before. At the very least, it will force your dad and the people in this town to actually respect me."

"It makes me mad too, Mom. He didn't just abandon you; he abandoned me as well. I know you're doing your best, but so am I," Bobbi says. "You have to trust me."

Pippa stares at her skeptically. There's so much riding on this campaign for mayor, and any minor mishap could cause the whole thing to crash to the ground. Can she trust Bobbi to make the right choices?

"Have I ever gotten in trouble before, Mom?" Bobbi says, invading Pippa's thoughts.

She thinks for a moment and shakes her head. "No, you haven't."

"I understand how important being the mayor is to you. I'm not going to screw anything up. I promise."

"Okay, fine," Pippa says, relenting. "But when I come home tonight, you and I are going to make a plan so that you don't ever get pulled into the principal's office again. That includes practicing both my signature and your dad's signature."

"Okay," Bobbi says, stuffing her mouth with a syrup-covered piece of pancake.

"I wish things were different, Bobbi. I really do, but your

dad gave us no choice when he disappeared and took my name off all of our joint accounts. I promise I'm going to get us out of this hotel and back to the lifestyle we're accustomed to. We just need to work together."

Bobbi reaches over and grabs Pippa's hand. "We got this, Mom."

Pippa squeezes her hand and puts on a brave face, even though inside, she's terrified. So much is riding on this plan, and she can't afford for it to fail.

15

LIV

If you had asked me this morning where I would be at lunch today, I would have told you that I would be eating my salad at my desk like I do nearly every day. I would have never guessed I would be at a shoe store.

The heel broke off my pump this morning when I was getting out of my car. Thankfully, I didn't have any clients until this afternoon. I would have looked like a fool. I've been hobbling around the office all day, trying to make do, but walking with just one heel is impossible.

So, here I am on my lunch break, sitting in the shoe store just a few shops down from my brokerage, trying to pick out a pair of heels that won't give me a blister by the end of the day.

I would have just gone home and gotten another pair, but that would have taken too long. I can't remember the last time I bought shoes in a store like this. I usually order my favorite brand online. It's easy because I know exactly what size I am and how they will fit. This feels like I'm playing roulette, and not the fun kind.

I grab a black pair of pumps and slip them on my feet. They look nice. They're presentable, but I have no idea if they are going to wear a hole in my ankle by the end of the day. I sigh. I guess I don't have much choice.

I grab the shoes and walk towards the front counter. The girl behind the desk is helping a young woman with her purchase. As soon as the woman turns around, I recognize her. It's the same girl I met in the bar the day I got stood up by that potential client. I never heard back from him, which is weird. That usually doesn't happen to me.

The girl is scanning her receipt as she walks away from the counter and doesn't notice me.

"Hey," I say, trying to get her attention.

She looks up at me, and a smile forms on her face. "Oh my gosh," she says. "Hi."

"Strange to run into you again so soon," I say.

"I'm just here getting some shoes for a job interview later today," she says.

"Well, you look amazing," I say. She's dressed in a pencil skirt and pink blouse, but on her feet are white sneakers. "I can see why you needed new shoes," I chuckle.

She laughs. "Yeah. I just recently graduated from the University of Washington in Seattle. I haven't had much use for fancy interview clothes up until now. I got most of this at the thrift store. Can you believe it?" She asks.

My eyes widen. "No way," I say, genuinely surprised. "That's amazing."

"Yeah, the thrift stores here are really great. So many designer clothes."

"So, you said you have a job interview. Where are you interviewing?" I ask.

"I'm hoping to get the executive assistant job at Mason's

Medical Insurance. You know, the company on the other side of town?" She asks.

I nod. "Yes, I know exactly where that is." This girl doesn't belong in insurance. She's exciting and magnetic; they're going to eat her alive.

"Have you ever thought about doing real estate?" I ask her curiously. "It's not very hard to get licensed, and I know you would do amazingly well. You have the right personality for it."

"I don't know," she says hesitantly. "I was hoping to find something more consistent. I've heard you don't make a lot of money at first."

"That's true. It can be hard at first," I remark. "But think of it this way, if you're able to sell just one of the million-dollar homes we have for sale in this city, your commission would be close to thirty thousand dollars."

Her eyes widen.

I continue. "That's just one sale. How much does the executive assistant job pay?"

She shrugs. "I don't know exactly, but I think probably somewhere around fifty thousand a year?"

"So, sell two houses and you've got that beat," I tell her. I can see temptation dancing in her eyes, mixed with uncertainty. I reach into my purse and pull out a business card. "Here," I say, handing it to her. "Call me anytime if you change your mind."

"Thank you, Mrs..." Her voice falters.

"Call me Liv," I say, reaching out my hand to shake hers.

"I'm Eden," she says back. "Nice to meet you, Liv."

"Likewise," I say.

I leave the store a few minutes later with a large white bag in my hand. My old shoes are in the bag, and my new shoes are on my feet. I can't help but smile at my interaction with Eden. She's a diamond in the rough and doesn't even know it. She just needs a person like me to believe in her and change her life. If I could somehow convince her to become my protege, I know we could do great things.

16

SANDY

Sandy sits at the dining room table, sipping coffee and scanning the local newspaper. Today is her one day off in the middle of the week. She often works on Saturdays, showing homes or staging open houses, and she compensates by taking Wednesdays off.

She turns the page. A large advertisement fills nearly half the page, catching her eye: *The Cedric J. Stein Gallery Grand Opening.* Checking the date, she notices that it's for today. Excitement fills her. She would love to go to a gallery opening. This is the type of stuff she and Blaine used to do when they were dating, but ever since Melanie was born and Blaine's career took off, they barely go to dinner together, let alone a gallery opening in Seattle.

Blaine walks into the kitchen, dressed in a suit and tie. He still looks as handsome as the day she met him. He gathers his travel mug and prepares his coffee. "What are you planning on doing today on your day off?" He asks without looking up.

"I was thinking of attending the grand opening of this

new art gallery in Seattle. Maybe you could join me?" She asks, hopefully.

He looks over at her for the first time that morning, annoyed. "Some of us still have to work on Wednesdays," he says.

Her face falls. "I know. I just thought maybe you could take a few hours off and go with me. It could be fun," she says, standing and walking towards him.

"Babe, I can't just take off from work like you can, you know that," he says. "I have client meetings scheduled all afternoon, and it would be incredibly unprofessional of me to cancel them so I could go look at some art."

She stares at him, hurt. He always acts like her job is a hobby more than a career, less important than his.

"You should go with Liv. She would enjoy that," he suggests.

Sandy shakes her head. "You know, Liv. She has a routine, and she doesn't veer from it. There is no way she'd go to a gallery with me today."

He shrugs. "I guess then you go by yourself," he says, grabbing his coffee and giving her a peck on the cheek. He doesn't even wait for her response before exiting through the garage door.

She sighs and sadly looks out the window. She feels like he doesn't see her anymore and that they are basically living separate lives.

Several seconds later, Blaine rushes back in from the garage.

"Did you forget something?" She asks.

"Yeah, my lunch," he replies, opening the fridge.

Their seventeen-year-old daughter, Melanie, walks down the stairs and into the kitchen. "Were you not even going to say goodbye to me, Daddy?" She asks.

"I'm sorry, sweetheart. I'm late," he says, wrapping his arm around her and kissing her forehead before continuing to pull food out of the fridge.

Sandy looks at her daughter excitedly. They used to love doing things like this together; maybe she would go to the gallery opening with her. "Melanie, how would you like to play hooky today from school?" Sandy asks.

Melanie looks at her suspiciously. "For what?"

"Well, there's this gallery opening downtown, and I thought we could go together," Sandy suggests.

A look of disgust crosses Melanie's face.

"Don't you remember we used to do stuff like this all the time? It will be fun," Sandy says encouragingly.

"Ew," Melanie says as if Sandy's suggestion was the worst idea on the planet. She grabs an apple from the counter, takes a bite of it, tosses it into her backpack, and walks out the front door without even saying goodbye.

Blaine looks at Sandy and sees the dejected look on her face. "Don't take it personally. They're supposed to be like that at that age. Did you want to hang out with your mother when you were seventeen?"

"No," she says quietly, "but I had hoped things would be different when I had my own daughter. My mother was mean and neglectful. I've tried to create a warm and loving environment for Melanie."

"Teenagers have been like this for thousands of years," he says. "She'll get over it, and you will become friends when she's an adult. I promise."

She nods, but a lingering sadness remains that she can't quite shake.

He walks over to her in an uncharacteristic gesture of kindness and places his hand on her shoulder. "You'll find someone to go with. Don't worry about it."

Sandy squeezes his hand and nods, but she knows he's wrong. Other than Liv, she doesn't have anyone else to ask. Making friends has always been a challenge for her, especially since they moved to Aldercreek. She can't help but wish things were different — that she was different. Social situations have always been very uncomfortable for her, even though she wants more than anything to fit in. She's always just been the awkward girl who doesn't know what to say.

Blaine gives her a quick kiss on the cheek and rushes to the garage door. She sadly watches him leave.

As the door shuts behind him, the silence of the empty house surrounds her, and she feels utterly alone. She refuses to sit in this house all day by herself. She grabs her phone and starts planning her trip to the gallery. If nothing else, it will afford her a change in scenery, and maybe she'll have fun, even if she's alone.

17

EDEN

I open the door and step into the only coffee shop on Main Street. I look around and am taken aback by the luxuriousness of even this small coffee shop. Coming from Seattle, I'm used to espresso shops with hand-hewn wooden tables and eclectic artwork on the walls. Instead, this place has plush velvet booths and chandeliers hanging from the ceiling. I shake my head; they even want their coffee to be fancy here.

I step to the front counter. To the left of the register is a glass display case with delicious-looking pastries. My stomach growls. I haven't eaten yet today, and they look extremely tempting.

"Good morning," the girl working behind the counter says cheerfully. "What can I start you with?"

"I think I'll just have a sixteen-ounce oat milk latte, please."

"Sure, no problem. Will that be for here or to go?"

I hesitate. Maybe I could do my work from here while I drink my coffee. "Do you have Wi-Fi?" I ask.

"Of course we do; the name and password are on this sign," she says, gesturing to a frame next to the register.

I take note of the code and smile at her. "For here, please."

She nods, grabs a plain white mug from the counter, and sets it next to the machine. At least they haven't attempted to make the coffee cup fancy either, I note.

"Will that be all for you?" The girl asks.

I nod as I grab my wallet from my purse.

"Are you sure you don't want one of our freshly made scones? The organic bakery down the street makes them every morning."

I look longingly at the scones and am tempted. "How much are they?" I ask.

"They are a steal if you ask me. Only six dollars each," she says confidently.

I freeze momentarily and swallow hard. Six dollars for a glorified piece of bread? My stomach rumbles again, but I ignore it. "No, thank you. I think I'll just stick with the coffee."

"Sure thing," she says, ringing me up. "That will be eight twenty-five."

That's a lot more than I was expecting, but I shouldn't be surprised. Everything is more expensive here, even the gas for my car. It's as if the store owners know they can bump the prices up as long as they claim their product is more luxurious than average. These rich people will buy anything if they think it's exclusive.

I consider walking away, but don't want to appear out of place. It's important that I blend in with this community. I hand over my card and make a mental note to never come to this coffee shop again.

Moments later, I'm sitting in one of the booths with my

overpriced latte.in hand. I take a sip. I admit it's good. It's not any better than the places I love in my Capitol Hill neighborhood in Seattle, but it's decent.

I pull out my laptop and connect to the coffee shop's Wi-Fi. I need to figure out my way around this town, which has changed so much since I last saw it.

I search for a map of the city. The first result of my search is a map website, but it isn't much help. It's a standard map showing street names and not much else. I don't need to know the street names; I remember all of those from when I was here last. I need to know the significant landmarks and the layout of the businesses and neighborhoods.

I navigate to the Aldercreek City Council website and find a neatly drawn map posted on their main page. I click on it. This is exactly what I need. It lists all the parks, the major shopping centers and business parks, as well as landmarks throughout the city.

I study it for a long time. At the end of Main Street, there's a large totem pole. A brief glance at the Aldercreek City Council website tells me that the pole was erected five years ago to honor the ancestors of the land on which it was built. Apparently, as little as one hundred years ago, this land was the home to a Native American tribe. I wonder what happened to them. Did the Aldercreek founders drive them off? The thought of them being pushed out of their own land makes me feel sick to my stomach, but I can't worry about that right now.

I look back at the map and notice several large subdivisions of homes that have been built throughout Aldercreek. Most of them are located on the outskirts of town, while the businesses and shops are clustered towards the center. Maybe I should have taken Liv up on her offer to be a real estate salesperson. She's probably right; I would have been good at it. You'd never know it by how I act, but the lack of a steady income was not really an issue for me. I have enough money in my account to sustain me for a long time. The real issue I have is with the time it would take to get licensed. I'm not sure if it is worth it.

The interview for the medical assistant position the other day went well. In fact, I was offered the job almost immediately, but I turned it down. I could tell from the atmosphere that I would be working a lot of overtime, and at the end of the day, I'm not here for a job. It was going to pull me too far away from Liv. I'm only applying for positions in town to give the appearance that I'm trying to settle down here and be a part of the community. I'm not about to accept a job for a place that will require me to make the job my life. I just can't; my mission is too important.

Maybe doing the real estate thing is the best idea. It would allow me to remain close to Liv once I am licensed. I search for the real estate salesperson requirements for Washington. I easily find them on multiple websites. It doesn't look too bad. Mostly, I would just need to pass the licensing exam and get fingerprinted. Then, of course, I would have to pay the licensing fee. I could be licensed in maybe two months, three at the most.

Three months seems like an eternity to sit in my empty apartment doing nothing. I don't know that I have what it takes to be that patient. However, taking my time and slowly infiltrating Liv's world is probably best for my plan in the long run. People make mistakes when they rush.

However, every day I'm in Aldercreek, memories of the past haunt me. Each time I see something familiar, it sends me straight back, and I'm filled with rage. I don't know how much longer I can hold back. I've been waiting for this moment for far too long. I don't know if I have the restraint to keep calm and not put my plan into action for several more months as I wait for a real estate license to be approved.

I lean back against the booth and close my eyes. What would my sister do? I wish I could just call her and ask her. Growing up, she always gave the best advice.

One time, when I was in the third grade, a little girl at school kept saying the meanest things to me. She would make fun of my clothes because they weren't name brand and my hair because I always wore it in a braid. I didn't go to my mom for help. Instead, I went to Autumn. She didn't lie and tell me everything would be better and that the little girl would eventually get nicer. Instead, she taught me to love myself so that the girl's words didn't even affect me. She spent that night showing me how to do my hair and dress like her. She always knew what to do and how to handle every situation. I wonder what she would say about this.

I take a deep breath and close my laptop. I will never know. My sister can't say anything anymore... because she's dead.

18

LIV

I stand and stretch at my desk. It's been a long day. I look over at Sandy, sitting at the front reception desk. "You ready to get out of here?" I ask.

She closes the lid to her computer and nods. "Definitely," she says.

The rest of my agents are either showing homes or working from home, so Sandy and I are the only ones left in the office.

I walk over to her. "Got any fun plans for the weekend?" I ask.

She shakes her head. "Just the usual. Melanie has some cheer competition this weekend that I have to take her to, and I have an open house on Sunday. What about you?"

"Mitch and I are considering trying that new restaurant that opened on the other side of town. The Italian one," I reply.

"Oh yeah, I've heard great things about it. It looks really good," Sandy says. "It's been getting rave reviews. One of our neighbors who went there last weekend said it was almost as good as the food in Italy. If I didn't have to cart Melanie all over town tomorrow, I would invite myself to join you guys."

"You're always welcome to if your plans change," I say, knowing that she won't take me up on it. Sandy's life revolves around her daughter, and she rarely takes time for herself. She barely even does things with her husband. I have no idea how their marriage is still thriving.

I'm grateful that I don't have to spend my weekends carting my child to and from their activities. My weekends are for me. Having children right now would just take away from all of my responsibilities. I can't even imagine how hard it would be to have a baby while being the mayor. I know Mitch desperately wants a child, but I'm not convinced that we're ready. I've agreed to try, for his sake, but every month I don't get pregnant, I'm grateful.

"Other than going to eat Italian food, anything else fun planned?" Sandy pries. It's almost as if she's trying to live vicariously through me.

"I'll probably spend most of the day tomorrow in the office," I say. "I've got a couple of clients coming in that want to see some homes tomorrow, but other than that, we don't have much else planned."

Sandy looks thoughtful as she's packing up her purse. It's almost as if she's trying to decide whether or not to say something to me.

"What's going on in your head, Sandy? You and I have been friends for a long time. You can't hide things from me," I say.

She looks at me cautiously. "I just heard something the other day from the other mothers at school about Pippa," she says.

"Oh?" I ask.

"Yeah, I heard her kid was caught forging her dad's

signature on a permission slip. Apparently, Pippa marched into the school office and defended her. She even insinuated that Principal Evans was a racist."

"No," I say, truly shocked. "Principal Evans might be a lot of things, but the last thing she could be called is a racist. She's the one who initiated the Black History parade that Aldercreek High School puts on every February. How in the world could she be a racist?"

"I know, right? Pippa has lost her mind. You know, if she's defending her daughter for forgery, who knows what other crimes she is willing to commit? You really should run for mayor, Liv. We cannot afford to have that woman be in control of our town. She's obviously raising her child to be a criminal. Imagine what she will do to our community."

"I don't know. I'm not sure I've fully made up my mind," I say coyly, but the truth is, my hesitance is a lie. I made up my mind weeks ago. However, I really need Sandy to think that this is her idea so that she will help me run my campaign and drive Pippa into the ground. I'm one hundred percent confident I can be the shepherd Aldercreek needs to thrive. It's my destiny.

"If Pippa gets into office, she could affect your business. Mitch's business, too," Sandy says. "You know she doesn't like you, and she would probably do anything to see you go under."

I pretend to contemplate the idea. "I have thought about it," I say. "I'm just not sure it's the right move for me or my family."

"Well, all I know is that the last thing I want is for Pippa to be mayor, that's for sure. That woman shouldn't even be allowed to be in charge of a book club, let alone be the mayor of our city," she says with such conviction that it surprises me.

"That's true," I say as I cross my arms and pretend to contemplate her words for several seconds. I look up at her. I have to play it cool. "Alright, you've convinced me to think seriously about it. Goodness knows I'll do a better job than Pippa."

A huge smile spreads across her face.

I continue. "But if I'm going to make that kind of push, I will need to start assembling a loyal team — people who will work with me all hours of the day and night until this campaign is over. I won't do anything halfway."

"You know you can count on me. I will give you everything I've got," Sandy says with determination. It's as if the idea of helping me run a campaign has reignited something inside of her. I haven't seen this Sandy in a long time. She believes that she orchestrated this entire plan for me to run for mayor, and now she's fully invested.

19

PIPPA

Pippa pulls up to the front of the school. Large groups of students congregate on the steps and the lawn.

Bobbi looks over at her. "Mom, do I really have to go?"

"Yes, of course you do. If you stop showing up at school, then that will put attention on us, and we cannot afford that."

Bobbi sighs. "Fine, but this is so embarrassing. Everyone in the school knows that I forged that signature. You know they'll be talking about it behind my back all day, right?"

"Yes, they probably will," Pippa says, "but then they'll move on to something else, and you will no longer be the center of attention. I promise." She says this with confidence, trying to give her daughter some courage, but she's not convinced that what she's saying is true. Sometimes, people hold on to things way past their expiration date.

Bobbi opens the car door and begins to step out.

"Wait," Pippa says.

Bobbi looks back at her, annoyed.

"I love you, Bobbi," she says.

Bobbi's shoulders slump. "I love you too, Mom," she says before grabbing her bag and exiting the vehicle. She shuts the door behind her, rolls back her shoulders, and walks straight for the front door.

Pippa feels a pang of guilt. If she wasn't planning to run for mayor, she could keep Bobbi home and protect her, but instead, she has to send her into a potential pack of hyenas to fend for herself. She knows she's strong, but it's not fair. She remembers the entire reason she's in this position, and the anger boils over once again. If Bobbi's dad had been here, none of this would have happened. She wouldn't have to keep so many secrets. It's time for her to get her life back in order.

If she's going to run for mayor, she has to have an address within the city limits. It's one of the requirements for every candidate. She looks at the list on her phone of apartments she found last night while Bobbi was sleeping. She dials the number of the real estate agent who agreed to help her find a place to live.

The agent answers after the first ring.

"This is Brandy," she says cheerfully.

"Hi, Brandy. This is Pippa Halloway. I don't know if you remember, but we spoke last week."

"Oh yes, Mrs. Halloway, Of course I remember. You live in Aldercreek, right?"

"Yes, that's correct. I know you don't live here, but would you be able to meet me today to show me a few places? I have a list."

Brandy is silent for a few seconds before she responds. "Yes, I have some availability today. Why don't you text me the locations you're interested in? I'll meet you at the first one in two hours. Does that sound reasonable?"

Pippa looks at her watch. She had been hoping to get some work done from the office today, but going in now and then turning around and leaving almost immediately would obviously be unproductive. She'll have to call in sick. That's something she tries to do as rarely as possible. Even during the first days after her husband left, Pippa didn't call in sick one time. Appearances are everything to her. She'll have to make an exception today. "Yes, two hours will be fine. I'll text you the list," she says.

EXACTLY TWO HOURS LATER, Pippa pulls up to a small apartment building on the edge of town. From the outside, it looks like it has maybe eight units. The siding is painted a dull blue that is chipping in several places. Pippa cringes at the idea of living in a place like this. Just a few months ago, they were living in a million-dollar mansion. This is a ginormous step-down.

This drive to become the mayor and force people to respect her is exhausting. The apartment building in front of her is not just a step down from her previous home, but it would be something she would actively have to try and hide. No one is going to vote for her if they know she lives here.

There's a part of her that wants to just run away and buy a boat to sail around the world with Bobbi. Everything would be so much easier on a boat. She could homeschool Bobbi, and they could spend as long as they wanted in each port around the world. Honestly, it sounds like heaven to her, but she knows it's impractical. She'd have to find a job that would allow her to work from anywhere in the world, and she'd somehow have to get Bobbi on board. No, this was an impossible dream.

The realtor stands outside the front door, waiting for

her. As she exits the car, she forces a smile on her face, pretending to be excited about this possibility.

"Mrs. Holloway?" Brandy asks.

Pippa almost corrects her but then thinks better of it. She's no longer a Mrs, but she's not ready for the whole town to know what her husband Jesse has done. She sticks her hand out. "Yes, I'm Mrs. Holloway. I'm sorry; it's just me this morning. My husband is away on business."

"No problem at all," the realtor said. "I can show you the place, and if you decide to rent it, you can have him sign the documents digitally."

Pippa feels a wave of relief. If all she has to do is get a digital signature from Jesse, she can take care of that.

The realtor opens the front door and leads her into the building. "As you can see, this is quite a small complex. This particular building only houses ten units, five on the bottom floor and five on the top floor."

She walks Pippa to the far end of the bottom floor and unlocks the door. "This is the unit that's available. It's quite a decent size," she says. "Nearly twelve hundred square feet. It has two bedrooms but only one bath." She walks over to the sliding glass door. "As you can see, you have a view of the forest instead of other buildings, which is a huge plus. This unit offers tons of privacy."

Pippa looks around. She's not completely repulsed. It's simple and clean, although definitely dated. The kitchen cabinets are white melamine with oak trim, and there's tile covering the countertops, which Pippa imagines will be a nightmare to clean.

The agent shows her the two bedrooms and the one shared bathroom, which is nowhere near the standards that Pippa is used to, but it, too, is clean. It's as if this place was built in the eighties or nineties and never remodeled.

Pippa is not thrilled with it, but it's on the edge of town, which does provide her privacy. Maybe she can keep her secret for a little while longer by living here. "What are the signing costs?" She asks.

"The owners are asking for first and last month's rent and a deposit up front," Brandy says.

Pippa's heart sinks as she quickly does the math in her head. She knows it'll be close at the start, but she can make it work. After that, she can easily make the monthly rent payments, but giving up nearly all her savings to move in will make things difficult for a while.

She sighs. The paperwork for mayor is due soon. She has no choice. She needs an address in Aldercreek. "I'll take it," she says.

Brandy looks at her, surprised. "You don't want to see the other places on your list?"

Pippa shakes her head. "Not unless they have cheaper move-in costs."

"They all would be about the same," Brandy says.

"Then this one is fine. I only plan on living here for a short while anyway."

She nods, barely able to contain her excitement. Pippa has essentially just given her the day off. "That's wonderful, Mrs. Holloway. I will have the paperwork drawn up and sent to you by the end of the day."

"Perfect," Pippa says. She looks around the apartment one last time. "Would we be able to paint the walls at all?" She asks.

The agent looks at her notes. "It looks like the owner says yes, as long as you paint them back at the end of your lease."

Making this their own will be fun for her and Bobbi. No matter what, Pippa is determined to make the best of the situation. Her husband may have set her back, but nobody holds her down.

.

20

EDEN

I am sitting on my empty apartment floor with my journal lying open on my lap. I pull Liv's business card out of my wallet and stare at it. Being an agent would give me unprecedented access to her, more than I could have ever hoped for, to be honest. I've already been waiting for years for this opportunity. What are a few more months?

I pick up my phone. It can't hurt to ask for more information. I dial her number. It goes straight to voicemail. I leave a message.

"Good morning, Mrs. Mitre. This is Eden. We met the other day, first at the bar and then at the shoe shop. Anyway, I'm calling to ask you some questions about the real estate salesperson position you mentioned the other day. Please give me a call back at your earliest convenience."

I quickly hang up the phone. The palms of my hands are suddenly damp, and beads of sweat form on my brow. Why did that make me so nervous? I've been planning this almost my entire life; I should be ready, but the thought of it now being within my grasp seems almost unreal.

A few minutes later, Liv calls back.

"Hello?" I say.

"Is this Eden?" Liv asks.

"Yes, this is she."

"Eden, I'm so glad you called. I've been thinking about you, worrying about you, really. I've been hoping you were okay."

"Yes, I'm good, but I'm struggling to find a job. I thought maybe I would take you up on the salesperson position that you offered."

"Oh, that would be wonderful. You will be amazing at it, I'm thoroughly convinced."

"Yes, well, can you give me some more details on how the process works?"

"We have all the training materials that you will need to pass the test. I can give you a computer and access to our materials, but I can't really help you with much more than that until you have your license, and you obviously won't be able to sell anything until you pass the exam."

"That makes sense."

"Once you are ready, I will have you work directly under me so I can give you all the tips and tricks I've learned over the years. Trust me; I know exactly how to make you successful. The job is yours if you'd like it," she says.

I hesitate. From the sound of it, while I'm studying for my license, I won't have much access to Liv. Can I really wait that long?

I remember something my sister once told me that has stuck with me my entire life. We were baking cupcakes together one morning when I was eight years old. We put them in the oven, and she turned on the timer. After a few minutes of baking, I could smell them. "They're done," I said excitedly, looking over at her. "Let's take them out."

She smiled at me kindly. "No, they're not done, Eden. You must be patient."

"But can't you smell them?" I asked.

"Yes, and they smell amazing, but if you take them out now, you will be disappointed. The edges might be good to eat, but the middle is going to be mush. If you're patient and wait until the timer goes off, you'll see that the wait will be worth it. I promise."

She said those words to me about many things as I was growing up. *Be patient; the wait will be worth it.*

Maybe this too, is something I need to be patient about. I know I will get what I came here for eventually, even if it takes some time.

"Once I get my license, how long do you think it will be before I make a sale?" I ask. I don't really care about the money, but I have to make it seem like I am seriously looking into this as a career, and this seems like the most reasonable follow-up question to ask.

"I would say, on average, two to three months. Maybe longer," she says.

"Oh," I say, trying to sound disappointed. "I didn't realize it'd be so long. I might have to think about it," I tell her. I take a deep breath. The amount of time it would take me to sell my first house doesn't bother me as much as the time it would take me to get my license and start working in the office. However, as much as I don't want to wait any longer to start enacting my plan, this is the best opportunity I have to get near Liv. It's one more hoop to jump through, but hopefully, it will bring me that much closer to my end goal.

Liv interrupts my musings. "Eden, are you still there?"

"Yes, sorry. I was just thinking," I say.

"I might have a more stable opportunity to offer you,"

she says. "Something suitable for a college-educated person. You said you have your degree, correct?"

"Yes, I just earned it from the University of Washington," I say.

"Excellent," she says enthusiastically. "Why don't you come by my office tomorrow, and we can discuss this further?"

"Okay," I say hesitantly. Why is she being so nice to me? "What time?" I ask.

"How does ten a.m. sound?" She asks after a brief pause.

"I'll be there," I say and hang up the phone. Curiosity overwhelms me. This was an unexpected turn of events. Maybe I won't have to be patient after all.

21

SANDY

Sandy is sitting alone at her desk in the dark real estate office. Liv left nearly twenty minutes ago. Sandy stayed behind, telling Liv she had some paperwork to catch up on, but the truth is that she just didn't want to go home. The house is always empty these days. Her husband works late, and her daughter is usually at some activity or at a friend's house. Even when her daughter is home, she shuts herself in her room and barely speaks to Sandy. If she goes home, she knows that she'll just sit in her empty living room, staring at the television.

There will be no chores to do around the house because their housekeeper takes care of all the shopping and cleaning. She doesn't paint or draw, nor do any other types of crafts. She doesn't really have any hobbies, to be honest. Growing up, so much of her time and energy was spent perfecting her appearance that she neglected all the other skills. Now, she feels as if it's too late to cultivate those things, so she doesn't even try. Boredom is her most prevalent emotion.

When she brought up the idea of Liv running for mayor,

she probably came across as overly enthusiastic, but the thought of the campaign, the fundraising dinners and the tight deadlines all gave her a rush unlike anything she'd felt in years.

It's not that she wants to seem ungrateful about her life. She is, on the contrary, incredibly grateful. She knows that she's blessed, but she is lonely. Helping Liv run a mayoral campaign would give her purpose.

She sighs as she looks around the office and grabs her purse. She can't stay here forever. She exits through the front door, locking the door behind her.

She looks at her shiny red convertible and hesitates. She still doesn't want to go home. She puts her purse on her shoulder and walks past the car, continuing down the sidewalk in front of the small upscale boutiques that reside in the outdoor mall.

She walks slowly and deliberately, surveying each storefront and the items she can see through the windows. She can buy anything she wants from these shops. Money is not an object. Her husband has made sure that they are well taken care of.

She spots a vintage gown from a famous designer in one of the shop windows, wanders inside, and checks the price tag — *ten thousand dollars*. She knows intellectually that it's a lot of money, but she knows her husband wouldn't even bat an eye at the price, especially if she loved it. She drops the tag and takes a look around the rest of the store. Nothing else catches her interest. The gowns are beautiful, but her stylist does all her shopping for her. There are gowns in her closet still with the tags on them; she would have no use for any of these.

She exits the store and continues walking down the sidewalk. At the end of the block, she passes a shop with a bunch of trinkets — mostly signs with pithy quotations painted on them, glass vases, and ceramic bowls. This is not one of those low-end places where everything is made overseas. Instead, all of the items are handcrafted, hand-painted, one-of-a-kind pieces.

She enters the store. This is her kind of shop. She loves art, and she loves to marvel at things she knows that she couldn't create herself. Each item has a picture of the artist displayed below the piece. Each piece has been lovingly curated by the owner of the shop, who stands proudly behind the register.

"Welcome," the owner says.

Sandy looks at her and nods.

"Please let me know if you have any questions," she says and goes back to her papers.

Sandy looks around, finding several things that catch her interest: a hand-blown glass Chihuly piece, a ceramic vase hand-painted with tiny bluebells, and a wooden sign with delicate lettering that says *Home Sweet Home.* She thinks of her home and the design that she and her interior designer meticulously developed. Everything is in its place and fits the aesthetic perfectly. While she loves these things, she knows that they would change the entire feeling of whatever room she puts them in, so she passes them by and continues looking.

In the back of the store, on the bottom shelf, she eyes a small hand-painted purple pig wearing pearls and a gold crown. Sandy has had an obsession with pigs ever since she was younger, from reading kids' books. She tries to include them in every design she oversees. In her backyard, there are manicured and sculpted gardens, and she had the gardener sculpt one of the bushes into the shape of a pig. In her living room, there is a bronze pig statue on her bookshelf. She always makes sure they're tastefully done, but they make her smile every time she sees them.

Sandy looks around the shop, making sure that no one is watching. Assured that the owner is distracted, she looks at the price tag, *forty-five dollars*. She doesn't know if that's a good price or outrageous because, to her, it's merely pennies. She knows she could easily buy the figurine, but spending money, even on things she loves, no longer gives her a thrill, and she needs some excitement in her life. She glances at the shop owner, who is busy reading her ledger.

Suddenly, a woman walks into the shop.

"Welcome," the shop owner says. "Can I help you find something?"

"Actually, yes. I'm looking for a very special gift for my mother-in-law's birthday. Do you have any suggestions?" The woman asks.

The owner exits her perch behind the register and begins showing the woman several pieces around the shop.

When Sandy is certain the owner is distracted, she takes the pig and slips it into her purse. The rush of energy that she feels at the danger of taking something that doesn't belong to her is the type of high that she's always searching for.

The shop owner stops what she's doing and looks over at Sandy.

Perspiration beads form on her forehead, and anxiety makes her blood feel like ice. She holds her breath.

"Can I help you with anything?" The owner asks.

Sandy shakes her head, trying not to look guilty. "No, I'm good. Thank you."

The owner looks at her appraisingly for several more seconds before returning to help the other woman. As soon as she does, Sandy quickly exits the store.

The second she's outside, she lets out the breath that she had been holding since the moment she thought she might get caught. Relief floods her body. She's done it. A smile forms on her lips, and she feels almost giddy.

She lives off of the high for the entire drive to her house. She loves feeling alive and on edge. Twenty minutes later, she pulls into her garage and opens the trunk of her car. Inside are dozens of expensive, meaningless objects she has been collecting for months, carefully nestled in a medium-sized box. She takes the ceramic pig out of her pocket, gently places it in the box next to an elephant figurine, and slams the trunk shut. She sighs and stares at the closed hatch. The high never lasts long enough. By the time she enters her house, it's completely gone.

22

EDEN

I sit across from Liv in front of an expensive mahogany desk. My leg bounces obnoxiously as I desperately try to release the pent-up nervous energy that has been building for the past twenty-four hours. I arrived at the office fifteen minutes early, figuring that would give me some time to collect my thoughts before my conversation with Liv began, but the moment I walked in the front door, Liv grabbed me in a big hug and pulled me into her office.

It's not your typical office with four walls and privacy. Instead, it's just a raised platform in the corner of the room encased in glass. Liv's desk overlooks the rest of the desks as if she is sitting on her throne, looking over her subjects.

"I'm so glad that you were able to come," she says as soon as she's seated.

"I'm grateful for the opportunity," I say, anxious to hear what she has to offer.

I look around her desk and notice that it's mostly bare, aside from a small stack of papers and a framed photo of her in a wedding dress with a tall, dark-haired man. Liv looks amazing in her dress. The material hugs her body perfectly. Her husband looks equally as perfect. His teeth shine brilliantly white, nearly matching the color of Liv's gown. I wonder if he always gets what he wants when he flashes that smile at people. "Is that your husband?" I ask, even though it's obvious.

Liv nods, her face unreadable.

"How long have you been married?"

"It feels like forever," she says, forcing what sounds like a fake laugh. "We've been together as long as I can remember. We were high school sweethearts." Her tone is dismissive; it's clear she doesn't really want to talk about it.

She continues, changing the subject. "So anyway, I'm so glad you agreed to come. I think I have the perfect job for you."

"Okay," I say hesitantly.

"I am planning on running for mayor of Aldercreek, which is going to increase my workload significantly. I am going to need a personal assistant to help me manage the daily aspects of my life. Things like my schedule, my dry cleaning, anything that would take away from focusing on my campaign."

I can't believe my ears. This is perfect. It gives me the access that I need to do what I'm here to do without having to wait for months.

"Did you, by any chance, bring a resume with you, Eden?" Liv asks.

I nod and pull a white sheet of paper out of my purse. I slide it across the desk towards Liv.

She takes a few moments to peruse it before looking up at me. "It says here that you live in Seattle," she asks.

I nod. I don't want her to know that I've rented an apartment here.

"That's quite a commute. Is that going to be a problem?" She inquires.

I shake my head. "No, I know it's kind of far, but it's a reverse commute. As I'm driving here, I pass standstill traffic as I'm traveling sixty miles an hour," I chuckle. "It makes me feel like I'm speeding. Anyway, I listen to a lot of audiobooks, too, so it's productive. Eventually, I hope to move here when the time is right, but for now, I don't mind it."

"Are you sure it's not going to be an issue?"

"I have relatives a few cities over, and if I'm ever too tired to drive home or if I'm in this area late, I can always crash at their house."

"That sounds good. If you're really thinking about moving here, you should know that this community is growing fast," Liv says. "Most of Aldercreek was a swamp land about forty years ago before our founder bought large chunks of it and pumped out the water to develop it. He invested millions of dollars creating a system of waterways that would keep the land dry and drain the water into Puget Sound. It was a nightmare for him to get the permits to do that."

Yeah, he also displaced hundreds of Native Americans in the process. Such a philanthropist, I think sarcastically. I keep my thoughts to myself as Liv continues.

"He had to build a water treatment plant to ensure that it was the right chemical makeup and temperature so as not to kill the natural habitat in the sound, but he was eventually approved, and as you can see, it's no longer swampland around here," Liv chuckles. "We're now the weekend destination of many high-profile businessmen from Seattle. They love the exclusivity of Aldercreek and the high-end amenities we have to offer."

"I noticed that most of the properties here are high-end

condos or million-dollar homes. Were there not other people here before the land was developed?" I inquire, curious if she'll admit the truth.

"There were some small farming communities in the surrounding areas when Aldercreek was first founded, but many of them have moved away. I guess they found that the price they were offered for their land was worth the move. I'm not sure. There were even a couple of Native American tribes here for several years, but you don't really see them much anymore either," Liv explains.

"So, they were basically kicked out?" I ask, unable to hold back.

"No, nothing like that," Liv says. "It's not like the gentrification that they do in the inner cities, which is obviously horrible. This was different. It was mostly rural, probably less than a couple hundred families, and I'm sure they were offered large sums of money that made their lives much better. The town continues to grow even to this day," Liv says. "On the other side of town, we have a new development being built of around one hundred million-dollar homes with a view of the Cascade Mountain Range. Just last year, a large development of five hundred homes surrounding a golf course was finished. The golf course overlooks Puget Sound. It's breathtaking if you ask me." Liv smiles, clearly enamored at the man-made splendor.

My heart breaks at the overproduction of the natural land and the forced relocation of its people, but I can't let Liv see my sadness. "That's amazing," I say, forcing a smile to my face.

Liv stares at me as if she's trying to penetrate my soul. This makes me feel uncomfortable, and I squirm in my seat.

After several seconds, she folds her hands, and a small smile forms on her lips. "I like your spirit, Eden. You're a really beautiful person," she says, reaching over and grabbing my hand. "I already feel like we know each other so well. I think you get me. Would you be interested in being my assistant?"

My breath catches in my throat. This has all happened so fast and seems too perfect. What if I blink and find myself dreaming? I try to hide the excitement from my face as I nod, responding as evenly as I can. "I would love that," I say, looking Liv in the eye.

"Excellent," Liv says, clearly excited. "Can you start tomorrow?" She asks.

I nod. I don't even bother asking for the pay rate because it doesn't matter. I would take this job for less than minimum wage if I had to, but something inside me tells me Liv wouldn't be caught dead paying her personal assistant less than minimum wage. Maybe her housekeeper or her gardener, but I will be too high profile for that.

As I exit the office, I consider my luck. Things are going better than I had planned. I think about everything that happened to my sister when she was here and about how all the time I've spent planning and preparing my revenge is paying off.

Liv seems nice enough- collateral damage, maybe- but I know she's not innocent. No one in this town is. Getting close to her is going to help me get close to the person responsible for my sister's death — Liv's husband, Mitch Mitre. Justice is coming.

23

LIV

I set a nearly full glass of chardonnay in front of Sandy. We're sitting in my living room on opposite ends of the couch, both dressed uncharacteristically in yoga pants and sweatshirts. Mitch has a client dinner tonight and will be home late.

I invited Sandy over for drinks. It has been a while. She used to invite me to do things with her on a regular basis, but I guess after I turned her down several times, she finally gave up. Don't get me wrong, she is my best friend, but I don't have time to sit around and do nothing.

She takes a long sip of her wine before setting it down on the coffee table. "We should do this more often," she says, trying to hide her eagerness.

I nod. "I think we'll have to," I tell her, a small smile forming on my face.

"Oh really?" She asks, a hint of curiosity in her voice.

"I decided to take your advice. I'm submitting my application to run for mayor in the morning."

She can barely contain her excitement. "That's amazing,

Liv. I can't wait. Pippa had better watch out. There's no way you're not going to beat her."

I flash her a genuine smile. "I'm going to announce my candidacy publicly next week."

"How are you going to manage all of that and the agency, plus everything else you have going on?" She asks, concerned.

"Funny you should ask that. You know that girl that was in the office earlier today?"

"The black woman?" She asks.

I nod. "I've decided to hire her as my personal assistant."

Skepticism crosses Sandy's face.

I continue, hoping to dissuade her concerns. "Don't worry, I promise to train her. She's smart and driven; I know she's gonna do an excellent job."

"How did you even meet her?" Sandy asks. "It's not like you put an ad in the paper for a personal assistant, is it?"

I shake my head. "No, it's a funny story, actually. A few days ago, I went to meet a client at Dave's, like usual, but they didn't show up. Eden was sitting at the bar next to me, and we just got to talking. We immediately clicked. She just graduated from college and is looking for opportunities in town here. At first, I offered for her to join our team as a salesperson, but she was hesitant because of the time it takes to get a real estate license and the inconsistent income, which I understand completely. As soon as I decided to run for mayor, I knew that she would be perfect for the job."

Sandy looks hesitant. "I don't know. It seems awfully convenient. How well do you know her?" She asks. "I mean, she could basically be anybody. Did you even check up on her references?"

"No, not yet," I say dismissively. "I will, I promise."

"It just seems really risky bringing someone new into

our circle in the middle of a campaign for mayor. What if she has something in her past that comes to light in the middle of your campaign? That could look bad on you, Liv."

I wave my hand at her. "It'll all work out, I promise. I'm an amazing judge of character, and Eden has what it takes. Even if she doesn't, at the first hint of dishonesty, I'll just let her go and claim ignorance. Do you know how easy it would be for me to pretend like I'm the victim if she's lying about who she is?"

Sandy just stares at me quietly.

"It will all work out, trust me," I say.

Our conversation continues, mostly focused on Sandy. We catch up on her lonely life, the concerns she has about her marriage, and the struggles she's having with her daughter.

Suddenly, the alarm on my phone goes off. I panic, grab it quickly, and turn it off. How did I let that happen? I never let that alarm go off. I always catch it before it does. If Mitch had been here, he would have wondered what it was for. Thank goodness it was only Sandy.

"Excuse me for a minute," I say. "I have to go to the bathroom."

"Of course," she says, taking another long sip of her wine.

"If you want more of that," I say, pointing to her glass, "it's on the counter in the kitchen. Help yourself."

She looks at her almost-empty glass and nods. "I think I'll do that."

We both get up. I head to the basement door while she walks to the kitchen. I open the door and turn on the light. We rarely use this area of the house. When we first moved in, Mitch designed the space as a game room. He had to have a pool table built down here because it wouldn't fit down the stairs. In addition to the pool table, there are dart-boards and a bar. He was so excited about it, imagining all of the friends he would have over and the good times they would have in the basement.

The first few months we lived here, he had parties almost every weekend. It was annoying, but I knew he would tire of it eventually. To be honest, it took less time than I expected. I don't even think he's been down here for several months.

I walk down the stairs and open the door to a small guest bathroom. I open the cupboard under the sink, get on my hands and knees, and reach to the back of the cupboard. I pull out an empty toiletry bag hidden in the very back corner. Inside the bag is a tampon box that hasn't housed actual tampons in a very long time. I reach my hand into the box and pull out an object wrapped in toilet paper. It is my half-full prescription of birth control pills. Good thing Mitch is an idiot. He never questions why I go downstairs. I'm sure he assumes I'm just cleaning something or... I don't even know. He doesn't pay much attention to me unless he wants to try and make a baby.

Every time I take one of these pills, I feel a pang of guilt. I know how much he wants a child, but it's my job to make sure that our life runs smoothly and that we're both able to attain our goals. Having children is just not a part of that. Even though I know this is for his own good, I still feel bad about lying.

Once I become mayor, it'll become easier. I'll claim that I'm too busy or too stressed to get pregnant. Maybe I'll even fake a miscarriage or two during that time, make him believe I'm really trying. We'll see. I'll make that decision when the time comes. If I feel like Mitch is starting to ques-tion whether or not I can even have kids, I'll prove to him that it's possible. Give him just enough hope to not question me further and then fake a miscarriage.

I pop the pill into my mouth and swallow it without water before carefully repackaging the bottle and tucking it back under the sink.

As I walk back up the stairs, I think about Eden and what an amazing asset she is going to become to me and my campaign. Not only is she going to make my life easier as my personal assistant, but I know that having a black woman on my team is going to be great for the optics of my campaign. Of course, I would never say that out loud. I'm not daft. Even Sandy has to agree that the diversity will be good for us. I can't believe my luck in finding her right at the moment I needed her. Yes, Eden will do just fine.

24

EDEN

The grocery store looks almost nothing like it did the last time I was here. The layout is still relatively the same, but everything else has changed. The white linoleum floors are now a deep, rich, planked wood. The shelves, previously made of grey-painted metal with plastic signs displaying the prices, are now made out of the same wood as the floor, and the price tags are handwritten on miniature whiteboards. Someone has gone to great pains to make the whole store feel like a home pantry.

In the bakery section, you can buy all sorts of world-class baked goods in addition to bulk items that are stored in wooden barrels. I shake my head, overwhelmed by the opulence and the drastic change from what I remember.

I walk down one of the aisles and look out the main window of the store. The clouds are rolling in as if it's about to rain. I notice a large brass pig statue standing out front. How did I miss that when I came in? Maybe I am just so used to seeing it that my brain didn't even register its existence. Staring at it now, I realize it might be the only thing that hasn't changed since the last time I was here.

A memory from when I was five comes rushing back. We would come here sometimes after my mom picked me up from kindergarten. Autumn was still in school, and we had to wait a few hours before we could pick her up. We often did fun things together that year, just the two of us. It is probably one of the best memories I have with my mom.

She would let me sit on the pig for a few minutes each time we came to the store. It didn't move or do anything special, but climbing onto its back felt like a treat.

I also remember running through the store while my mom was shopping, the white linoleum floors squeaking underneath my feet. She would always yell at me to stop. Each time, I would slow down and wait for her at the end of the aisle, but the itch to run was just so great that I couldn't keep it up for very long.

I loved going to the grocery store and seeing all the different colors on the shelves and the foods that I loved. My mom was rarely able to buy the things I wanted, but I would dream of the big feasts that I would make when I was a grown-up and had my own money. Once a year, my mom would allow me to pick out my favorite cereal for breakfast. I always chose sugary ones because she would never let us have them any other time. Even to this day, I still love kid cereal, although I don't allow myself to have it very often.

I stand in the middle of the aisle and reminisce for several moments before forcing myself back to reality. The memories of a brightly lit store are slowly replaced by the mood lighting of this new version, and sadness washes over me. Why does everything have to change? Some things are good the way they are, and they should just stay that way forever.

I sigh as I walk toward the liquor section and grab a

bottle of whiskey from the shelf. I'm celebrating tonight. Getting this job with Liv was a stroke of luck.

I double-check the price to make sure I have enough cash on hand and put it in my cart. I'm trying not to use any cards, just in case. I'm going to need to pull some more cash out soon.

I back my cart out of the aisle and run into someone who is standing right behind me. I quickly turn around. "Oh my gosh, I'm so sorry," I say, and my heart drops. I recognize this woman.

I try to squeeze around her and get away as fast as I can, but she stares at me intently. "Kari-Anne, is that you?"

I swallow hard, trying to compose myself. "I'm sorry, what?" I ask.

"Oh, Kari-Anne. Wow, I can't believe it," she says, bringing her hand to her mouth.

"Oh no, I'm sorry, that's not my name. You have the wrong person." I continue to try and squeeze past her, but she places her hand on my shoulder, causing me to stop.

"If you're not Kari-Anne, then what is your name?"

"I'm Eden," I say hesitantly. "I'm sorry. I don't mean to be rude. I'm just kind of in a rush."

"Okay then, well, welcome home... Eden," she says, clearly unconvinced that Eden is my actual name.

I finally get past her and walk away as quickly as I can. I fumble with my wallet and pull out the money. I can't pay for the bottle of whiskey fast enough. As I wait for the woman in front of me to finish her transaction, I feel the eyes of the woman in the liquor section boring into my back. I quickly glance back and see her standing in the same spot, staring openly at me. I turn away. What am I going to do? Pippa Halloway knows that I'm back.

25

LIV

The sound of the doorbell ringing can barely be heard above the loud buzz of voices filling my house. A dozen women are clustered around the living room in small groups of two or three. Most of the conversations I hear, as I slowly make my way from group to group, are gossip about this town, veiled as concern.

"Did you hear about Regina Clark?" Marly Brown, the wife of one of the most prominent bankers in town, says in a loud whisper.

"No," Josephine Lund replies, a shocked expression on her face. "What happened?"

Mary continues. "Well, apparently, she walked in on her husband and some twenty-something-year-old flight attendant."

Josephine gasps. "How embarrassing. Have you talked to her? Is she okay?"

"I haven't, but I can only imagine how she's feeling right now," Mary replies.

I walk past, not even bothering to hear the end of the conversation. It's probably not even really true. Oh, it probably did happen, but the version that Mary is telling is most likely a gross exaggeration, as is everything else in this town. These stories always have some morsel of truth, but as they spread around from person to person, they gain a life of their own.

The doorbell rings again.

"I'm coming!" I yell, hoping the person standing outside can hear me. I exit the living room, walk through the foyer, and open the front door.

My new assistant, Eden, is standing on the front porch, an anxious expression on her face.

"Eden, I'm so glad you could make it," I say, hugging her. "Come on in."

She steps into the foyer and looks around. "Your home is beautiful," she says. "I'm not sure I've ever been in a place like this before."

"This?" I say humbly. "It's really nothing. Just a starter home for us, really. Our dream is to live on the golf course. One day, we will, once both of our businesses take off. Just a few more years, I hope."

"Well, I think it's wonderful," she says. "You're very lucky."

I pretend to be embarrassed by the attention and change the subject. "Don't be nervous. I know you don't know these people, but as my assistant, you're going to have to get used to being in the spotlight. This is honestly a pretty safe place to start."

"Okay," she says quietly. "Whatever you think is best."

"I can take that for you," I tell her, reaching for her coat. "I'll hang it in the hall closet. You're welcome to grab it at any time."

She looks hesitantly at me and slowly hands me her coat. It's as if she's afraid I'm going to do something with it.

"Trust me, no one is going to touch it," I say reassuringly.

I hang up the coat and turn back to her. "You ready for this?" I ask.

She nods and follows me into the living room.

I walk to the opposite side of the living room, towards the main chair set up at the head of a circle made of couches and chairs. Eden remains on the far side, standing behind one of the couches.

"Excuse me, ladies. It's time to get started," I say as loudly as I can.

The conversations slowly end, and the women make their way to their seats.

"First order of business is the east-side lake entrance."

Several of the women nod.

Amy Syler, a wealthy business owner in town, speaks up. "We must figure out a way to make it safer. What happened to Regina is just terrible."

The police don't know what caused her to drown, whether it was a terrible accident or a suicide, but I see this as an opportunity to bring the city together for a common cause.

"I blame the husband," Mary says from her seat on the couch.

"It's always the husband," the woman sitting next to her says in agreement.

A brunette woman on the other side of the room speaks out, "I heard he has an alibi. Apparently, he was in Europe or something like that."

I listen to the women go back and forth, gossiping about Regina's death for several seconds, and realize that if I don't stop it, they will continue on like this forever. We won't get anything done if I allow them to continue spreading gossip.

"Ladies, ladies," I say. "It doesn't really matter how it

happened. The fact of the matter is we just need to make it safer. What if it was one of our children or our spouses who drowned? Are we really willing to take that chance?"

The women around the room shake their heads.

I continue. "We need to raise enough money to put a lifeguard out there or something."

Jessica, a timid young woman seated on one of the chairs, raises her hand. "We could host a bake sale at the local school."

Several of the women nod approvingly.

"Excellent," I say. "Would you be willing to organize that?" I ask her.

She hesitates briefly and looks as if she is deciding to be brave. "Yes, I can do that. I'll get started right away."

I clasp my hands. "Wonderful. Now, next order of business. I would like you all to know that I have decided to run for mayor."

Several women gasp. Sandy sits in the corner of a couch, looking proud of herself.

I've been preparing these words for several days leading up to this event. "Regina Clark's death at the lake was the last straw for me. People in this town need to feel safe, and I believe I can help them do that."

"Well, I think it's a wonderful idea," Sandy pipes up. "You're going to make an amazing mayor."

"I won't be able to do it without a strong team supporting me. Sandy is going to be my campaign manager," I say, gesturing towards her.

She waves at the women in the room.

"I would also like to introduce you all to Eden." I glance over at her as everybody turns to stare at her. She waves to the women, flashing them a timid smile.

Just beyond Eden, I can see Nadia assembling a plate of

hors d'oeuvres in the kitchen. I've been keeping my eye on her rather closely since her odd behavior the other day. I haven't noticed anything so far, but I continue to be on my guard.

I look back towards Eden. "Please come stand by me."

She reluctantly heads in my direction.

"Eden is going to be my personal assistant during this campaign. I hope you all treat her with the respect I know you're capable of," I say, looking around the room.

Most of my guests are smiling at her kindly, except for Sandy. Sandy's face is hard and suspicious.

I put my arm around Eden's stiffened body. It's clear she's uncertain and uncomfortable amidst their gazes.

"Well, ladies, unless you have anything else to discuss, that concludes the business part of our meeting," I say.

Everyone shakes their head.

"Nadia is in the kitchen preparing some wonderful treats for all of you. Please help yourself."

Everyone stands. Most of them head into the kitchen, except for Sandy. She beelines her way directly to Eden, her hand outstretched. "I'm Sandy, Liv's best friend," she says, territorily.

Eden shakes her hand cautiously. "I'm Eden. Nice to meet you," she replies.

I know that look in Sandy's eyes. When she wants information about something, she's as good as a bloodhound at sniffing it out, and she has her sights trained on Eden.

Before Sandy can say another word, I hear the front door shut. Heels tap loudly on the tile floor in the foyer. The tapping grows louder as whoever it is comes closer. Several seconds later, Pippa walks into the living room. All conversation stops.

"It was nice for you all to invite me," she says sarcastically to Sandy.

"I'm so sorry," Sandy replies. "We didn't invite you because we assumed you would be working."

Pippa crosses her arms. "Even if I was working, I would have appreciated an invitation. I don't think that's why you didn't invite me, though."

She turns and stares at me while continuing her conversation with Sandy. "I think you didn't invite me because Liv is trying to gather support for her run for mayor, and that's easier to do when I'm not in the picture."

I stare back at her, wanting desperately to defuse the situation. This is not the place to have a debate with Pippa. I take a deep breath. "Yes, I'm running for mayor, but it was never my intention to step on your toes. I'm just so tired of the patriarchy in this town that I had to do something about it. Regardless of which one of us wins, infusing the city government with new blood will be good for the town. Don't you agree?"

She nods. "Of course, I agree. That's why I'm running."

"Well, I see nothing wrong with a little healthy competition," I say.

I can see the anger in Pippa's eyes, but she expertly stuffs it down and flashes me a smile.

I notice Eden standing awkwardly between us. "Pippa, this is Eden, my personal assistant."

"Lovely to meet you," Pippa says, a strange look on her face. "You do look familiar though. Are you sure we haven't met before?"

"No. People tell me I look familiar all the time," Eden says.

"Right... Well, like I said, it was nice meeting you," Pippa says.

"You as well, Mrs?" Eden asks.

"Call me Pippa."

"Would you like to stay for the rest of the meeting?" I ask. If you decide to, I'll have Eden make you a plate of food."

Pippa shakes her head. "No, that won't be necessary. I'm not staying for your little party. I'm going to head home and start planning for my campaign. Our town needs someone who actually cares about it."

"May the best woman win," I say, already completely convinced that I'm going to destroy her.

"I just wanted to make a little appearance here so you all don't forget who is actually working for the good of this community when it comes time to vote," Pippa says.

I scoff. Who does she think she is? None of these women are going to vote for her over me.

I turn to Eden. "Apparently, Pippa is not going to stay for the rest of the party. However, I would like some food. Can you please go grab me a plate?"

She nods and walks into the kitchen. Pippa's eyes follow her, openly staring for several seconds before turning back to me.

"Next time, do the right thing and invite me to one of these meetings. I'm not saying I will come, but it makes you look bad to leave me out," Pippa says, flashing me a brilliant, fake smile.

"Lovely to see you again, Pippa," I respond, ignoring her request. I glance towards the kitchen, indicating to her that our conversation is over. I watch from the corner of my eye as she exits the party, not saying a word to another person.

In the kitchen, I notice Eden standing at the island directly across from Nadia as she loads a plate with food. They seem to be talking to each other. Eden's gaze travels to

Nadia's wrists. Nadia notices Eden's gaze and tries to cover what looks like bruises with her sleeves before continuing to work on the tray of food in front of her, but I can tell from Eden's expression that it's too late. Eden has already seen it.

I stare at Nadia suspiciously. Something is going on with that girl. I need to figure it out.

26

EDEN

I notice the bruise on the woman's arm before she can hide it with her sleeve. I look at her face. She doesn't meet my gaze as she continues to place tiny quiches on a tray. Something has happened to her, possibly in this house. I should talk to her and make sure she's okay.

I look around the kitchen. Several women stand in groups, talking and mingling with each other. Now is not the time. I grab the plate of food and give the woman a small smile before heading back into the living room. I walk toward Liv and Sandy, who are engrossed in a conversation with a brunette woman whose back is to me. As I approach, I can hear the woman speaking.

"You'll never guess what I did," she says, talking animatedly. "My neighbors have an oak tree that overhangs six feet into my yard," she says, using her hands as much as she is using her voice to tell the story. "I asked them nicely to remove it, but of course, they ignored me. So, you know what I did?" She asks Liv.

"No," Liv says. "I have no idea." She sounds interested, but the look on her face tells me she couldn't be more bored.

"I got out my ladder, climbed that tree, and chopped those branches down myself. They all fell right on their property," the woman says proudly.

Sandy gasps. "You could have hurt yourself."

"But I didn't," the woman says proudly. "And now they have a mess to clean up. Not my responsibility." Liv notices me standing there with her plate of food and uses this as an opportunity to stop the conversation.

"Thank you so much," she says to me, grabbing the plate from my hands. I nod, knowing full well that she's not even going to eat most of the food on that plate.

Liv is thin. The type of thin you don't get from eating quiches and brownies, which is the majority of the food on the plate I just handed her. She's probably not even going to touch it. Taking the food from me is all just an act to make her seem normal.

I got a sense of the type of person she is just by watching her from a distance this evening. She's calculated and precise with everything she does. She may take a nibble from the plate, but then she'll just play around with the food for the rest of the night. I've seen dozens of women like her at the bar. They do what they have to do to fit in. Some of them do like Liv and pretend to eat, while others excuse themselves and go to the bathroom halfway through the meal.

"Let me know if you need anything else, Liv," I say, mustering a smile. "I'm going to introduce myself to some people."

Liv nods approvingly and returns to her conversation.

I take a deep breath and summon the courage to pretend to be something that I'm not — Liv Mitre's bubbly and friendly personal assistant. Over the next hour, I smile, nod, and shake hands, giving the best impression I can of a competent assistant.

Around 10 p.m., the women begin to trickle out and head home. I walk back into the kitchen and find Nadia standing at the sink, doing the dishes. I walk over to her. "Can I help?" I ask.

She looks at me, surprised. After some hesitation, she nods. "You wash, I dry," she says in a heavy accent.

I nod. "My name is Eden, by the way," I say.

"Nadia," she says.

"How long have you worked for the Mitres?"

"Not long," she says. "Maybe a year."

I stare back at her. I want to ask her about the bruises on her wrist — to make sure she's okay — but there are still too many people around. I don't want any of them to overhear what we're saying, and I want Nadia to feel safe. Instead, we stand and do the dishes in silence.

Occasionally, I glance at her wrists. The bruises are dark and encircle all the way around. She hasn't tried to hide them from me this time. She knows I've already seen them.

When we finish the job, I turn to Nadia. "It was nice to meet you. I hope we get a chance to talk more at a different time."

She nods at me and smiles.

I glance back at the living room. Sandy and Liv are the only two people left. I walk toward them.

"I think I'm gonna go home," I say to Liv.

She flashes me a grateful smile. "Oh, Eden, I'm so glad you came. I'll see you first thing in the morning," she says.

"Yes, of course. I'll be there," I say.

I grab my coat off the back of the chair and walk towards the front door. I pause briefly before I exit. I never expected to be invited into their home, but here I am. This has been much easier than I expected.

27

PIPPA

P ippa's back in her small cubicle after taking a few days off to prepare for her candidacy and find a new place to live. She's an associate at Warner and Lo, one of the most prestigious in Seattle.

The day she was hired as an attorney with them was one of the best days of her life. She can still remember it vividly. She was in her third year at law school. Bobbi was just turning five and about to start kindergarten the following year. She had applied to all the major firms in Seattle, but Warner and Lo was her top pick because they had the best reputation for winning nearly everything they tried.

She knew that getting hired by them was a long shot, especially because she was older than most of the junior associates they hired, but she didn't let that stop her. She had excelled in law school in spite of having so much on her plate as a wife and mother, and she knew she deserved a shot. When they called her and offered her the position, she felt validated — as if everything she had sacrificed to get there was worth it.

And it was, for the most part. She has had the opportunity to work on high-profile cases with some of the best attorneys in the city. Each case makes her a better lawyer, but the commute from Aldercreek to the firm is brutal. Most of the time, she has to leave an hour before Bobbi does in the mornings just to get to work on time. Her days are long, and she often comes home late at night after Bobbi has gone to bed. She didn't mind it so much when her husband was around because she knew he would take care of Bobbi, but now Bobbi's all alone, and it makes Pippa feel incredibly guilty.

For the most part, she loves working at Warner and Lo. They've always been good to her. When she first started, they helped her pay off her law school loans and paid her a salary while she was studying for the state bar exam. Because of their generosity, Pippa is not in debt like many of her other law school classmates. Over the last few years, she's worked her way up to a senior-level associate position and has been the lead attorney on several recent cases.

She can't even imagine leaving the firm after all they've done for her, but she also dreams of being a full partner in the firm one day. However, they've made no indication that they're considering her for a position in the near future. She doesn't have the money right now for the buy-in anyway. Everything she's saved is no longer accessible since Jesse completely locked her out of their accounts when he left.

Not having enough money to buy into the business is the least of her worries. What if the firm finds out about her criminal father? Would they deny her partnership because of her relationship with him? They shouldn't. She was one of his victims, not an accomplice. Her father had swindled her out of her entire savings when she was in her early twenties, leaving her penniless.

Her mom had left the house the moment Pippa turned

eighteen, saying she needed to find herself — or at least that's what she told Pippa. To everyone else, her mom claimed it was time she started putting herself first now that Pippa was an adult. She took off with her new boyfriend two months after Pippa's eighteenth birthday and never came back. Pippa occasionally heard from her mother, receiving calls from random places across the country, but she hadn't seen her in many years. At least Bobbi's whole life.

Pippa lived with her dad for the first few years after she graduated from high school. She took classes at the local community college, and by the time she was twenty, she had become a paralegal at a small law firm in town. She didn't make nearly as much money as she does now, but it felt like a fortune compared to what she had grown up with. Each time she received a paycheck, she would put half of it into a savings account. She had been saving up to move out someday and find a place of her own.

One day, in the middle of winter, she came home from work soaking wet, clutching an umbrella in her hand. The moment she walked through the front door, she sensed something was wrong. She set the umbrella down in the entryway and began searching the house. She quickly discovered that all of her dad's belongings were gone, along with anything valuable she had left behind in her room. Thankfully, she didn't have much.

On a hunch, she called the bank to check on the funds that she had been carefully putting away over the last few years. It didn't take long for the banker to confirm her worst nightmare. Her father had figured out some way to get into her bank account, and he had taken everything she had set aside. The account was empty.

She had felt sick to her stomach as she contemplated what he had done. She'd had no choice but to call the police. He had taken her entire life savings. It was gone in an instant, stolen by her own flesh and blood. She should have known better. It's not like this was new behavior for her dad. He did this all the time to other people. She just usually was not his victim.

A few years later, he came back into her life and apologized. He even paid back some of what he had taken, but not all of it. She didn't want to forgive him, but he was the only family she had, so she gave him another chance.

Now, here she was again, penniless. A few months ago, her dad had cleaned out her account once more. Jesse was furious. They had one of their worst fights the day she found out. He thought she had given her dad the account information and just let him take everything from her. It was absurd. Even though she had called the police and filed a report against her father, it wasn't enough for Jesse. He was convinced that she had allowed the whole thing to happen.

It didn't take long for the police to catch her dad. He was found at a nearby casino, drunk and penniless. Everything that had been taken from her was gone. He was arrested and charged with grand larceny. She watched the entire ordeal play out on the news. It felt surreal to see her dad in handcuffs. Jesse sat on the couch next to her, an unreadable expression on his face.

"What are you thinking?" She had asked.

He looked at her and shrugged. "It's all gone. Every last penny. How could you let this happen?"

She had just stared at him. Nothing she could have said would have convinced him she had nothing to do with it, and each time she tried to defend herself in the past, it only fueled his anger. So, she said nothing.

A week later, Pippa woke up to find Jesse gone. All of his clothes had been cleaned out of their closet. The worst part was that he left her unable to support herself and Bobbi financially. He hadn't taken money from her directly, but he'd locked her out of his accounts. She knows she could take him to court for her share of the marital assets, and she probably will, but the promise of a future court date doesn't fix the fact that Pippa is now struggling to pay rent. That money was both of theirs. She had all her paychecks deposited into those accounts to help pay the bills. The account her dad stole from held just a fraction of their joint assets. Yet here she is again, without a cent to her name.

She shakes her head and stares back down at the papers in front of her. The only way for her to recover from this is to move forward and no longer trust that anyone else has her best interest in mind. She tries to focus on the Supreme Court Opinion she's reading, but it's hard to focus. She forces herself to dial in because, without this job, she can't even afford the apartment that she just rented for her and Bobbi. She has to be patient. Someday, she'll be able to stand on her own two feet. And when that happens, she promises herself that she won't trust anyone else.

For now, she has to keep her head down and make sure she doesn't make waves. She doesn't want anyone to look too deeply into her life because if they do, her bid for mayor and all of her plans could be over.

28

EDEN

I've been working for Liv for almost a week now, and to be honest, it hasn't been that bad. She's a fair boss and never expects me to work for free. She is, however, a little demanding, always changing her mind about what exactly she wants me to do. One day, she'll tell me I'm in charge of making coffee, and then the next day, she'll tell me that being in charge of the coffee takes away too much of my time, so I have to stop doing that. I haven't quite figured out exactly what she wants from me yet. It still feels like a moving target.

The one thing that she is consistent on is requesting that I maintain the office display of white roses. There can be no browning of the petals. She is nothing if not obsessive.

Today, she wants me to take notes for her during a meeting with a client. He is a high-profile Seattle businessman looking to buy a two to five-million-dollar home here in Aldercreek. The thought of spending that kind of money on a house blows my mind.

The client arrives at the office at precisely 10 a.m. Liv greets him warmly, introduces me, and escorts him into her office. As soon as he is seated, she shuts the door and closes the office blinds, honoring his request for discretion. When the meeting concludes, she offers to walk him to his car. My heart starts to race. She's leaving me alone inside the office.

It's not that I haven't been in here myself before, but her office is usually visible from every corner of the brokerage. When I was alone before, I didn't have the opportunity to do any kind of investigative work.

The moment Liv exits the office with her client, I close the door behind her and quickly get to work. I'm not exactly sure what I'm looking for, but I'll know when I see it.

I look through the shelves first, but they're mainly just covered in decorative items for her office, along with a couple of books… nothing of significance.

Next, I sit at her desk chair and open the drawers. She's probably one of the neatest people I've ever met; everything has a place. There's no paperwork or anything like that in the drawers, which makes sense. Everything we do now is electronic.

I have to get into her computer. I wiggle the mouse, and the login screen comes up. I glance toward the door, hoping I have enough time for this. I inspect the outside of the laptop until I find the USB port and breathe a sigh of relief. Some of these newer laptops don't even have them anymore, but Liv's does.

I put my hand in my pocket and fish out a flash drive that I've been carrying around with me all week. I move my hand towards the laptop, ready to insert it, when I hear Liv talking loudly just outside the door. In a panic, I hide the flash drive in the palm of my hand, swiftly close the laptop lid, and grab a stack of sticky notes from the corner of her desk.

When Liv walks in, I'm seated on her chair, pretending

to jot down a note for her. She stops and looks at me. "What are you doing, Eden?" She asks.

"I'm just leaving a note. I need to run an errand real quick. It won't take me very long. I'll be back in about fifteen minutes," I reply, trying to sound casual.

She eyes me suspiciously for an uncomfortable period of time. Eventually, she nods. "Why don't you get us lunch while you're out?" She suggests. "Just go to the restaurant at the end of the block. I'll have my usual. You should ask Sandy what she wants as well. And get yourself something too, my treat."

I plaster a smile on my face that I hope looks grateful, but I had been hoping for a few minutes uninterrupted, and now I'm on a mission to bring back food.

The bell on the front door dings as someone walks into the brokerage. Liv turns around and walks out of her office to greet whoever it is.

I breathe a sigh of relief and quickly stuff the flash drive back into my pocket. I'll have to find another way to get the information I need from her computer.

I hurry from behind the desk and out the office door. Sandy used to share one of the desks in the main office area with the other brokers, but just last week, Liv moved her to an office in the back corner of the brokerage. Now that she's taken on the position of campaign manager, she needs the extra space.

I walk to the backroom and knock on the door.

"Come in," Sandy says from inside.

I open it and peek my head in. "Liv asked me to get your lunch order. I'm going to the place down the street," I inform her.

She gives me a long look that makes me feel uncomfortable, like I'm being sized up for no reason. "I'll have whatever Liv's having. I know she goes there often," she replies. I begin to exit the office when Sandy stops me.

"Sit down for a minute," she says, gesturing to the chair across from her desk. "I'd like to talk to you."

I nod hesitantly and sit in the chair she suggested. This is the first time I've seen her since the business meeting at Liv's house. I have a feeling, though, that this won't be the last conversation we have.

Her stare makes me wiggle in my seat uncomfortably. It feels like several minutes before she finally speaks. "You know this campaign is a big deal for Liv, right?" She asks.

I nod. Of course, I understand.

"During a campaign, secrets are bound to come out, including the secrets of the staff. You understand that, right?" She asks.

I nod again. Where's this going?

She continues. "It's imperative we know that everybody who works for us is squeaky clean. There can't be any skeletons in their closets. We don't expect them to be perfect, but we do expect them to disclose anything that might come out so we can get ahead of it. Because if we don't, anything negative that comes out will reflect on her and her ability to make good decisions."

"That makes sense," I say.

She continues. "Where are you from?"

"I'm from Seattle. I've lived there most of my life," I reply. "My last place was in Capitol Hill, but my family and I have kind of moved around everywhere."

"I think I know someone who lives there, a friend from high school. Maybe you know him."

"I don't know a lot of people; I worked a lot and kept mainly to myself. I probably don't know them," I say, hoping she'll drop it.

"What are you doing here in Aldercreek?"

My face flushes. "I just wanted to get away from the city. I just got my degree, and I thought Aldercreek would be a good place for me to start my career," I explain.

Sandy eyes me suspiciously. "Okay. Liv trusts you. I guess that means I have to trust you too, but just know that I'm going to be watching you," she warns.

I nod nervously and step to leave the office. "I'll be right back with your food," I say.

She doesn't respond, only nods.

I turn around and walk back down the hallway towards the front of the brokerage. The entire way, I feel her eyes burning into me with each step I take.

29

EDEN

L iv is a creature of habit. This has become even more apparent now that I can observe her every move in the office. I'm sitting in my nearly empty bedroom, jotting down everything I observed Liv do today at work in my journal. I've been doing this for several days, and it's clear that, just like in her personal life, she doesn't deviate much from her routine. She arrives at work at precisely the same time every morning. She takes her lunch at the same time each day, ordering the exact same food from the same restaurant. She schedules appointments with the same number of clients each day and either drives them to their homes or meets with them at Dave's to discuss their needs. She rarely has clients in the office, only those who are so wealthy they value discretion.

She doesn't have much for me to do yet. She says she's still trying to figure out what the demands of the campaign will be so she can determine what to delegate. As a result, I find I have a lot of time to think and watch.

No matter how hard I try, I can't figure out a way to get close to Liv's husband. From my observations, I think they barely talk to each other. She's never mentioned going to dinner with him or meeting him for drinks. As far as I am aware, the only time they are together is after Liv comes home at night and early in the mornings when they drink their coffee together on the porch.

Maybe I should suggest helping Liv out at her house to prepare for the campaign. I can help make sure her clothes are dry cleaned and everything is in order. As a bonus, it will give me the type of access to Mitch that I don't currently have. I don't want to make Liv suspicious of my intentions, so I need to somehow make her think it's her idea. Working in their home is the best solution to my problem. I have to get inside.

The wind blows through the open window. I don't want to close it. The fresh air in the room feels nice. I grab my black sweatshirt off of my bed and pull it on. I run my hand along the faded numbers and smile briefly. The sweatshirt used to be my sister's. I remember the first time she wore it; she was seventeen, and I was ten. We had just taken the bus to the mall and were headed home. Every once in a while, our mother would hand us some cash and tell us to go buy ourselves some school clothes. We got really good at stretching that money by mostly shopping the clearance aisles and thrift stores.

Autumn found the black 1989 sweatshirt at a thrift store inside the mall; it was only two dollars, and she fell in love with it.

"Why are you wearing that?" I asked her.

"Because it's cool. It's vintage," she said.

I rolled my eyes at her. "What makes it vintage?" I asked. "It looks practically brand new."

"I know, right?" She said. "It's in excellent shape. It's

vintage because of the date printed on it. It's obvious it was made a long time ago."

I finger the faded numbers, and a small tear escapes the corner of my eye. I miss her. As much as I've tried, I have never been the same since she's been gone. I don't even know if I want to be. She taught me how to appreciate even small things. I'm overcome by grief. I sit in the corner of the room and cry until no more tears remain.

30

LIV

"I think I'll go with you today to your showing," I say as I walk into Sandy's office.

She stares at me, surprised. "Why?" She asks.

"I saw on the calendar that you're showing that new house on Green Street. I've been curious about that house, especially since it has an outdoor pool. As you know, it's not very common in the Pacific Northwest, and I wonder how they designed it to protect it from the weather."

"Yeah, it is definitely unique. My clients are desperate to have a pool. I tried to warn them about the maintenance costs in the wintertime here, not to mention the cost to heat it, but they don't care."

"Let's go a little early so we have a chance to look around before your clients get there."

"I've already previewed it for them, but sure, if you want to," she says affably.

THIRTY MINUTES LATER, we arrive at the front gate of the large estate. From the details on the listing, I expected a grand entrance, but nothing quite like this. Large wrought iron gates covered in ivy stand at the front of a long, winding driveway that leads through the canopy of trees. Sandy gets out of the car and punches in the code to the front gate. The gate swings slowly open. Before getting in the car, she sets a rock in front of the gate to keep it from closing.

We drive towards the front of the house down the winding path. As we get closer, glimpses of the large house are gradually revealed, eventually coming into full view. From the front, we can see the floor-to-ceiling windows that dominate one side of the house, letting in the natural light as it peaks through the trees. The house backs up to a stunning view of Puget Sound, unobstructed by other houses. It is nestled on top of a cliff. There's no direct beach access from the house, but the impressive view stretches for miles.

"Wow," I whisper under my breath.

Sandy smiles. "It's amazing, isn't it?"

I nod. "This is the type of place I want to live in someday. It feels like the house is almost in another dimension."

Sandy laughs. "Kinda like a storybook castle, right?"

"Absolutely," I agree.

We walk towards the front door, and I watch as Sandy enters the code into the lockbox in order to access the key to the house. Once she retrieves the key, she unlocks the large door and turns to me. "Are you ready to be amazed?"

I nod.

She pushes the door open into a large foyer surrounded by rustic woodwork and stone accents. The designer has clearly taken inspiration from the outdoors and brought it inside, making a warm and inviting entry.

"I love it," I say to her. "This outdoor aesthetic is completely unexpected in a home in this price range, but I can see that it's going to appeal to the right kind of buyer.

"It really only gets better," she says. "Wait 'till you see the wine cellar."

We spend twenty minutes investigating every aspect of the home. I can't help but dream that someday, this home might be mine and Mitch's. I double-check the listing. Three million dollars. It's going to be a while before we can even dream of owning this home. Disappointment fills me. I wish I could move us more quickly towards our goals.

Suddenly, I hear Sandy calling my name. "Liv. Earth to Liv. Are you in there?"

I look at her, embarrassed. "Sorry, I was completely wrapped up in my thoughts. Can you imagine owning a home like this someday?" I ask.

She nods. "I can. I actually think we could afford this house now if we wanted it, especially if I combine my income with my husband's, but we're comfortable where we're at for now. Besides, I like having my own money to spend; it makes me feel more independent. If we bought a house like this, everything I make would go towards paying the bills."

I flash her a fake smile. Deep down, I envy her. She has the financial freedom I've always dreamed of having, and she barely even has to work for it.

"It's been a long time since we showed a home together," Sandy says, changing the subject.

I nod. "You don't need me anymore to help you with showings. You've become a darn good agent, Sandy. You should be proud of yourself."

She beams at me. "Thank you for giving me the opportunity. It's exactly what I needed."

The doorbell rings, and Sandy walks hastily toward it, opening the wide door and letting her buyers into the house. She gives them a quick tour downstairs and offers to let them explore the house on their own. They agree and wander up the stairs, talking in hushed whispers the entire way.

I walk over to one of the back windows and stare at the ocean.

A few moments later, Sandy joins me. "What would you do if you had this view?" She asks.

I shake my head. "Never go back to work."

We both laugh.

Sandy turns to me. "There's something I've been meaning to talk to you about," she says.

"Oh?" I ask as I look at her with concern.

"I'm not sure about Eden," she says. "There's something about her that makes me not trust her."

"Like what?" I ask.

"I don't know. It's nothing I can pinpoint exactly, but just a gut instinct."

"Thank you for sharing with me. I'll keep it in mind."

"You know I love you and just want to make sure you don't get hurt."

I nod, but I'm not sure I believe that is her only motivation. Deep down, I think Sandy is just jealous. This young, beautiful woman comes into my life to be my assistant. She spends more time with me now than Sandy does, even as my campaign manager. I know Sandy works for me, but we were friends first, and I haven't had as much time for her recently as I used to.

I don't want to believe it's jealousy, but what else could it be? Eden is great. She has been an excellent assistant so far, always assessing my needs before I even see them myself. I can already tell she's going to be a valuable asset to this campaign and to my life, but I'll keep an eye on her. I can't afford to let my guard down, and if Sandy is remotely right about her, I need to make sure my eyes are open and that I can see the danger before it's too late.

31

EDEN

I can't believe my luck. Both Sandy and Liv are gone at the same time today. As soon as they walked out of the door, I wanted to rush into Liv's office, but there was another agent still sitting at her desk, working on her laptop. She isn't really paying attention to me, but I don't want to risk it.

Twenty minutes later, the other agent gathers her things and exits, barely looking at me on her way out. I probably could have done anything, and she wouldn't have noticed. I'm that invisible to her.

The door closes behind her, and I spring into action. Now is my chance.

I quickly walk into Liv's office and draw the blinds. If anybody comes into the brokerage, I don't want them to know I'm in here. I rush to her laptop and pull one of the flash drives Derek gave me out of my pocket. It is loaded with a program that can crack most computer passwords, especially those that are made from real words. I suspect Liv's is not overly complicated. I open the lid of the laptop, and the password screen comes on the computer. I insert the flash drive into the USB port and watch as the computer program does its magic. It only takes a few seconds for it to figure out the password. I quickly save it on my phone and use it to log into the computer. The screen unlocks. I breathe a sigh of relief. It worked.

I remove the flash drive from the computer and swap it for an empty drive. I don't have time to find exactly what I'm looking for right now, so I copy the entire hard drive onto the flash drive. Thankfully, I have one of those multiple terabyte drives, and it easily holds everything on Liv's computer. I anxiously watch as the progress bar slowly creeps toward one hundred percent.

A few minutes later, the front door jingles, and I panic. If that's Liv, I need to think of a reason why I'm in her office. I grab a notepad and a pen, and I start writing quickly. I glance at the percentage of Liv's files that are copied to my flash drive; it says ninety-nine percent. "Come on," I whisper under my breath. "Just one more."

A few seconds later, the job is complete. I pull the flash drive out of the computer and back into my pocket, quietly closing the laptop lid just before Liv walks into the office.

She stares at me, surprised. "What are you doing here?" She asks.

"I'm just finishing up the grocery order," I say, feeling her suspicion burn through me like a laser.

"The what?" Liv asks.

"You know, the grocery order you asked me to place for you?" I ask.

"Oh yes, that," she says, sounding relieved. "I had completely forgotten I had asked you to do that. It's usually something I take care of myself."

"Not that I mind, but I'm curious. Why don't you just

have Nadia do the store run for the house? She makes all the food, so wouldn't that make more sense?"

Liv looks at me with daggers in her eyes. "That's not her job," she says dismissively. "Her job is just to take care of the house... at the house. I don't want her running all around town." She crosses her arms. "Why are you so curious about Nadia, anyway?"

The look on her face tells me I need to back off. "It was a dumb question. I just thought it would be easier on everyone if she did the grocery shopping, but I'm happy to do it."

Liv nods. "Place that order, and then I need you to run an errand for me."

"Where to?" I ask curiously.

"I need you to go to Mitch's work and pick up a package. It's imperative that it is done today. As soon as possible, really."

I try to contain my excitement. This is it. My opportunity to get closer to Mitch. I work to keep my voice steady. "Where does he work?" I ask.

"I'll text you the address. I need your assurance that you will use the utmost discretion in this," Liv says.

I nod. "Of course, Liv." My curiosity piqued. I wonder what's in this mysterious package.

"Good," she says. "Finish what you're doing and leave immediately."

I nod, walk towards my desk, and breathe a sigh of relief. She could have pushed me on the reason why I was in her office, but she didn't. And for that, I'm grateful because I had no real excuse. Instead, she gave me the perfect way to insert myself into Mitch's life. This is my chance, and I'm not going to waste it.

32

EDEN

I sit in my car outside the construction site and take several deep breaths. This is the moment that I've been waiting for ever since I came to Aldercreek — an opportunity to confront Mitch face to face.

My hand grips the steering wheel tightly. I try to center myself and calm my nerves. I feel like everything is riding on this moment. I take another few deep breaths before exiting the vehicle.

A chain link fence surrounds the construction site. I scan the fence for my way in and find a small gate at the end of the fence that appears to be unlocked. I walk toward the gate and open it. I am immediately greeted by a scene that looks almost like pure chaos to me.

White trailers are scattered throughout the site, interspersed between various construction projects. Several holes are being dug using backhoes and other equipment I can't name. They beep loudly as they excavate dirt and drive the dirt to a pile on the other side of the site. Men wearing hard hats stand around and supervise, occasionally moving to action when something requires their attention.

It looks unorganized to me, but somehow, they make it work.

This is Mitch's family's construction company, and they've been around for decades. They're highly respected in the area, so who am I to question their methods? Besides, I'm not here to critique their work. I have a much more important mission. I have to find Mitch.

My eyes land on a white trailer labeled *office*. I shake my head; it's succinct and to the point. I gingerly make my way over to the trailer, careful not to step on any tools or fall into any holes. No one seems to question my presence; it's as if I don't exist at all. I expected catcalls and inappropriate behavior from men on a construction site, but I did not expect to be ignored. Maybe they just don't see me.

A few moments later, I make it to the trailer and knock on the door.

A voice inside booms. "Why are you even knocking? Come in."

I cautiously push the door open and peek my head inside. It's dark in there. It takes a moment for my eyes to adjust, but as soon as they do, I see Mitch at the other end of the trailer, lounging with both his feet on the desk.

My heart stops. I never actually believed this moment would come. I had hoped it would, but so many things had to fall into place for me to be standing here. It feels almost like my destiny. I take several steps into the trailer and allow the door to close behind me.

I freeze momentarily. Here I am, standing face to face with the man I have spent years planning to confront. There's a huge part of me that wants to scream at him for what he did, but I can't. That wouldn't be wise. I would probably end up being arrested for assault or something crazy like that and lose all the advantage I have gained by being employed by Liv. There's no way she would keep me on staff after something like that.

No, I have a plan, and I need to stick to it, no matter how convenient this moment seems. I put on a fake smile and walk toward the desk.

"Good morning, Mitch. My name is Eden. I am Liv's new assistant," I say, extending my hand to him.

Confusion crosses his face, followed by recognition. "Oh, yes, right. She told me about you," he says as he slides his feet off the desk and onto the floor. He attempts to stand, wobbling a little as he gets up to shake my hand.

I'm close enough to him that I can smell the alcohol — whiskey, to be more precise. The sour smell hovers around him as if he's been drinking for so long that the smell is oozing out of his pores. I glance at his desk. Sitting in the middle of the desk is a white coffee mug, half full of an amber liquid that is definitely not coffee.

"Liv never mentioned you look like that," he says, looking me up and down appraisingly.

What exactly did he mean by that comment? He looks me up and down like I'm some sort of snack, and his intentions become excruciatingly clear. My skin crawls under his gaze, and I'm uncertain how to respond. If I were at the bar, I would just give him some kind of mean response that would ensure he would back up and never talk to me again. I can't do that in this situation. I need him to trust me.

"Have we met?" He asks.

I swallow hard. "Not unless I served you drinks at the dive bar I worked at in Capitol Hill," I say, trying to sound flirtatious back.

He laughs. "No, I've definitely never been to a dive bar on Capitol Hill. And if I had, I would have remembered you."

"I'm that memorable, huh?" I ask, trying to keep my tone light.

"Very memorable," he says.

I attempt to change the subject. "Well, anyway, Liv sent me here to get a package."

"Yes, right," he says, shaking his head. He opens his desk drawer and pulls out a manila envelope stuffed with something unidentifiable. "Please make sure she gets this today."

"Of course, I'm heading right back as soon as I leave," I assure him.

He hands it to me. It's heavier than I expected. I wonder what's inside. Honestly, it's probably nothing. I push the questions to the back of my mind and tuck the package in my purse.

"Don't be a stranger around here," Mitch says hopefully.

I raise my hand to wave goodbye as I exit the building. "I'm sure I'll see you around," I say, keeping my tone friendly.

I keep the fake smile plastered to my face until I'm outside of the fence and convinced I'm out of sight. As soon as it's safe, my face falls, and I double over to take several deep breaths. I did it. I stood before him and pretended that everything was fine.

As soon as my breathing returns to normal, I stand and walk toward my car. As much as I wanted to call him out, today was not the time. I have to keep pretending that everything's fine until the right moment. Anger seethes through me. I can't believe he's allowed to sit there, acting as if he's never done anything wrong. The fact that he single-handedly destroyed my life seems to have no impact on him. Well, he can enjoy his little white throne for now, but I know what he did. I know who he hurt, and soon enough, everyone else will, too. He will pay for what he's done. That, I can promise.

SANDY

Today is one of Sandy's days off, and she's determined to make the most of it, knowing that Liv's campaign will soon ramp up and consume her time. She never made it to the art gallery on her last day off. She decides that today is the perfect day to visit. She asks her husband and daughter again if they want to join her, but their responses are the same as before. This time, though, she is prepared for their rejection. Asking them is more of a formality than a genuine request; the truth is, she wants to go alone.

It takes her about an hour to get there, and by the time she pulls into the parking lot, it's eleven a.m. Her day is nearly half over.

As Sandy steps out of the car, the salty sea breeze from the Puget Sound blows through her hair. She takes a deep breath, savoring the city's excitement and fast pace. It's so different from living in Aldercreek, where everything moves slowly and everyone knows each other. In Seattle, she can remain anonymous if she wants. She could reinvent herself and become somebody else. Sometimes, she dreams about moving to the city and creating a new identity. She imagines herself as Vivian, a Harvard-educated businesswoman, who is here to become an entrepreneur. In Seattle, she could become anything, limited only by her imagination.

She walks down the sidewalk toward the gallery. It's nondescript from the outside, with only a small sign hanging above the door indicating its presence. The moment she steps inside, she's blown away by the talent dripping from the walls. The artist specializes in steampunk paintings and designs. Each painting depicts an elaborate scene set in a world filled with airships and clockwork machinery. Many of the artworks feature actual working metal gears that create movement and sound, accentuating the intricate scenes. She stands in front of a large piece, admiring it. She could easily spend hours examining every detail. Lost in thought, she is unaware that someone has walked up next to her.

"It's pretty amazing, isn't it?" A man asks in a British accent.

Sandy turns to look at the stranger, and her heart skips a beat. She hasn't seen a man as handsome as this in a long time. "Yes," she manages to choke out, her mouth going dry. "It's astonishing, really."

"Do you come here often?" He asks.

She shakes her head. "No, this is my first time, but I think I'll definitely be coming back."

"I'm Grant, by the way," he says, extending his hand.

She places her hand in his, feeling a blush creep up as their skin touches. "Vivian," she says, giving him the name of the alter ego she created only moments before. She isn't sure why she didn't just give him her real name, but something about this interaction feels slightly dangerous.

"Nice to meet you, Vivian," he says. "I came here on a

whim during my lunch break, but I didn't expect to meet such a beautiful woman hiding amongst the art."

Her face flushes again. She hasn't had a man talk to her like this in a very long time. "I'm flattered," she says. "You're too kind." She places her left hand on his shoulder and gives it a gentle squeeze.

Grant glances at her hand, and she realizes her mistake. Her wedding ring is still on that hand.

He looks at her quizzically.

She hesitates, unsure of what to say, and quickly recovers. "My husband passed away a few months ago. I'm a widow. I just haven't felt ready to take it off yet." Her cheeks burn, and her voice catches as she lies. He doesn't seem to notice. "Maybe it's time I move forward."

"No, you take that off when you're ready. I understand," he says kindly.

A small pang of guilt pricks at her conscience, but she quickly dismisses it. She's not going to do anything she would regret. What's the harm in a little pretending?

"Where do you work?" She asks, attempting to change the subject.

"I'm an investment banker. I've been here for a few months as a consultant. It's pretty boring stuff if you want to know the truth, but I'm loving Seattle," he replies.

"I've lived in this area most of my life. It's easy to take it for granted," she muses.

"You shouldn't," he says, his voice warm and inviting. "I find something new every day that takes my breath away. Just yesterday, I was walking along the pier when I saw a group of sea otters just hanging out in the water. I'd never seen an otter before, except on TV. It was amazing."

She smiles, feeling a small flutter of excitement. "I should have you give me a tour of the city," she says flirtatiously. "Maybe you'd show me something that I've somehow missed."

He gives her a boyish smile, and she can't help but melt inside. "Would you like to grab some coffee?" He asks.

She checks her watch. It's noon, and she has about an hour before she needs to leave and head home. "I'd like that," she replies.

"There's a shop just down the street. I noticed it as I was walking here," he says.

"Perfect," she says, tucking her arm into his elbow. It's just coffee. What harm can it do? Besides, he doesn't even know her real name. She'll pretend to be Vivian for an hour and then go back to her real life. No harm done. However, no matter how much she tries to convince herself that she's not doing anything wrong, she can't shake the feeling of guilt that lingers in the pit of her stomach.

34

LIV

The sun shines brighter than usual this morning as I enjoy my morning coffee. The birds sing loudly in the trees behind our house, and steam rises from the grass as the sun burns off the dew.

Mitch sits next to me, wearing his sunglasses and reading his paper. "Did you hear about the new gallery opening in Seattle?" He asks.

"Sandy was talking about going to that. I wonder if she ever went." I make a mental note to ask her about it later.

"It looks pretty interesting. We should go sometime."

"I have so much work to do for this campaign. Maybe when it's over."

He nods without even glancing in my direction.

I grab my tablet from the coffee table beside me and look at my schedule for the week. Today and tomorrow, I'm booked solid with appointments with clients and prospective donors. I don't even think I'll be able to come into the office. There's no point in Eden coming in if I won't be there.

I pull up my phone and quickly text her. *Work from home today and tomorrow. I'm going to be incredibly busy and won't be in the office. You can handle all the phone calls and emails from wherever you like; maybe find a cafe somewhere. It's up to you.*

I close the case on the tablet and stand. "I'm going to leave early today. I have a busy day," I say, looking at Mitch.

He puts down the paper and looks at me. "What's going on?" He asks.

"Just a lot of meetings. Nothing really. I just want to get a head start."

"Okay, have a good day," he says. His phone buzzes. He glances at it and flips it over.

He thinks I didn't notice his urgency. Unlike him, I notice everything. I'll deal with it later. I pat him on the shoulder as I pass him. "You have a good day, too."

35

EDEN

I see Liv's text message as soon as I wake up. I roll my eyes. She thinks she's doing something nice for me, but little does she know I live in an empty apartment. I would much rather be doing this work from the office, and the last thing I want to do is buy one of those overpriced lattes again so I can use the internet at a coffee shop. No, I'll stay here.

I get up from my mattress and pull my laptop out of my bag. I cross my legs, set the computer on my lap, and begin to work, just as I did when I was in college. I used to do all my work on the floor. Even though I had a desk, I always felt like I had more room on the floor to spread out all my books.

Going to college was one of my best accomplishments in life. For a long time, I didn't think it was in the cards for me, especially after what happened to my sister. The first day I stepped foot on campus, I knew I was exactly where I was supposed to be.

I started during the spring quarter at the University of Washington. I was captivated by the beautiful cherry trees blossoming everywhere. They made the entire campus look like it was covered in pink snow.

After my first two classes that day, I ate lunch in the cafeteria. Afterward, I made my way to a library in the middle of campus.

To say I was amazed would have been an understatement. The outside looked like a Gothic castle with arched windows and imposing towers. The inside was equally impressive. The main reading room resembled a library from a fantasy novel. Its ceilings were several stories high, and dozens of stained-glass windows let in natural light.

I stood in the middle of the room for several minutes, staring at my surroundings. I felt like I was in another world. Eventually, I moved from my spot and found an empty table. I sat my things next to me on an empty chair and opened my laptop.

I was at the library for only a few moments when I was interrupted.

"I've never seen you here before," a man said, sliding into the seat across from me.

I looked up from my computer and stared at him. "Do I know you?"

"No, but you should," he said.

I took a good look at him and liked what I saw. His shoulder-length locs were pulled back into a ponytail, and he was dressed in jeans and a black polo shirt. His dark brown eyes and friendly smile disarmed me. "Do you go to school here?" I asked.

He shook his head. "No, I just love this campus. I know it's kind of weird, but I like its energy, you know? Especially the library."

"I've never been here before. I honestly feel like I'm in another world."

"Yeah, it kind of does feel like that sometimes." He glanced over at my computer. "What kind of laptop you got there?"

I stared at it, uncertain. "I don't know exactly; I just bought the one the salesperson recommended," I laughed.

"Can I take a look?" He asked. I know a thing or two about computers.

"Oh, really?" I asked skeptically. "That's convenient."

"I do — trust me."

"Fine," I said.

He got up, walked around the table, and sat next to me. "Oh, it's one of those kinds of laptops," he said as he rubbed his chin.

I side-eyed him. "You don't really know anything about tech, do you?"

"What do you mean?" He asked, looking offended. "I'm an expert."

"Right..." I said sarcastically. "Just like I'm an expert in martial arts."

"Oh wow, that's cool. What kind of martial arts do you do?"

I looked at him like he was stupid. "I was joking."

"Oh, right," he said, looking sheepish. "Well, I wasn't joking about the tech. I've just never heard of that brand of laptop before."

"You think it's bad?"

"It's probably fine, as long as you're not trying to write massive computer programs or anything like that."

I laughed. "No, I think I'll just stick to using it for doing my homework and surfing the internet."

"Then you're golden," he said, smiling. He looked at me for several seconds. "You know what? I like you."

My cheeks flushed, and I looked back at my computer to avoid his gaze. "You don't even know me," I said.

"Let's fix that. I'm Derek," he said as he reached out his hand, a small smile on his lips.

I hesitated as I sized him up. Is he the type of guy I really want to get to know? He gazed at me expectantly, and his puppy-dog eyes eventually did me in. I grabbed his hand and shook it firmly. "Nice to meet you, Derek."

"What, you're not going to give me your name?"

I shrugged. "I guess you'll have to earn it," I said coyly.

He stared at me, shocked. Slowly, a small smile tugged at the corners of his mouth. "Okay, mystery woman. Bet."

36

EDEN

I sit cross-legged on my bed inside my small, barren apartment. I still don't have any furniture besides the mattress on the floor. It hasn't seemed like a priority to buy anything since I try to spend as little time as possible in this space. The only times I'm here are when I'm watching Liv and Mitch's house and when Liv forces me to work from home. I have no intention of making this apartment my permanent living space. It serves its purpose, but it's not home. I did get a few dishes at the thrift store this last week-end, so at least I'm not eating out of takeout containers anymore, but spending money on anything else feels wasteful.

This is my second day working in this room, and I don't know how much more I can handle. I need to get out of here. The walls feel like they are slowly caving in on me. I don't work for Liv because I need a job. I have enough money. I work for Liv because of the unprecedented access it should give me to Mitch, but I can't accomplish any of my goals by just sitting here alone. I need to figure out a way to interact with him, and I'm not going to do that if I'm stuck inside these walls.

I walk towards the sliding glass door and stare at Mitch and Liv's house. Over the last two days, I've developed quite a routine. I sit on my bed and answer emails for about forty-five minutes. Afterward, I get up and watch their house for about the same amount of time, sometimes longer. If I ignore her for too long, Liv will start to notice that I'm not responding immediately, so I have to watch myself.

Occasionally, I get so caught up staring at their house that I completely lose track of time. It's not that their house is all that interesting. It's nice, don't get me wrong, but it's really just a house. It's the fact that the one person who destroyed everything and everyone I ever loved sits in that house every day, enjoying his life. Just the idea that I'm close to him sends me deep into my memories, and I am overcome by things in my past that I have painstakingly shoved into the recesses of my mind for self-preservation. Being here has dragged them all to the surface. An hour will have gone by, but it will only have felt like five minutes.

Mitch's car pulls up to the front of their house. Each time I catch a glimpse of him, my stomach twists into knots. This is the second day in a row that he's come home in the middle of the day. I wonder how often he does this. Is it a daily occurrence, or did I just happen to see the only two days it's happened? I doubt the latter is true. Coincidences like this don't usually happen.

I grab my notebook from my bed and jot down my observations. Whatever is happening, it can't be just a coincidence. He must be coming home often, maybe even every day. I stare at the house for a long time, waiting to see if I catch a glimpse of him, but all the blinds are drawn, and I can't see anything inside.

My phone buzzes in my pocket. I take it out. It's Liv.

Did you get the email I sent you a few minutes ago? Her text reads.

I quickly grab my computer and check my email. She wants me to preview ten new homes that are coming on the market this weekend.

I roll my eyes. How am I supposed to do that? I don't have a real estate license. The best I can do is just drive by them, but what's the point of that? The pictures of the homes are already on the internet; there's very little I can glean from just driving by.

Sometimes, I feel like Liv makes up tasks just to keep me busy. I pull up the addresses to the homes and quickly realize that this little tour she's sending me on is going to take me the rest of the afternoon. I sigh and pick up my phone to respond to her text. *I got the email. I don't have my license, so I can't go inside them. Is there anything specific you want me to look for?*

Her reply is quick. *I mostly just want to know if they are owner-occupied or if they are empty. You should be able to tell that from the front door.*

Great, now I get to seem like a crazy stalker or worse. I spend the next few hours driving from house to house. I don't even get out of my car; the last thing I want is to draw attention.

I pass by one of the addresses, and an elderly woman glares at me from her front porch. I drive away as fast as I can. How could Liv make me do something sketchy like this? This could have gone very badly for me. It might still. What if that woman got my license plate number? What if she calls the cops and reports a suspicious person outside her home? The last thing I need is for the authorities to start asking questions.

My whole body shakes as I start to think that I could have gotten this far into my mission for nothing. I'm forced to pull over. I take several deep breaths before I am able to center myself and calm myself down. I spend a few minutes convincing myself that nothing bad is going to happen. That I'm okay. By the time I am ready to keep driving, it's nearly five o'clock. I skip the last house. I'll just tell Liv I ran out of time.

As soon as I get home, I send her an email and update her on my findings. When I'm done, I close my laptop and walk back over to the sliding glass door. Mitch's car is gone. The lights in the house are dark. Whatever Mitch was doing inside that house remains a mystery, and I'm pretty sure Liv knows nothing about it.

37

PIPPA

Pippa looks at her computer, and her eyes glaze over. She's been staring at the same document for what feels like hours, combing through it, trying to correct all the mistakes. It has to be perfect. It's not like she's writing a social media post. She's writing memos and giving legal opinions. She can't make any errors because people's lives depend on her accuracy.

She rubs her eyes and stands briefly, stretching her legs and her arms. She grabs her phone and heads to the break room. She walks inside and takes a deep breath. It smells like someone just brewed a fresh pot of coffee. She grabs a cup and fills it nearly to the brim with the hot liquid. At least they keep this stuff flowing here. She doesn't know how she'd survive without the caffeine.

Her phone buzzes in her hand. She glances at it and quickly silences it. She recognizes the number; it's not saved into her phone, but it's called her before. She can't answer right now, not right here. This is not the kind of conversation she can have in public.

She quickly finds an empty conference room and closes

the door. She lowers the shades, trying to shield herself from view. As soon as she's confident that no one can peer inside, she sits in a chair and sets the phone in front of her. She can't call the number back, so she waits. It doesn't take long. Thirty seconds later, her phone buzzes once again. This time, she answers it on the second ring.

"Clark County Correctional Facility. Will you accept a collect call from Martin Chan?" The operator asks.

"Yes," Pippa says succinctly.

Several seconds later, Martin comes on the line. "Pippa, I'm so glad you answered."

"What do you want, Dad?" She asks, annoyed. "You're not supposed to call me at work."

"Not even a little bit happy to hear from me?" He asks, laughing.

She doesn't even answer the question. Instead, she reiterates herself. "Why are you calling?"

"I want you to come see me," he says.

Fear grips her chest. "I don't have time for that, Dad. It takes an entire day for me to come down there and see you, and that's if I hop on the first flight out of here and come back home the same day. I can't do that anytime soon."

"You can catch the hyperloop."

"I'd still lose a day on the train. Either way, it's the same thing."

"Well, I don't know how long things are gonna be okay for me in here. Someone I screwed over on the outside just got placed in my cell block. I don't think he's recognized me yet, but when he does, I know something's gonna go down," he explains.

Pippa rolls her eyes. "You made your own bed, Dad. You're the one who treated people like crap on the outside.

Why should I care about someone you screwed over being on the inside with you?"

"You don't get it, Pippa. This place is dangerous on a good day. If I make enemies, I'll have to sleep with one eye open."

"Well, whose fault is that? I can't keep caring, Dad. You ruined everything for me. You took all the funds that I worked so hard for. You ruined my marriage. Of course, I don't want you to die, but I can't keep wasting time and energy worrying about it," she says firmly.

He replies, sounding defeated. "Fine. I understand. I have something for you, though," he says hopefully.

"What is it?" She asks, annoyed.

"I can't tell you over the phone. It won't make up for what I took from you, but it will change your life. Just come and see me, please. One last time, so I can give it to you."

"I don't know. I'm tired of all the broken promises. Do you know how many times you've promised me a better life or that you'd give me something to repay me for what you've done to me? And what have you actually followed through on?"

"This is different, Pippa. I promise."

"I can't do this anymore, Dad," she says and hangs up.

She feels a little guilty at first. Maybe he does have something important to give her, but she doesn't know. What she does know is that she can't waste any more energy trying to connect with him. That relationship is dead to her. It has to be for her own sanity.

38

SANDY

I t's been two days since Sandy met Grant. The conversation had been so easy; it had felt like he was truly interested in her, like he saw her. They had been in the coffee shop for just over an hour when she glanced at her watch and panicked.

"I'm so sorry. If I don't leave now, I'm going to be late picking my daughter up from school."

"You didn't tell me you had a daughter," he said, surprised.

"Yes, she's seventeen and has almost zero patience," Sandy said, laughing more lightheartedly than she felt. Inside, she was panicking. She felt like Cinderella when the clock struck midnight. She was convinced that if she didn't get out of there as fast as possible, the entire persona she had created would fall apart right in front of him, leaving the real her exposed.

She hastily grabbed her things. "I had a wonderful time. I'm so sorry to rush off like this."

"Don't worry about it; I completely understand," he said

as he stood and helped put away the ceramic cup she had been drinking from.

He walked her to her car and opened the door for her. He stood outside with the door between them, a hopeful look on his face.

Sandy allowed her gaze to meet his, and when it did, her stomach did flip flops.

"It was lovely meeting you, Vivian," he said. "I'd love to do it again sometime, maybe for dinner instead."

She was caught off-guard; she almost forgot that she had given him a fake name. Sandy nodded in agreement, but she was so ashamed and confused that she couldn't speak.

He pulled out a business card from his wallet and handed it to her. "Text me sometime. I'm here for another couple of months before I have to go back home."

She took the card and tucked it in her purse. "Goodbye, Grant. It was lovely to meet you," she said as she ducked into her car.

She closed the door and drove away. She didn't even have the courage to look back, but she knew he was still standing there, watching her leave.

For the last few days, Sandy has been playing their inter-action over and over in her mind. Why did she even open herself up to this? She's usually so careful about protecting herself. She should have said no to coffee. She should have stopped herself, but she didn't.

She can't even remember the last time Blaine looked at her the way Grant did. It's as if she's just a fixture in Blaine's life now. She's something he's used to being around but doesn't actually pay attention to. It's as if she only exists in his world to be his arm candy. He parades her around at his work events like she's a prize, but any time she tries to have a real conversation with him, he's too busy.

.   .   .

SANDY WANDERS AIMLESSLY through the grocery store, lost in thought. Liv hasn't been in the office for the last few days. Sandy is supposed to be managing the campaign for her, but it's nearly impossible when Liv refuses to delegate anything. Sandy is actually amazed at the number of tasks Liv has found for that girl, Eden, to do; she's never known Liv to relinquish any kind of control. She wonders what it is about Eden that makes Liv trust her.

Sandy was excited when Liv asked her to manage the campaign. She thought it might give her some sense of purpose. So far, however, the things Liv has allowed her to do have been very minimal. They feel mostly like tasks made up to make Sandy feel like she's a part of things, but they're obviously not really important. With Liv away the last two days, even those trivial tasks have been non-existent.

Today, Sandy even ran out of real estate tasks to do at the office. She didn't have any showings or appointments this afternoon, so she closed up shop at four and left early. Liv would be furious if she knew; she insists on the office doors being open until precisely five p.m., but Sandy just couldn't sit there any longer.

Instead, she's walking aimlessly up and down the grocery store aisles. She doesn't even have to shop for food in her house — their cook does all the grocery shopping. Sometimes, Sandy misses cooking for her family. In the early days, before Blaine made all his money, she did the cooking and cleaning. It made her feel useful, as if she had a purpose. Now, she just wants to feel needed again or even just alive. Most days, she feels like a zombie as she navigates through her life, dead inside.

Grant made her feel alive.

She takes out his business card and stares at it. Maybe she could meet him for dinner, and it wouldn't do any harm. They could just be friends. As she stares at the card, her wedding ring flashes in the store's overhead lights, and she feels a pang of guilt. No matter how dismissive her husband is, she can't do that to him. It wouldn't be fair. At least, that's what she tries to convince herself.

Sandy tucks the business card back into her purse, frustrated. She feels like a caged bird, desperately yearning to be free. All she wants is to feel something again — anything. She's tired of feeling like nothing she does matters to anyone. She needs a purpose, but all she feels is invisible.

As she walks down the next aisle, she notices the left side is covered in greeting cards and magazines. Before she can talk herself out of it, she grabs a magazine off the shelf and stuffs it into her purse. She quickly looks around to make sure nobody has seen her, but the aisle is empty.

Adrenaline courses through her body, and her heart beats fast. She holds her purse close to her body as she continues walking through the store as casually as possible. She occasionally glances around, expecting to see a security guard or manager rushing toward her, but they never do. It seems like she got away with it.

As soon as she gets to her car, she pulls the magazine out of her purse and stares at it. The adrenaline continues to course through her, causing her entire body to pulsate and buzz. The rush makes her forget about Grant, Blaine, and her feelings of insignificance, if only for a few minutes. Instead, she feels alive. She wants to do it again.

39

EDEN

L iv has me working from the office today, thank goodness. I learned some valuable information the past few days working from home, but I also nearly went stir-crazy just sitting in my apartment.

After the first day, I caved in on my resolve to avoid the coffee shop and spent a decent amount of time there on the second day. In fact, I was there for so long that I almost wore out my welcome. There's only so long you can utilize a business's free internet before they start to notice. I started getting strange looks from the barista after a few hours. I pride myself on being able to read people, and her body language clearly told me that I needed to leave.

I took the hint. I had only purchased a cup of black coffee, which I drained in the first fifteen minutes I was there. Their Wi-Fi was for paying customers, and clearly, I had lost that status a long time ago. Feeling uncomfortable under her gaze, I grabbed my stuff and headed back home, spending the rest of the day in my apartment.

I guess I'm glad that I was forced to go home because I

was able to witness Mitch coming home in the middle of the day again. I never would have seen that if I'd stayed at the coffee shop.

Liv has me completing more mundane tasks today. I spend the first three hours of the morning looking up addresses and assessing homes that she is planning to list in the next few weeks. I can't even imagine the type of money she makes, especially selling these homes. Most of them are worth more than a million dollars.

I walk into her office at eleven to inform her that the real estate task is complete. She barely acknowledges me. "Great," she says dismissively. "I have another task for you. I want you to gather a list of names and phone numbers of potential campaign donors. Find all of the prominent business owners in Aldercreek by any means necessary."

"You want me to just randomly look up the businesses in Aldercreek and figure out who owns them?"

She stares at me as though my question is obvious. "Yes. That is precisely what I want you to do. Have it to me by the end of the day."

I sigh as I walk back to my desk. This is going to be excruciating, but that's not the worst part. These mundane tasks tether me to my desk all day, keeping me from my true mission. I had been hoping to make myself so invaluable to Liv that she would ask me to assist with the campaign from her home. Being in her home is the only reliable way to access Mitch. Instead, I'm stuck doing busy work that I'm not even certain is all that necessary.

I sit at my desk and rub my temples. If something doesn't change soon, I may have to quit my job and find another way to get close to Mitch. For now, I am focusing on creating a donor list for Liv.

It takes all my detective skills to complete this task. I begin by looking at the map I found on the city's website and calling the prominent businesses in Aldercreek. If they don't answer or if the receptionist doesn't know the owner's name, I hunt them down on the internet. Several hours later, I have a list of around one hundred business owners, along with their phone numbers. I email the list to Liv and blind carbon copy myself on the message. The information I was able to gather is a valuable resource, and there's no way I'm not keeping a copy for myself.

About five minutes before five o'clock, as I'm preparing to go home, the brokerage's front door opens. From my little desk right outside Liv's office, I have a straight view of the front door.

In walks Mitch, impeccably dressed in a designer suit and tie, his shoes shining and his hair slicked back. I'm not gonna lie — he looks amazing. I get what Liv sees in him, but I can't stop the visceral response I feel each time I lay eyes on him. Instead of being struck by how handsome he is, I feel sick to my stomach.

He stands in the entranceway for several seconds before I realize that it's my job to greet him. I hastily stand and walk toward him. "Mr. Mitre," I say. "Are you here to see Liv?"

He stares at me for what feels like forever before composing himself. His gaze makes me feel uncomfortable. He pulls his eyes away from my face and glances toward Liv's office, clearing his throat. "Yes. We have dinner reservations tonight. Is she here?" He asks.

I nod. "Just one moment. I'll go get her," I say. I knock on the door to her office.

"Come in," she calls loudly.

I open the door and peek my head into the room. "Your husband's here, Liv," I say.

She looks up from her computer, a confused look on her face, but a few seconds later, realization dawns. "Oh right, yes, dinner. Thank you," she says. She quickly grabs her things and stuffs them in her purse. She types a few more lines of response on her computer and closes the lid on the laptop.

I leave the room and return to my desk. I get off at five and could technically leave now as well, but there's no way I'm leaving without witnessing the exchange between these two.

Seconds later, Liv rushes out of her office. "Mitch, I nearly forgot we had dinner plans tonight," she says as she walks toward him. She stands on her tiptoes and gives him a quick peck on the cheek.

"Me too," he says. "I've been working without a break nearly every day this week at the site. I've barely even had time for lunch. My assistant has been calling it in for me every day. I step into my trailer at eight a.m., and most days, I don't leave it until five o'clock. I haven't even had time to walk around the site in two weeks."

I stare at him incredulously as he spews lies directly to Liv's face. I'm shocked at how naturally they come out of his mouth. Of course, he hasn't been working nonstop. I saw him on multiple days come back home, and it's not like he just dropped by for a few seconds, grabbed something, and left. No, he was there for a long time, not to mention the fact that his work is nearly thirty minutes away from their house.

Yet, the look on Liv's face is one of complete trust. She believes everything he says. She rubs his arm. "I'm so sorry, baby. I'm glad you were at least able to get away tonight."

She must have no clue that he comes home on a regular

basis. There is no way I witnessed the only times this has ever happened; he must be doing it frequently.

I wish I could say I felt bad for Liv, but I don't. She uses him just as much as he uses her, but it does make me curious. I wonder what he's up to. If he's hiding it from her, it can't be anything good.

40

PIPPA

Pippa and Bobbi moved into their small apartment just a few days ago. Boxes litter the rooms in between large pieces of furniture. It's hard to consolidate everything one owns into one thousand square feet when the last place was five times bigger.

Pippa's already gotten rid of a large percentage of the things that were in storage, but she's probably going to have to get rid of more, or they won't ever be able to walk around in the small space.

While it's safe and clean here, it feels to her like a huge step backward. However, she's trying desperately not to see it that way. Instead, she tries to envision the apartment as a first step towards becoming independently powerful and wealthy. If she can accomplish her goals, she'll never have to rely on a man again.

She sets a bowl of cereal down in front of Bobbi and one in front of herself. "I'll do some grocery shopping later this week," she tells her, "as soon as my paycheck comes in."

"Cereal's fine, mom," Bobbi says, shaking her head. "Don't worry about it."

But she does. She knows that Bobbi is used to finer things and that living here in this apartment, having to take the city bus to school, and the complete change in her diet can't be easy for her. Bobbi hasn't complained once, though. Each day, when she leaves for school an hour and a half before school starts to catch the city bus, she does it without getting mad or upset. She has never lost her temper or yelled at Pippa. Instead, she has shouldered the burden right along with her.

Bobbi is quiet this morning as she chews her cereal, clearly lost in thought.

"What's on your mind?" Pippa asks.

Bobbi doesn't respond immediately. It's as if she's carefully architecting her words. Finally, she speaks. "I'm thinking about dropping out of high school and getting my GED," she says.

"What?" Pippa says loudly, shock evident in her voice.

"I'm not trying to quit going to school, Mom. I just thought that if I got my GED now, then I could go to community college next semester. The sooner I graduate from college, the sooner I can get a job and help you pay for things."

Pippa is livid. "No. There's no way I'm letting you drop out of high school. What would people think if they found out? My campaign would be over with before it even started if they thought my own child was a rebel."

"Are other people's opinions of me all you really care about?" Bobbi asks angrily.

"Of course not. I'm also worried about your future. There's no way you're going to be successful if you don't finish high school, Bobbi."

"That's not true," she says, composing her thoughts.

"Plenty of people are successful without following the path dictated to us by society."

"Oh yeah?" Pippa asks, challenging her.

"Yeah, even some celebrities and billionaires. Besides, if I graduate college, it won't matter whether I have a diploma or GED."

"It will impact which college you get into."

Bobbi continues. "Not for me. I'm going to go to community college and get my AA and then transfer to a major university. There's just no point in me continuing to go to high school every single day. Everybody looks at me weird, Mom. It's like they know Dad is gone, even though I've never said anything. People whisper behind my back all the time."

"I get it, I really do. Finishing high school feels like an unnecessary chore, but those celebrities and billionaires you're talking about are not like us. They had families that could fund their mistakes. It's easy to drop out of high school when you've got millions of dollars supporting you. We don't have that. We barely have enough money for food right now. We have to do things the way that society tells us to do them, or we will never be accepted by them. We don't have any choice."

"I'm doing this to help you, Mom, not hurt you," Bobbi retorts.

"But it's not that simple," Pippa says. "One wrong turn, and I can very easily not be elected mayor of this town. And if I don't get elected mayor, then I don't get the prestige and the power I need to stand on my own two feet. We have to keep our optics perfect. It's already bad enough that your Dad isn't here. People aren't going to believe the lies I've been telling about his disappearance much longer. If they find out that not only my marriage has fallen apart, but my daughter has dropped out of high school, I'm done."

Bobbi stares at her sadly. "It shouldn't be like this, Mom. I shouldn't have to do something just because it makes you look good. I should do things because they're right for us."

"But this is right for us," Pippa says confidently. "When I become mayor, our whole lives are going to change. For now, we just have to keep our heads down and not make any more waves. I promise I have a plan."

"I hope so," she says doubtfully.

Pippa stares at her daughter, both proud of the strong, independent woman she's becoming and terrified that she's going to make a mistake that ruins her life. Pippa knows that this run for mayor has to go flawlessly. Both their lives depend on it.

41

LIV

E den is the best assistant I've ever had. Every day, I trust her with more real estate tasks, which frees me up to work on the campaign. I wasn't sure if I'd be able to trust her enough to make it worth it, but she has not messed up, not even once. Each time she completes a task, she does it on time and with impeccable accuracy, and I assign her a more important responsibility.

I pride myself on giving her an amazing opportunity to work her way up in my company, but I'm starting to wonder if what I have to offer is enough for her.

Yesterday, I called her into my office to double-check a few contracts for me. I know she can't practice real estate, but I just wanted her to look for typos in the names or addresses and make sure the sales price and commission amounts were correct. Obviously, she agreed to the task, but there was a flash of something in her eyes that concerned me. I'm not sure what it was exactly, possibly boredom or frustration, but I could tell she wasn't happy with my request. I'm afraid that she's going to quit, and I can't let that happen.

I check the time on my laptop. It's nearly five o'clock. I can see Eden through my office windows, packing up her desk. What can I do to help her be content with the work that I have for her? I know it's not glamorous, but I'm starting to think that without her, there's just no way for me to run a successful campaign. I have to convince her to stay.

This is what I do for a living. I convince people all the time to do things they are not sure they want to do. When selling homes, the key is to paint a future for my clients that is appealing to them and convince them it's attainable if they purchase the home they are looking at. I don't exactly lie to them, but I tell them what I know they want to hear, and their doubts start to dissipate.

I need to do the same thing with Eden. I need to help her see a vision of the future that she can aspire to, and then I need to help her make the connection between that future and working for me. If I can get her to see the end goal, she'll stay. She has to stay. The success of my entire campaign depends on it.

I double-check my calendar. I don't have any client meetings this afternoon. Now would be the perfect time to put my plan into motion.

I walk to my office doorway and call to Eden while leaning on the doorframe. "Have any fun plans this evening?" I ask.

She looks up from her desk and shakes her head. "No, I think I'm just going to go home. I'll probably order some takeout Chinese food or something like that. Nothing very exciting."

"I don't have any clients this afternoon. Would you care to join me for a drink? My treat."

She hesitates for a second as if she's trying to contemplate the wisdom of taking me up on my offer, but she eventually nods. "Yeah, I could use a drink."

"Great. We can go to Dave's, the place where we met the first time."

A smile spreads across her face. "You really like that place, huh?"

"Yes, I guess I'm a creature of habit. Besides, they make the best cocktails in town, so why would I ever settle for second best?"

"Can't really argue with that logic," she says as she puts the rest of her things into her bag.

"Are you ready to go now?" I ask.

She nods.

I glance at my open laptop on my desk and back at Eden. "Give me five minutes."

I EXIT my vehicle and walk towards Dave's. Eden is already standing outside waiting for me. "How in the world did you beat me here?" I ask.

She shrugs and smirks. "I guess I'm a better driver than you."

"Impossible. I must have gotten distracted or something. Either that or you know a faster way here," I say, eyeing her suspiciously.

"No, nothing like that," she insists defensively. "I followed you most of the way here. I only passed you at that last light while you were looking at something in your car. I don't have any kind of secret backway or anything like that." Her body is tense, and her hands are clasped tightly in front of her.

I stare at her for a second. Why does she seem so on

edge? Am I really causing her that much fear and anxiety? I don't think so, but her behavior right now is a little odd. Maybe she just needs a drink.

"Are you ready to go in?" I ask.

She nods. "Lead the way."

We step into the dimly lit space and stop for a few seconds just inside the entrance to let our eyes adjust before walking back to the bar.

The two seats we both sat in last time are available. I gesture towards them. "It's like they knew we were coming," I say.

"How nice of them to save our seats," she says, seemingly more relaxed than before.

The bartender walks towards us, folding a towel and setting it aside. "What can I get you ladies?"

"I'll get a Moscow Mule with pineapple juice."

I glance over at Eden. She gives me a half-smile. "Still ordering the drink I recommended?"

"You were right. It really does kick it up a notch. I don't think I'll ever be able to go back to a plain one after this."

Eden looks at the bartender. "I'll just have a gin and tonic."

I shiver. "I can't stand gin. It tastes like pine trees to me."

"It's definitely an acquired taste, but it grows on you."

A few seconds later, the bartender sets our drinks down in front of us. I grab the copper cup my mule comes in and raise it towards Eden. "Cheers to a successful partnership."

She hesitates for a few seconds before clinking her glass on mine. "Cheers."

What is going on with her? Why is she unhappy? I need to make her feel indispensable and give her a sense of purpose because I can't do this campaign without her.

I take another sip of my mule and clear my throat.

"Eden, I just want you to know how helpful you've been to me the last couple of weeks. You are doing an amazing job. I can't imagine doing this without your help anymore."

She looks down at her drink, and it's clear she's trying to contemplate whether she should speak up.

I continue, hoping I can convince her to talk. "Look, I know it can be a little scary to express your thoughts, especially to your boss, but I can tell there's something bothering you. I want to assure you that no matter what you say, I'm not going to fire you. I need you, Eden. So if there's anything I can do to convince you to keep being my assistant, please tell me."

She hesitates for a few more seconds and eventually looks up at me. "It's just when you hired me, I thought I'd be helping more with the election stuff."

Relief floods my body. Is that all she's really worried about? "You will in time, I promise, but right now, as my assistant, I just need you to make my life easier. That's the fundamental job description."

"I see," she says quietly.

"By doing the real estate and personal tasks for me, you free me up to meet with potential donors and promote my campaign. If I still had to do all that busy work for real estate, this campaign would be impossible."

"I understand that," she says. "It's just not exactly what I had been expecting." Her hesitation seems to dampen a little, but it's not totally gone.

"That still works for you, right?" I ask before she has a chance to speak. I need to convince her. "I get that the work is not exactly challenging, but you should really just see this as a stepping stone in your career. This is not the end of the line for you, especially when I become mayor."

She takes another sip of her drink and nods. I can tell that I'm getting through to her.

I continue. "I promise, once I'm elected, I'm going to make you my chief of staff. You'll be so busy managing everyone around me that I'll probably have to hire people just to be your assistants."

She lets out a small laugh, and I breathe a sigh of relief. I think I've convinced her to keep assisting me, at least for now. I go to take another sip of my drink and realize, to my chagrin, that it's empty.

I raise my hand, signaling to the bartender that I need another one. She nods and promptly begins making it.

Eden smiles. "It's gonna be that kind of party, huh?"

"These are going to be the death of me. I try my hardest to be very strict about what I eat. My success depends on making sure I look the part."

"It really shouldn't be that way, but I understand," she says sympathetically.

"The truth is, I honestly can't say no to these," I say, pointing to my cup. "I force myself to leave after two of them, or I know without a doubt I will order a third and undo all the hard work I've done to keep in shape."

"Makes sense. It's important to set boundaries for yourself."

The bartender sets the drink down in front of me, and I hold it up. "To the best assistant I've ever had," I say.

"And to being able to set personal boundaries," she says, smiling.

"I'll cheers to that," I say, laughing back.

We clink our glasses together and both take a sip.

I watch Eden relax a little bit more, and I feel a sense of relief. I think, for now, she's going to stay. I need her to stay. Most of that stuff I told her about being chief of staff someday wasn't true. I don't even think the mayor of Alder-creek has one of those, but it sure sounded nice. I would have honestly said anything if I thought it would have convinced Eden to stay working for me. I trust her, and it's imperative that I start gathering more people around me whom I can trust.

42

SANDY

The thrill Sandy got from stealing the magazine in the grocery store lasted for only a few hours before she was back to feeling lonely and insignificant.

Later that night, as she is sitting in bed alone, waiting for Blaine to come home, she pulls Grant's business card out of her wallet and stares at it. She knows it is wrong to even think about seeing him again, but she feels like an external force completely out of her control is pulling her toward him. He was kind and a good listener, the opposite of Blaine. She desperately needs someone to talk to.

She wishes that Blaine was sitting next to her so she could talk to him about her day and all the thoughts going through her mind, but she wouldn't feel safe enough to talk to him even if he was there. She knows he would judge her. She can hear it now. *How could you even think about stealing a magazine? What's wrong with you?* He wouldn't understand. So, even if he was here, she would still keep quiet about the things she's struggling with and the hopelessness that she feels day in and day out.

She looks back at the card, and the pull towards Grant overwhelms her. She convinces herself that they will talk and be friends, nothing more. She quickly grabs her phone before she loses her nerve and opens the text messaging app. She punches in Grant's number and types a message. *Hey, this is Vivian. We met at the coffee shop the other day.* She hits send before she can talk herself out of it. That same rush of adrenaline that she got when she stole the magazine comes back, and she feels alive once more.

It doesn't take long for Grant to respond. *Vivian! I was wondering if you were going to message me. I almost lost hope,* it says.

Sandy throws all caution to the wind. *I was hoping I could take you up on your offer for dinner.*

Yes, of course, Grant replies quickly. *How does Thursday night sound?*

She quickly looks at her calendar and sees that Blaine will be at a work event that night. *Thursday night is perfect.*

There's this Italian place that I love down by the market called La Trattoria. Meet me there at six? He asks.

Six it is, she replies. She quickly deletes the entire message thread from her phone. The last thing she wants is for Blaine to find it. She adds a new appointment to her calendar for 6 p.m. on Thursday night and titles it *Dinner with Liv — Seattle.* Blaine and Sandy share calendars. It's one of their best forms of communication. He won't even question a night out with Liv, especially since he's been trying to get Sandy to spend more time with her anyway.

THURSDAY COMES QUICKLY FOR SANDY. Between work and carting her daughter to and from her various practices and events, it creeps up on her without her even realizing it.

Earlier in the week, Sandy suggested that Melanie hang out with one of her friends. Conveniently, Thursday was the only day that she didn't have other obligations. She found a friend to spend the night with on Thursday night, and Sandy was in the clear.

She left for Seattle around five p.m., wearing a dress she had purchased from a local boutique earlier in the week. Normally, her stylist buys all her clothes, but she wanted to do something for herself for a change, and this dress made her feel beautiful. She is also wearing a pair of earrings and a necklace that she had swiped from the store counter and stuffed into her purse while the girl was ringing up her purchase.

She can't explain the thrill she gets from taking something that doesn't belong to her. Something that she could easily pay for, so it's not about the money. The high it gives her is addictive.

SHE ARRIVES at the restaurant just before six and sees Grant standing out in front, waiting for her. He's dressed in slacks and a button-up shirt, with a sports jacket over the top. Her heart flutters; he looks amazing. She walks towards him, and the moment he sees her, she can feel the blood rushing to her cheeks.

"Wow," he says. "You look stunning."

She looks down at her dress and back at Grant. "Thank you. So do you."

He escorts her inside to a table by the window.

"I've never been here before," she says. "It's beautiful."

"The food is to die for," he says. "Might I recommend their fettuccine Alfredo or their stuffed sole? Both are exquisite."

"Why don't I let you order for me? Maybe we can share a few things."

"Excellent idea," he says.

Just as Grant predicted, the food was world-class, but the company was even better. She can't remember the last time she connected with another human being like she's connecting with Grant. When the check comes, it's clear that neither of them wants to end their night.

"Want to do something impulsive?" Grant asks.

She nods without hesitation. Impulsiveness has been her thing lately.

"There's a glass exhibit nearby; all the pieces are made by the famous artist Chihuly. Would you like to go?"

She looks at her watch. Blaine will probably be home in a couple of hours, but he thinks she's with Liv. She has an excuse. "Let's do it," she says.

They both ride in Grant's car to the museum. As he drives, he places one arm around her back, and she leans in to smell the warmth of his cologne. It feels nice being close to him.

As they're walking around the exhibit, Grant puts his jacket over Sandy's shoulders and grabs her hand. Sandy feels like she's in another world. This is the kind of thing she usually tries to drag Blaine to, but he never wants to go. He always suggests that she go with Liv, but Liv is always too busy.

Standing here now, she feels a sense of fulfillment as she stares at the pieces, their beauty seeping into her soul. She knows it sounds crazy, but it's almost cathartic.

An hour and a half later, she and Grant stand by her car. A cool breeze tousles her hair. Grant gently tucks the strands behind her ears. The touch of his fingers on her face sends a chill down her spine. Their chemistry is electric.

Grant moves closer and leans down in an attempt to kiss her. She almost lets it happen, but a flash of guilt hits her, and she puts her hand on his chest to stop him and backs up.

"I'm so sorry," he says. "I didn't mean to..." His voice trails off.

"No, you didn't misread the signals. I just need to take things slow," she says.

He glances at her ring, his brow creasing in contemplation. After a moment, he grabs her hand. "I know that you lost your husband not that long ago, so of course, we can take things slow, but I need you to know that I like you a lot."

Sandy stares at him, the same emotions coursing through her body, but she doesn't feel brave enough to say them out loud. "I had a great time tonight," she responds instead.

"Can I see you again?" He asks.

Sandy hesitates. Tonight was amazing. It was honestly the best night she's had in a long time, but she's afraid that if she sees Grant again, she will give in to temptation. "I'll text you," she says.

He nods in disappointment, not convinced she means it. "I really hope you will," he says.

Sandy opens her car door and slides into the driver's seat. As soon as she does, she realizes that Grant's coat is still on her shoulders. She thinks about keeping it but realizes it would be almost too big for her to hide from Blaine. "I almost forgot," she says instead, removing the jacket from around her shoulders.

He takes it from her and sadly closes the door.

As he walks away, Sandy stares at him for several

seconds. She wants to stop him from going, but deep down, she is concerned that if she does, everything she's worked for all these years will come to a crashing halt. She's pretty sure Blaine will never forgive her.

43

PIPPA

Pippa has resorted to doing all of her grocery shopping late at night, the hour before the grocery store closes. At that time of the night, there are not as many customers, and the ones that are around are usually not the social elite that she is worried about running into.

Each time she takes a trip to the store, she takes extra precautions to avoid being identified. She wears a hood and sunglasses, even in the dark, to conceal her identity as best as possible.

Tonight is no exception. As soon as she steps out of the car, she pulls a black hoodie over her head. She hopes that the hoodie will make her blend in and be as unrecognizable as possible. Even with all the precautions she takes, she is still terrified that she will run into someone who knows her or her situation. All it takes is one person to blab, and her entire campaign is over.

She walks into the store armed with a shopping list organized by aisle. She knows precisely where everything she needs is located in the store. She starts at one end and works her way up and down the aisles, attacking her list in a precise and efficient manner.

She's three-quarters of the way through the list when someone taps her on the shoulder. "Miss Pippa?" A voice says from behind her.

Pippa's heart races. She turns around to see her former housekeeper standing behind her, holding a package of flour in one hand and a shopping basket in the other. She is a small Russian woman with auburn hair pulled into a tight bun.

The housekeeper's eyes light up. "It is you, Miss Pippa. Oh, I'm so glad to see you," she says, setting down the items and opening her arms wide for an embrace.

Pippa reluctantly accepts the embrace and steps back.

"You too, Yvette," Pippa says, trying to sound as cheerful as possible while each fiber in her being wants to run in the opposite direction. "What are you doing here? I thought you were going to look for work elsewhere?"

"Yes, I had planned to, but my sister said I could come live with her for free while I looked for work. So I'm going to be able to stay," she says, smiling.

Fear grips Pippa's chest. What if Yvette tells people about her money problems or her problems with Jesse? Pippa didn't think Yvette was going to be an issue because she swore that she was leaving Aldercreek, but now, she stands in front of Pippa with plans to stay in town, and her mere existence poses a threat.

"How are you, Miss Pippa?" Yvette asks.

"I'm fine," Pippa says hesitantly. "I'm so sorry I had to let you go. We sold our house and decided to move. I didn't think it was fair to you not to have a job while we looked for a new home. I hope you understand."

"Yes, yes, of course, I understand. Thank you for your

kindness. Will you at least think of me when you get your new house?" She asks.

"Yes, of course. You did a great job," Pippa notes. She glances at her watch and realizes that the store is set to close in fifteen minutes. "I have to run, but it was so nice to see you."

"You too, Ms. Pippa. And please tell your daughter I said hi."

"Of course," she says, knowing deep down that she won't. She really needs to get back on her feet so she can squash any rumors that are out there immediately. Until that time, she has to stay far away from Yvette.

44

EDEN

The window in my apartment is open. I can hear the sound of the wind rustling through the trees, which is relaxing. I lie on my bed and stare at the ceiling. I can't remember the last time I talked to someone outside of my workday. My nights are filled with loneliness: solo dinners on the floor in my apartment and journaling all of my observations from the day. The isolation is starting to get to me.

I miss Derek. If he were here, we'd be eating take-out together and discussing the events of my day. He'd help me strategize how to implement the next stage of my plan. Why did I tell him not to come? I'm starting to wonder if it was foolish of me to think I needed to do this alone. Why did I think he couldn't be an asset? He's part of the reason I felt confident enough to do this in the first place.

A memory comes rushing back to me. Derek and I were hanging out in his apartment one night. We had just finished Thai food takeout, and the white cardboard cartons remained open on the dining room table. I'm sitting on the couch next to him, and my head is lying on his shoulder.

"We should eat Thai food every night," I said.

He chuckled. "I don't know if I could eat it every day. I'm pretty sure I'd get tired of it, but we could definitely eat it more often."

"It really is the best," I sighed.

We sat in silence for several minutes, watching whatever show Derek had turned on the TV. I wasn't paying attention to it. Instead, I was working up the courage to ask him for some help.

I'd been planning my return to Aldercreek for some time now — years, really — but I still needed to learn some skills to make sure it was successful. One of the things I hadn't learned yet was some basic hacking skills. I needed to know how to get into somebody's computer to find information that they were hiding there. I remembered Derek saying something about hacking the other day, and it stuck with me.

I sat next to him and contemplated whether I should just ask him to teach me. What if he didn't know how to hack, and I just misunderstood his comment the other day? Would he look at me differently if he knew that I was trying to learn how to break the law? But this is Derek. I was pretty sure he would do almost anything for me, even if it was technically illegal.

Eventually, I worked up the courage to ask. I sat up and turned towards him. "Babe?" I asked quietly.

"Yes," he said as he turned towards me.

"Do you think you could teach me how to hack into a computer?"

He muted the television and looked at me, confused. "Why do you need to do that?"

I shrugged. "It's just something I've always wanted to learn how to do."

He hesitated for several seconds. "That's not something a normal person just wants to learn how to do. What are you not telling me?"

I sigh. I knew I shouldn't have asked him. "Please, just teach me, Derek. I can't tell you why I need to know right now, but trust me, it's for a good reason."

I could see his emotions as they crossed his face. First, confusion, then concern, followed by resignation. "Okay, let me get my computer."

He didn't bother to ask me why I needed to know again. He knew I wouldn't tell him. I had secrets that I kept even from him. Not because I didn't trust him but because I was afraid that if I spoke them out loud, I would lose the upper hand and that all those years I'd spent planning my revenge would be for nothing.

He grabbed his laptop and sat next to me. For the next few minutes, he taught me the basics, most notably how to use software to crack a person's passcode and get into their computer.

"How did you learn all this?" I asked.

"My brother taught me before he died. He had been sick for a long time, and in his last few months, he tried to share everything he had ever learned in his life with me."

"He loved you," I commented.

Derek nodded. "You wouldn't believe the random things I know now because of him."

I looked at his face. Did talking about his brother make him sad or angry? I didn't see either of those emotions. Instead, he talked about him as if he was still around. "How do you do that?" I asked.

"Do what?" He responded.

"How do you talk about your brother and be okay? Every

time I talk about my sister, I am overwhelmed with emotion."

He shrugged. "Time, I guess. The more I talk about him, the easier it gets. In a way, talking about him keeps him alive to me because all I have are memories of him. If I don't share those memories, it's as if he never existed." He placed his hand on my knee. "I know it's not like that for you."

Tears welled in my eyes.

He removed his hand from my knee and gently wiped away the single tear that had escaped. "I know it's so hard. Maybe it's different because your sister wasn't sick. I knew for a long time that my brother was going to die. I was forced to come to terms with it well before his death, but you didn't know."

"I've never gotten over the shock," I admitted. "Maybe you're right. I should talk about her more. I don't want to forget her. She was so goofy. I remember this one thing that she would do at the dinner table. My mom would always reprimand her for it."

"I'm listening," he said.

"She would take her spoon, blow hot air on it, and stick it to her nose. She thought she was so funny, but my mom was always so exasperated with her. 'Get that thing off your nose,' she would say. I always giggled, and she would wink at me. I knew she was doing it to make me laugh."

Derrick chuckled. "She sounds like she was a lot of fun."

"She was," I said, as a small smile formed on my lips.

"Tell me more," he said.

I spent the evening talking about my sister for the first time ever. It felt cathartic. I didn't even know all the weight I had been carrying around until I allowed myself to release some of it that night.

45

SANDY

S andy and Blaine sit at the kitchen table as the sun streams in through the large window that overlooks the backyard. Sandy is eating her usual nonfat Greek yogurt with blueberries and raspberries while Blaine has a bowl of cereal. He is fully dressed in his suit for the day, with his tie flipped up over his shoulder to make sure he doesn't accidentally dip it in the milk.

"Do you have a lot planned for today?" Sandy asks.

Blaine shakes his head. "No, just the usual. I should be home around seven tonight," he says.

She nods, but she doesn't really hear him. Instead, she's caught up in the memory of her night with Grant. She hadn't had that much fun in a long time, especially not with Blaine. A small smile forms on her lips.

"You look happy," Blaine comments. "In fact, you've been seeming much more upbeat the last few days. Is there something going on?"

Sandy panics. Her brain races to come up with an excuse. After a few seconds, she takes a deep breath and shrugs. "I don't know. I guess I've been working out more lately. They say that endorphins can help your mood."

He stares at her skeptically.

Sandy could kick herself – she always works out. This is nothing new. She should have come up with some other excuse, but it's too late now. She has to stick with it.

Blaine stares at her for a few seconds longer.

Sandy holds her breath as she waits for him to question her further, but he doesn't. Instead, he nods and goes back to his cereal.

"Well, whatever it is, I'm happy for you," he says in between bites. "I was worried that you were depressed or something. You seemed so sad all the time. You were always moping around here like you had a gray cloud over your head, but it seems like that cloud is gone. I'm glad."

She stares at him in shock. She didn't even think he noticed her, let alone realize that she'd been so unhappy.

"I gotta go, babe," he says as he grabs his bowl and puts it in the sink. He walks over to her and kisses her on the forehead. He doesn't notice her change in mood as he walks out the door.

She stares at the door, stunned. Did he really know she was depressed? Why didn't he say anything? He never even checked in with her or made any kind of effort to cheer her up. In fact, he got busier the moment she started to feel lonely. Did he not care? Is having a perfect wife that he can parade around this town the only thing he cares about? Does he want her to be happy and cheerful just because that looks good for him? It clearly didn't matter to him when she was going through a rough time. The realization that her husband doesn't care about her strikes her at her core, and she can't let it go.

46

LIV

I walk into the office at my usual time and find Eden already sitting at her desk.

"Good morning, Mrs. Mitre," she says with a smile.

"Good morning, Eden. You're here early."

"I had a few final things to complete from the tasks you assigned me yesterday, and I was hoping to get them done before you came into the office. Besides, I'm a morning person. I prefer to get up early."

"I lucked out with you," I say as I unlock my office door. "I don't think I could even contemplate running for mayor if you weren't here."

"Don't be silly. You would have figured out a way even if I wasn't around. One thing I've learned about you since I've started working here is that you don't let anything or anyone get in your way."

I chuckle. "That obvious, huh?"

"It's not a bad thing at all," she smiles back. You probably just don't need me like you think you do, but I'm glad I can help."

"Well, I appreciate you. That is all I'm trying to say." I open the door to my office and step inside, leaving the door open. I have an open-door policy in the office. I want all of my employees to feel like I am accessible to them, so I leave the door open unless I make an important phone call or meet with a client.

I sit at my desk and pull a stack of envelopes out of my bag. This morning at breakfast, I realized the mail was beginning to pile up on the counter. Usually, Mitch handles the bills, but he's been out of town for the last couple of days, so I grabbed them on my way out and shoved them into my bag.

I sift through them. Most of them are junk, but one catches my eye. It's from the electricity company. The word *Urgent* is stamped across the front in red letters. I furrow my brow. I swear we paid this bill. In fact, I don't think we've ever been late on the electric bill since we moved into the house.

I grab my letter opener, slide the sharp end underneath the flap, and slice it open. I pull the paper out of the envelope and scan the letter. *Dear Mr. and Mrs. Mitre, the card you used to pay your most recent bill was declined. Please call us at your earliest convenience to give us another form of payment.*

Declined? How is that even possible? I run my fingers through my hair. What is going on?

I grab my laptop out of my bag, open it, and log in. I pull up my credit card account and look at the most recent transactions. The last five have all been declined, everything from the last four days. What the heck is going on? How has this been going on for four days, and I didn't know? I should have noticed this sooner.

I grab my cell phone and dial the credit card company. I

wait on hold for ten minutes before someone finally answers.

"First National," a cheerful voice says on the other end of the line. "How can I assist you?"

"Hi. This is Liv Mitre. I'm calling because several of the most recent transactions on my credit card have been declined, and I don't understand why."

"Right. Mrs. Mitre, let me confirm some information with you before we proceed. Can you please verify your date of birth?"

I give him my birth date and the last four digits of my social security number.

"Thank you, Mrs. Mitre. Let me pull up your account and see what's going on."

The line is silent for several seconds as I wait for his response.

"Mrs. Mitre, are you still with me?" He asks.

"I am," I say, annoyed.

"Excellent. I think I've found the problem. It looks like there were several large purchases made in St. Petersburg a few days ago that flagged our fraud department."

"St. Petersburg?" I ask, flabbergasted.

"Yes, St. Petersburg — in Russia."

"I know where St. Petersburg is," I snap at him. "I'm just confused. I definitely didn't make those purchases. Why would I be in St. Petersburg?"

"We figured it wasn't you, Mrs. Mitre. When things like this happen, it's our policy to cancel the card and send out a new one. Someone should have contacted you and informed you of this."

"I didn't talk to anyone," I say, my temper rising.

"I see here that we called you three times in the last

week, but there was no answer. We do not leave messages regarding sensitive matters such as this."

"Well, you should," I say, frustrated. "I never answer numbers that I don't recognize."

"I apologize, Mrs. Mitre."

"What the heck did somebody buy in St. Petersburg anyway?"

"I'm not sure, ma'am. I can only give you the names of the stores where the purchases were made."

"Do I have to pay for these purchases?"

"Absolutely not. Since we know it's fraud, we have already refunded you the money. Don't worry. That's why those transactions are not listed on your account."

"Oh, okay. Good," I say, relieved. "Because I did not make those purchases. I'm about as far away from Russia as one can possibly be."

"Of course. We would not want you to be held accountable for purchases you did not make."

"Thank you," I say. "When can I expect new cards?"

"They should arrive in the next five to ten business days."

"What? There's no way to expedite that?"

"I'm sorry, Mrs. Mitre. If we had been able to get in contact with you, we absolutely could have sent them to you via priority mail, but since we were not able to, they were sent through regular mail this morning."

"Great," I say. "What am I supposed to do in the meantime?"

"Well, do you have any other credit cards you could use?" He asks. "If so, you could use those until you receive your new cards from us."

I grow more and more annoyed with every second this

overly cheerful person speaks. "No, I don't have any other credit cards."

"I'm so sorry, Mrs. Mitre, there's not much more I can do."

How did this even happen? Anger boils inside, threatening to overflow. Did Mitch have something to do with this? I have to get off the line. I hang up without even saying goodbye.

I rest my head in my hands. Can't anything go smoothly? Every turn I take, there's some sort of hiccup. This run for mayor is going to be a challenge. I have to stay on top of things. I can't allow something like this to happen again, especially not in the middle of my campaign. I'm going to have to talk to Mitch.

I grab my bag and walk out of my office. "Eden, I'm going to be out the rest of the day. Why don't you just finish your work from home?"

A disappointed look crosses her face, but she quickly hides it. "Sure thing, Mrs. Mitre."

I leave the office, determined to find a solution, but first, I need to run a few errands. I open my purse and check my wallet. There's a couple of twenties. I'll need to stop by the bank and withdraw some cash. My irritation rises. What a hassle. This is the last thing I needed to happen today.

47

EDEN

I can't believe Liv made me go home. The sky is dark and cloudy, making my apartment feel more like a tomb than it usually does. I sit next to the window on my mattress.

After completing a task that Liv assigned me yesterday, I sit at the computer and stretch my arms. The dreariness is making me sleepy. I can feel my eyelids getting heavy. I need to do something to help me stay awake. I need a cup of coffee.

I stand and walk into the kitchen. I pull my new coffee maker out of the cupboard and plug it in. As good as the lattes at that coffee shop downtown are, there's no way I am buying those ridiculous, expensive coffees. The last time I worked from there, I vowed never to go there again. After I left, I drove straight to the store and bought myself this coffee maker. Today will be my first time using it since bringing it home.

I use a spoon to scoop the coffee grounds into the basket, not even bothering to measure. I've made coffee so many times in my life that it's become second nature. I fill the carafe with water, pour it into the reservoir, and turn it on. The sound of water percolating begins immediately. I breathe a sigh of relief.

Five minutes later, I have a fresh cup of coffee in my hand as I return to my mattress. I carefully sit, making sure not to spill, and set the mug on the ground next to the mattress. I open the computer and log into my email. There are several emails from Liv giving me instructions on what to do today. I read those first, taking notes as I read them to make sure I understand all of my tasks.

Once I have read through Liv's emails twice, I move on to emails from other people trying to contact Liv. I have access to her inbox, and part of my job is to filter through her emails so she doesn't have to. Some of them are junk, and I immediately delete them, while others require some attention.

Several prospective clients have emailed to attempt to set up meetings with Liv. I reply to each one with a proposed time and location for the meeting. She has given me strict instructions for what types of meetings I can book in each of her available time slots, and the clear parameters have made this part of my job simple.

Finally, I go through the remaining emails. I read them and forward many of them to Liv for her to deal with directly. Most of these are bills or interview requests now that she has officially announced her campaign.

There's one email that catches my eye. It is from the assistant to the County Executive. I read the email carefully. It looks like Liv has requested a meeting with him. This email specifically requests confirmation of the date and time of the appointment. This must be an important meeting for the campaign. The last line in the email gives me an idea. *Please reply to this email and confirm your appoint-*

ment. If I do not hear from you in the next three business days, I will open your time slot for another reservation. The County Executive's time is limited and valuable. I hope you understand.

This would be a perfect opportunity to throw a wrench in Liv's plans. My finger hovers over the delete button for a brief second before I click it. The email disappears from my inbox. I navigate to my deleted items folder and remove it from there as well.

I know it's not going to totally derail her, but not responding to the confirmation email for the meeting she set up is going to make her look incompetent, and she's going to have to do damage control. She'll look like she ditched the county's top politician, which will put a tiny question mark on her ability to manage Aldercreek. This could come in handy later on.

I feel a sliver of guilt for interfering with her campaign like this. Especially since she's not really the one I want to destroy, but deep down, I know she's not innocent. I'm not exactly sure what role she had to play in everything, but I'm certain it was something.

I close my laptop and decide to take a break. I look down at my coffee mug and realize it's empty. I must have been mindlessly sipping on it as I was working. I grab it and take it to the sink in the kitchen, where I rinse it out and load it into the dishwasher. A part of me wants a second cup, but I know if I do, I'll be jittery.

I close the dishwasher, walk to the sliding glass door, and look at the Mitre house. I wish that they would leave their blinds open just once so I could see what was going on inside. Aside from the blinds in the breakfast nook area, they have never even once opened the rest of the blinds during the entire time I've been watching their house — not even on the weekends when both Liv and Mitch are home.

How do they intentionally live in only artificial light? I don't get it.

I check my watch and continue to stare at the house.

Several minutes later, Mitch's car approaches the house like clockwork. Every time I've ever observed him at this time of the day, he's come home. I wonder what he's doing?

My mind flashes to the one time I was inside their home for Liv's meeting, and I remember the bruises on Nadia's arm. Someone was hurting her, and she was obviously trying to hide it. It dawns on me. I don't think I've ever seen her leave that house in all the time I've been watching. Not even once.

My stomach twists into knots as I put two and two together. Mitch comes home every day, and Nadia never leaves. What is he doing to her? Panic grips me. He must be hurting her. I have to figure out what's going on. I am frustrated all over again by my inability to see into their house. I pace in my living room for several minutes. What am I going to do?

In a moment of impulsiveness, I grab my keys and my purse and rush out of the house. I have to get there before he leaves, and I have to find a window that's open just enough for me to see inside.

I know that it's a dangerous plan. I could easily get caught and lose my job, but I don't care. If he's hurting that girl, I need to know so I can protect her. She's not safe.

48

EDEN

I park a block away from the Mitre home. I don't want my car to be recognized by any of their neighbors, so I make sure to park around the corner, out of sight.

I put on a baseball cap and sunglasses to hide my identity and check my appearance in the rearview mirror. Pretty good. Before I left my house, I put on jeans and a black sweatshirt that was nondescript enough to suit my purpose. I'm hoping no one will be able to identify me like this.

I walk up to the Mitre's house and immediately head towards the side. A narrow gravel pathway leads to the back of the house, and I follow it to the porch. I quietly climb the stairs and walk across the porch, careful not to make any noise.

The kitchen blinds are slightly parted, and the window is partway open. I creep up to the glass and slowly peek inside.

I can't see anything. I press my ear to the glass, hoping to hear something. At first, nothing registers, but then I hear light moaning and grunting. My body wants to rush inside, but I don't hear any indication of a violation. Maybe I'm walking in on a consensual affair? No. Nadia is their employee. There is a power dynamic being exploited. But what if she is a willing participant? I don't know what to do. I can't even see for sure if it is them. The sounds I'm hearing could be something on TV for all I know.

Eventually, I am able to move, and I step back from the window. I stand in the shadows formed by a corner in the house to avoid being seen and try to process the millions of thoughts swirling around in my mind. I remember the bruises Nadia quickly covered up when I saw her last. I wonder if they're from him and if he hurts her every day when he comes home. Anger boils inside of me. She needs help. I can't just call the police; they would never believe me, but I can talk to Nadia and beg her to get help.

I stand motionless and wait for Mitch to leave — beads of sweat form on my brow. When I hear his car drive away, I walk back to the open window and stare inside. Now, I can make out a figure that I am certain is Nadia. She is sitting on the ground, and it sounds like she is softly crying. A wave of guilt washes over me. How did I not do something? I didn't know for sure. Am I just lying to myself? I could never forgive myself. Forget my mission, my revenge. This is a live human who may need my help. I have to make this right.

I knock gently on the window. She walks towards the window and opens the curtain, tears streaming down her face. She sees me and is frightened, as if I'm some sort of thief. Eventually, she recognizes me, and the look on her face goes from fear to shame.

"Please, leave me alone," she says through her tears.

"I can't do that. You need help. Please let me come in," I beg.

She closes her eyes and wipes her tears.

I wait patiently. I'm not leaving her like this.

Eventually, she gingerly stands and gestures towards the back door. I walk to it and wait for her to open it. When she pulls it open, I take a look at her from head to toe. There are fresh bruises on her arms. She avoids eye contact with me and quickly covers them with her long sleeves.

"Are you okay?" I ask.

She nods silently.

"Someone needs to know. This is not okay, Nadia."

"Please, don't tell Mrs. Mitre. She will call the police. Please, no police." She looks at me with a pained expression, and I can tell she wants to tell me more, but she stops herself.

"You have to do something. You can't just let this go on," I plead.

She shakes her head, her eyes wide with fear. "Please don't say anything," she begs. "If you do..." Suddenly, a terrified look crosses her face.

I hear the sound of the garage door opening.

She glances at the door and back at me. "You have to go," she says, her voice filled with desperation.

"I can't leave you like this."

"You must. Now." She shuts the back door in my face and locks it. I sneak back over to the window and watch as Liv walks into the house. I quickly back away, my heart pounding furiously. I can't be caught; I will lose everything.

Nervously, I sneak back around the house and walk back to my car as quickly as possible. I'm grateful I had the foresight to park it around the corner. Liv would have easily recognized it. I wonder what she's doing at home during the middle of the day. It's unlike her. She almost caught Mitch. If she had, what would have happened to Nadia?

I desperately want to help her. Why is she so terrified to go to the police? I have to do something. She doesn't deserve to be trapped with her abuser, but even worse, if she doesn't get out of there, she could end up dead.

49

SANDY

B laine insisted on hiring an additional housekeeper. Sandy isn't exactly sure why since their house is always immaculately clean, but he wouldn't budge.

When he mentioned the idea, she protested. "You know, I could do the additional cleaning myself."

"No, you shouldn't have to do that. I make plenty of money for us to hire help. You can focus on your hobbies or exercise. I don't care, but I'm not having my wife clean the house."

She rolled her eyes. Blaine could be so pretentious sometimes.

So, here she is, sitting in her kitchen across from the third prospective housekeeper of the day. She reads her resume, and her eyes widen. She looks up at the housekeeper. "You used to work for Pippa Holloway?"

The woman nods. "Yes, I did."

"What happened?" Sandy asks curiously. "Why do you no longer work there?"

The woman is quiet for some time as if trying to craft

her words carefully. Eventually, she responds. "Ms. Pippa did not need me anymore."

"Were you fired?" Sandy asks, looking at her skeptically.

"No, no, no," she says, raising her hands in protest. "Nothing like that. She just didn't…" She hesitates before continuing. "She didn't have the money to keep me."

Sandy sits back in shock. "Pippa Holloway?" She asks. "The woman who's running for mayor?"

She nods. "She was a very good employer. I would have stayed if she had let me."

"I see," Sandy says, contemplating her words. So, Pippa is having financial problems. She decides to pry a little further. "Is Pippa cleaning her house herself now?"

The woman hesitates. "No. She's not living in that house anymore. She moved out the day she let me go. I don't know where she went, but I saw her the other day at a grocery store on the edge of town. Maybe she moved over there."

"I see," Sandy says, sitting on the edge of her seat. "How long ago were you let go?"

"Last month," she says quietly.

Sandy tries to hide her excitement. If Pippa is not even living in her house, something big is going on. She takes out her phone and writes herself a reminder to do some research once the interviews are over.

She puts her phone away and focuses on the candidate's resume. For the first time during the interview, she looks at her name. "Yvette? Is that right?"

She nods. "Yes, ma'am."

"I see here that you've been cleaning houses for over ten years?"

"Yes, I'm very good at it."

"You understand this is just a part-time position, probably only ten to fifteen hours a week?"

"Yes, I understand. I will find another part-time job when I'm not working here."

"Okay, great. I have several more interviews today. I'll let you know in the next couple of days what I've decided," Sandy says as she stands and begins walking toward the front door.

Yvette stands and follows her.

Sandy opens the door and stands next to it. She puts out her hand to shake Yvette's. "Thank you for coming today."

"Please, I will do a good job for you," Yvette pleads as she shakes Sandy's hand.

"We'll be in touch," Sandy says, businesslike.

Yvette exits the house, and Sandy closes the door behind her.

Her mind is whirling with hundreds of thoughts. She wonders what is going on with Pippa Holloway. What else is hiding under the surface that she and Liv can use against her in this campaign? There must be more than anyone even knows. That woman is digging her own grave.

50

LIV

As I pull into the garage, the sun is beginning to set. Mitch's car is already parked in its spot. Good.

I came home earlier today to see if I could find one of his business cards to use at the grocery store, but I had no luck. There weren't any cards in his office or our bedroom.

Nadia was in the kitchen when I got here earlier and was acting strange. She seemed nervous — like I'd walked in on her doing something she shouldn't have been doing. I tried talking to her for a few minutes, but she wouldn't say anything, like usual. I didn't have time today to pry, but one of these days, I am going to sit down with her and make her tell me what's going on. This kind of behavior isn't acceptable.

When I head back to the kitchen, Nadia is doing the dishes.

"Good evening, Nadia," I say.

She turns toward me, her hands covered in suds. "Hi, Mrs. Mitre." The shiftiness from earlier is gone, and a small smile forms on her lips. She continues. "Dinner is in the refrigerator. I made Indian curry."

"One of my favorites, thank you," I say, genuinely excited. "Nadia, have you seen Mitch? I need to talk to him."

A flash of fear flits across her face, which is immediately replaced by her typical blank look. "I think he's in the office."

What was that about? Is she afraid of Mitch? I should ask her, but right now, I need to figure out the situation with this credit card.

I walk down the hall and knock on the door to Mitch's office.

"Come in," he yells from behind the door.

I slowly push the door open and peek my head inside.

"Liv," he says. "Come in."

There's a half-drunk glass of scotch sitting on the desk in front of him, and the entire room smells like alcohol. I wonder how many of those he's had since he got home.

"What's up?" He asks. His words are slightly slurred.

"I need to use one of your credit cards. Mine isn't working."

"You can't."

"Why not?" I say, my anger rising.

"Because they aren't working right now, either. Some sort of fraud charges were made overseas, and they shut them down."

"Yours too?" I ask, shocked. "Don't you have more than one?"

He nods. "Yeah, I have several, but they are all not working. Even my business cards are shut down. I called all the companies, and they've all been declined for similar reasons."

"What the heck did you do, Mitch?" Rage fills me as I

consider all the possibilities. Is he living a secret life, or is he just an idiot?

"Why do you think this is my fault, Liv?" His face turns red, and beads of sweat begin to drip down his forehead. "I had nothing to do with our cards being fraudulently used. Besides, the banks are fixing it, and we'll get new cards soon."

"How soon?" I ask, my voice rising. "Because when I called today, they told me two weeks. I don't have that kind of time. I have a campaign to run," I yell.

Mitch puts up his hands. "Woah, woah, woah. Simmer down."

"Oh, I know you did not just tell me to simmer down," I say, barely able to control my rage. "How long have you known about this? Days? And you didn't think that maybe I should know about it too?"

"I don't know; the first one was declined last week, I think?"

"A week? Are you freakin' kidding me? I thought we were partners, Mitch. Why would you keep something like this from me?"

"I wasn't keeping anything from you. I was handling it. I know you're busy with your campaign, and I didn't want you to worry." He takes a long drink of his scotch and downs the rest. He reaches for the decanter on the cart next to his desk and fills his glass to the brim.

I roll my eyes. "This is BS. Just look at yourself. The whole room smells like alcohol. How am I supposed to trust that you're handling it when you can't even handle yourself? You're wasted."

"If you need money, there's some cash in the safe in our bedroom. Just go take some of that," he says, ignoring my accusation.

"I can't pay for everything in cash, Mitch. I need my credit card to work. You need to be more responsible. Whatever is going on with our accounts is your fault; I'm sure of it."

Anger erupts on his face. "You blame me for everything. I can't live like this. Did it ever cross your mind that we were the victims of identity theft or something like that? Maybe I'm not actually the screw-up that you want to portray me as."

I hesitate; maybe he's right. Maybe I've been too harsh on him. The reality of the situation hits me once again. He knew about the cards being declined, but he didn't tell me. "No. If you were innocent here, you would have just told me. Instead, you kept it secret from me and just hoped I would never find out."

He stands and grabs his coat from the back of his chair.

"Where are you going?" I ask as he walks towards the door.

He turns around and glares at me. "I'm going upstairs. I'm done talking about this. By the way, I have to leave town for a few days for work. Just thought you should know."

I stare at him, shocked. "You have a business trip? Next week?"

"I leave first thing Monday morning. I'll sleep in the spare room tonight. Don't bother coming after me. I think we both need some time to cool down."

I stare at his back as he exits the office. Does he really have a business trip already planned, or is he just trying to get away from me? If it was already planned, that's just another thing he didn't bother to tell me, proving my point. He's hiding something. At the very least, he's being incredibly irresponsible.

I run my fingers through my hair, exhausted from the

fight. Nothing was resolved. My credit cards still don't work, and now I have to get into the safe to get some cash. I hope that nothing important comes up that I can't pay for with cash in the meantime.

After several minutes, I exit the office and head up the stairs to our bedroom. I hope I gave Mitch enough time to grab his things and get out of there. There's no way I want to see him again right now.

When I enter the bedroom, it is dark and quiet. I turn on the light and head toward the closet. Mitch's suits hang neatly on one side, a line of greys and blues. My side is filled with colorful blouses and skirts, also neatly arranged.

I push aside several of Mitch's suits and reveal a safe we had recessed into the wall when this house was built. The passcode is our wedding date. Predictable, but one that both of us can remember. Our wedding was one of the happiest days of my life, and now look at us. We barely have a conversation anymore that doesn't end in an argument.

I input the code and open the safe. Inside is a large stack of cash, several twenties and hundreds bound together by a rubber band. Lying next to the cash is a handgun. Mitch bought it a few years ago when our neighborhood had a few break-ins. "I just want us to be safe," he said when he brought it home. I was less than thrilled by the purchase, but I agreed that we needed some kind of protection.

I grab a stack of cash and stuff it into my purse. I stare at the gun for several seconds and shut the door. The bolts of the safe slide shut.

51

EDEN

The moon is hidden by clouds, plunging Aldercreek into nearly pitch-black darkness. As I drive to Liv's house, the street lamps and my headlights are the only things lighting my way.

Liv called me twenty minutes ago. I almost didn't answer the phone. It was nearly nine p.m., and I was supposed to be off the clock, but I forced myself to answer. When I did, it took everything I had inside me to remain professional.

"Hello, Liv. What can I do for you?" I asked as politely as possible.

"Eden, I'm so glad you answered. I need you to come over right now and grab a folder I forgot to give you earlier; it's very important. Are you still in the area?"

"I'm not far. Is this something that could wait until tomorrow?" Every inch of me did not want to go.

"No, it cannot wait. I need you to begin working on this first thing in the morning."

"Fine," I said reluctantly. "I'll be right there." I hung up the phone and got dressed as quickly as possible. I needed to just get it over with.

Now, as I drive towards her house, I'm desperately hoping the exchange will be quick, but something tells me I'm in for a long night.

"Eden, thank you so much for coming," Liv says, slurring her words. She holds a glass of white wine in one hand and uses the other to hug me.

I awkwardly pat her back. "I don't have much time, Liv. Can we make this quick?"

"Of course. Come inside, and we'll get this over as fast as possible."

I walk into the foyer, and she closes the door behind me. I follow her down the hallway toward the kitchen. Halfway down the hall, she stumbles briefly and catches herself on the wall. How much has she already had to drink?

We enter the kitchen. All the lights are on, and Nadia is cooking a late dinner for the Mitres. She's at the stove, and her back is turned toward us as we walk in. I half-expect her to turn around, but she doesn't. She remains focused on the meal she's preparing as if it's open-heart surgery.

I think about her and Mitch. I should say something to Liv. She needs to know what kind of man she's married to, but I notice Nadia staring at me from the corner of her eye. A pleading look is on her face, and I reconsider. Maybe now is not the right time. Nadia clearly doesn't want me to say anything, and I have so much more that I need to accomplish before I out Mitch to the world. His day will come soon. Besides, I'm not totally convinced that Liv doesn't already know.

"Eden," I hear a voice say, breaking through my thoughts. "Eden, are you still with me?" Liv asks, waving her hands to get my attention.

I clear my throat and look at her. "Yes, sorry. I just got

caught up thinking about something. What were you saying?"

"I was just wondering how everything was going for you at the office. Do you have any questions or concerns about the job?" She takes a long sip of her wine and sits it on the counter.

I stare at her incredulously. Did she really make me come over in the middle of the night just to ask me how I liked my job? I take a deep breath and sigh. "No, everything is going fine. Everyone has been very kind and helpful. I have no complaints."

She walks towards the cabinet and pulls out another wine glass. She sets it on the counter next to hers and fills it nearly to the brim. "Here," she says, handing me the new glass. "Drink."

I reluctantly grab the glass from her. The last thing I want to do is drink with Liv. Before I came to town, I promised myself that I'd always be at the top of my game when I'm around her, but I can tell she won't take no for an answer.

I take a small sip from the glass and set it in front of me. I watch as she drains her cup and pours herself another. How much has she had? As far as I know, this is not like her. She's always in complete control of herself. Something's going on.

"I'm glad you're here, Eden," Liv says. "I needed someone to talk to."

She makes it sound like I had a choice. "What's going on?" I ask, trying to mask my annoyance.

"Supposedly, Mitch is going out of town for a few days next week. At least that's what he told me."

I look at her, confused. What does any of this have to do with a work assignment? This information seems way too personal to share with an employee. However, I play along. The more information I can learn about Liv and Mitch, the better. "You don't believe him?" I ask, hoping Liv will keep talking.

She shakes her head. "No. I don't," she says quietly. She stares out the window for several seconds before turning back to me. "My mother wouldn't deal with this kind of crap. She'd laugh at me for being so weak."

"Why don't you believe what he says?" I ask, trying to bring her back to the conversation.

She turns her head to look at me. "I don't know; call it a hunch. We've been having some problems lately, and I think he just wants to get away from me."

I need her to talk more. She can't shut down now. I take a chance. "Do you want to talk about it?" I ask, giving Liv the most sincere look I can muster.

She stares through me for several seconds, her expression cold. It's clear she's calculating how much she can trust me. My heart races as I silently will her to let me in.

Eventually, her face softens, and she takes another sip of her wine. "Mitch desperately wants children."

"That's not a bad thing. I'm not sure I see the problem."

"Well, we've been trying for a few years now and..." She touches her belly and looks away. "He's getting desperate. I can see it in his eyes. He wants them so badly that I think he might do anything to get them. He'd probably kill me if he knew..." she hesitates.

I remain silent, hoping she will forget I am here and say what she's clearly holding back.

She continues. "Never mind about that." She looks at me with a look of resignation and changes the subject. "I think he's cheating on me."

I try to act surprised. "What makes you think that?"

She waves her hand. "I installed spyware on his phone several years ago when I was suspicious he was doing something behind my back. To be honest, it was scarily easy. I've been monitoring his text messages ever since."

"He has no idea?"

She shakes her head. "As far as I know, he's clueless. If he's not, he's an amazing actor. However, I think he might be using a secret phone or something because I don't always see the entire story. It's like there's stuff missing."

"Maybe he deletes things before you can read them," I suggest.

"Yeah, maybe. Or maybe he finishes the conversation when he sees whoever it is in person. I don't know."

I look over at Nadia. Her face is bright red, and she's staring at us from the corner of her eye. Maybe now would be the best time to tell Liv about what Mitch is doing to Nadia. Perhaps she would be willing to help Nadia out of the situation.

Nadia's eyes plead with me once more, and I groan inwardly. I don't know why she doesn't want me to say anything, but I need to respect her wishes for now. I would never forgive myself if I said something and destroyed things for her in the process.

"You know what's crazy?" Liv continues. "It's not the affair that bothers me the most. It's the lying and sneaking around behind my back. I can't stand knowing he's living this life I know nothing about."

Liv continues to rage, and I do my best to stay focused on her words when it dawns on me that Mitch should be home at this time of the night. "Is he here?" I whisper.

She waves her hand. "He's in the guest room at the end of the hall upstairs, fully passed out, I would expect. He was already several drinks in when I came home. Besides, we intentionally built that room to be soundproof so our guests could have some privacy." She rolls her eyes. "I bet he uses that room regularly for his other women."

"I'm so sorry, Liv. That must be hard," I say, trying to coax her to continue talking.

"It's whatever. I'll figure out who the current woman is and take care of her just like I've done before."

My chest tightens. "What do you mean like you've done before?"

"This isn't the first time I've caught him, you know. He's cheated on me several times before. Most of them are just flings; those women come and go quickly, but two of them were full-blown affairs. The first one was when we were in high school."

I hold my breath. She has to keep talking. This is the kind of information I desperately need.

She continues. "It was so stupid, really. The girl was..." her voice trails off. She changes the subject once again.

Come on, Liv, I silently plead. Finish your thought.

But she doesn't. "Anyway, I made sure they all stopped coming back. It's not like Mitch would have ever gotten rid of them. He's too weak. He can't even figure out what he wants with his life, let alone his relationships."

"What do you mean you made sure you stopped them from coming back?" I say quietly.

She stares at me for several seconds.

I hold my breath.

She ignores my question. "You know, that's the whole reason he just runs the construction company, right?"

I shake my head, disappointed. Even inebriated, she's somewhat in control of her words.

She continues. "It was basically handed to him on a

silver platter when his dad retired. He's never had to make any hard decisions for himself."

She stops talking and stares through me. She shakes her head and takes a deep breath. "That's a story for another time."

I nod. What else can I say? It's clear the conversation is over, and I won't be able to convince her to say more without seeming suspicious.

Liv grabs her bottle. "I'm going to bed. Goodnight. Nadia, please lock up after Eden when she leaves." She doesn't even wait for a response before walking towards the door.

I stare at her as she exits the room. What the heck just happened? She didn't even give me this mysterious assignment that she was so insistent I have for work tomorrow.

I glance at Nadia. She's openly looking at me, a look of gratitude on her face.

I sigh and stand, speechless. Grabbing my things, I exit the house without another word, completely stunned by what I witnessed and heard in the last thirty minutes. It has changed everything.

52

EDEN

Moonlight peeks from behind a cloud, illuminating the sheer curtains over my windows and gently bathing my apartment in its silvery glow. I pace around my kitchen in the dark, processing the bits and pieces of new information I just gleaned from Liv. What did it all mean?

Mitch has been unfaithful to her for a long time; that much is clear, but what I can't work out is what role Liv played in those affairs. What did she mean when she said she took care of them? Did she mean that literally or just metaphorically?

"Think, Eden," I chastise myself. I put my hands to my temples and force myself to assemble the pieces. Liv knew about two women Mitch had full-blown affairs with.

An image of the local newspaper story about the woman drowning in the lake comes to my mind, and I stop pacing. Was she the most recent one? Her body was found at the lake, the same place where my sister had died.

Grief overwhelms me. I can't believe how stupid I've been all these years. I've had such tunnel vision that I saw only what I wanted to see, but the truth has been staring at me this entire time. What else don't I know? It's as if a blindfold has been removed from my eyes, and I can finally see the truth.

I grab my black sweatshirt, the one I've worn since I was a child, and put it to my face. I scream into it as loud as I can. The sweatshirt barely muffles my cries as tears stream down my face. "I'm so sorry, Autumn," I whisper through the sobs.

A memory of her face invades my mind, one that I have clung to for years. She's wearing the same black sweatshirt I'm currently clutching in my fists, a broad smile on her face. She was so happy. I desperately wanted to be just like her, and now she's dead.

The pieces of the puzzle have been in front of me for years, and I just couldn't put them together. This whole time, I've been blaming the wrong person.

I think of the woman who was recently found dead at the lake. She must have been the other woman. It's all so clear to me now. Liv must have killed her. The implication of my words strikes me hard in the gut, and I sink to the ground. If that's true, then she also killed my sister.

53

LIV

I stare at my computer screen, my head pounding from the bottle of wine I drank the night before. I don't remember exactly what happened before I went to bed. I know I called Eden over, but after she arrived, the rest of the night was kind of a blur, and trying to remember it makes me furious at Mitch all over again.

I would have never even drunk that bottle of wine if it wasn't for his nonsense. He always makes everything so difficult. All he had to do was be upfront with me about the cards, but no, as usual, he just pretended like nothing was wrong, and I had to find out the hard way and try to do damage control. It's times like these that make me wonder if I made the wrong choice when I chose to marry him. I mean, I do love him, but he's made my life much more difficult.

I rub my temples and down a glass of water, forcing myself to push thoughts of Mitch out of my mind. I need to focus on the spreadsheet in front of me. Over the last few weeks, I've been building a list of community members who might be willing to support my campaign. My goal is to connect with at least fifty of the most prominent business people in Aldercreek in the next few weeks. I have already scheduled meetings with several of them. At the top of my list is a meeting I have planned for tomorrow with the County Executive. I contacted him a couple of weeks ago, even before I had made my campaign official.

I check my inbox for a confirmation email from his office, but find nothing. That's strange. I swear his assistant said he was going to email me to confirm. I check my deleted items folder and still see nothing.

I pick up my phone and dial the number for his office.

His assistant answers after a few rings. "Bruce Jenkins's office," he says cheerfully.

"Hi, this is Liv Mitre," I say in the calmest and most professional tone I can muster, but deep down, I am starting to panic. Something is wrong. "I'm calling to confirm my appointment for tomorrow with Mr. Jenkins."

"Just one moment, please," his assistant responds.

I wait in silence, and the only sound I hear is his keyboard clicking as he types.

Several seconds later, the assistant comes back on the line. "Mrs. Mitre, I'm so sorry, but we don't have an appointment scheduled for you today."

Panic rises in my chest. Without the County Executive's support, my campaign is likely dead in the water. "I made it several weeks ago. Are you sure?"

"Yes, I'm sure. It looks like we tentatively had it on the schedule, but you never confirmed the appointment, so we removed it. Mr. Jenkins's time is incredibly valuable, so we make sure every minute is booked. We have a strict confirmation policy to ensure there are no gaps in his day."

"It was never confirmed?" I ask, confused.

"No, Ma'am. I'm so sorry about the misunderstanding, but there is no way for me to squeeze you in tomorrow. Mr. Jenkins is going to Olympia for the weekend and won't be back until next week."

"Are you kidding me?" I exclaim, my panic swiftly turning into anger. I muster every ounce of self-control to stay composed.

"I wish I was," he replies.

"I never received a confirmation email. I've combed through my inbox, and it's not there. This is completely unacceptable," I say, my voice rising despite my efforts to stay calm. My grip on my temper is slipping. "This appointment was crucial. It needs to happen within the next week. You need to find a way to fix this."

"I'm sorry, right now I can't do that. We sent the confirmation to the email address you provided. I can see it right here in the sent items folder."

He verifies my email address. "I can offer you the next available slot if that works." His voice remains frustratingly calm, as though my words don't faze him at all.

Beyond frustrated, I search my email again for this phantom message. It's still nowhere to be found. Everything in me wants to tear into this man, but I know from his tone that it won't help. I take a deep breath and release it slowly. "Yes, please do," I say, forcing calm into my voice.

"It looks like his next available appointment slot is until January tenth at eleven a.m. Should I put you down for that time?"

"You have nothing sooner?" I ask, fighting to hold back angry tears.

"I'm so sorry, Mrs. Mitre, but that's the best I can do. I

can put your name down for a cancellation, though; due to our confirmation policy, appointment slots are always coming available."

I'm seething inside. How could they just cancel my appointment without calling and talking to me first? Who does that?

"Mrs. Mitre?" the assistant asks, interrupting my thoughts. "Are you still on the line?"

"Yes, sorry, I'm here. What date was available?"

"Tuesday, January tenth."

I look at my calendar, and my heart sinks even further. "But that's after the election. It's imperative that I sit down with him before the votes are cast. Preferably several weeks before."

"I'm so sorry, ma'am, but there's nothing I can do other than put your name on the waitlist."

"I see," I say, seething. "I guess put me on the list then."

"Will do. Now, is there anything else I can assist you with?"

I end the conversation, hang up the phone, and put my head in my hands. Why can't anything go right for me? I'm tired of having to always manipulate things to go my way. Frankly, I need·just one thing to happen without my intervention. This is a huge setback.

A knock sounds at the door to my office. I look up and see Sandy standing in the doorway with a strange smile.

"Can I come in?" She asks.

I nod and gesture towards the chair across from my desk. She closes the door behind her and sits in the chair.

"What's up, Sandy?" I ask, a little annoyed at the interruption.

"You would never believe what I found out," she says, not even noticing my obvious irritation.

I roll my eyes. "Why do you have to make everything so dramatic? Just tell me."

She leans forward. "My husband wanted me to find another person to help around the house, so I was interviewing potential candidates yesterday. Guess who applied for the job?"

"Who?" I ask, hoping she'll just spit it out.

"Pippa's housekeeper," she says, crossing her arms, a satisfied look on her face.

My irritation with Sandy quickly dissolves. "Why would she be interviewing with you for a job?"

"Apparently, she was let go a few weeks ago because Pippa couldn't afford to keep her anymore. Not only that, she's also no longer living in her home."

"Are you serious?" I asked Sandy, shocked. "Does the housekeeper know where Pippa went? Does she still live in Aldercreek?"

Sandy shrugs. "I'm not sure, but the housekeeper did say she ran into her at a store on the outskirts of town."

"If she doesn't live within the city limits, we can push her out of the election. You have to be a resident of the city to run for office. Even if she still lives in town, this is perfect material for an attack campaign. We could destroy her," I say, my mind reeling with the possibilities. My desire to end Pippa is fueled by some unquenchable anger. I love it when people make me get like this.

"Isn't that a little harsh?" Sandy asks.

"No, this is politics. Politics is always harsh. If someone can't run their own family, they shouldn't be able to run a town."

Sandy stares at me, a devious smile on her face. "I like this side of you. You're cutthroat."

"You have no idea. I will say and do almost anything to

become the mayor of this town. If Pippa is destroyed in the process, that's her own fault for going up against me. I want you to find anything you can on her. We're going to take her down."

54

SANDY

S andy's eyes feel like sandpaper from staring at the computer screen. She's spent the last few hours trying to track down any information about Pippa that she could find; even the smallest detail could be used against her. There's not much. She's done a good job of covering her tracks, but Sandy has found bits and pieces of information that make the situation even more of a mystery.

She stretches her arms and starts back at the beginning; maybe there's something that she's missed. She scours Pippa's social media pages once again. She's very active on social media, always posting and sharing a curated version of her life with her potential constituents. She rewatches Pippa's campaign videos when it hits her. About a month ago, Pippa started filming them from locations outside of town. Maybe that was just a coincidence. She needs more proof.

She runs a simple background check on Pippa. It doesn't tell her much other than that her address changed to another location in Aldercreek just last week. From the information she gathered from the housekeeper, it seems that there was a gap between when she left her home and when she moved into this new place. All the evidence points to her living temporarily outside of town.

She rubs her temples. There has to be something else. She looks up Pippa's new address in the real estate database and is shocked to discover that it's an apartment in the older section of town. Sandy would not be caught dead shopping in this area, let alone live in it.

She opens her email and types a quick message to Liv, highlighting the things she just discovered along with her speculation. This is a goldmine of information, and she believes that she's only scratched the surface.

She looks at her watch. Where has the time gone? Melanie has an appointment this afternoon, and if she doesn't leave now, she's going to be late. Grabbing her laptop from her desk, she carefully places it in her bag.

Just when she's about to leave, her phone rings. The name on the screen stops her in her tracks. Why is John Hawkins calling her? It's been years since she's talked to him. The last time she remembers seeing John was at their ten-year high school reunion, but she's not even sure she talked to him while she was there. He moved to Aldercreek from their hometown years before her. She ran into him once when she relocated, but other than that, she hasn't really spoken with him.

She and John were close in high school. When she was eighteen, she thought for a brief moment that they might get together someday, but when he graduated from high school, he went off to the police academy, and they drifted apart. Now they never talk, even though they live in the same town.

She answers the phone hesitantly. "John?"

"Hi, Sandy," he says, his voice apologetic. "I'm sorry to

bother you at work, but I was hoping you could come to the station. There's something we need to discuss."

Sandy's chest tightens. This can't be good. "Okay. I have to take my daughter to an appointment, but I can come down right after that if that works."

"Actually," he says, "I'm outside your work. Can you please meet me in the parking lot?"

"Outside?" She asks. "Was that really necessary?"

"I'm afraid it was. I didn't come into your office because I didn't want to make a scene and embarrass you, but I need you to come with me."

Sandy's mind is reeling. What could possibly be going on? Did one of the store managers catch her stealing on camera? Is she going to jail? She eventually responds, her voice shaky, "I'll be right out. Thank you for being discrete."

After hanging up the phone, she pauses for a few seconds, taking several deep breaths. It's probably nothing, she tries to reassure herself, but the anxiety refuses to subside.

She quickly messages Blaine. *Babe, something's come up, and I can't take Melanie to her appointment. Can you take her? It's in an hour.*

His response is immediate. *Yes. I don't have any more meetings today. Is everything okay?*

She hesitates, unsure how much to reveal. Maybe John wants to discuss something entirely unrelated to her shoplifting. There's no need to worry Blaine unnecessarily. *Everything's fine. Just dealing with a difficult client. You know how they can be*, she replies. Without waiting for his response, she slips her phone into her purse and puts it on her shoulder.

She walks through the office, her head held high. A few real estate agents sit in the main work area. Sandy flashes them a confident, fake smile, even though inside, she's terrified. "I'll be back in a few minutes, just going to run an errand."

One of the agents looks up at her briefly and gives a half-wave before returning to her computer screen.

As soon as she walks out the door, she spots the police car in the far left corner of the parking lot. John is standing outside the car, leaning on the trunk.

Sandy waves cheerfully, trying to maintain the facade that nothing out of the ordinary is going on. As she approaches, John opens the passenger door for her. Her brows crease in confusion. "Am I being arrested?"

He shakes his head. "If you were being arrested, you wouldn't be sitting in the front seat."

Confusion floods through her. If she wasn't being arrested, then what the heck was going on? She stares at John's face, but it's stoic and unreadable. "Is everything okay, John?"

He looks her in the eyes briefly, his expression unreadable. "Please just get in the car," he says. "We will discuss it at the station. FYI, when we're there, refer to me as Detective Hawkins."

"Oh, wow, okay," she says, reluctantly lowering herself onto the seat. This must be more serious than she realizes. He closes the door behind her. She lowers her head, desperately trying not to be seen by anyone she knows. Whatever is going on, it can't be good.

55

LIV

The sounds of a busy restaurant surround me as I sit patiently and wait at the bar in Dave's. When I found out about Pippa's living situation, I contacted her and asked her to meet me. She was leery at first, as if she could sense that I had ill intentions toward her, but she eventually agreed.

Our meeting wasn't supposed to start for another five minutes, but I came early. I find there's an advantage in being the first one to arrive. You can control the situation — where you sit and what direction you're facing. The other person walks into the scenario that you create, and they are at your mercy. I sit facing the door. I want to see her face the moment she walks through the door before she's had a chance to paint on her politician smile.

At precisely five p.m., Pippa walks in. She stands for several seconds in the entranceway, allowing her eyes to adjust to the dim light. She looks perfectly put together and poised. Her designer clothes are pressed and hang neatly from her frame. Her expression is a mixture of annoyance and fear.

After looking around for a few seconds, Pippa finally spots me staring at her from the bar. She immediately puts on her fake smile and waves at me. I return the gesture, playing the perfectly poised politician.

When she's a few feet from me, I stand and give her a light hug, air-kissing both of her cheeks. "Pippa, it's so good to see you."

"Likewise," she says without conviction.

"What are you drinking? My treat," I say as she takes off her suit jacket and carefully hangs it from the back of the stool.

"Oh, I'll just have a soda water with lime," she says. "I'm trying not to drink alcohol, especially during the middle of the day."

Her words are meant to sting me, but they don't. I respond calmly. "There's nothing like a good drink at the end of a work day. Of course, I would never abuse it. I have strict control over myself. Just one is all I allow."

"Well, that's good for you, but I will stick with my water." She flags down a bartender and orders her drink.

I analyze her appearance closely. Her light blue suit is couture, although I believe it's from a collection from a few years ago. Aside from a small black mark on the skirt, they are in near-pristine condition. Her fingernails are neatly trimmed but not manicured, an obvious sign of a change in circumstances. Pippa has always had her nails done.

The bartender brings Pippa her soda water, and she takes a long sip. "Alright, you got me here last minute. What do you want to talk about? I assume it's important," she says.

"Yes, I have something I want to discuss with you, and it can't wait," I say.

"Are you finally going to endorse me for mayor?"

I smile amusedly. She has no idea what challenges she's about to face. "No, not exactly."

"Not exactly? What does that even mean, Liv? Just come out and say it. I don't have time for your stupid games."

"Oh, this is not a game to me," I say. "I believe the people of Aldercreek deserve to have someone as their mayor with a proven track record of managing their own businesses and lives. I mean, how can someone run an entire city if they can't even keep their own house in order?" I stare into her eyes, waiting for her to break.

"What are you insinuating?" Pippa says, her voice low and menacing.

"I'm not insinuating anything. I know about your financial troubles. I also know that you have moved out of your mansion and now live in an apartment at the edge of town. It is rumored that while you were in between the two places, you stayed somewhere outside the city limits. Does any of this ring a bell?" I ask, taking a sip of my drink.

Pippa's face is no longer difficult to read; she's furious. Her neck turns beet red, followed by her cheeks. "Why is it anyone's business where I live? Is living in a mansion a requirement for being mayor?" Her voice rises above the crowd's noise, and several other restaurant patrons turn toward us.

"Lower your voice," I hiss. "You're going to cause a scene, and I can guarantee you don't want that."

She gains control over her emotions and leans forward. "What do you want, Liv? It's obviously not to endorse me for mayor."

I ignore her question. I'm not done making her squirm. "I also know about your daughter's little forgery incident at the school."

Pippa's eyes narrow. It's clear I've hit a nerve. "Leave her alone. You are not to use her as a pawn in this crazy game you're playing. In fact, I'm done. I don't need to subject myself to this anymore."

"All I'm trying to say, Pippa," I respond quickly, hoping to stop her before she walks away, "is that running for office might be too much for you. You should probably get your life and your family issues straightened out before you embark on such an intense endeavor."

"You have no idea what you're talking about," she says, her eyes burning straight through me.

"Don't I?" I ask, a small smile forming on my lips. "I think you know that your living situation right now doesn't look good, which is why you've been keeping it a secret."

"No, I just don't think it's anyone's business. My address doesn't determine my qualifications." She hastily puts her phone in her purse and grabs her jacket.

"Do you really think the constituents of this town are going to vote for someone to be mayor who lives in the ghetto?"

Pippa stands, clearly done with this conversation. "First of all, it's far from the ghetto. Besides, my track record will speak for itself."

"I'm not sure that's how it really works," I say, gesturing for her to sit back down on the stool. She doesn't move. "I have a proposition for you."

She rolls her eyes at me, annoyed. "Spit it out, Liv."

"Fine. I'll keep your financial problems, along with everything else I know, a secret as long as you stay out of my way."

"Stay out of your way?"

"You heard me right. I'm ramping up my campaign as we speak, and I need you to back off."

"Why should I?" she says, her eyes dancing with fire.

"Because you know it's the right thing to do. You should withdraw. If you continue forward, you will only suffer more humiliation. If I am able to find out this information about you, that means anyone else can, too. It will eventually become public knowledge. Most people fall on hard times at some point in their lives; I understand what you're going through, but I am just not sure that the voters of Aldercreek will be as understanding. These people are born into wealth. Do you really think they are going to vote for someone who has nothing?"

Her face is filled with rage, and I can tell I have rattled her to her core. Without saying another word, she grabs her purse and storms out of the restaurant.

I'm slightly amused at her reaction. She knows I have the upper hand here. We'll see if she takes my advice and withdraws from the race. If she doesn't, I'll have no option but to play dirty.

56

SANDY

The police station is hauntingly quiet. The phones aren't ringing, and the deputies are either quietly working at their desks or sleeping.

Sandy is embarrassed as she walks behind John to his desk. A few deputies quickly glance at her and return to their screens as if they couldn't care less about why she was there.

When they reach John's desk, he gestures towards a chair next to it, indicating she should sit.

She glances around the room and slowly lowers herself down, clutching her purse in her lap as if it were a shield. She's not quite sure what's happening, but she knows it can't be good.

He settles himself in his chair and looks at her silently. His gaze feels like it's boring through her, and Sandy squirms uncomfortably in her seat. She glances around the room and realizes how little privacy they have out here in the open like this. She clears her throat. "Do you think we could talk somewhere else? This is just so public."

He glances around the room and shrugs. "These guys aren't even going to pay attention to us, but if you'd rather use one of the interrogation rooms, we can go in there instead."

She nods. "Please."

Without another word, he stands, grabs his computer, and walks toward the back of the station.

Sandy stands and follows him. The moment she walks into the interrogation room, she knows she's made a mistake. On the wall hangs a two-way mirror, and just the sight of it fills her with anxiety. She feels like a fish in a glass bowl. Anyone who walks by can now see her and hear her without her knowledge. No, this is definitely not better, but she doesn't want to be seen as high maintenance, so she swallows hard and forces herself to sit.

John sits across from her. He places both feet on the table and interlocks his fingers behind his head. He stares at her, resuming his earlier intensity.

She squirms uncomfortably under his gaze. She wishes he would just get it over with and tell her why she's there.

Eventually, he clears his throat and finally speaks. "How are you, Sandy? It's been forever since we talked last."

She looks at him, confused. Did he really just bring her here to make small talk? "I'm good," she says hesitantly.

He nods. "Good. How's your family? How's Melanie? She's got to be at least thirteen now, right?"

"Seventeen." She quips. His nonchalance makes her nervous.

"Oh, my word, seventeen already? She's almost an adult."

She nods. "Why did you bring me here, John? I'm fairly certain it wasn't to find out how my daughter is doing."

"Right, he says. Let's get to business." He lowers his feet off the table and opens the laptop. His brows crease as he navigates towards something that Sandy can't see. After a few seconds, his brows relax. "There it is."

He turns the laptop towards Sandy and taps the space-bar. A video on the screen comes to life. For thirty seconds, she watches herself at the grocery store, putting a magazine into her pocket. Her face turns beet red as she realizes the implications of what she's watching.

As soon as the video is finished, Sandy looks hesitantly at John. She doesn't say anything to defend herself. What could she say? The evidence of her guilt is right in front of her.

"No police report has been filed about this incident... yet," he says, looking at her with concern.

"What?" She asks, confused.

"The grocery store owners gave me the footage. They said you've always been a loyal customer and wanted me to talk to you first and figure out what happened."

Relief floods her face.

John continues. "When I first saw it, I was convinced it must have been an accident. I mean, you obviously just forgot to pay, right?"

Sandy laughs nervously and thinks quickly. "Right. I put it in my bag so I wouldn't have to carry it around and completely forgot it was there. It was a total accident. I'm so sorry. I can obviously afford a magazine," she says as if her wealth is ironclad evidence of her innocence.

John doesn't respond. She can almost physically feel him staring at her. It's clear he knows she's lying. She shifts uncomfortably in her chair as silence fills the room. She wishes he would just say something — anything.

He finally speaks, changing topics. "How have you been managing since the death of Regina? Weren't you two friends?"

She looks at him, confused. What does Regina have to do with shoplifting? "No, we weren't that close. She was more like a friend of a friend. We hung out occasionally at major social events, but that's it."

"I see," John says, as if contemplating her every word.

She continues nervously. "It was truly terrible what happened to her. We don't get deaths like that here in Alder-creek. Most of the residents here die either from old age or car accidents. Regina's death was unlike anything I've seen here." She glances at John. His expression is unreadable.

Silence lingers in the air for several seconds. Sandy glances at the door, contemplating leaving the room. They can't hold her here indefinitely, especially without charging her.

John clears his throat before she can work up the courage to walk out. "Well, I think that's all the questions I have for you today, Sandy."

Relief floods her body.

He leans forward and places his hand on hers. "We're not going to press charges here today. The store owners were content with just a warning. However, I really think you should talk to someone who can help you figure out what's going on with you. If there are a few more incidents like this, I won't be able to make them go away. Do you understand?"

Sandy nods.

"Mistakes like this can derail a person's entire life," he says sincerely.

She quickly stands and extends her hand to John. "Thank you, John. I mean it."

He nods. "Good to see you again, Sandy."

"You too." She says.

She turns towards the interrogation room door and can't open it fast enough. As she leaves the station, she vows never to step foot in one again.

57

PIPPA

Pippa seethes under her breath, her steps quickening towards her car. "That pompous, arrogant, evil woman. How dare she threaten me." The urge to scream is overwhelming, but she reins it in, not wanting to create a scene in front of the judgmental stay-at-home moms in Aldercreek.

She walks as quickly as she can across the parking lot. The vibration of her heels striking the ground jolts her knees, causing sharp stabs of pain with each step. However, she doesn't mind the pain because it helps fuel her anger.

The moment she reaches the vehicle, she slides into the driver's seat, slamming the door behind her. When she is relatively sure that no one can hear, she screams at the top of her lungs and pounds the steering wheel with her fists.

Why can't Liv just leave her alone? Would it be too much to ask for her to fight fairly? She slumps back into the chair. She's known Liv for years — that woman has never fought fair.

It's not like the accusations Liv was making were false. If she were to go public with them, Pippa couldn't claim slander or libel. She was living outside Aldercreek for a few weeks, and Bobbi did get in trouble at school for forging a signature; it was all true. However, these were things that were all entirely out of her control. She couldn't help it that her convict dad took her life's savings and her worthless husband left her penniless. Probably half the women in this town would be in the same position if their husbands left them and took their names off of all the accounts.

Even though none of it was her fault, she knows she'll continue suffering the consequences anyway. She will have to figure out how to fight back and get revenge.

Her entire life, she's never been accepted by the popular crowd. No matter how hard she has tried to fit in, they have always rejected her. She had thought that things would change when she married into a wealthy family and that the women here would finally see her as an equal. However, it became evident that those hopes were unfounded when Bobbi started kindergarten.

She had been so excited to volunteer for the PTA. She'd desperately hoped that she could make some friends and finally become a part of the social elite in Aldercreek, but unbeknownst to her, it wasn't enough to have money; you practically had to be born with it to fit in here. The woman always looked at her with disdain and gossiped about her behind her back.

She could never figure out what it was about her that made them not like her. She copied their hair, their clothes and even their mannerisms. She did everything she could to try and fit in, but each time she attempted something new, they would either not even notice or laugh at her, making her feel small and insignificant.

Today was the last straw. As she left the restaurant, she felt empowered by her rage. She is tired of being shoved aside like trash. Those women who have pushed her aside her entire life deserve to feel the same way they've made her feel. She wants revenge.

As she sits in the car, a plan starts to form. They'll never see it coming, but they'll wish they had.

58

EDEN

Liv and I sit at her dining room table, working on her campaign. She rubs her eyes and leans back from her computer. She had insisted we work here the entire day. Papers, everything from zoning maps to constituent email lists, are spread over the whole surface. If Liv thought it might be pertinent to the campaign, she printed it.

We've spent the entire morning creating a route for her to take when she canvasses the neighborhoods in the upcoming weeks, trying to gather support from the community. We had to consider not only a family's financial status but also their likely availability at different times of the day. For example, it would be a waste of time for her to canvass a neighborhood during the middle of the workday if that particular area was filled with dual-income households. No one would be home.

It's the end of the morning. We've both had several cups of coffee and are obviously frazzled.

Nadia, noticing our distress, places a tray filled with deli-cious-smelling food on the kitchen table. "It looks like you need a break," she says hesitantly. "This is my abuela's pastelitos recipe."

"They are delicious. Eden, help yourself," Liv says, gesturing towards the plate as she stands. "I need to take a break. I'm going to run a few errands. I'll be back in about an hour. You should take a break yourself. Have some pastelitos, or I'm pretty sure the salad Nadia made last night is still in the fridge. Whatever we have here is yours."

I select a piping hot pastelito and take a bite as Liv grabs her purse and exits through the garage door. The crust is crispy and flaky, while the filling is savory and warm. I have not had food as comforting as this in a long time. I take another bite and close my eyes; it is almost an out-of-body experience.

"You like it?" Nadia asks hesitantly.

"Are you kidding me? These are amazing, Nadia. It's no wonder you kept your abuela's recipe. Sit down, have one."

"Oh, I don't know," she says, glancing towards the garage door. "I probably shouldn't."

"Don't be silly. She's not going to be back for at least an hour. You deserve to take a break, too."

She nods and sits in the chair previously occupied by Liv. Her back is stiff, and she looks uncomfortable.

I slide the plate towards her. "Eat," I command.

She slowly grabs a pastelito and brings it to her mouth. I visibly watch her relax as she takes a bite. "When I eat this, it makes me think about my abuela and how much I miss her."

I take a long look at her. Her face is worn but beautiful. The furrow between her brows is a permanent fixture, as if she's continuously contemplating something heavy or worrisome. The lines on her face suggest she's in her mid to late thirties, but something tells me she might be much younger and that the hardness of life has etched itself on her face. I want to know more about her. "Where are you from? Tell me about your abuela."

A small smile forms on her lips. "She was the best. Back in El Salvador, before I moved to America, my grandmother would spend all day making food for our family. She's the one who taught me how to cook. My favorite was her pollo encebollado. Sometimes, I can still smell it."

"What happened?" I ask. "Why did you leave your home?"

"When I was ten, my mama and papa died in a car accident." She lowers her eyes as she says this, the memory obviously still fresh so many years later.

"Oh my gosh, I'm so sorry. Where did you go after they died?"

She slowly looks up. "My abuela and abuelo took me and my sister in. They were old, but they had a lot of love to give. It was a good life. My abuelo died when I was fifteen from a heart attack. I knew my abuela missed him, but she never let her grief show. She was so strong."

"Sounds like she was an amazing woman. So how did you end up in America?"

"When I was sixteen, my sister, Maria, moved to America to go to school. After that, it was just me and Abuela. I didn't mind it so much. She taught me how to cook all of her recipes. She would make dozens of pupusas and pastelitos every day to sell to neighbors and tourists. It was the only way we were able to keep our house. When I wasn't in school, I would help her as much as I could."

I smile at her, silently encouraging her to continue.

"When I was nineteen, my grandmother got very sick. She had cut herself when she was cooking. It was a pretty bad cut. I thought it needed stitches, but she was a stubborn old woman who didn't ever want to go to the doctor, so she just put a bandage on it and continued on. The infection got so bad that she developed a fever. By the time I got her to the hospital, the infection had spread to her whole body. No matter what the doctors did, she got worse and worse. Three days after being admitted to the hospital, she died, and I was all alone."

I reach across the table and squeeze her hand. "I'm so sorry, Nadia. I know what it's like to lose someone so close to you. It's a pain you can't even describe."

She nods as a single tear runs down her cheek. She wipes it away with her free hand and continues. "I couldn't stay there. Everything reminded me of Abuela and all I had lost. I gathered as much money as I could and hired some people to take me across the border into the United States. I was trying to get to Miami to be with my sister, but the people I hired could only get me to Scottsdale, Arizona."

"How did you end up here, in Washington?"

She shakes her head. "It was all a mistake. I had found some work in Scottsdale and was trying to earn enough money to get to Miami. I didn't speak very good English yet, so it was hard to understand everything being said around me. I heard about this bus program, which provides immigrants free transportation to other states. I thought it was my chance to get closer to Maria. There was a bus going to Washington. I looked at a map and saw that Washington was closer to Florida than Arizona was, so I volunteered." She looks at the ground, frustration evident in her features.

"You didn't know about Washington State," I surmise.

She shakes her head. "I thought I was going to Washington, D.C., but by the time I got here, it was too late. There was no going back.

"I'm so sorry," I say, feeling genuine empathy for this girl who just can't seem to catch a break. "Have you talked to your sister since you came to America?"

She nods. "I talk to her every week. She never graduated from college, so she's working at a restaurant in Miami. She's also married and has a daughter." A small smile forms on her lips at the mention of her niece. "I can't wait to be her tia."

"So, what's stopping you now from leaving Washington and heading to Miami?"

Sadness washes over her face. "I've been trying to save up enough money, but it's hard." She looks around her to make sure that Liv and Mitch are still not around and lowers her voice. "Since I am here illegally, they don't pay me very much. It's taking me a long time."

Anger surges through me. How dare they take advantage of her like that. Who cares that she's not here legally? She deserves to make a living wage.

She continues. "I can't just hitchhike there; I'm afraid the government will find me and deport me. I am trying to get enough money to buy the right papers, but it's hard." She lowers her voice even further. "They won't let me leave the house, so I can't even look for someone to help me."

My eyes widen. "What do you mean? Liv and Mitch make you stay here?"

She shakes her head. "No, not Liv. She barely even knows I exist most of the time. Mitch. I've tried leaving a couple of times, but he always stops me. I don't even get to go to the grocery store to get the ingredients for the meals I make for them. He makes me give Liv a list, and she orders it for delivery."

A sick feeling forms in the pit of my stomach. He is basically keeping this poor woman hostage. "Why won't he let you leave?"

She shrugs. "I think he's afraid that if I do leave, I won't come back. He makes me do things..." her words trail off. "He doesn't want me to stop."

"Nadia, you know that this isn't right."

She nods. "But I don't know how to make it stop. I stay in the guest house in the backyard. There are cameras all over the place, and I know he checks them all the time. He has told me that if I even step foot off the property, he'll have me deported." She looks at me, her eyes filled with fear.

Her words fill me with a white-hot rage. That sick, worthless excuse of a human being should be rotting in prison. "I'm going to help you. I don't know how, but I will figure something out."

59

SANDY

The setting sun casts a pink glow on the dining room wall. Sandy meticulously sets the dinner table for two. She pulls two servings of their best china bowls, along with two sets of silverware, from the cabinet. A thin layer of dust covers the surface of the dishes. She can't remember the last time they used them. Maybe last Christmas? Wiping off the evidence of neglect, she sets the dishes neatly on the table.

She walks back into the kitchen and checks the coq au vin simmering on the stove. The savory aroma fills her nostrils as soon as she removes the lid. "Perfect," she whispers. She could have just had the cook make this, and she's pretty sure it would have been better, but she wanted to make tonight's meal herself. Maybe it was silly, but she thought Blaine might notice her again if she cooked him his favorite dish. He barely even looks at her these days. She can't even remember the last time they had been intimate. It's been months. Food is supposed to be the way to a man's heart, and this is her last-ditch effort to win back his attention.

Grabbing a large glass bowl from the cupboard, she assembles a salad. Earlier, she had asked the cook to chop up all the veggies for the salad, so all she had to do was put it all together. She knows that she can't honestly say she made the entire meal, but she did ninety percent of the work, so she's going to claim it.

FIFTEEN MINUTES LATER, dinner is finished, and Sandy puts the finishing touches on the table. She fills each bowl with a generous helping of coq au vin and cleans off the edge with a paper towel to ensure it looks perfect. Selecting a loaf of sourdough from the bread box, she cuts two generous slices, placing one on each bowl and carefully carries the bowls to the table.

She grabs a candlestick and a lighter from the side table drawer, places the candle in the middle of the dining table, and lights the wick. She finishes by selecting two wine glasses from the china cabinet and a bottle of wine from the wine rack and sets them on the table. Uncorking the bottle of wine, she leaves it open on the table to breathe.

Stepping back from the table, she surveys her work. Pleased with all she's done, she hopes it's enough to get him to notice her. It's nearly seven. Blaine should be home at any time.

Realizing she doesn't have long, she quickly walks to the powder room to freshen up her appearance. A long, heavy, blue robe covers her body from her neck to her ankles. Taking it off, she hangs it on a hook in the bathroom. She stares at her reflection in the mirror. Black, lacy lingerie clings tightly to her body, covered by a loose, flowing, sheer black robe.

Sandy works hard to make sure her body is always in the

best shape possible. She spends nearly five days a week at the gym, and she's careful about the calories she puts in her mouth. When she's wearing clothing, her body still looks trim and youthful. However, in the harsh light of the bathroom, with barely anything on, she can see the cellulite that now covers parts of her thighs.

It's not just her body; her face is also showing signs of aging. Fine lines and wrinkles have formed around her eyes and mouth. No amount of wrinkle cream has kept them at bay.

Maybe that's why Blaine has been so distant lately; he can't even stand to look at her. What if he wants to trade her in for a newer model? Could she blame him? The negative thoughts threaten to overwhelm her, and she forces them aside.

"You are beautiful, intelligent, and worth your husband's attention," she says with forced conviction to her reflection in the mirror.

The sound of the garage door opening interrupts her self-talk, and she rushes back to the dining room. She dims the light, knowing that the wrinkles and the cellulite won't be as evident in the dark, and stands seductively at the end of the table.

Her heart races almost as fast as it did years ago when she was waiting for him to pick her up for their very first date. She can remember the day they met as if it happened last week.

SHE AND BLAINE were both freshmen at Western Washington University, and it was the first day of World History. Sandy had arrived at class fifteen minutes early. She didn't like being stressed, so she made sure she had plenty of time to get herself settled.

One minute before class started, a tall, handsome, dark-haired boy threw himself onto the seat next to her and looked at her with a mischievous grin. "Ready to be bored to tears?"

"Excuse me?" She asked, confused.

"Come on, who actually wants to learn about a bunch of dead white guys?" He said, crossing his arms.

She shrugged. "I don't know, I kind of like it."

He stared at her appraisingly and reached out his hand. "I'm Blaine."

She grabbed his hand back, his hand dwarfing hers. "I'm Sandy. Nice to meet you."

"I think you and I should be study partners. I have a feeling you're going to ace this class."

She hesitated. "I don't know."

"Come on, it will be fun. I'll take you to dinner tomorrow night, and we can discuss this partnership."

Staring into his emerald green eyes, she knew she was in trouble. It wouldn't take much for her to fall madly in love with him. She wasn't sure if being his study partner was wise, but she couldn't help herself. "Okay," she said. The words escaped her mouth before she had even finished analyzing the situation.

"Awesome," he said, turning towards the stage.

On the way out of class, Blaine suggested he pick her up for dinner at seven p.m. the next day. Reluctantly, she agreed, although deep down, she was excited and anxious.

By the next day, her nerves were on edge. She was ready thirty minutes early, and she spent those thirty minutes convincing herself he was not going to show up. By the time he finally arrived, her heart was pounding from the anxiety, and beads of sweat were forming on her brow.

The moment he saw her, he wrapped his arms around her as if they had known each other forever. Sandy didn't mind. She inhaled the smell of his cologne. It was over for her. She knew she was already falling in love with him.

From that day on, they were inseparable. It seemed Blaine had been as into her as she was into him. In their second year of college, they moved in together in an apartment just off campus. It had been small and simple, but that was where they had fallen in love.

When Sandy found out she was pregnant with Melanie during their Senior year, Blaine didn't even hesitate to propose. They got married just after graduation, and Sandy believed naively that their love would continue to grow forever. And it did, for a while.

But by the time Melanie was in middle school, everything had changed between her and Blaine. She wasn't even really sure what happened. He just slowly became less and less interested in her. He worked longer hours and often disappeared on the weekends to play golf, leaving Sandy alone with Melanie.

NOW THAT MELANIE was nearly an adult, Sandy found herself contemplating what life would be like as soon as she left the house, and the picture she had conjured was terrifying. If something didn't change between her and Blaine, she was going to be very alone.

For the last few months, she's been trying to woo him back. So far, nothing has worked. It's as if he doesn't even recognize she exists anymore. Tonight's dinner is a last-ditch attempt at rekindling what they once had.

She stands in the dim light, her heart racing. The house alarm beeps as soon as the door to the garage opens. She brushes stray hairs from her face and adjusts her negligee.

"I just came back to get my laptop," Melanie yells as she runs up the stairs.

Disappointment lands in Sandy's gut like a heavy brick, followed by panic. Melanie can't see her dressed like this; she would be mortified. She wraps the see-through robe around her and steps into the shadows in the corner of the room, hoping desperately that she can remain hidden.

As soon as she is safe in the shadows, she responds. "Are you still staying at Jessica's?"

"Yeah," Melanie yells from upstairs. "We are going to make some videos for our channel. I wanted my computer to edit them. It's just easier than the phone."

Sandy hears her rushing back down the stairs. "Okay, honey, have fun," she says, mustering all the cheerfulness she can.

"It's super-dark in here. What are you doing, Mom? Sitting in the dark?" She asks snarkily.

But before Sandy can even respond, Melanie is already in the garage and headed back to Jessica's car.

Relief washes over her, followed by disappointment. She and Melanie used to do everything together. Every weekend, they would get their nails done and then go have lunch at this little bistro downtown. They were inseparable. Now, Melanie just looks at her like she thinks she's stupid. She doesn't even know when it changed. Hopefully, it's just a phase.

She sits in one of the dining room chairs, waiting for Blaine to come home. After thirty minutes, the food has grown cold, and Sandy is starting to wonder if he's ever coming.

She grabs her cell phone from the dining room table and dials his number. He answers after only two rings. "What do you want?" He asks, clearly annoyed.

"I'm just wondering when you'll be coming home tonight," she says quietly.

"I have a dinner meeting tonight. I thought I told you about that. I won't be home until late."

Disappointment floods her veins, followed by apathy. What's the point of fighting anymore when he clearly doesn't even care? "Okay," she says, hanging up the phone without saying goodbye.

She stares at the plated food in front of her. There's no way she's going to let it go to waste. Grabbing a fork, she begins shoveling the food into her mouth. It is delicious. Blaine is missing out.

A few bites into her meal, she stops abruptly as an idea comes to her. She doesn't have to eat this alone. She puts the fork down and glances through the contacts on her phone until she finds the one she's looking for — *Grant Art Gallery.*

60

EDEN

I'm driving home from Liv's house, my mind spinning. I can't believe that Liv and Mitch are keeping that girl hostage just to satisfy Mitch's sick whims. Even if Liv doesn't know what's happening, she's still to blame. There's no way she could have missed the bruises on Nadia's arms. She does her best to cover them up, but they are glaringly obvious. If Liv hasn't done her due diligence and checked up on Nadia, then she's being willfully blind.

The anger builds in me as I turn the corner to my street. Rage nearly blinds my vision, and I pull over to the side of the road just a few blocks from my apartment.

I glance around to ensure no one is nearby. The street is silent. Nearly all the houses are dark except for one apartment on the top floor of the building I'm parked next to. Confident I won't be heard, I scream at the top of my lungs, gripping the steering wheel tightly. I have to do something to help her. I can't let Mitch and Liv destroy the rest of her life.

Impulsively, I grab my phone and call Derek. He answers after the first ring.

"Hey baby," he says as if I just saw him yesterday. "How you doing?"

"That was quick. It's almost as if you were waiting by the phone for my call," I tease.

"Nah, I was just on it already," he says defensively.

"You know I'm just teasing you, right?"

"Yeah, I know. I am glad you called, though. I miss you," he says softly.

I sigh. I miss him more than I can let on. I have to stay focused on my mission. I can't allow myself to get caught up in whatever this is with Derek right now. "Me too," I say simply.

"So tell me everything. What's been happening?" He asks.

I can hear the genuine interest in his voice. I want to tell him everything — about working for Liv, the bruises on Nadia's arm, everything, but I know that if I give in, I'll drive all the way back to Seattle tonight to be with him. I have to keep him at a distance for now.

Instead, I change the subject. "I need your help."

"That's it? You won't even tell me what you've been doing?" He asks, frustrated.

"You know I want to, Derek. I want to spend hours talking to you, but I have to stay focused for now. Talking to you is a distraction I can't afford."

Derek is silent on the other end of the line.

I continue. "The best kind of distraction, but still a distraction."

Derek sighs. "Fine, how can I help?"

61

SANDY

Sandy stands in the lobby of Grant's upscale Seattle condo. It's the type of building that has security guarding the elevators. The floor is covered in marble, and sconces dripping with crystals line the walls. For the last few years, she and Blaine have been living a wealthy lifestyle, but beautiful places still strike her.

She looks down at her tight-fitting black dress and brushes away invisible imperfections. Glancing at her reflection in a mirror hanging on the side of the lobby, she confirms that her dress is perfect and she looks fantastic.

Nervously, she glances at the waiting elevators. What if Grant is just being polite and doesn't really want her? What if Blaine somehow finds out? It would be the end of her marriage. She shakes her head, trying to push away the doubts. Grant would be crazy not to want her, and there's no way Blaine's going to find out anything, she tells herself. When he's at these work events, it's like she doesn't even exist. He won't even notice she's gone. She convinces herself that she deserves this, but deep down, a kernel of doubt takes root in her gut. She shouldn't be doing this.

She walks towards the security guard. His eyes are closed, and he's leaning back in his chair. "Excuse me," she says quietly at first.

He snores loudly.

"Excuse me," she says even louder.

The security guard startles. "Oh, I'm so sorry. I must have dozed off."

Sandy nods. "It looks like you were in a pretty deep sleep there."

"I was. I just started this graveyard shift, and I'm still adjusting to the new hours. I'm so sorry. How can I help you?"

"I'm here to see Grant..." She hesitates, embarrassed. "I'm sorry, I don't know the rest of his name, but I have his phone number."

She gives him the number, and he dials it on the front desk phone. "Hello, sir? There's a woman down here, her name is..." He pulls the receiver away from his ear and whispers, "What's your name, sweety?"

"Sandy... I mean Vivian," she says, quickly correcting herself. "Sorry, Sandy is my middle name. I often go by it." Warmth floods her cheeks as she realizes the mistake she almost made. She has to pull it together, or she will ruin everything.

"She says her name is Vivian," the guard says into the phone. He eyes her suspiciously. Seconds later, he replaces the receiver and looks at her. "Mr. Harwood says to come on up. He's on the thirty-fifth floor, apartment thirty-five twenty."

The elevator takes forever to reach the thirty-fifth floor. With each passing second, she is plagued by more and more doubts. What if he doesn't answer the door? What if he answers the door but then tells her to leave? The palms of her hands are sweaty, and the hair at the nape of her neck is starting to curl from perspiration.

Finally, the elevator door opens. She takes a deep breath. Exiting the elevator, she pauses briefly in the hallway to read the sign describing the hallways' layout.

"Vivian," a voice calls from the end of the hallway to her left.

She turns and sees Grant standing outside an open doorway at the end of the hall. Waiving her hand, she walks towards him, all of her previous anxiety dissipating. "I'm glad you were free at the last minute," she says as she approaches him.

"It was perfect timing," he says, a genuine smile on his face.

She stands in front of him, her hands clasped together.

He continues. "I had just gotten home from a work function when you called. Please, come in." He steps to the side and ushers her into the condo.

She walks into the large space and gasps. The entire apartment has an open layout from the front door to the windows. To the right is a large kitchen with a marble-topped island and stainless steel appliances. Next to the kitchen is a cherry wood dining table, large enough to seat at least twelve people. To the left of that, a sunken living room is nestled right next to a window that covers the entire wall and overlooks a balcony. Beyond the balcony, the view of Seattle and the water is breathtaking.

"Wow," she says. "That view is unbelievable."

"It's my favorite part about this place," he says, closing the door behind him. When the sun sets in the evening, the pinks and oranges in the sky reflect in the Puget Sound. Before I moved to Seattle, I'd never seen anything like it."

Sandy turns towards him, their eyes locking. "I'm not sure how you ever leave."

They stare at each other for several seconds, tension building between them.

Grant breaks eye contact and gestures to the kitchen. "Would you like something to drink?"

She nods. "Scotch, if you have it."

"I do. It's my drink of choice." He grabs a bottle from the cabinet.

Sandy raises her eyebrows. That's a nice bottle of scotch.

"So why the late-night phone call?" He asks as he pours a small amount into two glasses.

"I don't know. I was feeling a bit lonely and your name came to my mind. I really enjoyed our dinner together, and I guess I just wanted to see you," she shrugs.

He hands her a glass, and she takes a sip. "Wow, this is some of the smoothest scotch I've ever had."

"I don't do the cheap stuff. That's just torture."

She smiles and takes another sip. "I could get used to this." Her eyes glance up at his, and she notices him staring at her, not even sipping his scotch.

He sets his glass down and steps around the island towards her. Her breath catches in her throat and heat rises to her cheeks. He stops just a few inches away and grabs her hands. She lets him. His eyes bore into hers; the attraction between them is palpable. She's pretty sure he can hear her rabidly beating heart in the silence.

Suddenly, the tension is broken by Grant's ringing phone. He breaks his gaze and grabs his phone from the counter, checking the caller I.D. His brow creases. "I'm so sorry, it's work. I have to take this. It'll only be a few minutes."

He walks toward the balcony and steps outside to answer the phone.

Sandy sits on the bar stool and takes several deep breaths to calm her racing heart. What is she doing here? Reality sets in. The chemistry between her and Grant is almost palpable. She knows that if she stays here for much longer, she will end up in his bed. Guilt seizes her, causing her chest to constrict and her mouth to go dry. She takes another sip of her scotch. As good as Grant's attention feels, she can't do this to Blaine.

She glances at Grant through the window. He looks at her, flashes her a brilliant smile, and turns towards the water. Sandy's heart feels like it's being pulled in two directions. There's a huge part of her that wants to stay. She hasn't had this kind of attention in months, maybe even years. She feels alive again when she's with Grant, but her loyalty to her husband wins out as the anxiety she feels threatens to overwhelm her.

She stands and glances around the room. On the far wall stands a bookshelf filled with books and several art pieces. Tucked away towards the back hides a small glass vase. Sandy glances at Grant as she walks towards the bookcase. He's still looking out over the water.

She grabs the small piece of glass and marvels at it. It's clear with swirls of blue and orange. It reminds her of the large Chihuly pieces she's seen. She wonders if this could also be a Chihuly but decides she doesn't care. She glances out the window one last time. Grant is still not looking in her direction. Confident she won't be seen, she shoves the glass vase into her purse. Adrenalin immediately floods her body, masking the anxiety.

She quickly heads towards the front door. Walking past the kitchen, she notices the bottle of scotch still sitting on the counter. Glancing at Grant one last time, she grabs the bottle and walks straight out the door into the hallway.

As soon as she's in the elevator, heading toward the lobby, she breathes a sigh of relief.

As she exits the building, a pang of guilt seizes her. She quickly tries to push it down, but the weight of the stolen items in her purse forces them to the top of her mind with each step she takes to the car.

Just as she is reaching her car, her phone rings; she pulls it out of her purse, careful not to pull the vase out with it. It's Grant. Maybe she should answer it and tell him that there was some kind of emergency that called her away. She looks down at the bottle of Scotch in her hand and realizes there's no good excuse for the fact that she stole his things. He'll never understand.

She lets out a breath and silences the phone. Grief overwhelms her as she opens the car door and gets inside. Once inside the safety of her vehicle, she allows the tears to flow. She hasn't cried this hard in years. Her sobs wrack her entire body. Every hurt she's felt and every instance of loneliness is within her tears. She cries until she has nothing left.

62

EDEN

I pull into the parking lot of a small 24-hour diner about thirty minutes south of Aldercreek. Despite the late hour, several cars and a dozen semi-trucks are parked in front and to the side of the building.

Before parking the car, I spot Derek inside the diner, and my heart catches in my throat. He's sitting in a booth right next to the front window; a cup of coffee sits untouched in front of him. He checks his watch and glances outside. I'm certain he can't see me, considering it's the middle of the night and nearly pitch black out here. After a few seconds, he turns his gaze from the window and back to the front door of the restaurant.

I park in a spot right in front of where he's sitting and turn off the engine. Knowing he can't see me, I watch him for several seconds before opening the door. His locs are pulled back into a ponytail, revealing the shaved section of hair underneath. His face is strong and hard, but his eyes tell a different story. Even from here, I can tell they are weary. I'm not sure if that's from the lack of sleep or something deeper. I suspect it's the latter. My one regret about this whole plan has been walking away from Derek. Looking at him now, I wonder if I've made a mistake.

I take a deep breath, grab my purse, and exit the car. The moment I open the door to the restaurant, Derek's face lights up. Butterflies erupt in my stomach as if this is my first time seeing him.

He waves me over.

"Sorry I'm late," I say as I slide into the booth across from him.

"I'm not worried about it," he says, reaching both his hands across the table towards me. "I'm just glad you came."

"Me too," I say, allowing him to wrap his hands around mine. They are warm and familiar.

"How you holding up?" He asks, concern in his eyes.

I glance away and stare into the blackness outside the window, contemplating my next words. Tears threaten to spill from my eyes as the loneliness of this journey hits me. I force them back, unwilling to burden him with my feelings.

When I'm confident my emotions are under control, I turn towards him. "It's been hard, but I'm holding on," I say, staring into his eyes.

"You know you don't have to do this alone. We could do it together. I've got your back," he says, almost pleadingly.

I stare at him for several seconds, my resolve wavering. Things would be much easier for me if he were in Aldercreek. Having someone to talk to about everything I have been witnessing would be nice, but I know I can't. If he were here, he would also be a distraction. I can't afford to lose focus.

I squeeze his hand. "I know you do."

He stares at me, longing in his eyes, and sighs. "Are you at least finding what you were looking for?"

"I don't know yet. Maybe? I'm working on it."

He squeezes my hand and grabs a small package wrapped in brown paper from the seat next to him. He hands it to me. "Everything you asked for is in there."

"You're the best, Derek. I mean it," I say, setting it on the table.

He nods. "Do you want to check it?"

I shake my head. "I trust you." The realization of how true that is hits me hard. I've never trusted anyone the way I trust him.

"Anything else you need..." his voice trails off as the waitress walks up to us and interrupts.

"Can I take your order?" She asks me, clearly bored with her job.

I look at her. "No, thank you, I'm not staying."

Glancing at Derek, I see hurt flash across his face, but he quickly hides it.

The waitress turns to him and gestures towards his cup. "Refill?"

He shakes his head. "No, I'll just get the check."

Without another word, the waitress walks away.

"You can't just stay for a few more minutes?" He asks sadly.

"I don't trust myself," I say quietly.

We sit in silence for a few seconds, exchanging thoughts without words. My heart feels heavy. If I sit here much longer, I might change my mind.

As soon as the waitress returns with the receipt, I quickly stand and exit the booth. Derek follows me. He wraps his arms around me. Their weight on my shoulders makes me feel safe and protected. Knowing that the longer I stay here, the more my resolve will crumble, I take a deep breath and force myself to leave. "Bye, Derek. Thank you again for driving all this way to bring me this." I grab the package from the table.

He nods. "Anything you need, I'm here."

I look into his eyes one last time and can tell he means it. My heart breaking, I turn towards the front door and walk away. No matter what happens, I can't look back. I know deep down that if I do, I will lose my resolve. This all better be worth it because I'm walking away from the best man I've ever known.

63

SANDY

S andy sees Blaine's car parked in his usual spot as soon as she opens the garage door. She glances at the clock; it's almost eleven. The lights in the house are all off except for one towards the back. She wonders what time he got home. Has he been waiting for her? She highly doubted it.

Glancing at her phone, she sees no missed calls or texts from him. He's probably in bed. He couldn't care less about her. Tonight was evidence of that. She should have been home hours ago, but after stealing from Grant, her adrenaline spiked, leaving her nerves on edge. She cried in her car for a long time. By the time she was done, her adrenaline had tanked, leaving her weak and exhausted. It took a long time before she felt capable of driving.

She kept expecting Grant to find her sitting in her car, but he never did. He called her one more time and sent a few messages, but the last one she received was nearly two hours ago.

I see you took my scotch. His last message read. *That was an expensive bottle. I'm not mad. I just hope you're okay.*

His words gutted her, the pain almost unbearable. Why did she take the vase and the bottle of scotch? She glances at the bottle sitting on the passenger seat, and a pang of guilt cuts through her like a knife. She didn't need Grant's things, but she just couldn't help herself. Taking them had quieted the anxiety building in her chest, if only temporarily.

Sighing deeply, she grabs the bottle and her purse and gets out of the car. She opens the door to her house and steps inside. Everything is quiet and still. She walks into the kitchen only to find the remains of her earlier cooking spread all over the countertop.

She shakes her head as she thinks about all the times Blaine has let her down. She almost expects it now, but deep down, a small part of her keeps thinking this time will be different. It never is.

She sighs and walks towards the dining room. Turning on the lights, she sees Blaine sitting at the head of the table, staring at her. "What the heck are you doing, Blaine?" She screams.

He gestures at the table. "What is all this?"

She looks away to compose herself. The last thing she wants right now is for Blaine to see her vulnerable. Confident she has her emotions under control, she looks back at him. "I just thought we could have a romantic meal together — you know, try and reignite that spark or something. It was stupid."

She sets the bottle of scotch down on the table and glances at Blaine.

He raises his eyebrows but says nothing.

She pulls her purse off her shoulder and grabs the small vase, setting it next to the scotch.

Blaine crosses his arms and looks at her quizzically but still doesn't comment.

"There's food in the fridge if you're hungry. I'm going to bed," she says wearily.

"I was just about to call you. Where did you go?" He asks.

"Out. I just couldn't be here anymore."

He nods. "I'm sorry, Sandy. I know I've been messing up lately."

She stares through him, uncertain if his words are even sincere. Dark circles are underneath his eyes, and his face looks drawn. His eyes are on her, pleading.

She sighs, pulls out a chair, and sits, facing him. He grabs both of her hands and envelops them.

She stares at him, confused. Why is he suddenly acting like he cares about her? She eyes him suspiciously. Did he somehow already find out about Grant? Her instincts tell her to walk away, but she doesn't. A small part of her still hopes that things could change between them. All she wants is for him to put her first, above his job and his friends. She's tired of feeling like she's always his last priority.

He squeezes her hands. "I know I've been gone a lot lately, and I'm sorry for not being here for you. I want that to change. I miss us. The way we used to be when we first started dating."

She nods and replies, her voice barely above a whisper. "Me too." She wonders what he would say if he knew where she just was. Who she was with. The image of Grant's smiling face fills her mind. She silently berates herself. Why did she take his stuff and just leave like that? What is wrong with her? She completely destroyed any hope of something working out with him. She pushes him from her mind and tries to focus on Blaine.

"I love you, Sandy," Blaine says. "I know I don't always show it, but I do."

A small smile crosses her face. She's not sure she believes his words, but they sound nice.

He continues. "Things are going to change, I promise," he says earnestly.

They sit in silence for a long time. Blaine stares at her while she stares out the window.

Finally, he breaks the silence. "Say something, please."

She sighs and grabs the bottle of scotch from the table. "Care for a drink?"

A look of hurt briefly flashes across his face, but he quickly hides it and nods.

She heads to the kitchen and grabs two glasses from the cupboard.

Blaine follows her hesitantly, uncertain of what's about to happen.

Sandy pours two shots and hands one to Blaine.

"Oh, we're taking shots of this? Isn't this scotch?"

"Just drink. Cheers. To fresh starts."

They clink glasses and down the shots.

"Are you mad at me?" He asks quietly.

She shakes her head. "Not right now, but I've been mad at you for a really long time. I think I'm just too tired to be angry anymore."

"I'm sorry. I know I hurt you. I hope you'll give me a second chance."

"I don't know, Blaine. I can't put up with much more disappointment." Her mind flits briefly back to Grant. She shoves the thought aside.

"I promise," he says urgently. "It's going to be different this time."

A sad smile forms on her lips.

He steps closer to her. His handsome features still take her breath away. She sighs. "I'm willing to try if you are, but you can't mess this up. I don't have much left to give."

A broad smile lights up his face. He grabs the glass from her and fills it again. "I like that plan."

He hands her the glass and holds his up toward hers. "Cheers, baby," he says hopefully.

She lifts her glass and clinks it with his. "Cheers." As she takes a sip of the scotch, she wonders if things are really going to change or if this is all just smoke and mirrors.

64

EDEN

I open the front door of the office and step outside. The sun blinds my vision. I grab my sunglasses out of my purse and slip them on, but it barely helps. The parking lot is bathed in sunlight, making it practically impossible to see more than a few feet in front of me.

I take out my keys as I approach the location where I parked my car, preparing to hop in as quickly as possible. I press the button on the keyfob and hear the car beep just in front of me. I still can't see it, but I know I'm heading in the right direction. It's not until I'm less than ten feet away that I notice someone sitting on the hood of my car.

The figure stands and walks toward me. The light shines off their back, casting their face in shadow. It's impossible for me to discern who it is.

I take a step back and reach my hand into my purse. My fist wraps around the pepper spray I keep on me at all times, just in case something like this happens. "Who are you?" I ask. I struggle to keep my voice strong and clear.

The figure puts up both hands in surrender. "It's just me. Pippa."

Relief floods my body, and I release my grip on the pepper spray. "What do you want, Pippa?" I ask, annoyed.

She crosses her arms and stares at me for what feels like forever.

"I know it's you, Kari-Anne. It took me a while to figure it out, but once I did, all the pieces fell into place."

"I don't know what you're talking about," I say, taking another step back. "My name is Eden."

"Oh, I know that's what you're calling yourself, but that's not what your name used to be when you lived here."

My heart is racing a million miles a minute. What do I do? If Pippa has figured out who I really am, then it's only a matter of time before I'm outed to the rest of the community, and my mission will be over.

Pippa continues quietly. "I'm not sure what you're doing back here in town, but you didn't just come back for fun." She steps towards me, and I take another step back. "I just want you to know that I'm available to help you in any way I possibly can. What happened to you and your family has never sat right with me. I'm not sure what you're planning, but you can count on me."

I stare into her face, her eyes boring into mine. I don't detect even a hint of deception. It's obvious she's figured out who I am, but maybe that's not such a bad thing. She could have gone to anyone with that information and destroyed everything I've been working towards, but she didn't. She came directly to me and offered me her help.

I take a deep breath and look Pippa directly in the eyes. "You're right. I am Kari-Anne."

"I knew it was you," she says, her voice raising slightly.

"Please, I don't want people to know I'm back," I plead with her. "They need to keep believing I'm just Eden, a recent college graduate from Seattle."

"Of course. Your secret's safe with me, I promise. Now, tell me what I can do to help."

I hesitate. Do I trust her with anything? She could already completely ruin my plans with one loose sentence. I'm going to have to trust her a little. Since she's already figured out who I am, maybe she could be an ally. It helps that she's basically mortal enemies with Liv. She would probably do anything if it meant bringing Liv down in the process.

After contemplating for a few seconds, I decide to trust her with a minor task. If she can accomplish this one without leaking additional information about me, maybe I'll be able to trust her with more.

I glance at her conspiratorially. "I may have something you could do to help me."

She grabs my hands, and I let her. "I promise I'll do anything."

65

LIV

"What is all this?" Mitch asks as he walks into the dining room. The table is covered with piles of papers in chaotic stacks.

"Constituent lists, bids for catering and entertainment, blank invitations…" I say, rubbing my eyes. "I've been staring at them for hours, trying to devise a plan for my fundraiser, but I feel like I'm just going around in circles."

"It looks like total chaos," Mitch says, chuckling. "This is not like you. I can't remember you ever letting things get out of control like this."

"I know. This event is just so pivotal to my campaign. I can't mess it up. I almost feel paralyzed when it comes to making a decision. What if I make the wrong one and the event is a complete dud?"

Mitch walks over to me and places his hands on my shoulders. "Nothing you have ever done has been a dud, but maybe you should think about getting someone to help you. Someone a little more unbiased than you."

I consider his words. Maybe he's right. I have so much riding on this that I can't be objective. My whole future depends on me winning this election. I need someone to help ground me.

"I guess I could ask Sandy to come over here and help me out."

Mitch looks at me as if I've lost my mind. "I know you like Sandy, and I'm fine with her being around whenever you want to invite her over, but are you really sure she's the most reliable person to help with your campaign right now?"

"I don't know. She does like to drink a lot, and the last thing I need is to be distracted like that."

Mitch nods. "What about that new assistant of yours?"

"Eden?" I ask, surprised. I think about everything Eden has done for me over the last several months and realize she would be the perfect person to help with this. "Good suggestion, thank you. She's reliable and unemotional. She'll help me regain my focus."

Mitch places a small kiss on my forehead. "I'm going to head upstairs and possibly go to bed early. It was a long day at work today."

I barely process the words he's saying. "Good night," I say absentmindedly.

He chuckles. "There you go, already so focused on this event that I cease to exist."

I turn towards him. "Don't be silly; of course, you exist. I just can't focus on anything else right now. The deadline for this fundraiser is quickly approaching."

Mitch sighs. "I know. Do your thing. I'll be upstairs."

"Okay," I say dismissively.

It's not that I'm trying to ignore him, but I have a one-track mind when I'm trying to accomplish something. Nothing else around me matters except for achieving my goal. This is the biggest goal I've ever set for myself. This event has to be the best campaign fundraiser anyone in Aldercreek has ever attended. It needs to be so amazing that people continue talking about it for weeks. If I can remain at the top of their minds, then they will remember to vote for me when the time comes.

I grab my phone and dial Eden's number. It rings several times before going to voicemail. I try again. Same result. Where could she be? I know she doesn't have to be at my every beck and call, but she could at least answer the phone. Frustrated, I sit at the table and put my head in my hands. What am I going to do?

I call her again. Maybe she just didn't hear the phone the first time.

66

EDEN

I retrieve an empty black duffel bag from my closet and place it on the mattress next to a meticulously arranged pile of supplies I had just spent the last thirty minutes gathering. I unzip it and turn it upside down to ensure it's empty. I unzip the side pockets and check them too. This bag needs to have no trace of me anywhere.

When I am sure the bag is completely empty, I open it wide and begin to fill it. First, I carefully place a brand-new container of pepper spray and a mini stun gun at the bottom of the bag. I make sure both are in the locked position. The last thing we need is for either one to discharge accidentally.

I open the brown paper-wrapped package Derek had given me earlier. Inside are cash and a passport. I grab several stacks of twenties and place them in the bag. I hope it's enough. I take the passport and double-check it. The guy who made it did a good job — it looks real. Satisfied, I lay it on top of the cash.

Suddenly, my phone rings. I grab it. It's Liv. I check the time. Why in the world is she calling me so late? I ignore the call and continue packing.

I cover the contents of the bag with a couple of sets of clothes and socks, zip up the bag, and slide it under my bed.

My phone rings again. It's Liv once more. I roll my eyes. "Take a hint, Liv," I say as I send the call to voicemail again.

I glance out the bedroom window. A single light shines from the first floor of Liv's house. "What are you doing over there that is so urgent?"

My phone vibrates. This time, it's a text message. *Eden, please call me back. It's important.*

I immediately put my phone on silent. I can't allow Liv to ruin my plans.

I walk to the sliding glass door and glance outside once again. The sky is dark. Clouds cover the moon, blocking most of the nighttime light. Good. What I'm about to do needs to be done in secret.

I grab my purse and pull a white slip of paper out of the side pocket. On it is a phone number. I grab my phone and dial the number.

The person answers after one ring.

"I'm ready," I say.

67

EDEN

The night has grown even darker as clouds now cover the sky. Soft snowflakes fall outside my window as I look at Liv's house one last time. All of the windows are now dark and have been for at least an hour. Now is our chance.

I open the laptop and navigate to the website that controls Mitch and Liv's cameras. I log in with the username and password I found on Liv's computer when I copied her hard drive. I carefully check each one to make sure there's no movement. Everything is still. I click the drop-down menu and select the *shutdown* option. A warning box asks if I really want to shut them all down. I click the yes button and watch as the images, one by one, go black.

Satisfied, I grab my black down winter coat, the duffel bag, and a stocking cap to cover my head and leave my apartment. I have to be quick. Who knows how often Mitch wakes up in the middle of the night and checks his cameras? The faster we can get this done, the safer we'll all be.

I park my car around the corner and walk the remaining distance to the Mitre's house, being careful to stay in the shadows. The last thing I need is to be identified on someone else's camera.

As soon as I get to the house, I slip around to the back as I had done the other day, but instead of heading to the back door, I keep walking towards the small cottage at the back of the property where Nadia lives.

The lights are off in her place as well. The front door is entirely made of glass and covered with a curtain. I knock on it quietly, not wanting to draw attention to myself. I hear no movement inside. I knock again, a little louder this time. "Nadia, it's Eden. Wake up."

This time, I hear a shuffling sound on the other side of the glass door. "Coming," a voice says quietly.

I take another quick look at the Mitre house. It's still dark. I breathe a sigh of relief. Maybe we will actually pull this off.

I turn back toward Nadia's door and find her staring at me from behind the curtains, fear evident on her face. "Nadia, it's me, Eden," I assure her. I take off my stocking cap so she can really see me.

The look of fear changes to one of confusion. She quickly unlocks and opens the door. "Why are you here, Eden?" She asks as she gestures for me to enter. She's wearing a white, almost see-through nightgown, and a feeling of disgust washes over me. I bet he makes her wear that in case he has urges in the middle of the night. The thought makes me sick.

I step into the small studio apartment. On one side of the room is a twin bed, and on the other is an immaculately clean kitchenette. Nadia closes and locks the door behind me.

I turn towards her, anxiety now the dominant expression on her face. "Why are you here?" She repeats, glancing towards the Mitre's house and wringing her hands.

"I came to help you out of here." I hand her the duffel bag. "Inside, you will find everything you need to get to Florida."

She pushes the bag back to me, refusing to take it. "No. I can't take this. He will know I left and will find me. He always does."

"You have to go, Nadia. Things are about to get really bad here, and I would never forgive myself if you were caught in the middle of it. I have no idea what Mitch will do when he's under stress. I can't risk it, knowing you could get hurt."

She looks at me, confused. "I don't understand."

I shake my head. "I know. You don't need to understand. Just know that I have set everything up so you can get away from him, but you have to leave tonight." I hand the duffel bag back to her. This time, she takes it cautiously.

"What's in here?" She asks quietly.

"A few changes of clothes, some cash, pepper spray and a mini stun gun to keep you safe. There's also an American passport with your name on it."

Her eyes widen.

"Hopefully, you won't have to use the weapons, but they are there just in case," I reassure her.

She sets the bag on the bed and wrings her hands. "But the cameras? They will see us."

I shake my head. "Don't worry. I turned them off. We're good for now, but I don't know how much time we have before he wakes up and realizes they are not working. We have to go now."

Nadia stares at me for several seconds, her facial expressions switching between fear and hope. Eventually, she nods. "Okay, I will go."

With her words, I spring into action. I unzip the duffel bag and gesture for her to hand me more clothes. She quickly changes out of her nightgown into jeans, a sweatshirt, and tennis shoes. Once dressed, she grabs a handful of clothes from her dresser and hands them to me.

"You got everything you need?" I ask.

She nods. "I don't have much."

I open the front door and hold it open for her. She begins to exit and stops abruptly in the middle of the doorway. "Mi hermana," she whispers. She rushes back into the room and straight to the fridge. She grabs a picture of her sister off the fridge, kisses it, and holds it close to her heart. "Sorry," she says, clutching the photo.

"It's okay, I understand, but we need to go now."

She nods and rushes through the open door.

We walk in silence past the Mitre's home to the sidewalk. I gesture towards the end of the block, in the opposite direction of where I parked my car.

We walk away as quickly as possible, careful not to make any noise. My heart is pounding wildly in my chest. We might just pull this off.

We turn the corner, and relief floods my body when I see Pippa sitting in her car. The engine is running, but the headlights are off. Good, she listened.

I grab Nadia's hands, and we jog towards the car. I hear the doors unlock when we are a few feet away.

I open the back door and get in the car first. I try to pull Nadia's hand, but she hesitates.

"It's okay, I promise. Pippa is here to help you."

Nadia glances between Pippa and me, trying to decide whether to trust us. I pull gently on her hand. She looks scared but doesn't put up any resistance and climbs into the back seat with me.

"Okay, I will trust you," she says to Pippa. "But only because Eden says to."

Pippa laughs. "You have no idea how badly I want to take the Mitres down. I'll do anything as long as I know it hurts them. You can definitely trust me."

Nadia nods and sits back in her seat, allowing herself to relax a little.

"It looks like you guys got away without alerting the neighborhood," Pippa says.

"Yes, it went better than I expected," I say distractedly. "You remember where to take her, right?"

"Yes. It's not like you didn't drill it in my head at least thirty times. I got it."

I nod. "Okay, good." I turn to Nadia. "You go find your sister. This is your only chance."

Tears stream down her face, and she wraps her arms around me in an unexpected hug. "Thank you," she whispers.

I wrap my arms around her and hug her back. "You're welcome," I say. "Get out of here and never look back. Pippa will take care of you. Trust her."

She pulls away from me and nods.

I turn towards Pippa. "Thank you for helping," I say sincerely.

She waves her hand at me. "Don't even worry about it. It's my pleasure."

I hesitate for a few seconds. "Text me when it's complete."

"Of course," Pippa says.

I exit the car and watch as they drive away. Maybe Nadia

will find the life that she has been dreaming about since the day she left for America. I can only hope.

I walk around the block the long way, not wanting to pass the Mitre's house again. Now that I know Nadia's safe, I can begin the next part of my plan. Thoughts of what needs to happen next consume me. It takes everything I have to shove them aside and pay attention to my surroundings, but I can't afford to get caught now, so I force myself to focus. The time to plan will come.

68

PIPPA

Nadia sits silently in her seat, tightly clutching her bag and staring out the window.

"I'm going to take you to the bus station. In your bag, you'll find your papers. Everything is in order," Pippa says kindly.

Nadia looks over at her, terror filling her eyes. "He will find me."

Pippa shakes her head. "No. He won't. By the time he figures out you're gone, you'll be far away from here, heading towards Florida. I think Eden put enough cash in your bag to make sure you get there safely."

Nadia opens the bag and looks inside. Her eyes widen at the stacks of cash. "It's too much," she says quietly.

"No, it's not. Please use it and get yourself to your family. We just want to make sure you get out of here. Aldercreek can be a cruel place. Get out while you can."

Nadia nods, her eyes wide.

"I grew up here. I know," Pippa says softly, her voice trailing off.

Her mind drifts back to a different time...

. . .

THE SUN BEAT down on the metal roofs of the Aldercreek trailer park, casting long shadows across the cracked asphalt. Pippa stepped outside of her trailer and slipped on her sunglasses.

From the looks of her, you would never guess she grew up poor. She worked hard at the local ice cream shop, often working more hours than was legal, just to make enough money to buy whatever was in fashion. She was always embarrassed about where she came from and worked diligently to ensure she could get out as soon as she graduated from high school.

Pippa's grandmother sat on the porch, rocking back and forth in her old wooden rocking chair. Grandmother rarely left her roost at the corner of the porch. From her position, she saw everything that happened in the park. Who was getting in fights, who was cheating on their wife or husband — if it happened in the park, she knew about it.

"Where you going, girl?" Grandmother asked in her heavily accented English.

"Work. I have a long shift today. I won't be home until late."

Grandmother shook her head. "You work too much."

Pippa sighed, exasperated. "I'm trying to save up enough money to get out of here and go to school. I want to make something of myself."

"Why?" She asked.

"Do you really enjoy living here? In this run-down dump?" Pippa countered.

"I don't mind," Grandmother said.

"Well, I do. If I can go to college and make something of

myself, I could move us out of here into a better home. I could give us a better life."

"At what cost?"

Pippa stared at her, confused.

"Come here, child," Grandmother said.

"I can't. I'm going to be late."

"You can be late one time. I want to tell you a story."

Pippa sighed and walked towards her, crossing her arms. "Fine, I'm listening."

Grandmother smiled gently and began. "Once, there was a successful businessman on vacation in a small island village. He saw a local fisherman unloading his catch and struck up a conversation.

'Why are you finished so early?' the businessman asked.

'Because I caught enough fish for today,' the fisherman replied. 'Now I can go home, play with my kids, take a nap with my wife, and spend the evening with my friends.'

The businessman was puzzled. 'But if you stayed out longer, you could catch more fish,' he suggested.

'What would I do with more fish?' the fisherman asked.

'You could sell them, earn more money, buy a bigger boat, hire more fishermen, and expand your business. Eventually, you could open your own seafood processing plant, move to the city, and run your business from there,' the businessman explained.

'How long would that take?' the fisherman inquired.

'Maybe fifteen to twenty years,' the businessman replied.

'And then what?' the fisherman asked.

'Then you could retire, move back to a small village, fish a little, play with your kids, take naps with your wife, and spend your evenings with friends,' the businessman said.

The fisherman smiled and said, 'Isn't that what I'm doing now?'"

Pippa's grandmother paused, letting the story sink in. "You see, Pippa, the fisherman already had what he needed to be happy. Sometimes, we chase after things we think we want, only to realize we had what we needed all along."

Her words struck Pippa. Was everything she was doing for nothing? No. She remembered the way other kids treated her. They made fun of her when she wore clothes from the thrift shop or had holes in her pants. She had suffered nearly eighteen years of shame and ridicule. She was going to make things better for herself and her family. Some situations were not worth staying in.

"Thanks, Grandmother, for the story, but I think the fisherman can have both power and his family. He doesn't have to give up one for the other, and he can set up their future by sacrificing time now."

Grandmother sighed. "Can he?"

Pippa nodded. "I really have to go, Grandmother. I promise I won't forget why I'm doing all this." She kissed her on the cheek and left with an even stronger resolve to do what was necessary to get ahead.

Pippa waited outside the trailer park for the city bus. Having to take public transportation everywhere was the one aspect of being poor that Pippa had not yet been able to remedy.

When the bus arrived, she climbed aboard and approached the back. As she did, she passed ten-year-old Kari-Anne and her sister Autumn, laughing together, clearly enjoying each other's company. Pippa was struck by how much love they shared, and she envied it.

Kari-Anne glanced up at her as she passed by and waved. Pippa nodded her head at her and continued past towards the back row of seats. She spent the whole ride envying the bond the two sisters had. It further fueled her desire to make something of herself so she could find that kind of love. If she could have a family of her own, they would be happy like that, especially if they didn't have to live in poverty.

THE MEMORY BEGINS TO FADE, and Pippa realizes she's been driving on autopilot for several minutes. She shakes her head. All these years later, she is still driving down the roads of Aldercreek. Yeah, now she has fancier clothes and a daughter she adores, but what does she really have to show for all her hard work? She is still spinning her wheels, trying to make things better for herself and her family. Not much has changed. She doesn't get to spend the time with her daughter that she would like, and her marriage is in shambles. Was it all worth it?

She glances over at Nadia. Her expression remains the same — a mixture of fear and hope.

They pull up to the bus station. Pippa parks the car in an almost empty lot. The terminal also looks empty. The bus is already parked outside the station, and its engine is running.

Pippa hands Nadia a ticket. "Hurry up and take this. It should get you all the way to Florida."

Nadia takes the ticket. "Thank you. You and Eden have been so kind."

"This place will hold you hostage if you let it. Take the chance now to get free from it."

Nadia nods, puts her bag on her shoulder, and gets out of the car.

Pippa watches her walk towards the waiting bus, both envious of her and hopeful for her. She wishes she could disappear like that and start over in a place where no one even knows who she is. Would things be different? The thought is stupid even to entertain. She could never relocate her daughter while she's in the middle of high school.

Pippa sits and watches the bus until it drives away from the curb into the darkness of the night.

"Goodbye, Nadia. I hope you find what you're looking for," she says before backing out of the parking space and heading home.

69

EDEN

The sound of my phone buzzing draws me out of a deep sleep. Confused, I glance at the clock next to my bed. It's 8:30 a.m. on a Saturday morning. Who in the world is calling me? I grab my phone, look at the caller I.D., and inwardly groan. Liv. Has she already discovered that Nadia is missing? Did she somehow catch me on camera?

"Don't be ridiculous, Eden," I chastise myself. "You turned those cameras off. She can't possibly know anything."

I need to answer it. If I don't, she'll track me down at home, knowing Liv. I press the button and slowly raise the phone to my ear. "Hello?"

"Eden? I need you to come to my house as soon as possible. There's been an incident," Liv says abruptly.

"An incident? Is everything okay?" I ask, feigning concern.

"No, I don't think it is. Please hurry," she says, hanging up the phone, not even giving me the chance to respond.

I rub my eyes and run my hand through my hair. After

helping Nadia escape, I only managed to get a couple of hours of sleep. As soon as I got home last night, I paced in my living room, unable to relax until I heard from Pippa that Nadia was safe. I didn't receive that message until nearly five in the morning. I thought I would have all day to rest and recover, but instead, I'm at the mercy of Liv's whims.

I throw on a dress and some flats, trying to look somewhat presentable. I pull my hair back into a low ponytail and check my reflection in the mirror. There are dark circles under my eyes. I grab some concealer from my makeup bag and try to cover them. The makeup lessens the intensity of the circles, but they don't completely disappear. After a few more attempts, I give up. This is as good as it's going to get.

AN HOUR LATER, I pull up to Liv's house. She still thinks I live in Seattle, so I took some extra time to keep up the illusion and grabbed a coffee from the nearby coffee stand. Unlike the previous night, I park the car in front of the house and slowly make my way to the front door.

Liv opens the door before I even get to the front steps. She looks worse than I do. Her hair is disheveled, and she looks like she hasn't slept in days. "Hurry, please," she says urgently. "I don't want the neighbors to see me like this."

I nod and pick up my pace. It's just like Liv to care more about appearances than anything else.

I step into the foyer, and she quickly shuts the door behind me. Without saying a word, she walks towards the back of the house, expecting me to follow her. I do.

"What's going on, Liv?"

She doesn't respond. The only sound is that of our footsteps on the hard floor. Fear grips me. I'm about to get fired or worse.

Liv walks into the kitchen and directly to the window overlooking her backyard. She stands in front of the window and stares at the guesthouse. I stand beside her, my heart racing and beads of sweat forming on my brow.

We stand like that for what feels like forever; neither one of us talks. Just as I'm about to ask Liv what is happening again, she turns towards me.

"Nadia is missing," she says matter-of-factly.

"Nadia?" I ask, pretending to be surprised.

She nods and turns back toward the guesthouse. "She's always in the kitchen by seven a.m. getting our breakfast ready, even on the weekends. However, this morning, I came down at seven-thirty, and the kitchen was still dark."

"Maybe she just slept in," I say.

Liv immediately shakes her head. "No, I went to the guesthouse to wake her up. I pounded on the door for at least five minutes before I let myself in using my key." She glances at me. "I have tried to give her as much privacy as possible back there, but I knew something was wrong."

I nod, silently encouraging her to continue.

"Anyway, not only was she gone, but all of her stuff was gone too. She must have left in the middle of the night."

"Oh wow, where do you think she went?" I ask.

Liv looks at me, her eyebrows furrowed. "Maybe I should be asking you that question."

"Excuse me?" I ask, shocked by the accusation. "What are you trying to say?"

"I'm not trying to say anything just yet, but what do you know about Nadia's disappearance?"

"Nothing. Why would I know anything?"

Her face is unreadable and cold. "I don't know; it's just a hunch I'm starting to develop. You were pretty friendly with her every time you came here. Maybe you helped her skip town."

I shake my head. I need her to believe I'm still on her side. "No, I know nothing about it."

She nods, seemingly accepting my denial. "Well, when Mitch found out, he almost lost it. I've never quite seen him like that, actually. I've had my suspicions about him and Nadia for a long time, but his reaction basically confirmed it. He's out there somewhere right now, driving around, trying to find her. Did you know about the two of them?"

"About what? Was there something going on between Nadia and Mr. Mitre?"

Liv looks at me skeptically. "You really knew nothing?"

I shake my head. "Nothing, I promise." A rising tide of panic threatens to overtake my ability to reason and think coherently. It clicks in my mind that Liv has just admitted she knew at least somewhat what her husband was doing to Nadia, and she did nothing. This makes her complicit. She needs to be held accountable. I hold back my rage and force myself to look Liv in the eyes.

She stares at me, and I hold her gaze. It feels as though she's trying to peer into my mind and uncover all of my secrets. Her relentlessness makes me uncomfortable, but I refuse to back down.

"Do you have friends in St. Petersburg, Russia?" She asks.

I blink, break my gaze, and take a step back. "I'm sorry, what?" I ask, pretending to be confused, but deep down, I'm terrified. What exactly does she know?

"My identity was stolen by someone in St. Petersburg. Fraudulent charges were made on my accounts. Let me guess, you know nothing about that either," she says sarcastically.

"Absolutely not."

"I see," she says, turning to stare back out the window. "I'm not sure I believe that. I'm starting to wonder if anything you told me was true. You convinced me that you were just a simple bartender who had worked hard to earn her degree."

"I am," I say quietly.

"Oh, I know that's what you wanted me to believe, but I'm starting to think there's more to you than that."

"I think you're just being paranoid, Liv. Not everyone who works for you will betray your trust like Nadia did." I try to keep a calm expression on my face, but deep down, I'm getting increasingly worried.

Liv turns back to me, her eyes hard. "I wish I could believe that. I know that you've been talking to Pippa behind my back."

My eyes widen. I thought we were so careful.

She continues. "Pippa, my main competition in this mayoral race. What could you possibly have to discuss with her behind my back?" She crosses her arms. "Still think I'm being paranoid?"

I stare at her silently, unable to speak for fear of further incriminating myself.

Liv continues. "From the beginning, I've told you I need people I can trust to help me run this campaign. And for a while, I thought you would be one of them, but ever since you came to Aldercreek, things have been slowly falling apart. Every move I make seems to be sabotaged in some way."

"I think you're being a bit dramatic," I say in an attempt to calm her down. It doesn't work.

"Am I?" She asks, her voice rising. "I'll show you drama.

You're fired. I don't want to see your face around my house or my business again."

"Are you seriously firing me? After all I've done for you?"

"And what exactly have you done for me, Eden, that I couldn't have done myself?"

"That's not the point. I freed you up to focus on more important things, like your campaign."

"Did you? Or did you just orchestrate things to make my life even more difficult?" She asks.

I laugh, genuinely amused by the accusation. "What kind of control do you think I have over any of this? Your life has been falling apart for years; you just never noticed. It started way before I showed up. What kind of damage could I have really done in a few weeks? Your life was already a mess, Liv. I had nothing to do with that."

She glares at me, her eyes brimming with fire. "Get out of my house," she says in a low whisper.

I stand tall and stare back at her. "You are awful to work for. You think of no one other than yourself. I quit."

Liv stares at me, her mouth hanging wide open, as I exit the room. I keep my head held high and my posture straight as I walk down the corridor and out the front door. It's not until I get in my car that I allow myself to succumb to the emotions. "What have I done," I whisper through the tears.

70

EDEN

I get in my car and scream. A light turns on in the house across from Liv's. I have to get out of here.

I wipe the tears from my eyes, turn on the car, and begin driving. As I'm pulling away, a car passes me. I glance at it and see Mitch pass as he heads back to his house. A chill runs down my spine, and I increase my speed. Just the sight of him makes my blood boil.

I drive fast. My hands grip the steering wheel, and my knuckles turn white from the pressure. I pass the turn to my apartment, anger fueling me to keep moving.

What have I done? I pushed too far and too fast in my effort to destroy the Mitres. What do I have to show for it? Why couldn't I have just been more patient?

At least I got Nadia out of there. I would have never been able to live with myself if I had allowed her to stay in that monster's house for one more second.

Maybe I should have let Derek come with me, as he repeatedly suggested. Perhaps if he were here, Liv wouldn't have figured out I was responsible for all the bad things happening in her life. He would have helped me be patient and slow down. But no, I had to keep him at arm's length and stubbornly do this whole thing by myself. And here I am, driving away from the Mitre's home, probably for the last time, without finding any semblance of justice for my sister. I've been such a fool.

From the very beginning, Derek has been on my side. No matter what decision I have made, he has backed me up one hundred percent. Even from a distance, he has always been just a phone call away. How did I not see?

I laugh and shake my head as a memory from just a few months ago fills my mind.

DEREK WAS AT MY APARTMENT. Boxes of half-eaten takeout lined the kitchen countertops.

"I'm stuffed," I said, setting down the carton of chow mein I had been slowly working on.

"I never get full when I eat Chinese food. It's kind of sick, actually," Derek said. He grabbed my half-eaten box of chow mein and stuck his fork inside. "I think they put some kind of chemical or drug in it that makes it so addictive."

"Yeah, it's called MSG," I quipped sarcastically as I slowly stood from my chair.

He set the container on the table, walked towards me, and wrapped his arms around me. The warmth of his embrace felt good. It felt right. I wrapped my arms around him and stared up at him. His rich, brown eyes felt like they were penetrating my soul.

"I want to do this every night," he said.

"What? Eat Chinese food and get fat?" I said jokingly. I knew exactly what he was talking about, but I wasn't ready to have that conversation.

"No, Eden. I want to spend every night with you. I want us to move in together."

Anxiety gripped me, and I pushed him away. "You know I can't do that, Derek."

"Why not? We've been dating for how long?"

"A while," I said softly.

"That's even more reason for us to move in together. We're good together. Don't you want this every day?"

I looked up at him, torn between my heart and what I knew I had to do. "It's not about that. Of course, we're great together, but I can't stay here much longer. I have to leave."

"I'll come with you. I'll help you."

I shook my head and stepped backward, forcing him to release me. "You know I need to do this alone."

"But why?" He said desperately. "I wouldn't get in your way. I would just be there for you to help you decompress or process stuff. I'm good for that. Especially the decompressing part," he grinned.

I smiled at him softly. "Yeah, you are."

"So, let me come with you," he pled.

I stared at him and almost gave in, but this was my battle to fight, not his. I had to do this alone. Or at least that's what I had thought at the time. Now, I wasn't so sure I was right.

He continued. "Fine. I don't want you to go, but I know you have to. You're ready. At least let me put together a package with everything you need. I'll even throw in a few extra things to help you."

"Okay," I said sadly. "You know I don't want to leave you, right? You're amazing. I wish I could just stay here with you forever."

He wrapped his arms around me once more. "I know. I am pretty amazing, right?"

I laughed and slapped him playfully on the shoulder. "Always so humble."

He stared at me and touched my face. "I'll be here when you get back. I promise."

His words calmed me. What did I do to deserve him?

THE MEMORY BEGINS TO FADE, and I look around. I'm on the freeway, heading towards Seattle. How did I even get here? I must have been driving on instinct, the memory compelling me back to him.

I clock the next exit and ease my car off the freeway to turn back around. As much as I miss him, I can't give up now. I have to find another way to get my sister the justice she deserves.

But first, I need to grab anything I can from the real estate office before I lose access. I don't know how much time I have, but knowing Liv, it's not much.

71

LIV

I sit at the dining room table, resting my head in my hands. The sun shines brightly through the kitchen window, bathing the table. On any other day, I would sit on the back porch, wrapped in a blanket, and enjoy my morning cup of coffee, but not today. Today, I feel like a bystander as my entire world implodes.

The garage door slams open. That must be Mitch returning from his fruitless search for Nadia. I told him he wouldn't find her. I knew in my heart that she was gone for good, but he didn't listen to me, as usual.

"Liv?" I hear him yell from the kitchen.

I say nothing. I don't want to talk to him right now. I stand and walk toward the corner of the room as quietly as possible and hide myself in the shadows behind our china cabinet.

"Liv, I know you're here. Your car is here. Where are you?"

Maybe if I stand here long enough, he'll go away and leave me alone again. I need him to go away.

He briefly glances into the dining room but doesn't turn

on the light. I hold my breath. He doesn't come into the room. I can see the look on his face from my hiding place. I haven't seen him this angry in a long time.

I sink deeper into the shadows and close my eyes. I feel like a kid playing hide and seek. Maybe if I can't see him, he won't be able to see me. I know it sounds crazy, but for some reason, I feel safer with my eyes closed. After scanning the room for a few seconds, he moves on to the rest of the house.

I let out a small breath, standing as still as possible in the darkness. Time seems to tick by incredibly slowly. I wish he would just go away.

Finally, after what seems like forever, I hear the garage door open again, and I breathe a sigh of relief.

I wait for several seconds before exiting my hiding place and sit back at the table, resuming my previous position with my head in my hands.

How did everything go so wrong? Just a few months ago, I firmly believed that my life was on the precipice of real success. All the hard work I had done since I was a teenager was beginning to pay off. My real estate business was thriving, and I was about to finally start my career in politics. I thought the sky was the limit, but now, I feel like I'm one wrong move from complete destruction.

I second-guess every decision I've made since the day I met Eden. Even the decision I made today to fire her. What if I am wrong? What if it's all just a coincidence and she really had nothing to do with any of it? I don't have any real evidence that she did anything; Everything I do have is all circumstantial, but it can't all just be a coincidence, can it?

I hear my mother's voice echoing in my head. "There are no coincidences, Liv," she would tell me growing up. "If someone shows you who they are, believe them."

What has Eden even shown me about herself? I think hard about every conversation we've had and realize I know almost nothing about her. I was so caught up in my own little world that I let a total stranger into my business and home. I shake my head. How could I have been so stupid?

Maybe she hasn't even done anything on purpose. Maybe she's just bad at her job and somehow let stuff leak that should have been kept private. That's the point. I didn't even really check into her qualifications. Everything she told me the day we met at the bar could have been a lie, yet I believed her without even questioning if what she was telling me was true. Who is she really? I chastise myself for not doing my due diligence in the first place. I was too trusting. I'll never make that mistake again.

I know it's probably too late, but I'm going to do what I should have done from the beginning. I'm going to figure out who Eden really is.

I grab my laptop from my bag and type her name into the search engine. To my surprise, I find practically nothing. Of course, there are a few people with the same name, but after clicking through several of the links and looking at the associated pictures, it is clear to me that the Eden I know doesn't exist online.

The little hairs on the back of my neck stand on end. Who in the world did I let into my home? I feel so stupid for not doing this before I hired her. She could be anybody.

I grab my phone and open the small app with the video camera icon. Several months ago, I had my own set of cameras installed around the outside of the house. They're all the size of a pin and practically invisible unless you know where to look. Mitch has complete control of the main camera system, but I've never trusted him. I wanted to make sure I knew exactly what was going on at all times.

I find last night's footage from the camera pointing toward the guesthouse. Fast-forwarding through it, I spot a figure dressed in all black. I pause and zoom in. "Is that Eden?" I whisper. I press play. Slowly, the figure turns toward the camera, and I get a clear shot of her face as if she were staring directly at it. "What have you done?" I mutter, panic rising in my chest. I turn off the video. I don't need to see any more. Time is running out.

I pull up Eden's resume. The address she has listed as her home address is somewhere in Seattle. If I'm going to find out the truth, this is the best place for me to start.

I grab my coat and my purse and glance around my silent home. Nadia's absence makes the house feel suffocating. She was always around — cleaning, making dinner, cooking — a comforting presence. Now that she's gone, it feels like the light in the home was extinguished.

I shake my head. I'll worry about Nadia later. First, I need to figure out who Eden really is. I rush to my car and slip into the driver's seat. I grab my phone to put the address into the maps and see seven missed calls from Mitch, plus several increasingly angry text messages. I ignore them. He too, can wait.

As I pull onto the freeway, heading towards Seattle, I feel a semblance of control coming back. I can fix this. I just need to know exactly what I'm fixing.

72

EDEN

I speed towards the office, going as fast as possible without breaking the speed limit. The last thing I need is to get pulled over. The light in front of me turns red, and I reluctantly slow down to a stop. What if she's already told Sandy or someone else who works in the office not to let me in? All the information I've been gathering for weeks will be lost.

The light turns green, and I take a deep breath. Almost there.

I pull into the mall parking lot. It's nearly empty. It's still too early for the stay-at-home moms to be out and about, shopping with their baby carriages. The only people out at this time of day are the ones who have to be — for work or school. Maybe I'll be the first one there, and I can grab everything I need before anyone else shows up.

That hope is dashed the minute I step out of the car. A haggard-looking Mitch opens the office door and steps out of the building. He slips on his sunglasses and looks directly at me. He raises one hand and gestures for me to come closer.

Great, just what I didn't need. The last thing I want to do right now is talk to him. I walk towards him hesitantly, unsure of what he knows about my current employment with his wife.

He waves for me to join him again, this time more urgently.

I pick up my pace. Maybe he doesn't know yet that I've been fired.

"Hey, Mitch," I say when I'm a few feet away. "What are you doing here so early? Where's Liv?" I ask, knowing full well she's not here.

"That's exactly what I was going to ask you. Have you seen her this morning?"

"No, I just got here. She's not in the office?" I say, desperately trying to hide the truth. I force my face to look concerned. Hopefully, it's working.

He shakes his head. "No, I just checked. Sandy hasn't heard from her, and no one else is in yet."

"Well, it is still early. Maybe she's still at home," I say in the most encouraging voice I can muster. "Have you checked the house?"

"Yes, I just came from there. She's not home. The weird thing is that her car was there, but I couldn't find her anywhere."

I look at him, genuinely surprised. "Are you sure?"

"I went into every single room, and they were all dark and empty."

"That's so strange," I say, mostly to myself. She was literally just there; where could she have gone? "Did you check the back porch? You know she likes to sit there and drink her coffee in the mornings."

He nods. "That was one of the first places I looked. It's

like she vanished. First Nadia, now Liv," he says, absently running his hand through his hair.

I really get a good look at him for the first time. His eyes are bloodshot, and his hair looks like it hasn't been combed in days. His clothes are wrinkled, and he already has sweat stains under his arms. I wonder if they're the same clothes he wore the night before. I shake my head. He looks like he's about to lose it. Good. "What happened to Nadia?" I ask, hoping that he has no idea.

He responds quietly. "She was gone when I woke up this morning. She's not answering her phone. I have searched the entire town and haven't seen any sign of her."

"Maybe she couldn't sleep and decided to run some errands before starting her day?"

He shakes his head vigorously. "No, Nadia doesn't run errands."

"Oh?" I question, trying to sound innocent, but deep down, I'm screaming at him. She never runs errands because you're a psychopath who holds her hostage for your own sick pleasure. If I do nothing else while I'm here, at least I got her away from you. I concentrate on maintaining a calm look on my face. I must seem serene and unemotional to him, even while I rage inside.

"I have called her cell phone several times, too and it just goes straight to voicemail," he says, increasingly agitated. "I don't know what to do anymore."

I glance inside the office. It is dark, save for a light at the back, coming from Sandy's office. I have to get as much information as I can before everyone finds out I've been fired. "Give me five minutes," I say to Mitch, "and then I'll help you find her."

He nods at me absently, clearly only halfway listening.

I rush inside to my desk as quietly as I can. I don't want

Sandy to know that I'm here. I quickly take a few flash drives I had stored in the office drawer, along with a few notepads with random information on them. I need to get into Liv's computer to grab the information I really want. I look at her desk. Her laptop is not there. She must have brought it home.

Suddenly, it dawns on me. If Mitch doesn't know I've been fired, maybe he'll let me back in the house to help him find Liv. I grab a few more things and rush back out the door.

Mitch is standing against the wall with a faraway look in his eyes. He pulls away from the wall as soon as he sees me emerge from the building. I step up next to him. "Have you checked Liv's master calendar at the house?"

He looks at me, confused. "What master calendar?"

"She keeps a paper calendar in her office where she writes down all her appointments for the day. It helps her make a plan before she leaves in the morning. It's really her backup for the digital one in case something is wrong with the cloud." I can't believe how easily that all came to me. Liv doesn't keep a paper calendar, but it sounds convincing, even to me.

"Liv always has contingencies. That makes sense," Mitch says. "No. I didn't check her calendar."

"I'll come too and help you find it. Maybe it will give us a clue as to where she went."

He nods. "Okay, that makes sense. I'll meet you at the house." He pulls his keys out of his pocket and walks towards his car.

"It will be okay, Mitch," I call to him.

He slowly turns around. Doubt fills his eyes.

"We'll find her," I say as reassuringly as I can muster.

"What about Nadia?" He asks, his face downcast.

I don't want him to shut down, so I lie. "Yes, I'll help you find her too." Knowing full well that Nadia should be hundreds of miles from here by now. "But first, let's figure out what happened to Liv."

He nods silently and walks to his car. I rush to mine, not wanting to lag too far behind him. This is my chance to access Liv's office without her eyes peering over my shoulder. I can't waste it.

73

SANDY

Mozart is softly playing in Sandy's office, and she's slowly scrolling through social media. She hesitates. She wants to look Grant up but knows it will only make her sad. Maybe they could have had something. Her marriage with Blaine has basically been over for a long time. Maybe Grant had been her way out, but she'd screwed it up — like usual.

She can't help herself. She types his name into the search bar. Immediately, she sees his face and brilliant white smile at the top of the search. She clicks on the link to his page. His account is pretty private, so she can't see much, but there's enough. She pauses on a smiling picture of him and some buddies playing golf in Redmond at a fancy country club. He looks tan and happy. A stark contrast to Blaine. She can't help but regret what she'd done to Grant. Panic fills her as the memory comes flooding back in despite her efforts to block it.

She hasn't heard from Grant since that night. Not that she can blame him. A woman he barely knew entered his home and, a few minutes later, walked out with a very expensive bottle of liquor and a prized vase. He probably thought that she had planned it all from the very beginning — that she was always just there to rob him blind. She wishes he understood why she did it. She wishes *she* understood why she did it.

Every time she takes something, the initial high is almost like a numbing agent. The bad feelings are temporarily replaced by adrenaline, and she feels free for just a moment from the crushing weight of her sadness. As soon as she comes back down, the feelings hit her like a train, much worse than before. On top of the already existing misery, she now has an added layer of guilt. Usually, she can push the guilt aside because she takes things from businesses, not people. She figures they budget for losses, so it won't hurt them. Besides, she only takes small items that are of little value. However, Grant was a person she cared about, and she broke his trust.

She scrolls to the next picture on social media and sighs. He really is handsome. Not that Blaine isn't handsome; he is. Probably even more handsome than Grant, but some time ago, he just stopped looking at her as anything more than an employee of his household. At least, that's how she's felt for a long time.

However, in the last few days, Blaine has been trying to be more attentive and present. To be honest, she's not sure how she feels about it. She had gotten so used to him not being around very much and always being alone that his constant presence is almost suffocating.

This morning, he brought her breakfast in bed. It was a lovely gesture, but his attention made her feel panicky.

He set the food on her lap and climbed into bed next to her, wrapping his arms around her. "I could get used to this," he said.

"What part?" She asked.

"Just being around each other all the time, like we used to be. I don't know how I got so far off track. I'm so sorry."

"It's really okay," Sandy said.

"No, it's not. I'm going to make up for it, I promise."

She stared at the bacon and eggs he placed on her lap and felt an overwhelming urge to throw them across the room. She closed her eyes, trying to convince herself to calm down. This was exactly what she'd wanted for years. Wasn't it? Now, staring at the plate of food, she no longer knew what she wanted, but she was one hundred percent certain that if she didn't get out of the house right now, she would explode.

She set the tray on the side table next to her bed. "I'm so sorry, babe. I totally forgot. Liv asked me to get into work early today to open the office for a client." She quickly got out of bed and rushed to the bathroom.

He stared at her suspiciously as she threw off her night-gown and replaced it with a silk button-up shirt and a pencil skirt with black heels. "Why can't she do that herself?" He asked, clearly suspicious.

"I don't know. Something about having a meeting first thing in the morning that she couldn't miss. All I know is that I have to be there in fifteen minutes. I totally forgot."

"Okay," he said, disappointed. "Dinner tonight, then?" He asked hopefully.

She inwardly sighed. "Yes. Seven?"

He nodded. "I'll pick something up on my way home."

"Sounds good," she said as she rushed out the door.

THERE WAS no early morning client. As soon as she walked into the office, she grabbed a cup of coffee and sat down in the silence, breathing a sigh of relief. Blaine is a good guy, but he's going overboard. She just needed her space.

She turned on the music and allowed the violins to soothe her anxious soul even more. It wasn't long before she logged into social media and contemplated looking up Grant. She wondered how different her life could have been if she had married Grant instead of Blaine. She closed her eyes and allowed her mind to wander.

She is lost in thought when Mitch interrupts her, looking for Liv. Annoyed, she barely gives him the time of day. "I'm sure Liv is fine," she says, trying to calm Mitch down. "She'll be back before dinner. Just you wait and see." He leaves abruptly, not even acknowledging her response.

She stares at her computer screen, her brief conversation with Mitch already dissolving from her mind. Liv is not lost. She's the last person she would ever worry about. She's pretty sure Liv has nine lives like a cat.

She resumes her stalking efforts, scrolling through more pictures posted on Grant's page, when suddenly, a small banging noise sounds in the front office.

Panic grips her. There isn't supposed to be anyone here for several more minutes. She turns down Mozart, hoping to better hear what is happening in the main part of the office. She hears what sounds like the front door opening.

"Hello?" She calls loudly. "Is anyone there?" Maybe Mitch had forgotten something and came back to get it. If it's him or one of the other agents, surely they would respond, but there is only silence.

She peeks her head out of her doorway. The office looks quiet and uninhabited. "Mitch, is that you?" She pleads, but she's met with silence.

Movement outside the shop catches her eye, and she walks towards the glass doors, stopping a few feet away. Two people are standing in front of the agency, their backs turned to her. The man is Mitch. She can tell from their brief conversation with him earlier. He was wearing faded jeans and a red and white flannel shirt. He's impossible to miss. She has no idea who the woman is. From her vantage point, she can see only a portion of her back.

Sandy continues to walk slowly towards the front door, carefully staying in the shadows. Suddenly, Mitch and the mysterious woman both look back toward the building. Sandy's breath catches. Is that Eden? Curiosity propels her forward even closer. They speak in hushed tones, and she can't discern what they are saying through the glass. Suddenly, they part ways, each heading towards their respective cars.

What were they doing here together? Does Liv know they were here? Every question she thinks of leads to even more questions. Something strange is happening. She takes out her cell phone and dials Liv's number. This is something she is going to want to know.

74

LIV

The Seattle sky is growing dark, and the clouds create a gloominess that feels almost physically heavy. I pull up the address Eden provided on her resume on my phone and walk briskly down the sidewalk. As I walk, the wind blows at me sideways, and I wrap my jacket around me even more tightly.

I'm regretting my decision to park so far away. I didn't want to park so close that someone related to Eden could somehow identify me or my car, but I also didn't want to park my car on the streets down here. Crime in this area of the city is notoriously high, and I have a nice car. All I could picture was coming back to it, only to find the windows smashed in and my stereo ripped out.

I parked ten blocks away in a well-lit and monitored parking garage that's probably going to cost me an arm and a leg. I'm not sure it made me that much safer in the long run. Instead of subjecting my car to a potential crime, I'm now subjecting myself to being mugged or worse. I grab the pepper spray out of my bag and grasp it tightly in one hand. If anyone tries anything on me, they are going to regret it.

My phone vibrates almost audibly in my coat pocket. I grab it and see that it's Sandy. Annoyed, I answer the phone. "What do you need, Sandy?" I say, my irritation evident.

"Mitch was just here looking for you," she says in that voice she uses when she has gossip she can't wait to share.

"I don't care. He can look for me all he wants. I'm fine," I respond, unable to keep the irritation from my voice.

"Oh, that's not the interesting part," she says conspiratorially. "Guess who he was with."

"Just spit it out, Sandy. I am not in the mood to play a guessing game today."

"Fine. He was with Eden." She pauses to let her words land. After a few brief seconds of silence, she continues. "I'm not quite sure what they were talking about because they were standing outside in front of the store, but they left at the exact same time like they were on a mission."

I stop dead in my tracks. "Eden?" I question, wanting to make sure I heard her right.

"Yes. It was Eden. I would bet my life on it."

I stand silently in the middle of the sidewalk, fury building inside me, ready to explode. "I fired her this morning."

"What? You did? Why?" Sandy peppers me with rapid-fire questions, wanting to know everything.

"Yes. Do not, under any circumstances, allow her back into the building. I'm not exactly sure how, but I think she's been somehow sabotaging me."

"Are you serious? I knew there was something off about her from the beginning," Sandy says.

"Yeah, well, I don't have any proof yet, but I'm looking for proof now. I can't come back and deal with Mitch at the moment. He's going to have to wait. Please make sure that

Eden has no access to anything. Do not even let her back in the door."

Sandy hesitates as if she's contemplating whether or not to tell me something.

"What is it, Sandy? Spit it out," I say, my voice tight with frustration.

"Nothing. It's nothing. I'll make sure she can't get in. I promise."

"Thank you. And if Mitch asks you where I'm at, please tell him you haven't heard from me."

I hang up the phone without waiting for a response. This news makes me even more determined to figure out who Eden is. I need answers that I'm not going to get in Aldercreek.

I look at the map I've pulled up on the phone, and there are only a few more blocks.

75

EDEN

Mitch and I arrive at the house at approximately the same time. I followed him the entire way here, even though he drove like a crazy person. I couldn't give him time to change his mind, so I stayed on his tail.

He opens the garage door and pulls in while I park on the street. I quickly get out and jog up the driveway toward the house.

Mitch gets out of his vehicle. A distressed look on his face. "Her car is gone. It was here earlier, and now it's gone."

"I'm sure she's okay," I assure him. "I'll find her calendar, and maybe we can get a better idea of where she went."

He nods and points towards the door. "Yeah. Go ahead and look in her office. I'm going to look around the house and see if maybe I missed something."

My heart is racing a million miles a minute. I will never get this chance again. I just need enough time to copy the information from Liv's hard drive.

Mitch opens the door and lets me inside. I must remain calm and not rush to the office. I can't look like I'm too eager to get in there, or he will become suspicious. I take a deep breath to calm my nerves.

"You know where her office is, I assume?" He asks, barely paying attention to the answer.

"Yes, I've been there a few times when we've worked from the house."

He nods and walks away, not even waiting to make sure I head in the right direction. "Let me know if you find anything. I'm going to see what I can find upstairs," he says with his back to me as he walks up the stairway.

The house feels empty somehow — dead. I walk as quickly as I can toward the office without raising suspicion. I open the door and leave it open to hear what Mitch is doing. He shuffles up the stairs. His footsteps are heavy and slow. After a few seconds, they stop. I quickly close the door to the office and get to work. I don't have much time.

Opening my purse, I grab a flash drive from a side pocket. I rush to Liv's computer. I grab the mouse, and my sweaty palms slip slightly on the plastic. "Gross," I say as I wipe them on my pants. The last thing I need is to leave a bunch of DNA all over this place. I grab the mouse again and move it slightly. A login screen pops up. Crap, I need a password. I could ask Mitch for the password, but he might begin to question my motives. No, I need to figure out her password on my own.

I know the password to her computer from when I used that computer program to crack it. I would use the program on this computer, too, but the USB drive is at the apartment. I can't risk losing this opportunity to go home and get it. Maybe she uses the same password on this computer?

I type in the password and hold my breath as I wait for it to authenticate. *Welcome,* the computer says, and I breathe a sigh of relief. "Thank goodness," I whisper.

I plug the flash drive into the computer and begin copying everything from her hard drive to the flash drive. The computer estimates it will take ten minutes. I check my watch. I've been in here for less than five minutes, but I have no idea how much time I have left before Mitch realizes I'm not supposed to be here and kicks me out.

Wringing my hands, I look around the room. Maybe there's something else in the room that I can use. As quickly as possible, I pull out the drawers on the desk. If Mitch comes in here while I'm snooping, I'll just tell him I'm looking for the calendar. He should believe me... I hope.

The top drawers contain nothing except obsessively organized office supplies. In the bottom drawer, I find several books that look like journals. I flip through them and find nothing interesting, just information about former clients and listings.

I glance at the computer — thirty more seconds. I close the drawers and look at the office door anxiously. Mitch could walk in here at any minute. No matter what the circumstances, he would not be okay with me copying Liv's hard drive. I tap my foot on the ground. "Come on," I whisper under my breath.

Suddenly, the message on the screen says the transfer is complete. I breathe a sigh of relief and eject the flash drive from the computer.

I take a second to look at the folders I just copied to my flash drive. Most of them seem business-related and useless to me, but at the bottom of the list is a folder labeled *Mitch and A*. The last time it was accessed was several years ago.

My heart races. Is this folder about my sister? I quickly open it. Inside, I find hundreds of photos of Autumn and Mitch together at various locations. "What is this?" I whisper. "It is obvious now that Liv knew that Mitch and

Autumn were together. What really happened that night at the lake?"

I scroll through the folder, my heart constricting as Autumn's face fills the screen. At the very end of the list is a text file titled *Fix*. I hesitantly open the file. What I read chills me to the bone. On its surface, it looks like nothing. Autumn's name isn't mentioned, and everything is written in code. None of this is solid proof, but I can read between the lines. If Liv acted on this plan, then I've been focusing on the wrong person this entire time.

The ceiling above me creaks. I quickly close the file and lock the screen. I have to get out of here without Mitch realizing I'm gone.

I quietly open the office door. The hallway is dark and silent. I carefully make my way down the hallway, ensuring my footsteps don't make any noise.

Just as I reach the front door, I hear Mitch's voice from the top of the stairs. "Are you leaving already? Did you find something?" He asks as he slowly walks down the stairs.

I only have a few seconds before he can grab me. I have to get out of here. Placing my hand on the front door handle, I turn to Mitch. "No, I didn't find it."

"Then why are you leaving?" He asks, his steps getting quicker.

I ignore his question. I don't owe him anything. He may not have been the one to kill Autumn, but he has done terrible things to Nadia. Anger rages inside me as I open the door. I glare at him and allow the anger to fuel my words. "Why do you think it was okay to keep a woman hostage?"

Mitch stops briefly and stares at me, confused.

I continue. "You treated her like she was some kind of household pet. What kind of sick person does that?" I ask.

"I... I don't know what you're talking about," he says, the

expression on his face turning from worry and exhaustion to rage.

I don't even give him a chance to finish his descent down the stairs. I throw the door open the rest of the way and run to my car, fishing my keys out of my pocket on my way there. I glance back and see his imposing figure barreling toward me.

"Stop! Come back!" He yells, stumbling down the front steps.

I pick up my pace and use my key fob to unlock the car door. Opening the handle, I slip into the driver's seat, locking the door behind me. I glance through the window and see Mitch less than ten feet away.

I shove the keys into the ignition and start the car. Mitch bangs on my window. "Eden! What did you do? What did you take from Liv's office?" His face is red, and his eyes have a crazed look.

Ignoring him, I pull away from the curb. I glance in the rearview mirror. Mitch is standing on the sidewalk, both hands on his head. My heart is pounding, and tears are threatening to spill down my cheeks. This wasn't how this was supposed to go. What am I going to do?

LIV

The clouds in the sky darken, and I know it's only a matter of time before snow begins to fall. I look at the map. Eden's address should be just around the corner.

I stop for a second and survey the area. I've passed through the worst section of town. The streets in this part are virtually empty and mostly clean, aside from a stray coffee cup lying on the ground beside a nearby garbage can. My earlier fear of being mugged lessens, and I put my pepper spray back in my purse.

I glance across the street at a towering apartment building. I know I've seen that building before. A small golden plaque next to the door reads *The Broadmoor*. Realization hits me. I've never physically seen this building, but I've seen pictures of it. My mom sent them to me last year when my brother John moved into the penthouse apartment.

Your brother is really moving up in the world. Look at his new home. He has the entire top floor. Can you believe it? This is what you could have, too, Liv, if you would only focus and apply yourself.

I remember looking at the pictures and wanting to throw my phone against the wall. I didn't. I have learned to keep it together no matter what she says to me, but it's never easy. John has always been the golden child, and he knows it. I'm older than him by two years, and for us, birth order psychology is insanely accurate. As the oldest child, I had all the responsibilities and expectations, and John got away with everything. He could literally do nothing wrong in my mother's eyes.

I REMEMBER one time when we were both in middle school. I came home at the end of the semester with my report card — straight A's, as usual. I handed it to my mom, expecting some sort of praise.

She looked at it. "Good," she said without even looking at me. Turning toward the fridge, she walked the report card to the drawer next to it and shoved it inside, not even bothering to fold it.

My heart had been broken. I had worked so hard for her to be proud of me, but it was never enough.

"You need to take more challenging classes," she said instead of praising me. "You'll never get into a good school if you continue taking things like drama or art. Those are easy A's."

I stared at her in shock. "Those were required classes, Mom. I had to choose electives. I can't just take all math classes, you know."

She shrugged her shoulders. "Then take something more useful, like something about computers."

My face burned as the hurt was replaced with anger, and I realized that nothing I did was ever going to be good enough for her.

"John," my mother called up the stairs. "Where's your report card?"

"I forgot it at school," he yelled from his room.

"Make sure you bring it home tomorrow," my mom replied.

Later that evening, I walked past John's room. His door was slightly cracked, and I could see him sitting at his desk, doing something on his computer. He had headphones on, and the music was playing so loudly that I could hear it as clearly as if I were listening to it myself.

I pushed the door open slightly to get a better look at what he was doing. I wasn't afraid of him hearing me. With his music on, I was pretty sure I could scream, and he'd have no idea.

His report card was displayed on his computer screen. On the right-hand side of the screen was a white text box containing lines of computer code.

I glanced at the report card. All D's and one F. I shook my head. Mom was going to kill him.

I watched as John edited the block of code. I glanced back at his report card and noticed one of the D's had turned into an A.

"What the heck are you doing, John?" I asked as I stormed into the room, unable to stop myself.

He didn't respond. I watched another D turn into a B.

I shoved his shoulder, and he ripped the headphones off his head. "Get out of my room," he yelled at me.

"How are you changing your grades like that? What are you doing?"

"It's none of your business," he said as he stood from his chair and pointed at the door. "Get out of my room, now."

"You think she's going to be fooled by this? What are you going to do, just print it from your computer?"

He didn't respond, but his expression told me everything. His eyes were wide and defiant.

"That's never going to work, and you know it. Besides, I'll just tell her that you forged it."

"No, you won't," he said with conviction.

"Of course I will. You're not going to get away with this."

He took a step closer to me. He was smaller than me by almost two inches, but he was scrappier than me and had been involved in martial arts his entire life.

I took a step back.

"You won't tell because if you do, I'll tell Mom you stole her credit card."

Fear gripped my chest. "What are you talking about?"

"Oh, I know you didn't steal her credit card, but who do you think she's going to believe if it goes missing?"

I hesitated. I wanted to think that she would believe me, but I knew he was right. She always took his side in every single argument we'd ever had. I stared at him with white-hot rage.

He crossed his arms, smirking. "Now, leave my room."

"Fine, but Mom is never going to believe that those are your real grades."

"We'll see," he said, turning back to his computer.

Of course, he got away with it. The next day, he presented the fake report card to our mother like he'd won the Nobel Prize. She showered him with praise, wrapping her arms around him and hugging him — completely opposite to how she reacted when I showed her my grades.

John looked at me smugly, and I wanted nothing more than to scratch the expression off his face. It was then that I realized that no matter how much I accomplished, I was never going to live up to my golden child brother.

. . .

I STARE at his apartment building, still experiencing the rage from that incident years ago. A figure walks towards the penthouse window. I stare at it for a few seconds before realizing it's John. I look away, hoping he doesn't recognize me from this distance. A chance encounter with him is the last thing I need.

I glance back at my phone and continue walking toward Eden's address. I turn the corner, walk three more blocks, and stop when the map indicates I've arrived. I look up at the building I'm standing next to. It's not an apartment building, but it looks like a local neighborhood pub. Confused, I double-checked that I had entered the address correctly. I had.

I walk up to the windows and stare inside. It looks ordinary. A brown wooden bar flanks nearly one entire wall of the place, while booths line the other wall. It's dark in there and dead right now in the middle of the day. Maybe there are apartments above the pub, and that's where Eden lives?

I take a deep breath and head inside. I'm immediately greeted with the smell of hops and fried bar food. A tall, blonde bartender stands behind the bar. He looks like a guy who would rather be surfing than stuck inside this dark place all day. I glance around; there are only two other patrons in the room. They both sit at the bar top, watching the soccer game displayed on the television screens mounted above the bar.

"How can I help you?" the bartender asks, clearly bored.

I walk over to the bar and sit in an empty seat. "Just water, please," I say. "For now."

He nods and quickly pours me a glass.

"You new to the area?" He asks.

"Kind of, not really. I live in Aldercreek."

"Oh, yeah. I've driven through there before. It looked nice."

"Yeah, it is nice," I say absently.

"What brings you down here?" He asks.

Maybe he knows Eden. I pull up a picture of her on my phone and slide the phone toward him. "Do you know this woman?" I ask.

He steps closer to the phone, and his eyes light up immediately. "Her?"

I nod. "I'm trying to find her."

"You could say I know her," he says with a chuckle.

"What's that supposed to mean?"

"She kind of owns the place," he says, a large grin on his face.

"No, you must be mistaken. This woman just graduated from college and..."

My thoughts trail off as I glance over the bartender's shoulder at a photograph hanging on the wall. There are several people in the photograph that I don't recognize, but Eden is standing right in the middle of the group. "That's her," I say, gesturing to the photograph.

"Yep, she took over the place a few years ago and has done a lot to restore it to the local neighborhood spot it used to be. She's been gone for a few months now. Not sure where she went."

"Can you tell me her name?" I ask, realizing that even her name was probably a lie.

"Kari-Anne," he says nonchalantly.

My heart stops beating, and I feel like I can't breathe. I haven't heard that name in years. It can't be her... can it? I look back at the photo and examine Eden's face. Could it be true? I stare at her picture for several seconds before the truth of the situation weighs down on my shoulders like a lead blanket. Eden is Kari-Anne, the sister of the first girl I ever killed.

77

EDEN

My nerves are on fire as I drive away from Mitch and Liv's house. Everything has gone so completely wrong. I was so close. I don't regret helping Nadia; I couldn't live with myself if I had allowed him to keep abusing her. She needed to get out. However, everything I've been working toward since coming to Aldercreek is now falling apart.

As I exit the neighborhood, I pass several large mansions. I imagine the housewives inside, sipping coffee and enjoying their morning in peace, utterly oblivious to the monsters who are their neighbors and friends. How do people like Mitch and Liv fool so many? It makes me angry just thinking about it. They are responsible for the death of my sister, yet everyone treats them like royalty. Autumn deserves justice for what happened to her, and I was so close to achieving it.

Hot tears prick my eyelashes, and I wipe them away with the back of my hand. At least things aren't totally lost. I pat the flash drive that I had stuffed in my pocket. There must be something on here that I can use to bring them down.

I pull out of the neighborhood onto the road that leads to town. The morning commuters clog the road, making it congested. My body itches to drive as fast as I can, but the rush-hour traffic forces me to drive achingly slow. I just need to get out of here and make a new plan.

I inch toward the light at one of the main intersections in town. On the corner is the brick business complex where the trailer park used to be. In front of the complex is a large, ancient oak tree, one that has been in Aldercreek for as long as I can remember. My mind flashes back to when I was maybe seven or eight years old.

"KARI-ANNE, GET DOWN FROM THERE," my sister yelled at me from the base of the tree.

"Why? I like it up here. You can see everything."

"You're going to break a leg or something worse. You can't just climb trees like that. What are we going to do if you hurt yourself? Take a bus to the hospital? There's no way Mama can drive us anywhere right now. You're being stupid."

I stared into the distance, watching a flock of birds soar over the blanket of trees. I wished I could fly with them, free to go wherever I wanted.

"Now, Kari-Anne!" she yelled at me, her hands on her hips.

"Fine," I said, slowly making my way back to the bottom, branch by branch.

As soon as my feet hit the ground, my sister turned on her heels and stomped away from me in frustration. "You can't be doing stuff like that," she said, her back to me. "You can't just go around being so impulsive and risking your life. You're going to get yourself killed."

I ran up to her and grabbed her hand. "Sorry," I said. "I won't do it again."

She stopped and looked at me, a small smile on her face. "You know I just care about you, right? I don't want anything to happen to you. I could never live with myself."

I nodded and leaned against her arm.

She wrapped an arm around me. I always felt safe with her.

A WAVE of grief washes through me as the memory fades. She was the sensible one. She had a plan for her life and was always making safe, responsible choices. Mitch was her only weakness, and she died because of it.

"I'm going to figure it all out, Autumn. I promise."

The light in front of me turns green, and I continue to drive through the city, being pulled to the place where it all started.

78

LIV

Blood pounds in my ears. Eden is Kari-Anne. How could I have missed that? I've let her into our lives, my business, my home. What have I done?

I walk towards the front door of the bar without saying another word. I have to get out of here. I have to talk to Mitch. I push the front door of the bar open. The sun shines brightly, temporarily blinding me. I squint as I look around, trying to will my eyes to adjust so I can figure out the way back to my car.

Within seconds, my vision starts to return. I look to my right and see my brother's building. That's the way I need to go. I walk quickly, holding back an insane urge to run as fast as possible. Why did I have to park so far away? Panic sets in. I have to get home and find Eden. I have to stop her.

I dig into my bag and pull out my cell phone. I keep walking as I dial Mitch's number. "Come on, Mitch, please pick up," I say under my breath. After several rings, the call goes to voicemail. I immediately hang up and try again. It rings several more times. "Mitch, answer your dang phone!" I yell.

A homeless man, huddled in the doorway of a nearby building, looks up at me from his cocoon of blankets and cardboard.

"I'm so sorry," I say, picking up my pace towards my car. "I didn't mean to wake you."

He stares at me with bleary eyes but doesn't respond.

I look away uncomfortably. Normally, I would stop and give him cash from my wallet, but I don't have time. I have to deal with Eden.

I check my phone for messages. Nothing. Where is Mitch? When I left this morning, he had gone to look for Nadia. What if he found her and decided that she was what he wanted? What if they ran off together, leaving me alone to pick up this mess? Or what if he had found Eden and she's sunk her little claws into him too? The irrational thoughts cause the panic inside me to build, threatening to spill over.

Finally, after what feels like forever, I reach my car. Beads of sweat line my brow and the back of my neck. My breathing is ragged, as if I had just run a marathon to get to my car, and my chest feels as though a thick rubber band is wrapped around it. I have to get home. I have to find Mitch.

I start my car's engine and begin to drive, taking deep breaths to keep the rising panic at bay. I pull onto the freeway and set the cruise control on my car. The last thing I need is to get pulled over for going too fast. I breathe in slowly, counting to five, and then I breathe out. I cycle through the breaths in and out, but it's not working. The panic threatens to spread through my whole body and make me immobile. Stars dance in my vision. I know I have to stop driving, but every moment I'm not at home is one more second Eden has to dig her claws into Mitch further and destroy everything.

The stars in my eyes grow, and I reluctantly pull to the side of the road. I try Mitch's phone one last time without luck. Anxiety threatens to tear me apart, and I scream at the top of my lungs, pounding my fists against the steering wheel. My grip on reality feels tenuous. I need someone to tether me back to the present and help me refocus.

I open my contacts list and navigate to a name I have actively avoided most of my adult life. My finger hovers over the name as I hesitate. The last time I talked to her, I hung up the phone and wept for twenty minutes. She is unfeeling, and her words often tear into me like a harpoon, but she is always honest, and I know she'll know what to do.

I will my finger to push the button and let the phone ring. After two rings, an older woman's voice answers. "Hello?"

"Hi, Mom," I say quietly. My voice is no longer that of a strong, independent woman but meek and soft, almost like a child's.

"Liv," she says, matter-of-factly, almost as if she's disappointed. "What do you need this time?"

"Why do you always think I need something when I call you Mom?"

Silence hangs on the other end of the line. My mind fills the silence with her possible answers. Because you're so weak that you always need me, you can't get along in your life without me. At least your brother can take care of himself, unlike you. You'll never amount to anything.

My mother interrupts the barrage of negative thoughts that threaten to consume me. "What do you need, Liv?" She repeats.

I take a deep breath. "Mom, I have an emergency."

"Whenever you call me, you do," she states matter-of-factly.

Irritation floods my body, and I push it down. "I'm just... I'm having trouble keeping control."

"Your brother never has that problem. Have you talked to him?" She asks, void of any compassion.

I grit my teeth. "I am just trying to ask your advice on what I should do."

My mother pauses for several seconds. Finally, in a low voice so quiet and menacing that I can barely hear her, she replies. "There are no problems. There are only people. You know what to do."

The line clicks, and there's silence on the other end. "Mom?" I say, hoping that she is still here, but I know the truth deep down. She has given me the extent of the motherly advice I am going to get from her. Since I was little, she taught me how to stand up for myself and take care of my own problems, but she doesn't have that motherly instinct. I grit my teeth. Why couldn't she have been a normal mother? Why doesn't she ever listen to me?

I close my eyes and take a deep breath. I know what she would want me to do, what I have to do. I will my heart rate to slow and my breathing to stabilize. Calmness rushes through me along with a sense of purpose. I take one last deep breath and open my eyes. I'm ready.

79

EDEN

I exit the main road and turn down a well-worn dirt path. The frozen tire tracks are deep, forcing my car into their ruts. As I drive into the forest, the sun begins to disappear behind the canopy of trees. Darkness surrounds my car, and I turn on the headlights to illuminate my path.

The forest seems empty, though I know hundreds of animals are probably hiding steps away from my car. I brace my hands on the steering wheel in case a deer or a rabbit jumps into my path.

Thankfully, nothing jumps out. Five minutes later, I pull out of the darkness of the forest and back into the sunlight. In front of me is a rocky beach next to a lake. I pull my car to the side, put it in park, and turn off the engine.

The sun is partially hidden behind a cloud, preventing its rays from shining down in full force, but I can still feel the heat on my skin as I get out of my car, despite the bitter chill of the winter air. Most of the lake is surrounded by houses, many of them owned by wealthy businessmen and women. These houses are empty most of the year. Looking around the lake's edge, I see three houses with smoke billowing out of their chimneys.

The beach I am standing on is one of two public places on the lake. The other one is directly across from me and decidedly more popular. This is the beach where my sister died. I have avoided this place for years, but it's time I start facing those thoughts and allowing her memory some space.

I step towards the frozen lake. Sheets of ice extend as far as I can see. I gingerly step onto the surface. It seems sturdy, but with this lake, you never really know. The ice could support your weight for several feet until you hit a weak spot and end up in the water. I put my foot back on the rocks. The last thing I need right now is to fall through the ice.

I stare at the ice, my arms wrapped around me to ward against the bitter chill. Thoughts of Autumn taking her last breath in this very space invade my mind. I kneel to the ground as sobs wrack my entire body.

"I'm so sorry, Autumn. I wanted to find justice for you, but I've messed everything up." The icy wind blows my hair and bites my cheeks. I kneel to the ground, not even noticing the stiffness forming in my fingers. "Tell me what to do now," I whisper through the tears.

80

AUTUMN (PAST)

Kari-Anne, Autumn and Pippa stood outside the trailer park next to the main road. It was the end of August, and the hot sun beat down on their skin.

"How much longer until the bus gets here?" Kari-Anne whined.

Autumn glared at her. "How am I supposed to know? It's not like it's ever on time."

"But I'm hot," Kari-Anne said as she walked towards a tree twenty feet away.

"Kari-Anne, what are you doing? You know the bus isn't gonna wait for you. Either you're standing here when it arrives, or you're not getting on the bus."

Kari-Anne sighed. "Fine." She walked back to stand next to Autumn.

Pippa looked at Kari-Anne. "I'm surprised your mom lets you go to school on the city bus. Aren't you like nine or something?"

"I'm ten," Kari-Anne said, crossing her arms. "Besides, how else am I supposed to get to school? My mom's always sleeping on the couch in our living room. She'd never drive me."

Autumn glared at Kari-Anne.

She immediately shut her mouth. "Sorry," she whispered.

Autumn sighed. "I wish I had a car. I hate taking this bus every day. I'm late to first period like fifty percent of the time."

"Me too," Pippa said.

"There it is," Kari-Anne shouted, pointing to the bus as it turned the corner down the street. She waved her arms until the bus stopped directly in front of them.

The door opened, and all three girls stepped on the bus. They swiped the bus passes supplied by the school district and headed to the back.

The bus wasn't crowded yet, but their stop was one of the first on this route, and it would be standing-room only when they got to school.

Aldercreek didn't have many buses. Most of the people who lived there were wealthy and drove their own cars, so it didn't make much sense to the people who ran the city to pay for a bunch of buses. The ones they did have took long routes and were painfully overcrowded.

Kari-Anne laid her head on Autumn's shoulder. "I'm hungry," she said, clutching her stomach.

"Me too," Autumn said, wrapping her arm around Kari-Anne's shoulder. "Make sure you eat breakfast and lunch at school. After school, we'll go to the grocery store and get some food for dinner."

"Did Mama give you money for food since she's going to be out tonight?" Kari-Anne asked.

Autumn shook her head. "Don't you worry about it. I'm going to figure something out."

.   .   .

AUTUMN LOOKED at her watch as she walked quickly down the empty halls of the high school. She had gotten there so late that she'd missed breakfast entirely. Her stomach groaned loudly. Rubbing her belly, she willed it to stop making noises.

She walked up to Mr. Robertson's classroom and peered in the window. His back was to the class as he put a new math equation on the whiteboard. Now was her chance to sneak in unnoticed.

Glancing around the room, she noticed an empty seat next to Mitch, the captain of the football team and the hottest guy in school. She'd had a crush on him since they were both freshmen, but she'd never had the courage to even say hi to him.

Her heart raced. Now was her chance. Today, she was going to be brave. Mr. Robertson's voice filled the room. She walked as quietly as she could towards the empty seat.

"Nice of you to join us, Ms. Jones," Mr. Robertson said without even turning around.

"I'm so sorry," Autumn said quietly as she sank into the empty seat.

"I believe that's three times this week," Mr. Robertson said as he turned and stared at her. "Part of our job here is to teach you how to be successful when you enter the workforce, and being on time is crucial to your success."

Heat rushed to her cheeks as she sank even lower in her chair. "I know. It won't happen again," she lied, knowing full well she might be late again tomorrow.

Mitch leaned over and whispered to her. "You should just tell him."

She looked over at him in surprise. "Tell him what?"

He smirked. "I've been paying attention to you for a long time. I've seen you get off that city bus. You should just tell him that the bus is the reason you're late."

"I..." she stammered. "You've been watching me?"

"Of course I have," he said with a grin. "You're one of the prettiest girls in school. I just don't think you know it."

She quickly looked away from him, embarrassed. The warmth in her cheeks intensified.

"Today, I will give you a pop quiz on everything we've learned this week."

The entire class groaned.

"Did I also mention that you're one of the smartest girls in school?" Mitch asked.

Autumn looked at him in surprise.

"Would you mind if I looked at your paper while we're taking this quiz? Please?" He asked.

Autumn stared into his eyes and melted. She nodded. "Just don't get caught."

He shook his head. "Never. I'm a pro at this."

Her heart beat wildly as she worked on her test. Mitch Mitre knew who she was.

81

AUTUMN (PAST)

"Mama, what are you doing?" Autumn asked. She wore an oversized T-shirt and shorts, and she stood at the kitchen's entrance, rubbing the sleep from her eyes. "What time is it?"

Autumn's mother, Janice, was in the kitchen with a guy Autumn had never seen before. She glanced at the microwave clock, her hands on her hips. "It's three a.m., Mama. Why are you being so loud? You know we have to go to school in the morning."

Janice walked over to Autumn and wrapped an arm around her shoulders. Her breath reeked of alcohol, and she slurred her words. "Autumn, I want you to meet my new boyfriend, Jason."

Jason walked towards Autumn to shake her hand, but she ignored him.

"Mama, you can't just keep bringing strange people into the house in the middle of the night like this. It's not safe."

"You don't get to tell me what to do, Autumn. I'm a grown woman."

"You don't act like it," Autumn said under her breath.

"What did you say?" Janice asked, anger flaring in her eyes.

"Nothing, Mama. I don't want to get in a fight with you tonight."

"Well, I think it's kinda too late. You already started one."

"Fine." If her mama wanted to fight, she wasn't going to back down. "What kind of grown woman stays out all night while her children are at home starving? What kind of grown woman brings a complete stranger into the home where her minor children are sleeping? Does that sound like a grown woman to you?"

"You better watch what you say to me, Autumn."

"Or what, Mama?" She said, standing tall and challenging her mother to show her true colors.

Janice raised her hand to slap Autumn across the face, but Jason grabbed her arm and pulled her away. "Baby, don't do that. We have to get going."

"Get going?" Autumn asked as she glanced back and forth between Jason and Janice.

"I'll be in the car. Don't be too long," Jason said as he walked out of the kitchen.

Janice's anger seemed to dissipate, and a small smile formed on her lips. "Jason is taking me to Vegas for a while."

"What?" Autumn asked in shock. "You're leaving?"

"I'll be back in a few weeks, probably."

"A few weeks? Are you leaving us any money for food? How am I supposed to take care of Kari-Anne? I'm not even an adult yet, Mama."

Janice opened her purse and pulled out a twenty-dollar bill. "Here, take this for food."

Autumn stared at it in shock. "Are you serious?"

Jason honked the horn.

"I gotta go. Be good. Take care of your sister," Janice said, giving Autumn an awkward hug. Autumn didn't raise her arms to hug her back.

"Twenty dollars. That's it? Do you have any concept of what it costs just to buy a bag of groceries? Do you honestly think twenty dollars is going to cut it?"

"You'll figure it out," Janice said as she rushed out the front door and slammed it behind her.

Autumn stared at the door as she heard the car pull away from the trailer and into the night.

At the end of the hallway, Kari-Anne stood in her doorway, wrapped in her robe, her eyes wide. Her mama left without even saying goodbye. She is pretty sure she's never coming back. Tears stung her eyes, but she wiped them away angrily. How could she have done this to them? How could she have cared so little? From that day on, Kari-Anne vowed never to cry over her mama again.

THE NEXT FEW weeks were stressful for Autumn. Most of the twenty dollars her mom gave her was gone within twenty-four hours, even though Autumn did her best at the grocery store to stretch it. She was able to buy enough food for a couple of days, but she knew it wouldn't be enough.

That weekend, she took the bus to a grocery store on the other side of town. She wore a huge sweatshirt, one big enough to fit a bag underneath it. She wandered the grocery store and stuffed items under her shirt into her bag when no one was watching her. When the bag was full, she walked down the candy aisle and grabbed a chocolate bar. She had to look like a legitimate customer to avoid appearing suspicious.

She walked up to the cashier, her heart pounding in her ears, and placed the candy bar on the belt.

"Is that everything for you today?" the cashier asked, a bored expression on her face.

"Yup, that's it," Autumn said.

She paid for the candy bar and tried not to exit the store too quickly. The last thing she needed was to get caught on her way out.

Relief flooded her body as she stepped back onto the city bus without anyone chasing her. She did it. This food should tide them over for a few days, but she knew she'd need to figure out something else. Stealing didn't feel right to her.

82

AUTUMN (PAST)

Autumn walked into math class on Monday feeling better than she had felt in weeks.

Mitch waved at her, and her heart fluttered.

They'd been sitting next to each other in math class every day since the day he cheated on her test. He pretended like he didn't know what he was doing and constantly asked her for help, but Autumn knew better. She'd seen his homework, and it was always done correctly. She played along, though, because she liked the attention.

Mr. Robertson was writing on the board. "Next Thursday will be our unit seven test on three-dimensional solids. I will be posting a study guide for you on my website by the end of the day today."

Mitch leaned over and whispered in Autumn's ear. "What do you think about being my tutor?"

Autumn looked at him, her eyes wide. "Don't you have a girlfriend or something? Would she be okay with that?"

"Yeah, she'll be fine with it," he said dismissively. "This will be strictly business. I'll even pay you to show you how serious I am about this."

"You would give me money to tutor you?"

"Yeah, of course. How does twenty dollars an hour sound?"

Autumn hesitated; she could really use the money, and twenty dollars an hour was more than minimum wage.

"Fine, you drive a hard bargain. Twenty-five dollars an hour, final offer."

Autumn swallowed hard. "Yeah, okay. Deal," she said, shaking her head.

"Excellent," Mitch said, grabbing her hand to shake it.

Autumn laughed.

"Do the two of you have something you want to share with the rest of the class?" Mr. Robertson asked.

Autumn looked around and noticed the rest of the class was staring at them. Her cheeks flushed.

"Autumn has agreed to be my math tutor. I'm going to ace this test," Mitch said, a huge grin on his face.

Over the next several weeks, Autumn and Mitch met for an hour each day after school to work on their math homework and study together. True to his word, Mitch gave her twenty-five dollars in cash for each lesson.

At first, they met at the school library. Autumn made every effort to remain very professional, but she couldn't help but fall for him despite the fact that he had a girlfriend. He was funny and charming. He never made her feel bad because she rode the city bus to school and didn't have the designer clothes and shoes most of the kids at school wore. He made her feel like she mattered.

The day after the unit seven test, Mr. Robertson returned the test scores to the class. Both she and Mitch got A's.

"Nice work, you two. The study sessions are paying off for you, Mr. Mitre."

Mitch beamed at Autumn. "Let's celebrate this afternoon. I mean, we can still study, and I'll still pay you, but let's do it at Charlie's."

"Yeah, okay," Autumn said, not even hesitating. "You'll have to give me a ride to my sister's school after. I have to ride the bus home with her."

"Deal," he said as he wrapped an arm around her.

Butterflies formed in her stomach.

From that day on, the study sessions were held at Charlie's instead of the library. Mitch not only paid her twenty-five dollars, but he also bought her whatever she wanted to eat while they were there. She'd always get a meal and only eat half of it, pretending she was full, when in reality, she'd saved half for her sister.

Mitch and Autumn talked about everything, and she was surprised to find out how much they had in common. After a while, she and Mitch did very little math together and spent most of their study sessions talking about other things.

One day, as they were splitting a chocolate milkshake, Mitch abruptly stopped drinking and looked at her. "Hey, have you ever been to the watchtower at the top of the hill?"

Autumn shook her head. "I don't really get out much," she said.

"I'm going to take you there. You can see the whole town. It's amazing."

"But what about Liv?"

He waved his hand. "I'm thinking about breaking up with her anyway. I just want to get to know you better."

She hesitated. She didn't want to come between Mitch and Liv, but she couldn't help herself. Over the weeks, she fell madly in love with Mitch, and she wanted nothing more than for him to break up with Liv and be with her. "Okay," she said. "I'll give you my address. Pick me up at ten. My sister should be asleep by then, and I can sneak out."

A huge smile spread across his face, and he gave her a quick kiss on her cheek.

"Stop," she said. "Someone is going to see us."

"You're right," he said, backing away. "We have to be discreet. At least for now."

She nodded as a small pit formed in her stomach. What was she getting herself into?

83

AUTUMN (PAST)

The night was still. No wind was blowing, and the animals were surprisingly quiet. Autumn stood by the front window of her trailer, her nerves threatening to overwhelm her. Why did she tell Mitch to meet her here? Once he saw where she lived, she was fairly certain he would turn around and drive the other way.

She ran to the bathroom and checked her image in the mirror for probably the fiftieth time. She wore her best teal dress, one of the only pieces of clothing her mama actually bought for her before she left for Vegas. Most of her clothing came from donations delivered to the trailer park once a month.

Her brown skin was glowing, and her hair was pulled back into a sleek bun. She sighed and talked to herself in the mirror. "This is your one chance. Don't screw it up."

A horn honked from the front of her house.

"Shoot, he's going to wake Kari-Anne."

She ran to the front door, carefully opening and shutting it as quietly as possible. She locked the door and ran to the car. The driver's side window was rolled down, and Mitch smiled at her. His white teeth and dimples made her stomach do flip-flops.

"You can't honk the horn like that. You're going to wake my sister," Autumn said in a loud whisper.

"You look amazing," Mitch said, completely ignoring her request.

Heat rose to her cheeks. "Thank you," she said shyly.

"Get in. Let's get out of here."

Autumn ran around to the passenger side and slid in. Before she was even buckled, Mitch put the car in reverse and barreled out of the trailer park.

KARI-ANNE (PAST)

I nside the trailer, the sound of a car horn woke Kari-Anne. Bleary-eyed, she ran to her bedroom window and peered into the night. She watched as Autumn ran to a car. Kari-Anne tried to make out who it was, but it was too dark.

She stood in her bedroom and watched until the tail-lights completely disappeared. Fear and sadness washed over her as she lay back down on her bed and tried to fall back asleep.

AUTUMN (PAST)

Over the next few weeks, in addition to their regular tutoring sessions, Autumn and Mitch saw each other several more times after she thought Kari-Anne was asleep. They went to the drive-in movie theater, a small park just outside of town that overlooked the Puget Sound, and a diner in the next town over — all places where they could avoid being seen by people they knew.

Mitch never pushed her to do anything physically that she didn't want to do. He wrapped his arm around her shoulders and held her hand, but he didn't try to kiss her or anything like that. It seemed like he really respected her boundaries. At least, that's what she told herself. Aside from the fact that he still had a girlfriend, Autumn thought he was pretty perfect, and she fell for him hard.

Nearly a month after their first date, they met at the local diner as usual for their tutoring session. Autumn arrived first and placed their standing order: a chicken sandwich with a salad for her and a bacon double cheeseburger with fries for Mitch. Of course, she planned to steal a few of his fries. After ordering, she sat in the booth and waited.

Five minutes later, Mitch strolled into the diner. The moment he saw Autumn, a huge smile erupted on his face. He slid into the booth and immediately placed a hand on her thigh.

Autumn glanced around the room nervously. "What are you doing? What if someone sees us?"

"I'm not sure I care if someone sees us," he said.

"What about your girlfriend?" She hissed.

He shrugged. "I'm going to break up with her. I want to be with you."

She snapped her head to look at him. "Are you serious?"

He nodded. "You're way prettier than her and way more fun. I've only stayed with her because she's the most popular girl in school and it's good for my image, but she's actually pretty mean and I don't think I care about my image anymore."

Autumn's stomach twisted into knots. Mitch really wanted to be her boyfriend.

He grabbed her chin and gently forced her to look at him. "Would you want to be my girlfriend?"

She tried to think of something to say, but her mind drew a blank as she stared into his handsome, questioning eyes. She nodded.

A grin formed on his face. "Good."

The waitress delivered their food. Autumn and Mitch sat in silence as they ate. Once they both finished, she turned slightly toward him. "Ready to do our homework?"

He nodded. "I don't think this one should take very long."

Twenty minutes later, after they finished their last question, Mitch reached into his pocket and pulled out his wallet.

Autumn put up her hand and pushed the wallet away. "You don't need to pay me anymore. It doesn't seem right. It feels like you're buying my time. I don't like it. I would be sitting here spending time with you if you didn't pay me a cent."

He grabbed her hand and gently set it on her lap. "Of course, I'm going to still pay you. You need the money. You know I've seen where you live. Don't you think I haven't noticed you never bring your own food to school? You're always eating that nasty cafeteria food. I watch you. I can tell you don't like it. Take the money, Autumn."

Tears stung her eyes in utter embarrassment. Why did this have to be her life? Why did her mother have to leave her to take care of Kari-Anne by herself? It wasn't fair. She thought about her sister and how empty the fridge was at home, and the shame burned her face almost like fire.

She looked over at Mitch. He stared at her earnestly. His right hand held his wallet while he brought his left hand to her cheek. "Let me help you," he whispered.

She sighed. "I wish I didn't need the help, but fine."

He immediately opened his wallet and pulled out a wad of cash.

Autumn's eyes widened as she watched him count out ten one-hundred-dollar bills. "What are you doing? I can't take that."

He grabbed her hand and shoved the money into her palm. "You need it. As you can see, I have plenty."

She shook her head and tried to give the money back. "Mitch, I'm not your charity case. I can't accept all this money. I will take what I have earned and nothing more."

He grabbed her wrist and held it firmly.

She glanced in surprise at his tight grip. "You're hurting me."

He ignored her. "You're taking the money, Autumn. You need it. I have it. It's as simple as that. You're not a charity case, but I refuse to watch you and your sister go hungry. I care about you too much."

She stared at him, her mind a whirlwind of thoughts and emotions. She knew he was trying to do something nice for her, but the force with which he was doing it made her feel uncomfortable, almost as if he was bullying her into accepting.

He held her wrist even tighter, and the look on his face told Autumn that he wasn't going to take no for an answer.

"Fine," she said reluctantly. "I'll take it."

He released her wrist, and the relaxed, happy grin returned to his face. "That's my girl," he said as he watched her put the cash in her purse.

She grabbed her sore wrist and rubbed it as she stared back at him warily. She wasn't so sure she liked the person she just saw. Maybe it was a fluke. He really cared about her and Kari-Anne and didn't want them to starve. That's admirable, right? She pushed aside her feelings and allowed herself to be with this Mitch, the kind, caring, and gentle Mitch she'd been falling for, but she could not let go of that kernel of doubt.

AUTUMN (PAST)

Autumn's thoughts were restless the rest of the night. Her mind replayed the incident in the diner over and over. She tried to convince herself Mitch cared for her and he would never hurt her, but the image of him forcefully grabbing her wrist plagued her mind. She tossed and turned in her bed, trying to make sense of it.

Each time she replayed the incident, she convinced herself that she was overreacting. When the alarm went off at six the next morning, she had buried the doubts about Mitch far in the recesses of her mind.

She arrived at school fifteen minutes before the bell rang. The city bus was early today. She and Kari-Anne had barely walked out their door when they saw it turning the corner in front of the trailer park. They had run screaming and waving their arms, barely getting to the street before the bus drove past.

She walked towards her locker at the end of the math hallway. It was amazing how empty the halls were. Most students arrived with only a few minutes to spare. With so few people crowded around her, Autumn felt exposed. She held her backpack straps and walked down the hall quickly, hoping to avoid being seen. Ever since she started seeing Mitch, she'd been afraid of someone finding out. They did their best to go places where they would not be seen, but it was always a risk.

A locker door slammed as she turned the corner. She looked toward the sound, and her mouth went dry. Liv was staring at her, an angry look on her face. Autumn backed up slightly and walked towards the other side of the hall. Liv stepped towards her, blocking her path.

"Excuse me," Autumn said, trying to avoid looking at her. "I'm trying to get to my locker."

"That can wait," Liv quipped back.

Reluctantly, Autumn stopped and looked at her. "Do you need something?"

"Yeah, I need you to stay away from my boyfriend."

"I... I..." Autumn stammered.

"I know you're helping him with his math homework or whatever, but don't think I don't see you."

"I'm just his tutor."

"Whatever the case is, just know that you'll never be good enough for him. I have the whole package. Not only am I smart and pretty, but I have enough money to make things happen for us. You're just trailer trash."

Tears formed in Autumn's eyes, and she fought desperately to hold them back. She would not give this girl the satisfaction of seeing her cry.

Liv stared at her for a few more seconds before stepping aside. "You need to stop tutoring him. I don't care what you tell him, but I don't want to see you with him again."

Autumn silently walked past. She clenched her jaw as

tightly as possible, willing the tears to stay put. There was no way she was going to allow Liv to dictate her life.

Later that night, Mitch picked Autumn up from her house as usual.

"Where are we going tonight?" She asked.

"I thought we'd go get ice cream at the mall."

"Are you serious? Don't you think that's too public?"

He shrugged. "Maybe. I'm not sure I care anymore, to be honest. We can go to the mall on the other side of town if that would make you feel better."

Autumn stared at him for a long time. "I just don't want the kids at school to think I'm some kind of bad person for being with you while you're still with Liv. I thought you were going to break up with her."

He sighed and ran his fingers through his hair. "I am. It's just not that simple. The moment I end things, my life is going to be miserable. She's not the type of person whose bad side you want to get on. I have to do it gently. Better yet, I need to make it seem like her idea."

"Fine," she said, crossing her arms. "I just don't want to hide like this forever."

Mitch put his hand on top of hers and grinned. "You wanna be my girlfriend?"

She rolled her eyes and shoved him playfully. "Shut up. Just drive."

He laughed while putting his car in reverse. "You're cute when you're angry."

They pulled out of the trailer park onto the main road. A car that had been parked on the side of the road with its lights off turned them on and pulled onto the road behind them.

Autumn eyed the car suspiciously in the rearview mirror. Ten minutes later, the same car was still behind them. It made every turn they made, always staying about two car lengths behind. "Mitch, I think that car behind us is following us."

He looked into the rearview mirror. "Why do you think that?"

"It's been there since we left my house."

His brows creased. "I doubt they're following us. We've mostly been on main roads. It's possible they legitimately had to go the same direction."

"Maybe," Autumn said, still unconvinced.

"I'll try to lose them. If they are following us, it should become pretty obvious."

Mitch took several unexpected turns. The car made the first two turns with them but didn't make the third.

"See," he said. "You're just being paranoid."

She looked in the rearview mirror. Even though the car wasn't there, she still had a nagging feeling that something was wrong.

Five minutes later, they arrived at the strip mall with the ice cream parlor. The parking lot was empty except for a single car parked in front of the shop. Not many people ate ice cream in the winter.

Mitch parked the car at the far end of the strip mall, several stores away from the ice cream shop.

"Why are you parking here? There are plenty of spaces over there by the store."

"'Cause I want to walk with you and hold your hand. Got a problem with that?"

Autumn shook her head. "Are you sure?"

"Positive."

They got out of the car, and Mitch walked around to her, grabbing her hand. Butterflies filled her stomach.

"I'm going to break up with her this week. I promise. Just give me a couple of days," he said quietly.

She nodded. "Okay."

Several minutes later, Mitch and Autumn walked out of the shop with waffle cones in their hands.

"Let's go that way," Mitch pointed away from the direction they had parked.

"We're going to freeze to death eating these out here," Autumn said, gesturing to their cones.

"Come on, be adventurous," he replied.

She chuckled. "Fine."

They walked away from their car, shivering as they took bites of their ice cream.

The sound of footsteps echoed on the pavement behind them.

Autumn stopped. The footsteps stopped. "Do you hear that?"

"What?" Mitch said, oblivious.

"I think someone might be following us again. First the car and now I'm hearing footsteps behind us."

Mitch glanced back. "There's no one there."

Autumn looked and confirmed the walkway was empty. "I guess I'm just being paranoid. I don't want to become the laughingstock of the town."

He grabbed her hand. "I told you I would do it this week, and I meant it."

She nodded. She wanted to believe him, but she wasn't sure she did. They kept walking. The sound of footsteps behind them resumed. They both stopped abruptly and turned around. There was no one there.

She looked at Mitch. "What do you want to do?"

He squeezed her hand. "Whatever you feel is best. I don't care what people think."

"I think we should just go home."

"Home it is then," he said and turned back toward the car.

Autumn hated that their night had been cut short, but she knew it was for the best. Their time would come.

87

AUTUMN (PAST)

The next day, Mitch slipped into his seat next to Autumn in math class just thirty seconds before the bell was supposed to ring.

"Hey, you," he said with a grin.

She glanced at him. The feelings of unease from the previous night still haunted her. She didn't think she could do this anymore. "Hey," she said quietly.

"You look nice today."

"Mitch, I..." Before she could finish, the bell rang, and Mr. Robertson asked for everyone's attention.

Autumn opened her notebook and tore out a piece of paper. She scribbled a note and passed it to Mitch.

I need to see you. Tonight.

He quickly wrote back. *R u ok?*

No, we need to talk.

I have a game tonight. I'll be there at eleven.

Autumn nodded once and focused on Mr. Robertson. She didn't want to bring anything up here, so she did her best to ignore Mitch for the rest of the period. He made it difficult. He played footsies with her and tried to grab her hand multiple times, but each time, she moved away. She couldn't do this anymore. She couldn't be the hidden secret. Either he chose her, or they stopped this altogether.

At ten-thirty, when she was certain Kari-Anne was asleep, Autumn got ready to meet Mitch. She carefully did her hair and put on her best dress. Her hands shook as she applied her mascara. What if Mitch chose Liv? Even though he had promised to break up with her that week, there was a distinct possibility it had all been empty words meant to string Autumn along. Her heart constricted at the thought.

Five minutes after eleven, she watched from the front window as Mitch pulled his car to the front of her trailer. The headlights shone brightly through the window, illuminating the wall behind her. She quickly rushed out the front door before he could honk the horn and opened the passenger side door.

"Where do you want to go?" He asked.

"Let's go to the lake," she suggested. "There are no clouds out. We should be able to see a ton of stars."

He nodded and put his car in reverse. "Is everything okay?"

"I hope so," she said quietly, looking out the window.

As the car backed up, the headlights illuminated Kari-Anne's window. Autumn stared at it and turned to Mitch. "We can't be gone long. No more than an hour. I don't want Kari-Anne to wake up and find me gone."

"We always go out at night, and nothing's ever happened. Why are you worried now?"

"I don't know," she said. "I just feel kinda weird tonight. I don't know why."

"Okay," he said. "An hour it is."

Mitch put the car in drive and turned the wheel. The

headlights slowly moved to the right, illuminating Kari-Anne's window. Autumn looked away into the dark. Just as she did, the curtains in the window ruffled as Kari-Anne poked her head through and pressed her forehead against the glass.

88

KARI-ANNE (PAST)

K ari-Anne opened her eyes. The sun streamed brightly through her window, and she rolled over to look at her clock. It read *9:30*. Kari-Anne jumped out of bed. Why didn't her sister wake her up?

She ran to Autumn's room, which used to belong to their mother and knocked on the door. "Autumn, are you awake?"

There was no answer.

"Autumn? Open the door."

Still no answer.

Kari-Anne turned the handle and opened the door. Autumn's bed was still made.

A loud knock sounded on the front door. Kari-Anne ran to the window.

Standing outside the door were two police officers. "Police, is anyone home?" One of them shouted.

Kari-Anne slowly walked to the front door and opened it.

"Hello," a female officer said. "Is your mom home?"

Kari-Anne shook her head. "She hasn't been here in a long time."

"You're home alone?"

"My sister takes care of me, but she didn't come home last night."

Tears filled the officer's eyes, but she did not let them escape. "Can we come in?"

Kari-Anne nodded and let them inside.

"What's your name?" the female officer asked.

"Kari-Anne," she said quietly.

"Kari-Anne, I'm Officer Jones, and this is Officer Burt. Can we sit down?"

Kari-Anne nodded and pointed to the worn-out brown couch. She sat on the old chair across from the couch as both officers sat.

"This is not something I would normally tell a young girl, but since you are Autumn's only relative, I guess I have to. We found Autumn this morning in a stolen car."

"What?" Kari-Anne asked, confused. "Autumn wouldn't do that."

"That's not all," the officer continued. "The car was found in the lake."

"Why was she in the lake? Is she okay?" Kari-Anne asked, her heart racing.

"We think she got high and fell asleep with the car on and accidentally drove the car into the lake. I'm sorry, Kari-Anne."

"What are you sorry about?"

"Your sister... Your sister is dead."

"No," Kari-Anne whispered. "She's... No. You must have the wrong person. Autumn would never steal a car. She can't be dead."

"Her purse was found in the car with her. We know it's her," the officer said softly.

Kari-Anne shook her head. "No, she didn't do drugs

either. She always said people who did drugs ruined their lives."

The officer stood and wrapped her arms around her shoulders.

She shoved her off. "You're wrong. She didn't do any of that stuff."

"Sometimes, we don't know people like we think we do. I'm so sorry."

"No, you have to listen to me. Why would she steal a car? She doesn't even know how to drive. Besides, my mom left her car here. It's out front. She had no reason to steal one."

The officers stared at her, pity in their eyes. Their pity made Kari-Anne even angrier. She continued. "There was a guy who picked her up last night in his car," she said desperately, her whole body shaking. "His name is Mitch. He did this to her. You have to believe me," she screamed.

Officer Jones held her tightly as she sobbed. Officer Burt stood awkwardly next to the door.

Kari-Anne wanted to say more, but she knew it was pointless. She was just a kid. They would never listen to her.

"Kari-Anne, you're going to be okay," Officer Jones said quietly.

Kari-Anne knew she wasn't going to be okay. Nothing was ever going to be okay.

89

KARI-ANNE (PAST)

Aside from a social worker, a priest, and a few men who worked at the graveyard, Kari-Anne was the only one at Autumn's funeral. Not even her mother showed up. Not that she had expected her to; she hadn't seen or heard from her in months. She wasn't even sure she was still alive.

It was a gray and cloudy day. The cold wind blew steadily, whipping around her body like an invisible current. She pulled her thin coat tightly around her as she watched her sister's body being lowered into the ground.

As the casket disappeared into the dirt, she didn't cry. She was too angry to cry. She wanted to scream, but she didn't do that either. What would be the point?

After the police had left that day, she had tried desperately to tell anyone she knew about Mitch and Autumn. About how he picked her up that night from their house, but no one would listen. They kept telling her that Mitch had a girlfriend and that she must have been mistaken about what she saw, but she knew she hadn't. That knowledge festered inside of her like a cancer.

Kari-Anne stood next to the grave until the last shovelful of dirt was placed on top of Autumn, and everyone but the social worker had left.

"Kari-Anne," the woman said gently. "It's time to go."

She didn't respond. She grabbed the black sweatshirt with *1989* silkscreened in big, white numbers from the seat next to her. It was the only thing found on Autumn's body that Kari-Anne had wanted. She hugged it to her chest and walked straight toward the car. That day, she vowed to get justice for Autumn. She wasn't sure how or when she was going to do it, but she knew she wouldn't rest until it was complete.

KARI-ANNE BOUNCED from foster home to foster home for the next few years. She never wanted to be adopted. Anytime it seemed like someone was considering it, she would try to run away or steal something from them. She did anything she could think of to change their minds. Her sister had been her family, and no one could ever replace her. Finally, when she was thirteen, they placed her in a group home for teenagers who had not been adopted.

She knew that if she was ever going to get justice for Autumn, she would have to be smart, so she threw herself into school. It wasn't enough to be a straight-A student; she had to be at the top of her class. She often stayed extra hours when necessary to meet with her teachers just to gain that competitive edge. It was more than a want; it was a need. She was like a sponge, soaking up everything she learned, always craving more.

When she turned sixteen, the group home allowed her more freedom on the weekends. She could go and do whatever she wanted as long as she was back by nine p.m. She often took the bus to Seattle at six a.m. to wander around the city all day.

Her favorite place to go was the library. It was the strangest, most beautiful building she'd ever seen. To get to the reading room on the top floor, she had to walk through a long, dimly lit corridor. The floor, the ceiling and the walls were covered in a shiny coat of red paint. She felt at home in that hallway as it reflected her rage. At the top of a staircase at the end of the hallway was a reading room on the library's top floor. The walls sloped from the ground to several stories above the floor and were entirely made of diamond-shaped windows. There were tables and chairs near the windows overlooking the city. The moment when she walked out of the red corridor into the vast space always made her feel free.

The library offered all sorts of free programs on the weekends, especially for teenagers, and she took advantage of all of them. She took free coding classes, art classes and attended several lectures. It didn't matter what the topic was; she wanted to know everything.

One day, she attended a lecture at the library given by a psychology professor from the University of Washington on motivation and achieving your goals.

Kari-Anne sat in the front row with her notebook in her hand, sticking out like a sore thumb. Most of the attendees were middle-aged professionals trying to learn how to get ahead in their careers. She was the youngest there by at least fifteen years.

After the lecture, the professor walked straight toward her as she frantically scribbled everything she could remember in her journal.

"It's not very often that I see a young person in my lectures. Most of them are out having fun on the weekends."

Kari-Anne looked up in surprise. "Are you talking to me?"

He chuckled. "Yes, my dear. I'm Professor Martin, but I suppose you can just call me Albert."

Kari-Anne stood quickly and accepted Albert's hand. "Nice to meet you, Albert. I'm Kari-Anne. I really enjoyed your lecture."

"What are you doing here on a Saturday? I'm sure you have friends you could be hanging out with."

She shook her head. "Not really. Besides, I love learning. I attend all the free lectures I can."

He stared at her for several seconds, and his eyes felt like they were boring into her soul. She squirmed under his gaze.

"Well, Kari-Anne, I don't normally do this, but something tells me you're going to do great things one of these days. Would you like to come to work for me on the weekends at the university?"

"Excuse me?" She said.

"I'm asking if you'd like a job. I'd pay you, of course, but I could use a research assistant, and something tells me you'd be an excellent help."

She stared at him, not quite sure if he was being sincere. His eyes held hers, unwavering and kind. He could have ill intentions, but she didn't think so. She took a chance. "Yes, I would love that."

KARI-ANNE (PAST)

K ari-Anne started the following weekend and worked with Albert for four hours each day. It wasn't easy at first. He tasked her with finding and summarizing articles related to his current research. Finding the articles was easy. Writing a summary that met his high, exacting standards proved to be a different challenge.

Initially, she would rewrite the same summary two to three times before getting it right. First, it would be too long and contain too many details. Then, she would scale it way too far back, and it would be too vague. The professor was always patient with her but firm. Under his tutelage, she began to grow. Within a few months, she was getting it right on the first try.

When the weather grew cold, it became difficult for Kari-Anne to hide her threadbare clothes and shoes. One day, snow was on the ground, and she came to work wearing tennis shoes and a thin coat.

He looked at her, concerned. "Do you have nothing warmer to wear?"

She shook her head in embarrassment, and a sad look flashed in his eyes.

"Come with me. This will never do."

She followed him out of his office. He stopped at his secretary's desk. Gina was a thirty-something, warm, motherly type of woman.

He looked at her. "Gina, grab your coat. We're going shopping."

She looked at him in surprise but immediately got up and grabbed her coat.

They spent the next few hours selecting armfuls of warm clothes and shoes at a local department store. Kari-Anne had never had such nice things. When they were checking out, her eyes widened in surprise at the total.

"It's too much," she said. She began to grab several items off the counter to return to the racks.

"Stop," Albert said. "This is my money. I will choose how I'm going to spend it."

Her eyes filled with tears. "I can never pay you back for all this."

"You don't have to. Now put that stuff down so this nice lady can ring them up."

She nodded. Hot tears filled her eyes.

Gina wrapped her arms around Kari-Anne's shoulders. "He really cares about you, you know that?"

She buried her face in Gina's shoulder and allowed the tears to slip out of her eyes silently.

"How about some lunch?" the professor asked, clearly uncomfortable with all the emotion.

He took them to a small pub on Capitol Hill. It was nothing special, just a cozy, local spot that served good food. When they walked through the front door, it took Kari-Anne's eyes a few seconds to adjust to the darkness, but once they did, she looked around and liked what she saw. The wood floors and bar brought warmth to the small space. The booths that lined the walls were cozy and inviting.

"Professor!" the bartender said in greeting to Albert.

"Good afternoon, Jeremiah," he responded. "Please bring us a few menus."

"Of course, sir," Jeremiah replied, quickly grabbing a stack of menus and showing them to a booth near the front window. "Looks like your spot is open, sir," he said, setting the menus down on the table.

"Thank you," Albert said. "Who's cooking today? I haven't seen the schedule yet."

Kari-Anne looked at him quizzically.

"Elizabeth," Jeremiah said.

"Excellent. You two are in for a treat," he said to Kari-Anne and Gina.

"Let me know when you're ready to order. I'll be sure to let Elizabeth know you're here."

Albert sat across from Kari-Anne and Gina in the booth. Kari-Anne looked at him, confused. "Why would you look at the schedule?"

"Well, my dear. Because I own this place."

A look of shock crossed both Kari-Anne's and Gina's faces.

"What? How?" Kari-Anne asked.

"My uncle built this place in the fifties. When he passed away several years ago, I was his only living relative, so the place was left to me. I considered selling it, but it means so much to this neighborhood and these people. So, I figured out how to make it work. It basically runs itself now. I barely have to do anything, and I get all the free food I want," he said with a huge grin.

"I love it," Kari-Anne said. "It feels like home."

THROUGHOUT HIGH SCHOOL, Kari-Anne loved working for Albert. He was always kind to her. Occasionally, she would find a large brown paper bag sitting on her desk when she arrived at work, filled with clothes, shoes, and various other items that he knew she needed for school. He pretended to know nothing about the clothes, but she always knew they were from him.

By the time she graduated, he had become like a father to her. In fact, he was the only one who showed up to her high school graduation.

"I'm so proud of you, Kari-Anne," Albert said when she found him in the crowd after the ceremony.

"I couldn't have done it without you. In fact, I couldn't have gotten into college without you. I owe you so much."

"Stop it," Albert said. "You worked hard and deserved everything you've received. Valedictorian? I didn't do that for you. You could have gotten into any school you wanted without my help."

"Maybe that's true, but you're the reason I received a full ride. I don't know what strings you had to pull, but I can never repay you."

"You made it easy, my dear. Just look at your resume. How could they not want you?"

Heat rose to her cheeks as she wrapped her arms around him. He felt frail. It was as if he was wasting away. She took a step back and looked him in the eyes. "Is everything okay, Albert? Are you well?"

"Never better," he said, dismissing her.

She looked at him skeptically but let it go. "I just wish Autumn had been here to see me."

He patted her shoulder. "You know she is watching you and is so proud of all you have accomplished."

She nodded her head, knowing he was right. Still, the grief threatened to consume her.

Albert could tell she was about to sink into a dark hole. "Should we go to the pub to celebrate? Jeremiah has been asking about you."

She nodded eagerly, pushing thoughts of Autumn aside. "I've been dreaming about Elizabeth's grilled cheese for days," she said, a small smile forming on her lips.

KARI-ANNE EXCELLED IN COLLEGE. She was always at the top of every class she took, no matter the subject. It wasn't that she was the smartest student in the room, but she was always the most driven. She was on a mission to avenge Autumn, and learning as much as she could, she believed, would give her a necessary edge, especially since she couldn't rely on the police.

She continued to work for Albert several days a week. She watched as he became frail and weak. "Albert, you need to see a doctor," she told him one day after she had hugged him and felt only skin and bones underneath his wool sweater.

"I'm fine," he said dismissively. "If it's my time, it's my time. I'm not going to the doctor just to have them pump me with drugs to try and keep me alive beyond my time."

She looked at him sadly. This man was like a father to her, and she was watching him waste away.

"Please, Albert. Maybe it's something easy to fix, like a vitamin deficiency."

He stared at her for a long time and finally acquiesced. "Fine. For you, I'll go."

It wasn't a vitamin deficiency. Albert was diagnosed with stage four pancreatic cancer. He refused any kind of treatment except for pain medication as he neared the end. He was gone two months after he was diagnosed.

Kari-Anne felt the pain of losing Autumn all over again. Why did the only people she cared about have to die?

WHEN THE ADMINISTRATOR of Albert's estate read his will, she was shocked to find out that he left everything to her — his stock portfolio, his condo on Capitol Hill, and the pub. All of it was now hers. He'd lived a simple life and had amassed over a million dollars in stocks alone. Kari-Anne would never have to worry again. If only she could have shared it with Autumn.

91

EDEN (PRESENT)

I stare at the frozen lake, wishing my sister would walk across it and that all of this would have been a terrible dream, but the lake is still and quiet. The cold from the ice chills me to the bone. I open the car door and grab the black sweatshirt with *1989* printed on the front — my sister's sweatshirt. I've kept it with me all these years as a reminder of her. "I'm so sorry, Autumn," I whisper.

How have I been so wrong this entire time? Since the day Autumn died, I've been on a mission to destroy Mitch, but he's not even the one who killed her. His biggest sin back then was cheating on Liv and keeping her secrets when she *fixed* the problem. In the end, they are both to blame for Autumn's death. She for committing the act and Mitch for being a coward and doing nothing to stop it.

What about that other woman who died on the lake a few months ago? Was she another one of Mitch's affairs? Is Liv responsible for her death, too? What would have happened to Nadia if I hadn't gotten her out of there? The reality of the situation was much worse than I could have ever imagined. I had believed that Mitch just lost his temper or something and killed Autumn in a rage, but her death was planned, and the plan was executed precisely as Liv had written it. Every detail was calculated.

I feel sick to my stomach. Initially, I had believed that she, too, was a victim of Mitch's schemes, but she has been the author of them from the beginning. They both deserve to go to prison for what they did to Autumn and countless other women.

I wish I had more proof. What I do have is circumstantial at best, but not enough to put either one of them away. They're never going to be held accountable for what they've done, at least not by the criminal justice system. I learned that a long time ago. If they aren't held accountable, I know they will do it again. More women are going to die. Mitch can't keep it in his pants, and Liv has to control everything around her. It's inevitable.

For justice to happen, they both have to be stopped. There's no other way.

92

LIV

I return from Seattle to find Mitch gone and the house quiet. It is late. I have no idea where he went, but I honestly don't even care anymore. He can do whatever he wants... do whoever he wants. He has been a thorn in my side for years, and I'm tired of cleaning up his messes.

I grab a bottle of pinot grigio from the fridge and uncork it. I select a glass from the cabinet, fill it to the brim, and set the bottle on the kitchen counter. The sound of the glass hitting the marble echoes in the empty house. I take a sip of the wine. Before I set the glass down, the front doorbell rings.

"What now," I whisper.

I walk to the door and look through the peephole. Sandy is standing on the porch, a bottle of vodka in one hand. She looks anxious. I sigh as I open the door.

She gives me a small smile. "I thought you could use something a little stronger than wine," she says, handing me the bottle.

"You have no idea," I reply, stepping back to let her inside.

"Did you find Nadia?" She asks.

I shake my head. "I wasn't even looking for her. She could be all the way back in Mexico for all I care."

"Was she Mexican?"

I glare at her. "I don't care."

"What about Eden?"

I hesitate. "Let's pour this first." I gesture to the bottle.

Back in the kitchen, I put my glass of wine in the fridge and grab two liquor glasses, filling them with ice. "You want a mixer? I'm sure I have some sort of diet soda in the fridge."

Sandy shakes her head. "On the rocks is fine."

I pour the clear liquid into the two glasses and pass one to Sandy.

"So," she says. "Did you find Eden?"

"Not exactly," I say, unsure of how much I want to share with her. At this point, I have no idea who I can and can't trust. "I learned a lot about her, though, that's for sure."

"What makes you think she's been sabotaging you?"

"She's the one who helped Nadia get away."

A look of complete shock forms on Sandy's face. "What?"

I nod. "She came here this morning and drove away with her. She thought she had turned off all the cameras, but I have my own set of cameras that not even Mitch knows about. I watched her and Nadia walk away together, clear as day."

"Why would she do that?"

"I don't know. I guess she felt like Nadia was being held hostage or something crazy like that."

"Wow. I didn't really trust her, but I just thought I was being paranoid."

"Yeah, well, she isn't the person she claimed to be. She's been lying to me from the beginning," I say, being careful of what I reveal. If I'm going to fix this situation like I've fixed all of Mitch's previous entanglements, I need to keep most of what I know close to my chest.

"What do you mean?" Sandy asks, leaning forward.

"Eden's not even her real name."

"Are you serious? I knew there was something sneaky about her."

I nod. "I never checked her references. I don't know why. I guess I just trusted my instincts. When she applied, I didn't call a single one."

"That's not like you at all," Sandy says, surprised.

I shake my head. "I googled her this morning, and she doesn't even exist. No social media, no address, nothing."

"Whoa. Who is she really?"

I hesitate. Should I tell her? Maybe she could help me figure out my next step. If I tell her, I know she'll tell someone else. She can't help herself, and I can't risk anyone figuring out Eden's connection to Aldercreek if I'm going to have a chance to fix things.

"I don't know," I lie. "But she had access to everything. To my business records. My personal records. My finances." I consider telling her about the stolen account information, but she also has access to my computer. Who's to say Sandy's not the person responsible? She's been different lately... suspicious. I decide not to share that little detail with her. If she is responsible, it will come out eventually. Instead, I focus on Eden. "What kind of sick person does that to someone? She's been scheming against me for months now."

"Maybe it's simpler than that," Sandy replies quietly. "Maybe there's something inside her that makes her lie about who she is, and she doesn't even really understand why she does it."

"What are you even talking about, Sandy? You're not making any sense." Here it comes, her confession. I keep my face as placid as possible to invite her to tell me the truth.

She takes a deep breath and sighs. "I steal things."

"You do what?" I ask, not entirely shocked. I knew something was wrong. Chances are, she's the one responsible for the purchases on our credit cards. I wouldn't put it past her.

She nods. "For the last couple of months, every time I go into a store, I steal something. It's usually something small that I could easily buy, but instead, I shove it in my purse or pocket and walk out."

"Why in the world would you do something so stupid? You're not hurting for money. Why would you risk going to jail like that?"

"I don't know. I just can't seem to help myself. It's as if the thrill of it almost makes me feel less anxious or something. Of course, it never lasts very long. I've got a whole box of random stuff I've stolen hidden in the trunk of my car."

I stare at her for several seconds. It's clear Eden isn't the only person who has betrayed me. I call her out. "You also have had access to all of my files, including my financial information."

Her eyes grow wide. "What are you accusing me of, Liv? I've done nothing to hurt you, ever."

"Did you know that someone stole our bank account information and bought some random stuff overseas? Thousands of dollars worth."

"No, I had no idea."

"Do you honestly think I believe you after what you just admitted? You even said you couldn't help yourself. How am I supposed to believe that I'm immune from your compulsions?"

Tears form in Sandy's eyes. "It wasn't me, I swear. You have to believe me."

"Do I? You were always trying to convince me that Eden was sneaking around and that I couldn't trust her. Maybe that was all just a diversion, and you were the one I really couldn't trust."

"You've got to be kidding me," Sandy says, anger flaring in her eyes. "I've been nothing but loyal to you, Liv, even when you treat me like I'm an idiot."

"Look me in the eye and tell me it wasn't you."

"How could you believe I would hurt you like that?" Sandy asks, her brows furrowed.

"So, you don't deny it. Here I was thinking that you were the one person I could trust, and you've been stabbing me in the back this entire time."

"No, Liv. You have it all wrong," she cries desperately.

I stand, blood pounding in my ears. "How could you, Sandy? I trusted you."

"Liv, no. I didn't do it, I swear," she says, standing up.

"Oh, I understand perfectly well. You couldn't handle me having so much success. Owning my own business... running for mayor. You have been jealous of me from the beginning, and you've wanted nothing more than to bring me down. I can see it all so clearly now."

"I've never done anything to hurt you," she says quietly.

"I don't believe a single word you say. You're a piece of work. Get out of my house."

"But, please. You have it all wrong."

"Do I? I've seen the way you look at me... at Mitch. We have everything you have ever wanted. Of course, you would do anything to get it. You even admitted to me that you take things that don't belong to you for no reason. What more would you be willing to do when you actually had a reason?"

"You can't do this," she says, tears falling down her face.

"Watch me. If you don't get out, I will call the cops and tell them everything you just told me."

Her eyes widen in fear. "You wouldn't do that. I told you that as my friend in confidence."

"Yeah, well, I guess that's what friends do, right? Stab each other in the back."

She shakes her head and grabs her purse.

"I don't ever want to see your face again," I yell at her as she walks towards the front door. "Oh, and by the way, if it wasn't supremely obvious. You're fired."

She fumbles with the door handle, unable to get it open.

I walk towards her. "You can't even open a stupid door. You're utterly worthless."

Before I get to her, she finally manages to open the door and runs to her car.

I stare at her as she drives away, and a confusing mixture of anger and sadness fills my heart. I'm utterly alone. Everyone I trusted has betrayed me. I remember my mother's words: *There are no problems. There are only people.*

I need to find Mitch. We need to fix this together, or everything we've worked so hard to build will crumble. Kari-Anne needs to be dealt with.

PIPPA

P ippa pulls up to her apartment. It's late. The windows in the apartment are dark. Bobbi had texted her earlier, letting her know she was eating dinner and staying the night at a friend's house, so Pippa had not attempted to be home at a reasonable hour. She had worked until the sun began to set, and no one else was in the building.

After dropping Nadia off at the bus stop this morning, she went straight to the office. At first, it was difficult for her to focus on anything, but working on motions for her clients was a good distraction from other thoughts plaguing her. Being able to help Nadia felt good, but she was also scared. Liv and Mitch were dangerous; she knew that, and she knew she had woken a sleeping bear by helping Nadia get away. Her only hope was that maybe they didn't know she was involved. Perhaps they thought it was only Eden who helped Nadia. If she was in Mitch and Liv's sights, it was over for her... they could destroy her. However, the look Nadia gave her when she dropped her off at the bus stop made it all worth it. She had been so grateful.

Pippa parks her car in her spot and walks to the mail-box. It has been days since she checked the mail. She unlocks the door to her box and grabs the stack of mail that barely fits in the tiny container. A key is at the bottom of the stack, indicating she has a package.

She unlocks the door to the box for packages and grabs what is inside. It nearly fills the entire container, and she struggles to squeeze her fingers on either side to pull it out. What is this? she wonders, but it is too dark to read the label.

Bringing it inside the apartment, she turns on the light and sets the package on the counter. Her throat constricts as she reads the return address. It is from the prison where her dad is behind bars. She can't even remember the last time she'd received a letter from him, let alone a package.

She opens the package. The contents inside are a complete mess, as if someone had just shoved everything into the box without any care. On top of the box is an offi-cial-looking letter addressed to Pippa.

Dear Ms. Halloway,

We regret to inform you that your father, Martin Chan, was involved in an incident at the prison. Unfortunately, Mr. Chan was stabbed by another inmate during the altercation and did not make it. We are performing a complete investigation and will let you know when we have more detailed information.

Inside this box are all of his personal belongings. As his only surviving relative, they now belong to you...

Pippa can't read anymore. She sits at the counter and places her head in her hands. "What did you do, Dad? You weren't supposed to get yourself killed." She doesn't know how to feel. She has been mad at him for a long time for everything he has done, but she never wanted him dead. She feels a little guilty. She hasn't seen him since he was imprisoned. She wonders if she should have gone to visit him, but deep down, she knows better. If she had visited him, he would have turned everything around on her and made her feel worse. She blocked him from her life for a reason.

She stands and reaches into the box. There isn't much inside. A few books and magazines, a radio, and several snacks that had been purchased from the commissary. She laughs. Why in the world would they send her his food? Why would she want this?

At the bottom of the box, she finds a small bible. She looks at it, confused. Her dad had never been a religious person. Why did he have a bible?

She opens it and starts rifling through it. A white envelope drops from the pages and lands on the counter. She picks it up. It's addressed to her.

Slowly, she opens it, afraid of what's inside. The words are written in her dad's nearly illegible handwriting. Only a few people in this world can read the things he wrote, and she is one of them.

MY DEAREST DAUGHTER, it begins. Pippa is already sick to her stomach. *If you're reading this, I probably didn't make it out alive. I want you to know that I love you and never stopped wishing that we could go back to how things were when you were little and we were both happy.*

Just before being convicted, I put everything I owned that had any value in a secret spot just for you. Remember where we used to go when you were a little girl? The special place where you and I would hang out and fish? Behind the big rock, you'll find a red brick. Dig underneath the brick, and you'll find a metal tin that will give you further instructions. You'll never want for anything ever again. I promise.

PIPPA STARES at the letter in shock. Has this stuff been hidden all this time? Why did he wait until he was gone to tell her about it?

Tears prick her eyes as she thinks about those times she spent with her dad fishing. Those were some of the best memories of her life. She has been so mad at all the things he has done to her, but she never wanted him dead. She will always be his little girl.

She folds up the letter and stuffs it back in the box. A big part of her doubts if any of it is true. Just watch. She'll head to their spot and dig behind the rock like a fool, only to find nothing there. That would be like her dad, disappointing her even in death. Even with all the evidence, there's a small part of her that wonders if maybe he was telling the truth.

"Oh, Dad, why did you have to go like this?" She asks, putting her head on her arms. A confusing mixture of anger and grief swirls around inside of her. She doesn't really know how she is supposed to feel, but each emotion that comes to the forefront feels real and raw, leaving her feeling drained.

She makes her way to the couch and lies down. She needs sleep. Everything's better after sleep. In spite of how tired she is, she doesn't find rest even after closing her eyes. Her dad haunts her even in her dreams.

94

EDEN

I stand at the lake's edge until my fingers and toes grow numb, and I can barely move them. I sigh. I have to figure out a different way to bring Mitch and Liv down. Being fired may have changed my plans, but I will never give up. There has to be something on that thumb drive I can use.

As I walk back to my car, I wrap my arms around myself to stop my body from shaking. I hug them tightly around Autumn's sweatshirt. It has several holes near the wrist in the cuffs, and the numbers on the front are cracked and wearing away. No matter how beat up it gets, I'll never get rid of it. It's a constant reminder of the reason why I'm here, of everything my sister lost. It could be ripped in half, and I would still wear it.

I open the car door and immediately turn on the heat after starting the engine. It takes several minutes before the car is warm and my body stops shaking.

When I can feel my fingers again, I head back to my apartment in the dark. A part of me is nervous that someone might be waiting there for me, but as soon as I pull up, I see no one at my door, at least not in the light.

I grab my pepper spray out of my purse and tuck it into the palm of my hand. I place my thumb on the trigger, making sure I'm ready to use it at a moment's notice. There are several dark and hidden corners between my parked car and apartment door; I will be ready for anything.

Thankfully, the walk to my door is uneventful. I quickly unlock it and slip inside. Before turning on the hallway light, I lock the door behind me, ensuring the deadbolt and chain are in place.

I hold up the pepper spray and slowly walk from room to room, checking under the furniture and inside the closets. It doesn't take long. After finding nothing out of place, I take a deep breath and set my bag on the table.

I grab the thumb drive and place it in my laptop. What I found this morning was proof enough for me, but I know the police will need more to build a case against Liv and Mitch.

I navigate to the drive and double-click on the first folder in the list. It's full of pictures of houses that Liv has listed and sold. After a cursory glance at most of the pictures, I move on.

The second folder contains medical records, which I slowly begin to open one by one. The first set of records is from a fertility clinic. It looks like Liv and Mitch have gone through several rounds of in vitro insemination, spending thousands. The total on their last bill for everything was over twenty thousand dollars.

I open the next bill, and my eyes narrow. This bill is from a gynecologist in the next town over. What exactly was Liv doing? I read through the list of services provided until I come upon a line that explains everything. "She really is a horrible person," I say.

My phone dings, and I grab it. It's Liv. I hesitate. Do I want to even read the message? I stare at the phone for several minutes before finally giving in. I guess it can't hurt to see what she has to say.

Can we meet? It says simply.

I hesitate. Liv has proven to be dangerous. If I meet with her, who knows what she might do to me? I won't be able to confront her and learn the truth if I don't meet her.

I stew over my decision for several minutes until, suddenly, I have a plan. This is it. It's probably my one chance to avenge Autumn, and I have to take it.

Outside your office. One hour. I hit send.

Usually, I would run my plan by Derek, and we would spend hours shooting holes in it until there were none left, but I don't have that kind of time. For my plan to work, I have to move fast.

I open a new browser and navigate to the email I had set up specifically for this mission. Before I can second-guess myself, I open a new message and begin to type.

95

MITCH

Mitch is nursing his third vodka soda at a dark mahogany bar top. The sour smell of stale beer permeates the small space. It's definitely not a high-class joint; it's more like the type of place people come to hide, but that was the point... he was trying to disappear. After the whole fiasco with Eden this morning, he couldn't face Liv. How could he explain that he allowed Eden into her office alone? He was so stupid.

His phone vibrates in his pocket. At first, he doesn't even reach for it, but he gives in after the tenth vibration in a row. It's Liv. As afraid as he is of her, he's also pissed at her. Nadia would still be here if Liv hadn't let Eden into their lives. He loved Nadia, but now she was gone because Eden helped her escape.

Not only did Eden let Nadia go, but it now seems like she's hell-bent on destroying their lives. He's not quite sure how, but he can sense it. This is all Liv's fault, too. He wouldn't have even let Eden into the office if Liv hadn't trusted her in the first place. No, he doesn't want to talk to

Liv. He pushes the button on the side of his phone to ignore the call and sets the phone down in front of him.

The events of the morning run through his mind like a video on replay. Who was Eden, really? She obviously had some kind of hidden agenda against Liv, maybe even against him. What kind of person had Liv brought into their lives? Their home? No. None of this was his fault. There was zero reason for him to be scared about something he had no control over, but he knows his wife, and he's not sure she will see it that way. Somehow, she will blame him.

If Liv had only involved him in any of the decisions she made for their family, they wouldn't even be here. He would have made her run a background check on Eden before giving her so much access to their personal information.

Even in high school, Liv was always the one who ran the show. He was just her little yes-man. Anytime he tried to express his opinion about matters, she would shut him down and talk to him like he was an idiot. He was only supposed to do what he was told, like a good boy, and play the role of the doting husband. That's what he has done for years. Now look at him. He's hiding from his wife in a hole-in-the-wall bar. He shakes his head. What kind of life is this?

The only time he's ever put his foot down about anything was when he convinced Liv to start trying to have a baby. For some reason, he felt that having a kid would change their marriage. Maybe Liv would soften up a bit, and they would finally feel like a real family, but they had been trying for years without any success. They had spent thousands of dollars going through several rounds of in vitro, but nothing ever took. It was almost as if the universe had a vendetta against him. Maybe he doesn't even deserve a family after all he's done.

His phone buzzes in front of him. He grabs it and sees a

text message from an unknown number. Hesitating, he opens up his phone and slowly navigates to the unread message. A series of screenshots comes through in rapid succession.

He cautiously opens the first one. It looks like notes from a doctor's visit. Liv's name is at the top of the page. He doesn't recognize the doctor's name, and he takes note of the clinic's address, which is one town over. He looks down at the first recommendation, and his mouth immediately runs dry. Liv was prescribed birth control pills around the same time they started trying to have a baby.

He downs the rest of the vodka in his glass and raises it without even looking up.

"Would you like another?" the bartender asks.

Mitch nods.

He begins to scroll through every screenshot sent to him by the unknown sender. There are appointments, prescriptions, and notes from doctors that go back several years. There are even secret bank accounts in Liv's name containing thousands of dollars. She has been controlling everything, even the one thing he had believed she had given in on... starting a family.

His heart sinks as the realization begins to dawn. He was never going to have a kid with Liv. This was never going to be a real family. If he stayed in this marriage, he would be nothing better than a puppet in her sick games.

96

EDEN

I stand under the street light immediately in front of an ATM. I chose this location because cameras are always running to protect the machine. If Liv tries to do anything to me, it will all be caught on tape, and she won't be able to lie about what happened.

It's not as cold standing here as it was next to the lake, but I still shake from the wind whipping through my hair. I pull my jacket tighter around me and check my watch. I've been standing out here for more than fifteen minutes. Maybe she's not coming.

Suddenly, a car pulls into the empty parking lot. Its headlights point toward me. The driver ignores the painted lines and heads straight through the parking spaces, directly at me. I stand my ground even as the car comes dangerously close without slowing down.

When the car is less than five feet from me, it comes to a screeching halt. A few seconds later, Liv comes barreling out of the driver's side door, a crazed look in her eyes.

"I know exactly who you are," she says without pretext.

"Oh yeah?" I ask, not wanting to feed her any information about me that maybe she hasn't already ascertained.

"You're Kari-Anne. Did you think I'd never figure it out?" She yells, stepping closer.

I step back towards the ATM and point at the two cameras. Their little red lights glow, indicating that they are on and recording.

"You should really watch what you say and do, Liv; everything is being recorded. I'm not stupid enough to meet you alone without some kind of protection."

"So, did you come here to destroy me for what happened to your sister? I barely even remember her. She was so insignificant," Liv says with a sneer.

Rage fills me. I could step forward and end this right now. I could kill her and get revenge for what she and Mitch did to Autumn, but I stop myself. I have to be smart. "She was more beautiful and intelligent than you could ever hope to be. She didn't deserve what you and Mitch did to her."

"And what exactly do you think we did? She overdosed and was found in a stolen vehicle in a lake. Do you think I made her steal that car or take those drugs? When are you going to come to terms with the fact that your sister was a thief and a junkie?"

Tears fill my eyes. How could Liv care so little and be so cruel? I could attack her and end this all now, but if I did that, I would be throwing away the plan I'd spent years developing. I am smarter than that.

Liv continues. "You're the one who should be in jail. In fact, I should call the cops and have them arrest you for everything you've done to me in the last few months. Lying to me about your identity, breaking into my personal files, stealing from me." She grabs her phone and begins to dial 911.

"I wouldn't do that if I were you," I say calmly, though my heart is beating almost audibly in my chest.

"And why not?" She asks, hesitating.

"You shouldn't have been so meticulous with the files on your computer. You literally kept evidence of nearly everything you've ever done and all the laws you've broken. I took a copy of every single file. Please say thank you to Mitch for being such a gracious host."

Liv stares at me, eyes wide, her expression frozen in disbelief.

I continue. "If you call the cops, then everything I have in my possession, everything I stole from your computer, will become property of the state."

"You wouldn't," Liv hisses.

"You have no idea the lengths I would go to in order to avenge my sister. You better start looking over your shoulder, Liv. Justice is coming for you when you least expect it."

"They'll never believe you. All you have is a copy. You don't have the real thing."

"Are you really willing to take that chance?" I ask, taunting her.

"You'll never get away with this, Kari-Anne. You're going to pay for violating my privacy and trying to ruin my life. This is not over."

"You're right about that. It is definitely not over. Oh, by the way, where's your husband?"

The look of rage on Liv's face gives me a sense of joy. Her life is falling apart, and I have a front-row seat to the destruction.

Liv grits her teeth and rushes to her car. She hops in and slams the door shut, peeling out of the parking lot. I contemplate my next steps as I watch her go. It's not enough for the police to find out everything Liv has done. I need Liv to feel the pain and suffering that I've been living with for years. I won't stop until Autumn's death is fully avenged.

97

MITCH

"Liv!" Mitch yells as he storms into the house. He stumbles into the wall, struggling to maintain his balance. He definitely shouldn't have driven himself home from the bar, but he wasn't thinking straight after looking through all those screenshots. Rage has blinded his common sense.

His marriage to Liv has always been a mutually beneficial arrangement. He doesn't love her, at least not in the same way most men love their wives. Their secrets bind them together, and up until now, he had come to terms with the fact that they would never be capable of truly loving each other.

The one thing he had always wanted from this marriage was kids. If his relationship with Liv wasn't going to be loving, he had thought maybe he could find a different kind of love with his children. If only she had been upfront with him from the beginning and told him what she really felt about having kids. Maybe he could have mourned the loss of a family a long time ago and moved on.

Instead, she led him on for years. She made it seem like

there was some medical reason why she couldn't get pregnant when, in reality, she was taking pills to stop it. She has been lying to him from the beginning. The thought makes him sick to his stomach.

He walks from room to room, yelling her name, but each room he enters is as empty as the last. "Liv, where are you?" He yells in frustration as he closes the guest bedroom door.

He contemplates his next move as he walks slowly back to the kitchen. Should he stay here and wait for her to come home, or should he get back in his car and drive until he finds her?

Stumbling into the kitchen, he braces himself on the wall to avoid falling over. His head spins. Everything is falling apart, and he doesn't know how to stop it.

Opening the fridge, he grabs a beer. He twists off the top and takes a long drink, hoping it will drown this feeling of helplessness that he can't seem to shake.

Beer in hand, he walks over to the kitchen window and looks out into the backyard at Nadia's cottage. The feeling of loss intensifies. "Why did you have to go?" He asks sadly. "I would have left her for you in a heartbeat, especially with what I know now about all that Liv has done. Nothing is keeping me here. I love you."

He places his head on the window in despair. If he could go back to the beginning and change everything, he would... starting with Autumn. Just the thought of her rips at his heart. She didn't deserve what he and Liv had done to her. Her death had been the beginning of his destruction; he can see that so clearly now. He wishes he had done something to save her, but he has always been a coward.

His phone vibrates in his pocket. Apprehensively, he pulls it out and opens it. What if the stranger is sending more evidence of Liv's betrayal? He's not sure he is strong enough to see more.

He glances at the screen. He has received a new text message from an unknown number, different from the one who sent the images. He opens it cautiously.

MITCH, it's me, Nadia. I am so sorry I had to leave. I found out last week that I am pregnant. The baby is yours. I wanted to tell you in person, but I was afraid of what Liv might do to me if she found out. She is scary, and she watches everything I do. Yesterday, I caught her going through the trash in my room. I was afraid she had figured out my secret, and I couldn't risk staying any longer, so I left in the middle of the night for my own safety. I didn't want to leave you like that, but I didn't know what else to do. I was on a bus to leave town, but I realized I couldn't leave without at least saying goodbye to you, so I came back. I'm on the north side of the lake where there are no houses. I'll be waiting for you. Please come. If you're not here by morning, I will be gone for good, and you'll never see me again.

MITCH TAKES a deep breath as resolve fills him. This is his chance to have real love, not the facade he's had with Liv since high school. He grabs his keys and heads out the door without a second thought.

98

EDEN

T he night is so dark that my headlights barely illuminate the road. There are no street lamps on this country road. Everything, including the trees surrounding me on either side, is oppressively dark. My headlights reveal a small patch of asphalt directly in front of me, along with a small section of the white fence that lines both sides of the road — nothing more.

I slow down and proceed cautiously. The deer in this area are fearless, or maybe they are just stupid. They will jump in front of a car and then stare at it as the car plows into them. The term *frozen like a deer in headlights* is accurate. I can't afford to get into an accident now, not when everything I have dedicated myself to comes down to this moment. I have to be cautious.

Earlier today, I came out here and tied a silver ribbon on a white picket fence to mark where I needed to stop. Now, in the dark, I wish I had done something more obvious.

As I approach the location where I had placed the ribbon, I slow down to a crawl. I can't afford to miss it. A car barrels down on me from behind and honks loudly as it passes.

"Sorry," I say to the car as it speeds by, the anxiety inside me steadily building.

Just as I'm about to turn around and try again, I see a flash of silver on the fence as the ribbon reflects the light of my headlights. I breathe a sigh of relief and pull my car over to the side of the road.

I grab the beanie, gloves and flashlight from the passenger seat and exit the car. I stretch the beanie over my ponytail and turn on the flashlight. The beam is less bright than my headlights, and it barely illuminates more than five feet in front of me. It will have to do. I slip on the gloves and check inside my car to ensure I haven't forgotten anything. The passenger seat is empty.

I lock the car and take a deep breath. With the light from my flashlight leading the way, I hike into the dark woods.

99

LIV

As I drive home, the night air is almost completely still. The wind from just a few moments earlier has stopped its assault as if it's waiting for the right moment to strike again, harder and faster than before. As I drive through the streets of Aldercreek, I'm amazed by how peaceful it looks. The stillness of the town is inconsistent with my boiling rage.

I can't get Eden's taunt out of my mind. "Oh, by the way, where's your husband?" I say mockingly as I drive down the empty street. It's as if she knows something about him that I don't.

That idiot has been a liability since day one. None of this would have happened if he could have just controlled himself, but no, he can't keep it in his pants for two seconds. I always have to clean up his messes. Frankly, I'm getting tired of it. I wish I didn't have to keep him around. I would gladly cut him loose if I didn't think he'd destroy everything in the process.

The light ahead of me turns red, and I bring my car to a stop. No other cars are at the stoplight or on this road, for that matter. "Why did you turn red? This is pointless," I mutter to the light as if it could hear me. The cross light remains green even though no cars approach or drive through the intersection. You'd think a town as wealthy as this one would install sensors. I mentally put that on my list as one of the first things I will do as the mayor.

Normally, I would sit and wait for the light to turn green. I am a law-abiding citizen — at least on the surface — but not today.

I check my surroundings. Still, no cars are coming in any direction. I release the brake and slam on the gas, plowing through the intersection. The thrill of it propels me forward. Tonight, I'm going to put a stop to whatever Eden has planned. She's not even going to see me coming.

I pull up to the house. All the windows are dark, save for one light towards the back of the house. Maybe Mitch is home, drinking away his sorrows.

Boy, that man can drink. Most of the situations I have to fix are either due to the women he decides to sleep with or his drinking. His lack of common sense and control makes me ill.

I think back to the boy I knew in high school. Teenage Mitch was charming and popular, but that's all he really had going for him. From the beginning, he was the life of every party. He would go toe-to-toe with anyone in a drinking game and always came out on top.

I hated those parties. I always sat towards the back and watched as everyone lost their minds. I only went because it was necessary for my image. My goal since I was a kid has been to become the mayor of Aldercreek and eventually become a senator. Who knows, maybe I'll even become the first female President of the United States. I refuse to put limits on myself.

Everything I've done, every plan I've put in place, has been to achieve that goal. I shake my head. If I could go back and tell my younger self what I know now, I'd tell her to run far away from Mitch Mitre. I thought he might give me an edge if we partnered together. People like him from the moment they meet him. They tolerate me by proxy. However, he's been way more work than he's worth, and I'm done cleaning up his messes. I have to figure something else out.

I pull my car into the garage. Mitch's car is missing. Where could he be?

I open the door to the house and immediately call for him. "Mitch, are you here?"

I'm greeted by silence as I enter the kitchen. A beer can sits towards the edge of the island. I pick it up, and its weight surprises me. It's half-full. He never leaves alcohol undrunk. I wonder where he could have gone in such a hurry.

"Mitch?" I yell again. Maybe he's still here, and he went to bed in a drunken stupor. The only time he ever leaves alcohol untouched is when he passes out. I check the house for him. All of the rooms are dark and empty. Where did he go?

I run to my home office and log into my laptop. Years ago, when Mitch got his first smartphone, I installed spyware software on it to keep tabs on him. At first, it only gave me rudimentary information, such as the coordinates of his location and the telephone numbers of the people who called and texted him. Over the years, however, the software has drastically improved. Now, not only does it show me his precise location on a map, but I can also access his entire phone screen as if I were holding the phone in my hand.

I navigate first to his messages. Most of them seem to be

from his work buddies, but there are two messages from unknown numbers. The last one came in not too long ago. I click on it.

My heart drops as I read through the message. I know how much Mitch has wanted to have a baby, and now Nadia is pregnant with his child. My mind is racing. What if he decides to go with her? After all I've done for him and all the situations I've bailed him out of, does he really think he can just walk away from me?

The two words at the bottom of the screen make my blood run cold.

I'm coming.

He's going to do it. He's going to ruin everything. For what? For an illegal immigrant and a kid?

Tears of anger sting my eyes. I can't let him do it. I can't let him make this choice. He'll take me down with him, and I've worked too hard to get to this point.

I check his location on the spyware app. Sure enough, he's at the lake. I have to get to him before it's too late.

I rush to the bookshelf and pull several books down, revealing the safe. I quickly input the code and open it. Inside lies a stack of papers. On top of the papers is a handgun and a fully loaded magazine clip.

I grab the gun, tuck it into the waistband of my pants, and carefully put the magazine in one of my pockets. I'm going to end this once and for all.

100

MITCH

Mitch pulls his car right up to the edge of the lake. His headlights illuminate the frozen section of lake in front of him, while the rest of the lake is shrouded in the soft glow of the full moon. "Where is she?" He whispers, putting the car in park and getting out.

"Nadia?" He yells, but his voice echoes back to him across the lake through the cold night air.

He grabs his phone out of his pocket and rechecks Nadia's message. This is the north side of the lake; she should be here.

He walks down the rocky lakefront, stumbling several times on the uneven, frozen ground. "Nadia?" He calls again, but there is still no answer.

Maybe she got tired of waiting and already left. Doubts and fear creep into his mind and heart.

He had been dreaming about this moment for months. He fell in love with Nadia the day Liv hired her to work at the house. She was naturally beautiful, kind, soft-spoken — everything Liv was not.

At first, he just watched her work, and that was enough. She did everything with such grace and perfection. Her energy was like a beacon, a welcome difference from Liv.

Over time, he became bolder and would flirt with Nadia when Liv was not around. He'd touch her arm or her back when he walked past. She seemed to enjoy it. She always smiled at him and blushed. He wonders now if maybe he had misread her cues.

ONE NIGHT about six months ago, Mitch had come home drunk from the bar. He stumbled into the house, barely able to stand. Nadia was putting the dishes away in the kitchen, and Liv was at some book club or community meeting; he never knew where she was most of the time.

"Are you okay, Mr. Mitre?" Nadia asked, concerned.

He nodded his head. "I just need some water."

She quickly grabbed a glass and filled it with the water pitcher she always kept cold in the fridge. She handed it to him.

He downed it greedily. "Thank you, you really are the best."

Her cheeks flushed, and she looked down at the floor. He had never been quite sure what it had been about that night. Maybe it was the alcohol, maybe it was the look she gave him, but that was the first night he grabbed her, his mind filled with lust, and forced himself upon her on the kitchen floor. She barely put up a fight, and over time, he convinced himself that deep down she wanted it.

The next morning, after he had sobered up, a wave of guilt and shame washed over him. He had hurt her. The memory of her sobbing face and the fear in her eyes came back to him almost as if it were a dream.

He vowed never to hurt her like that again, but he broke his promise later that same night. He told himself that he just couldn't stay away. He knew he was the worst type of man. Not even a man in reality. There would be no mercy for him wherever he ended up when this life was over.

Guilt threatens to overwhelm him, and he is plagued with regret. He wanders back towards his car, his heart heavy. He convinces himself that things are going to be different now. She wants to be with him; she told him as much in her message. He's not sure why she's willing to give him a second chance, but he knows he's not going to waste it. He will be free of Liv and her judgmental, controlling ways. She is the reason he drinks so heavily. Without her constant presence in his life, he will have no reason to drown his sorrows in alcohol, and alcohol is the major contributing factor to all the times he hurt Nadia. Things are going to be different now; he can feel it.

Besides, Liv is usually the one who hurts people, not him. He thinks back to Autumn and all the women who came after her. In each case, he stood by helplessly as Liv hurt them in an effort to control her own destiny. Aside from being a coward and never saying anything, he played no part in her sick, sadistic ways. Surely, if he can get out from under her grasp, he can recover and become the man he is supposed to be, but deep down, he wonders if it's too late. Maybe standing by for years and watching Liv destroy people has caused some permanent evil to invade his mind and heart.

He shakes his head. He can't give in to thoughts like those. There has to be some hope for him. The idea of his child, his own flesh and blood, growing in Nadia's belly gives him the strength to push back against Liv and her evil ways. She has been keeping him from experiencing this kind of joy for years, pretending that she, too, wanted a child. He's been doing her bidding for as long as he can remember and has nothing to show for it but heartache. Now, he has something to fight for. The new life growing inside of Nadia gives him hope, and an unfamiliar surge of courage rushes through his veins.

He grabs his phone and dials Nadia's number. The line rings and rings until he is transferred to a voicemail box that has not been set up yet. He tries the number again with the same result. "Nadia, where are you?" He asks, frustration tinging his voice.

Just as he is about to try a third time, a light in the distance catches his eye. A car approaches him slowly, gravel crunching under its tires. The headlights grow larger and larger as the car approaches. They shine directly on him, temporarily blinding him. "Nadia?" He calls.

The car stops less than ten feet from him, and a woman opens the door and quickly gets out.

101

LIV

I stare at my lousy, good-for-nothing husband as he stands next to the frozen lake and shake my head. Why have I put up with him for so long? Hatred fills me, giving me the courage to face him and end this for good.

I grip the gun I grabbed earlier from the safe in my right hand and load it with the magazine from my pocket.

"What are you doing here, Liv?" He asks, his eyes wide and his breath ragged. It's as if he's on the verge of tears.

"Oh, were you expecting someone else?" I ask sarcastically. "Who'd you come out here to meet, Mitch? Was it your pregnant girlfriend, Nadia?"

"How could you... I..." he stammers.

"Did you honestly think I didn't know what you were doing to her in our own house? I've known for a very long time. I was just waiting for the right time to take care of it... like I always do."

"What did you do to her?" Mitch screams, rage filling his eyes. He rushes towards me.

I point the gun at him and hold my ground. "I wouldn't

take another step if I were you. I'll pull this trigger, Mitch, if I have to, and you know it."

He stops in his tracks, a crazed look in his eyes. "You did it, didn't you?"

"I don't know what you're talking about."

"You killed Nadia."

"I haven't seen Nadia all day, sadly," I say, playing with his emotions.

"Liar," he yells, tears streaming down his face. "You took away my best chance at becoming a father. It's not like you were ever going to give me children, were you?"

"We've been trying for years. It's not my fault that I've never gotten pregnant."

His face turns beet red as he reaches for his cell phone. "Lies. All you do is tell lies, and these documents are evidence that you never once intended to give me a family."

I look at him, confused. "What exactly are you showing me?"

"Medical records going all the way back to when we first started going through in-vitro. At the same time we were supposedly trying to have a kid, you were taking birth control." He spits the words out of his mouth in disgust.

I shrug. "I was never cut out to be a mother. Deep down, you know that. I was just giving you the hope you so clearly needed."

Anguish and hatred fill his face. "You are evil, Liv. There is not one shred of good inside you. You have been deceiving me and controlling me almost my entire life."

"Oh, my dear Mitch," I say. Looking at him, I'm filled with pity at how useless he is. Since the beginning, he has just been a puppet in my ultimate plan to propel myself to a place of power in society. For the most part, he's followed along like a good little puppy, but he has always been a bit of a loose cannon. I've had to clean up his messes more times than I'd like to count. "You act like I'm the villain and you're the innocent one, but you're not so innocent, are you?"

"What are you talking about, Liv?"

"Don't act stupid. This isn't the first time you've cheated on me. You act like you're so perfect, but those other relationships weren't always so nice, were they? I know you, Mitch. You have a temper. I saw the bruises on Nadia. I'm sure you did the same to the rest of them, too."

"I never meant to hurt them. I just can't always control myself." He runs a hand through his hair, something resembling confusion or regret present in his eyes.

"Oh, I know," I say mockingly. "You just love them so much, you can't help but hurt them."

"At least I didn't kill them," he yells, his gaze so intense I'm afraid it might actually pierce me.

"You've never had the guts to do what was necessary. If it weren't for me, you would already be in prison by now. Don't you see that I've been saving you from yourself all these years?"

"Is that how you live with everything you've done? You convince yourself that you're saving me? Don't you dare blame any of your actions on me. You killed the one woman I actually loved, and stupid me, I have helped you hide it for all these years. Well, I'm done."

I take a step towards him. "I'm done too. I can't be your fixer anymore. You've become a liability."

"How'd you even do it, Liv?" His shoulders slump. The rage in his eyes morphs into sorrow.

"Do what?" I ask, growing tired of him and his simple mind.

"How did you kill Autumn? Or any of them, for that matter?"

I stop and contemplate whether I should tell him. Should I share the secrets I've been keeping locked inside me for years? Yes, I think I'll tell him. I mean, what's the harm really? It's not like he'll be able to tell anyone. He's not leaving this lake alive.

"Okay, fine. I'll tell you since you want to know so badly. Killing Autumn was actually very easy. I had figured out that you and she had been seeing each other a few months before I made my move. I wanted to make sure nothing could point back to me, so I allowed your little thing to go on while I came up with the perfect plan."

As I TELL Mitch the truth, I am transported back to the day I killed Autumn as if it were yesterday. The night was cold, and the lake was icy but not frozen solid. Chunks of ice floated in the water. It was still cold enough that the ground was firm and not muddy like it would be later in the spring. Mitch and Autumn always thought they were so secretive, but they were easy to follow. Mainly because they rotated between the same four locations. I only had to follow them for a few weeks before realizing they didn't switch it up. If I wanted to find them, it never took long.

I pulled up to the lake the night of the incident to find Mitch and Autumn in each other's arms on the hood of his car. They were both holding cheap cans of beer, and a few empty cans were littered around the car.

I slipped on a pair of gloves, grabbed the mixed drinks I had made in water bottles, and took a deep breath. I knew that if I was going to pull this off, I had to put on the performance of a lifetime.

Autumn saw me first and immediately jumped out of Mitch's arms. "Liv, hi. This isn't what it looks like. We were just hanging out," she explained nervously.

I put on the biggest, fakest smile I could muster. "Don't you worry about it. I'm not the jealous type like that. Mitch can have his own friends."

Mitch looked at me like I'd grown a third eyeball. "Are you being serious?"

"I know that I haven't always been the nicest to you, Autumn, and I'm sorry for the way I've treated you. You have helped Mitch with his math grade so much. I should be thanking you," I forced a cute, bubbly laugh.

Autumn and Mitch exchanged a suspicious glance.

"Here," I said, shoving a mixed drink bottle into each of their hands. "A peace offering."

Mitch looked at it suspiciously. "What is this?"

"Some of my parent's vodka and fruit punch we had in the house. I know it's not the best, but it will definitely make you feel good."

Mitch unscrewed the top and took a sip. "Not bad. Thanks, Liv."

"What about you, Ms. Autumn? Are you going to try it?"

She shook her head. "No, I'm not feeling very well. I think alcohol is just going to make me feel worse."

I had to think quickly on my feet. If she wasn't going to drink the alcohol, I needed to figure something else out. "How about some water?" I asked. "I have some bottles in the car."

Autumn hesitated at first, then nodded.

I rushed to the car and grabbed an unopened bottle of water from my back seat. I grabbed the eye drops from my purse. I opened the water and took a few sips to make space, then poured the entire contents of the eye drop bottle into the water, resealed the lid, and shook it up. Most people don't know that something as simple as eye drops can kill you if ingested.

When I was done, I rushed back to where Autumn and Mitch were waiting.

"What took you so long?" Mitch asked. "I'm not feeling very well."

"I'm sorry, the water bottles rolled under my seat. Here," I said to Autumn, handing her the doctored bottle of water.

"Thank you," Autumn said, still eyeing me suspiciously. She took a long drink of the water, and I internally sighed with relief.

It wasn't long before she and Mitch were vomiting their guts into the lake.

"I can't breathe," Mitch said. "What did you do to me?"

"I don't know what you're talking about. I didn't do anything. Let me help you," I said as I led him to my car. "Sit back here, and I'll take you guys home."

He nodded and got in the back seat.

When I returned to Mitch's car, Autumn was lying against the hood, her breathing ragged. I had put enough eye drops in Mitch's bottle to make him feel sick, but I had put enough in Autumn's bottle that she would probably pass out and possibly never wake up again.

"Let me help you into Mitch's car," I said to her. "I'll take you guys home and make sure you get some help."

She nodded at me, so trusting. I helped her into the driver's side seat.

"Wait, what are you doing?" She asked, slurring her words. "I can't drive. I can barely keep my eyes open."

"I know. Just sit here for a minute while I figure stuff out."

She nodded and rested her head against the seat. Her eyes closed, and her breathing slowed.

I grabbed a pill from my purse and forced it into her mouth. I purchased these from the school drug dealer months ago. It was long ago enough that no one would make a connection between me and what happened to Autumn.

"What is that?" She asked, barely able to open her eyes.

"Just something to make you feel better," I said.

I waited five minutes to ensure the pill dissolved, and then I set a baggie full of pills in the console next to her. There was no way I was going to get blamed for this.

Autumn was unconscious. I grabbed her right foot and put it on the gas pedal. Next, I grabbed the keys that Mitch had stupidly left in the ignition and turned the car on. The engine roared to life as Autumn's foot pushed down on the gas. Finally, I reached over her body and shifted the car into drive. I jumped back as the car lurched forward towards the lake.

I watched as it careened into the water and immediately began to sink. If the drugs I had put in her system didn't kill her, the water certainly would. I stared at the car without remorse. Autumn had threatened my plans, and so she had to be dealt with. It was as simple as that.

OVER THE YEARS, Mitch had several affairs. Usually, they were short flings and ended barely after they started. Sometimes, however, I had to take drastic measures, just like I did with Autumn.

The most recent one was Regina Clark. The affair with her felt a little more personal because she and I were friends before she started sleeping with Mitch. I couldn't believe how she would smile at me and act like my best friend while sneaking behind my back.

Mitch had gotten a little better at hiding his behavior over the years. If it wasn't for the spyware I had installed on his cell phone, I would have never known what he and Regina were up to. Lucky for me, I watched the entire thing play out from the comfort of my home office.

Regina was a stay-at-home mom with no real commitments during the day while her kids were at school. I lured her to the lake in the late morning, pretending to be Mitch through the spyware app. I suggested she bring her canoe so she and Mitch could take it out on the lake. It was quite easy. I had watched them do this same activity several times, so I knew it would be believable.

I waited in the woods for her to show up, and when she finally did, I snuck up behind her and put a rag soaked in chloroform over her mouth and nose. She passed out within seconds and fell to the ground.

I grabbed her cell phone and held it up to her face to unlock it. It immediately opened to the home screen. I quickly navigated to the text messages and deleted the entire message thread between her and Mitch. I did the same with all her social media accounts. I was determined to leave no trace of their affair. I knew that this would not be enough. I had to give Mitch an alibi, so I scheduled this little rendezvous when I knew Mitch was at work. He would have dozens of witnesses.

I took Regina's shirt, wiped my fingerprints off the phone, slipped it into her pocket, and then dragged her to the lake. I walked into the water a few feet and then held her head under. She was unconscious, so she didn't fight me. However, her body shook towards the end in involuntary protest. I had anticipated this from my research and held firm until she went still.

When I was certain she was dead, I pushed her further out into the lake. I then grabbed the canoe that I had found strapped to the roof of her car and pushed it into the lake next to her body. I hoped it would look like an accident; fortunately for me, that's exactly what happened. No one ever suspected me or Mitch in her death.

THE MEMORIES FADE, and I find myself staring at Mitch's broken face.

"You're heartless," he says. "You didn't even care about any of them. They were just problems that had to be fixed."

I look at my fingernails, bored. "All of them were problems that you made. You should be thanking me."

"Why would I ever thank you for killing women that I actually cared about?"

I ignore his question. "I was going to have to switch it up for Nadia. It would have looked too suspicious if three women drowned in the lake in nearly the same spot. Besides, the lake is frozen solid at this time of the year. I hadn't figured out yet how I was going to do it before she ran away." I stare at him hard, trying to gauge his next move.

The rage in his eyes burns like a forest fire.

I tighten my grip on the gun in case he tries something stupid.

Predictably, he lunges toward me, his eyes trained on the gun. I step back and slip on a rock near the lake's edge. I fall hard on the ice, and the gun slips out of my hand, sliding several feet away toward the middle of the lake.

I get up as quickly as I can and scramble toward it, but

Mitch is faster than me. "Don't do something you'll regret," I say to him as I slip and slide toward the gun.

Mitch ignores me as he carefully makes his way toward the gun's position on the ice. I am just a few feet behind him and scramble to gain ground.

He gets to the gun first and leans down to grab it. A loud cracking sound fills the night sky. "Don't move," I yell at him. Not because I'm afraid of him dying, but because if he moves too much, the ice underneath me could crack, too.

He panics and rushes back toward the shore. The ice underneath him groans and breaks apart, sending him into the icy cold water.

"Help!" he yells as he frantically tries to grab hold of a sheet of ice to pull himself up.

Suddenly, the ice beneath me starts to shudder. I slowly crawl back toward the shore, but it's too late. The sheet beneath me gives way, plunging me deep into the water. "No," I yell. "This is not how this was supposed to end."

I look over toward Mitch, the cold water affecting his ability to fight. His limbs are slowing down, and I can see fear in his eyes. I watch as he slowly stops fighting and his head dips below the water.

Frantically, I look around for a chunk of ice large enough to grab hold of. I grab the nearest one but slip off it after using every ounce of strength I have to hold on. I do this a few more times, and each time, it's fruitless. I can feel my limbs becoming heavy as my body grows numb.

I look towards the beach. Maybe someone will show up who can help me. Hope fills my heart as I watch a figure step out of the woods into the moonlight. That hope is immediately dashed when I realize who it is. Eden... or Kari-Anne... The moment I see her cold, calm face, I know I'm going to die.

I fight as hard as I can until my limbs can no longer move. I stare at Kari-Anne the whole time, our eyes locked in a mutual understanding. I had killed her sister. This was her revenge.

I fight until there is nothing left. All my hopes and plans for my future are slipping. My body finally gives up, and as much as I want to continue fighting, I can't. Kari-Anne watches as I sink under the chunks of ice floating on the water.

102

EDEN

I started filming on my phone the moment Mitch arrived at the lake. I wasn't exactly sure what was going to go down between him and Liv, but I knew that whatever happened would be evidence of their guilt that I could take to the police. I never expected it to end like this.

I stare at Liv as she struggles for her life. Her eyes are locked on mine, but she doesn't even call out to me to help her. I think she knows that she's getting what she deserves, or at the very least, she knows that asking for my help is pointless.

I stand fixated in one spot until she disappears under the water for the last time. I wait several minutes to make sure that she doesn't come back up. When I am certain that Liv is down for good, I take a deep breath.

It has taken me years to get revenge for what Liv and Mitch did to Autumn. In the end, I didn't even have to exact it myself. The two of them self-destructed, and I had a front-row seat.

I never wanted them to die. I only wanted to make sure

that they would never hurt another person again. As much as I fantasized about killing them, if I was honest with myself, I knew that I wouldn't be able to be the one to do it. Maybe in a world without all those libraries, the Hillside Lounge, Albert or Derek, or any of the other things that saved me, I would have turned out different.

Either way, I still was a catalyst of justice, and now that Liv and Mitch are gone, I feel a sense of relief. I feel guilty because it was almost cathartic to watch them both die at the same place where Liv killed Autumn. Everything that happened was their own doing. My only crime was not intervening. Even if I had attempted to intervene, chances are that I would have probably ended up in the lake right beside them. It was always going to finish like this. There was no way for me to stop it.

I double-check the video on my phone and quickly back it up to the cloud so I can't lose it. Satisfied that it is safe, I turn towards the woods and walk back towards my car. The mission I have been planning since I was ten is finally complete.

103

PIPPA

Pippa knew exactly which rock her dad was talking about in his letter. When she was a kid, he used to take her fishing at a small stream in the middle of the woods. Next to the stream was a large, flat rock. They would sit on it and cast their rods into the stream from their perch. It's one of the best memories she has of her dad. During those times with him, she felt like life was perfect.

The stream is not easily accessible. The clearing where she and her dad fished lies at the end of a hiking trail in the Chuckanut mountains. Pippa parks her car at the base of the trail. The sun is barely peaking up over the horizon and no other vehicles are in the lot. She had left her house an hour ago before the sun had begun to rise, hoping to get to the trail before other hikers. Now that she's sitting in her car at the edge of the dark woods, she questions the wisdom of this decision. It would probably have been safer with more people around.

She takes a deep breath and gathers her courage. She double-checks her backpack. It is nearly empty, aside from a gardening shovel and a few bottles of water. Satisfied that she has everything she needs, she gets out of the car and begins the mile-long hike. By the time she reaches the stream, she is out of breath. It has been years since she last hiked.

The fishing spot is nearly the same as it was when she was a kid. The trees are a little taller and the bushes a little more dense, but the large fishing rock sits right where she remembers. She stands in the small clearing by the water as a wave of grief washes over her. Memories of the times here with her dad come rushing back to her like a flood.

WHEN SHE WAS LITTLE, he was her best friend. She did everything with him. When she was in elementary school, they would come here at least once a month to fish. They never caught much, but that never really mattered.

As she got older, her dad was home less and less often, and the fishing adventures became a thing of the past. He was driven by a desire to keep up with the wealthy citizens of Aldercreek, and it made him do risky things. At the time, she didn't know he'd been breaking the law, but she always wondered where he was and what he was doing.

As a teenager, she had been hurt by his lack of attention and had said some awful things to him, oftentimes giving him the silent treatment for weeks. Her mom would always tell her that he was away doing what was necessary to help their family get ahead.

Her dad bought them a brand new car one year with the money he was earning. He was so proud of it. To him, it was a symbol of what was yet to come. However, he was never able to really move them into the upper echelons of society. By the time she was in high school, they were still living in the trailer park on the edge of town.

The car gave him hope, though, that things were going to change eventually. For the next few years, he doubled down on his efforts and was gone even more. His absence hadn't just affected Pippa; she'd watched as her mom slowly sank into a deep depression during those years. She became a shell of herself, barely able to get out of bed most mornings. By Pippa's junior year in high school, she had almost forgotten what it was like to have a mother. She got herself up in the mornings, made her own breakfast, and forged her mother's signature for school activities — just like Bobbi had to do now. A wave of guilt crashes over her. Bobbi deserved better than the life she had been dealt.

Pippa's mom stayed depressed until her senior year. She's not sure what happened, but something in her mom began to shift just before Christmas that year. She'd started exercising and wearing makeup again. The vibrant, happy mother Pippa remembered from her childhood returned. Pippa had been confused by the change, but she was also happy. Those were some of the best months of her life.

Even though that time with her mom was good, she never fully trusted it would last forever. She wasn't too surprised when her mom walked away from everything after she turned eighteen. Pippa had wished she could walk away too, but she couldn't bear the thought of leaving her dad alone.

Looking back, Pippa realizes she would have traded all the nice things her dad bought just to have more time with both him and her mom. If he had paid more attention to her mom, maybe she would still be here. After her mom left, she was so angry at her dad that she'd spent years barely talking to him. Even though she had stayed so he wouldn't be alone, they became like strangers to each other.

Overcome by emotion, she drops to her knees. "I'm so

sorry, Dad," she whispers. "I'm sorry I pushed you away." She allows herself to grieve for several minutes. When the tears slow, she stands and looks over at the rock.

She takes a deep breath and walks towards it. A dense patch of ferns surrounds it. She walks around the rock, pushing through the vegetation, hoping no animals are hiding under the fronds. Behind the rock, she finds a brick that used to be bright red but has dulled to a brownish-red over the years. She picks up the brick and begins to dig.

It doesn't take very long for her to hit something hard and made of metal. She uses her hands to push aside the remainder of the dirt covering the box. Pulling it from the ground, she brushes off the lid and opens it. She finds a single piece of paper sealed inside a plastic bag with a small golden key.

There is very little written on the paper. The first line is an address in Aldercreek. Below the address is a combination of letters and numbers: *B105*. "What in the world, Dad?" She asks as she examines the box to ensure she hasn't missed something else, but it is now empty.

She puts the paper and the key back in the box and tucks it under her arm to make the trek back out of the woods.

NEARLY TWO HOURS LATER, she pulls up to the address she had programmed into her GPS. She double-checks the location with the address on the paper. "A post office," she says, realization dawning on her.

She exits the car with the key and the PO Box number and walks towards the building. As soon as she gets inside, she looks around to see if anyone is watching her. She feels a little strange accessing a box that doesn't belong to her, but no one is paying any attention.

It doesn't take her long to find *B105*. She takes the key out of the box and inserts it into the hole. It turns easily, and she pulls it open.

Inside, she finds an envelope with her dad's handwriting on the front. She slowly opens the letter and pulls out a single white piece of paper. Inside the envelope is also a small flash drive. She leaves the drive in the envelope and reads the letter.

My dearest daughter,

I know that I was not always the best dad growing up. I hope you know that I was just trying to give you and your mom the best of everything. I didn't know what I would have to sacrifice to make that happen until it was too late. I'm so sorry. If I could go back, I would do things so much differently.

If you are reading this, that means something has happened to me. I have prepared for this day and opened several bank accounts in your name. I am not sure what they are worth today, but just know you will never have to work again. Enclosed in this envelope is a flash drive that will tell you how to access them.

I love you, baby girl.

Dad

Pippa's tears flow freely. She hadn't realized how much she was like her dad until just now. For the last few years, she has worked tirelessly to get ahead. She works long hours at the law office and now this campaign. Meanwhile, Bobbi has spent so much time at home alone. She realizes that if she's not careful, she's going to push Bobbi away just like her dad did to her. All her drive to become the best at everything is really just a fool's errand if she loses Bobbi in the process.

She holds the paper to her chest. "I love you, Daddy. I know you loved me. I promise I will learn from you and not let the drive to be successful destroy my family," she whispers through her tears.

104

DETECTIVE HAWKINS

D etective Hawkins sits at his desk, drinking his third cup of coffee. He opens his email to find forty unread messages. He sighs. Most of them are probably junk mail, but he has to open each one just in case.

He slowly makes his way through the messages, deleting the ones that are clearly spam and leaving the rest to be dealt with later. He opens a message from an unknown address, briefly scans it, and immediately reads it again more thoroughly.

Detective Hawkins. The attached video will be the final evidence you need for two unsolved murders in Aldercreek. I trust that you will use them to close those cases and bring justice to the two women who lost their lives at the lake.

At the bottom of the message is a video attachment. His heart pounds as he double-clicks on the video and waits for it to be scanned by the virus software. Once it opens, it plays immediately.

It takes him a few seconds to understand what he is seeing, but his mouth drops wide open once he does.

"Yo, Bill. Come look at this," he yells at his partner.

Bill walks over to his desk and peers over his shoulder. "What am I looking at?" He asks.

"Isn't that Liv and Mitch Mitre at the lake?" John points to the two figures in the paused video.

"Oh yeah, man, I think it is. What are they doing?"

"I'm not sure," John says. "Let me turn up the volume."

The video is five minutes long and trimmed to show only Liv's confession. When it ends, the two officers look at each other.

"Is this real?" Bill asks, his eyes wide.

"If it is, that means that Liv was the one who killed both Autumn and Regina."

"No one is going to believe this, man."

John shakes his head and runs his hands through his hair. This could be the break of a lifetime.

EDEN

I stand in the middle of the empty apartment and look around at the small space. It didn't take me long to pack all of my belongings. Most of them are now tucked neatly into the trunk of my car.

I look out the window at the Mitre's dark house. So much has changed since that first day I watched them drinking coffee on their porch. They had lived their lives so carefree up until yesterday. Despite all the heinous things they had done, their life had been practically perfect. Now, the house will remain empty, and they won't be able to hurt anyone ever again.

I grab the last box from the kitchen floor and exit the apartment. As I load it into the trunk, a sense of peace washes over me. I have spent so much time planning how to stop the Mitres. Now that it's over, the possibilities for my future seem endless.

I drive away from Aldercreek, knowing I will never return. The past no longer haunts me. I am finally prepared to move on and live my own life. It's what my sister would have wanted.

NADIA

The hot sun beats down on Nadia through the small fifth-floor apartment window. The shades are open, and a warm ocean breeze blows tendrils of hair around her face. Her niece and nephews play loudly in the other room.

"Pásame esos tazones," she says to her sister, Maria, who is standing in front of the stove stirring a pot of chicken posole.

"Nadia, you need to speak English," she chides. "You can get much better-paying jobs if they can understand you, and that's just going to take practice."

"I speak English just fine," Nadia says, smiling. "I just don't want to."

Maria gives her a side-eyed glare.

"Fine, pass me those bowls... please," Nadia says sarcastically.

Maria rolls her eyes and hands her the stack of bowls they used to prep the meal.

Nadia dunks the bowls into the hot water in the sink. As she washes them, she thinks about how far she's come in just the last couple of weeks. At the Mitre's, she had begun to lose hope. If it weren't for Eden, she's not sure if she would have ever gotten out of there. With no way to transport herself, she had been nothing more than a caged animal.

"What's going through your mind, sister?" Maria asks.

"You don't know how bad it was there. All I wanted to do was make enough money to come to you, but even when I got the money, I had no way to leave."

"I'm so sorry, Nadia. I didn't know how to find you," Maria says. She walks towards Nadia and wraps an arm around her shoulders. "I'm so glad you made it here."

"Me too." Nadia looks outside. Her sister's apartment is only a few blocks from the beach. "The water is so blue. I've never seen anything more beautiful."

"That decides it," Maria says, placing her hands on her hips. "Tomorrow, we're going to spend the day at the beach."

Nadia looks at her. "Seriously?"

"Would I lie to you?"

She smiles and turns back to the dishes. This is the life she had been dreaming of; she just never really believed it would come true, especially when she was working for the Mitres. Someday, she would pay Eden back for saving her. She just wasn't sure how.

107

PIPPA

Pippa and Bobbi are in the car. Bobbi turns on the music and turns up the volume much too loud for Pippa's comfort. She looks over at her daughter. Her eyes are closed as she leans her head against the headrest, moving her whole body to the music.

When the song is over, Pippa turns the volume down until the music is barely audible.

"So when are you going to tell me where we're going?" Bobbi asks, crossing her arms.

"You'll find out soon enough. It wouldn't be a surprise if I told you."

"Lame," Bobbi says, but she can't help but smirk. "Whatever. I'm just glad to be hanging out with you."

"Me too, baby," Pippa says quietly.

Things have changed a lot since Pippa's father died. The first thing she did after opening the thumb drive her dad left her was drop out of the mayoral race. The next morning, she went to the county office to submit her resignation. The whole place was abuzz. People were standing in groups scattered about the large open office space instead of working at their desks.

"What's going on?" Pippa asked a group of four standing close to the entrance.

"Did you hear about the Mitres?" A tall, blonde woman with perfectly coiffed hair asked.

Pippa hesitated. "No, what about them?"

"They both drowned in the lake in the exact same spot as those two other women drowned. Autumn and Regina, I think, were their names," the woman said in a loud whisper.

Pippa stared at her in stunned silence. "Wait, so you're telling me Liv Mitre is dead?"

All four nodded at her grimly.

"Oh wow. I can't believe it." She thought about Kari-Anne coming to town and wondered if she'd had something to do with it. "Do they know what happened?"

A short man with brown hair and a handlebar mustache piped up. "They're saying it was an accident. I guess Liv and Mitch went out on the ice for some reason and fell through."

Pippa looked at him suspiciously. "I can't imagine Liv ever doing something so stupid."

The man just shrugged and turned back to his friends.

Pippa stepped away from the group and stood in the middle of the foyer for a few minutes to process what she'd heard. She couldn't shake the feeling that Kari-Anne coming to town just a few months before all of this wasn't a coincidence. She must have had something to do with their deaths. Even if she did, Pippa didn't care. Liv was one of the cruelest individuals she'd ever met.

As she and Bobbi drive down the road, she thinks about the Mitres. The police were never able to find any evidence of foul play. Video footage of an argument between Mitch and Liv, where Liv confesses to killing at least two women, leaked to the press a few days after their deaths and then spread like wildfire over social media. Someone had been there and had recorded them, but as far as Pippa knew, the police never identified who that person was. She knew deep down that it was Kari-Anne, but she would go to her grave before she shared that information with the world.

She remembered Kari-Anne and Autumn from the bus stop in front of their trailer park all those years ago. Kari-Anne had been devastated after Autumn died. She'd lost her mom and her sister in the course of a few months. If she was somehow able to exact revenge for what had happened to her, Pippa wouldn't be the one to rat her out.

She turns into a neighborhood full of brand-new and unfinished homes. Bobbi looks at her quizzically. "Why are we going here?"

Pippa ignores her and keeps driving slowly down the streets of the development. They are lined with cherry blossom trees on either side. It feels almost magical.

At the end of a small dead-end drive, the largest home Pippa has ever seen stands like the sentinel of the block.

Brandy, the same realtor who helped them get their apartment, is waving on the front porch.

Pippa pulls into the driveway of the home.

"Wait, what are we doing here?" Bobbi asks.

"I thought we might see if we wanted to live here."

Bobbi looks at her in shock. "Are you serious? How can we afford this?"

Pippa shrugs. "Your grandfather left me a little money when he passed away. I guess you can consider it his gift to us."

Bobbi immediately gets out of the car and walks toward the steps. Pippa shakes her head at her teenager's enthusiasm as she exits the vehicle.

"This is certainly an upgrade," Brandy says to Pippa from her perch at the top of the stairs.

"You can say that again," Pippa replies, chuckling.

Brandy gives them a tour of the house. Its beautiful marble floors and mahogany wood trim are of the highest quality. Pippa is overwhelmed by emotions as they walk through the space.

This is everything she had ever thought she wanted, but now, as she's walking through these ornate rooms, she's not so sure. For years, she has worked to earn enough money and respect to push her way to the upper echelons of society. Now that she's here, she's not sure she needs it. So much has changed since she found the note from her dad, and none of this feels necessary anymore.

The tour ends in the chef's kitchen. It's the most beautiful room Pippa has ever seen. The cabinets are painted a mossy green color. The stainless steel appliances and rich travertine countertops gleam in the morning light that streams through the window. Brandy steps away to give Pippa and Bobbi a moment to talk.

"What do you think, Bobbi?" Pippa asks.

"It's beautiful," Bobbi replies in awe. She turns to Pippa. "What do you think, Mom?"

"I agree. It's probably the most beautiful home I've ever seen. Would you like to live here?"

Bobbi nods. "It would kind of be a dream come true, but isn't it a little big for the two of us? I think I counted ten rooms. Do we really need all that?"

Pippa shrugs. "I'm not sure. I just want to do what's best for you, honey."

"Mom, I don't need something like this to be okay."

"I know, but you deserve the very best of everything."

Brandy walks back into the room. "Well, what do you two think?"

"It's stunning," Pippa says sincerely.

"Would you like to make an offer?"

Pippa hesitates. "I have the funds ready, but I'm not sure this is the route I want to go. I'll need to think about it a little more."

Brandy nods. "Of course. Houses in this price range don't move too quickly, so you have a little time."

In the car, Pippa grabs Bobbi's hand and smiles at her. Whatever decisions she makes, she's going to make sure that Bobbi's needs come first. She doesn't want to make the same mistakes her dad made by valuing wealth and status over her family. If she's learned nothing else over the last year since her husband left her, she's learned that she and Bobbi can be happy with practically nothing.

108

SANDY

Sandy and Blaine are cuddled next to each other on the couch in their living room. Ever since he promised to be better, Blaine's been true to his word. He is now home every weekend, hanging out with the family. If he has to work late, he always calls Sandy to let her know. It's like he's reverted back to the person she married all those years ago.

Sandy had become so comfortable being alone that it took some time to get used to him being around all the time, but now she feels happier and more confident in their relationship every day. After the video of Liv was released, the whole town thinks she got what was coming to her. Sandy wonders if Liv really felt loved like Blaine loves her — would she have been so evil? It bothers her that she misses Liv, but she can't help it; Liv was her best friend.

"Want to watch a movie?" Blaine asks, grabbing the remote.

Sandy nods. She really doesn't care what they do; she's happy just being around him. It reminds her of when they started dating and couldn't get enough of each other.

She looks towards him. "This doesn't seem real."

He looks at her, confused. "What are you talking about?"

"You, me... us. It just feels too good to be true."

He stares at her and runs a hand down her face. "I'm sorry, Sandy. I know I hurt you. I just got so caught up in my job that I lost sight of what was most important. I promise it's never going to happen again."

Blaine leans closer and softly presses his lips against Sandy's.

"Ewww, gross," Melanie says as she walks in from the kitchen.

Sandy and Blaine break apart.

"I mean, I'm glad that it seems you guys like each other again, but please, can you get a room?" Melanie says as she walks through the living room and exits on the other side.

Blaine and Sandy look at each other and laugh. This is exactly how life is supposed to be.

109

PIPPA

"**A**ll packed up?" Pippa hollers to Bobbi.

"Almost," Bobbi says from her bedroom. "Just a few more minutes."

Pippa walks into Bobbi's room. She is cramming as much as she can into a suitcase and duffel bag that are wide open on top of her bed. Pippa laughs. "Do you think you got enough stuff?"

Bobbi looks at her, her eyes wide. "Mom, we're going to be sailing around the world. It's not like I can just come back home to get the things that I missed."

"We'll be back here from time to time. I bought this whole building so we would have a place to stay when we decided to return to Aldercreek. Anything you forgot to bring, you will be able to get it again."

"What, in like six months? No, I'm taking as much as I can right now."

Pippa stares at her daughter, wondering if she's doing the right thing. "Bobbi, are you sure you're all right with this? It's really okay if you're not. I just want to do the right thing for you."

Bobbi stops shoving a pair of boots into the duffel bag. She grabs Pippa's hands and looks her in the eyes.

"Mom, I'm sure. What better education could I receive than learning from different cultures around the world? Besides, it's not like I have any friends here, and who knows where Dad is. This is going to be the best adventure." She wraps her arms around Pippa.

Pippa returns the hug, but the anxiety doesn't dissipate.

When she had come home the other day to figure out the financials for buying that mansion, she just couldn't shake a feeling of sadness and despair. The house was beautiful, and thanks to her dad, she had enough money to purchase it all in cash, but something just didn't sit right in her soul. It was everything she had been working towards all these years, but when she finally got it, she realized it wasn't what she really wanted. This had been her dad's dream, not hers, and even her dad regretted it in the end. She knew deep down that to break the cycle of neglect, she had to choose something different.

Bobbi releases her and takes a step back. "What are you worried about, Mom?"

Pippa sighs. "I just want to make sure we're making the right decision. We're going to be gone a long time."

"Mom," Bobbi says, exasperated. "How many times do I have to tell you I want to go? I'm excited about it, actually. We're going to have so many amazing experiences. So please, stop. I'm going to finish high school online, and I'll apply to college just like we planned. Nothing is going to stop that. I'm going to be fine, I promise."

Pippa looks at her brilliant, funny, and kind daughter. She knows she doesn't deserve her. She takes a deep breath. "Okay, let's do this."

Two hours later, they arrive at the marina where the

boat Pippa purchased is being prepared by the crew she hired for the voyage. The boat looms above them, dwarfing the other vessels in the harbor.

"There's our boat," Pippa says as she and Bobbi step out of the rideshare.

"Mom, to call that thing a boat is an understatement. Let's be real, that thing is a yacht."

Pippa grins. "It is pretty magnificent, isn't it?" She wraps an arm around Bobbi's shoulders and guides her towards the yacht. The steward comes rushing down the gangplank the moment he sees them.

"Ms. Holloway, so happy to see you finally made it."

"Thank you, Frank. Can you please grab our bags?"

"Yes, of course," he replies.

He immediately rushes for the bags while Pippa and Bobbi make their way up to the deck.

"Good morning, Ms. Holloway," the captain says. His Australian accent makes Pippa weak in the knees. Not to mention, he's beautiful. He's at least six feet tall with olive skin and a bright smile. Salt and pepper hair peeks out from underneath his captain hat and the outline of well-developed muscles is visible under his uniform. Pippa could stare at him all day.

"Good morning," she replies shyly.

Bobbi glances at her sideways, a look of surprise on her face.

"The crew has prepared your quarters," the captain announces. "Would you like me to show you to them?"

Pippa shakes her head. "No, we can find them ourselves. Thank you." She walks as quickly as she can towards the door that leads to the bedrooms. As soon as they are inside the corridor, Bobbi grabs her arm.

"Mom, what was that?"

"What?" Pippa asks in mock innocence.

"You like him," Bobbi says with a grin.

"So what if I do?"

Bobbi hesitates. "I approve. I just want you to be happy. You should go for it."

"You really think so?" Pippa asks.

"It's time for you to start living your life, Mom. Yes. If it would make you happy, you should."

Pippa can't wipe the silly smile off her face for the rest of the evening.

An hour after boarding, the captain announces they are ready to depart. Pippa and Bobbi make their way to the deck.

"Where should we stand?" Bobbi asks.

Pippa grabs her by the arm and leads her towards the front of the boat. "No looking behind us, only ahead."

The vast ocean stretches in front of them in every direction, and for the first time she can remember, Pippa finally feels free.

110

EDEN

"Are there any more, babe?" I ask as Derek stacks a large box on top of another one.

"I don't think so, but I'm pretty sure you packed enough stuff to fill an entire house."

I slap him playfully. "This is going to be my home, isn't it?"

He grabs me by the waist and brings me close. "Finally." The look in his eyes makes my knees buckle. He leans in to kiss me. I push him away. "Not right now. I'm all gross and sweaty."

"There's a shower right there," he grins as he points to the bathroom. "We can take one together."

Heat rushes to my cheeks. "As good as that sounds, I won't be able to enjoy myself until I get this stuff put away."

"You want to put it all away right now?" He asks, surprised.

"Not all of it, but I want to unpack a couple of the boxes just so I can feel at home."

A disappointed look crosses his face.

I roll my eyes. "Derek. We are living together now. We can do that whenever we want. Besides, I'm pretty sure you're going to get sick of me sooner rather than later."

"Never," he says. He puts both of his hands on the sides of my head and brings me to him. "I'm never letting you go again," he says, staring into my eyes.

"You know I had to do everything by myself, right? Losing Autumn almost broke me, and I had to figure out a way to move forward with my life, or I was never going to be good for anyone, including you."

"Yeah, I know, but from now on, we're a team. Deal?"

I look at him, my heart full. "Deal."

"Why don't you unpack for a little bit, and I'll order us some dinner. Any suggestions?" He asks, releasing me from his arms.

"Anything but Chinese food. We've already had that twice since I moved in yesterday."

He grins at me. "Okay, fine, what about Thai then?"

I tickle his side. "No, that's too much like Chinese. "

"Vietnamese?" He asks, pushing my hands away.

"You're incorrigible," I say. "You know what? I don't really care. Surprise me."

"You drive a hard bargain. Japanese?"

I turn away from him. "Your choice," I say, shaking my head.

I open the box marked *Important*. On the top of the box is a silver picture frame. I take it out and set it on the table on my side of the bed. The picture is of Autumn and me. I think Autumn was seventeen and I was ten. It was taken just two weeks before she died. "I did it, Autumn. I made sure the people who hurt you got what they deserved," I whisper to the picture.

I reach back into the box and pull out Autumn's sweatshirt, the one I had worn when I was in Aldercreek to remind me of my mission. I fold it and gently place it in the top drawer of my dresser.

I spend the next hour unpacking three boxes and finding spots for the contents of each one throughout the room. By the time I'm done, I feel like Derek's apartment is officially mine, too.

I glance around the room. The boxes containing all my clothes are stacked neatly in the corner.

"Dinner's here," Derek yells from the kitchen.

I sigh. I have so much more to do, but the smell of food wafts into the bedroom, making my stomach rumble.

"Is that Indian food I smell?" I ask, walking into the kitchen.

Derek gives me a wide grin. "I know how much you love it, and you deserve to have everything you have ever wanted."

I wave my hand at him. "I don't need anything. If all I have at the end of the day is you, then I'm good."

He walks over to me. "You sure you don't want to take that shower with me?" He asks, his eyes darkening as he looks at me with desire and wraps his arms around me.

"What about the food?" I ask without much enthusiasm.

"The food can wait." He picks me up, carries me to the bedroom, and lays me gently on the bed. He crawls onto the bed next to me, a look of genuine love on his face.

As I stare into his dark brown eyes, all thoughts of hunger leave my mind.

"I love you, Kari-Anne," he says.

The sound of my real name on his lips fills me with peace. I feel loved and seen for the first time in a long time. I couldn't have done this without Derek's support. Even from another city, I could always feel his presence. "I love you too," I say to him. It took some time, but I know now I'm right where I'm supposed to be.

ALSO BY WINTER K. WILLIS

THE WIFE INSIDE

HOW THE AFFAIR ENDS

BEHIND THE NEIGHBOR'S DOOR

THE PERFECT GIFT

THE PERFECT EX-WIFE

THE LAST CHANCE

A LETTER FROM WINTER

Dear Readers,

We hope you loved *The Assistant,* and if you did, we would be very grateful if you wrote a review. Reviews help us to reach more readers and continue to write books for you. Follow us on our Amazon page and all our socials, as well. We love connecting with our readers!

At our website below, you can sign up for our newsletter. It will keep you updated on our latest releases. Your info will never be shared, and you can unsubscribe at any time.

https://www.winterkwillis.com

Thanks!
Winter

CONNECT WITH WINTER

Winter K. Willis is a pseudonym for our two-person writing team. We like to think of it as our band name. We love telling our characters' stories and hope that you enjoy reading them.

Website: www.winterkwillis.com
BookBub: www.bookbub.com/authors/winter-k-willis
Instagram: www.instagram.com/winterkwillis
Facebook: https://www.facebook.com/winterkwillis

Made in the USA
Columbia, SC
26 May 2025